To Jesus Christ,
To Living Water

A Novel by
Marcia L. Boynton

This book is a work of fiction. Names, characters, places
and incidents are either the product of the author's
imagination or are used fictitiously. Any resemblance
to actual persons living or dead, events, or locales is
entirely coincidental. All characters are fictional,
and all events are imaginative.

To Jesus Christ, To Living Water

ISBN-10: 0692771166
ISBN-13: 978-0692771167

Unless otherwise noted, scripture references contained herein are taken from
the New King James Version, copyright © 1982 by Thomas Nelson, Inc.
Used by permission. All rights reserved.

On the cover: Destiny, Nikki and Brittany Boynton
Cover photo by Marcia L. Boynton

Cover design by Justin Q. Young, Firstborn Designs.
Email: accessjustinyoung@gmail.com.

For Nikki, Brittany, Destiny, Genesis and Syncere

Contents

Acknowledgements

To my First Love, my Lord and my Savior, Jesus Christ, thank you. Thank you for loving me unconditionally. Thank you for your grace and mercy. Thank you for forgiving me of my sins and for giving me another chance. You are worthy of the praise, glory and honor. For your glory, breathe upon this work, and move it according to your will for the glory of your name and the advancement of your kingdom. May the hearts of your sons and daughters be encouraged to look unto you, the author and finisher of our salvation. This, my first novel, would not be possible without you, Lord, and without every experience through which I have come to know you in the fellowship of your suffering. Glory to God! Thank you for the journey that it took to get here. Thank you for blessing our family with a church home.

Thank you to my daughters, Nikki, Brittany and Destiny, for your faith during the journey.

Nikki, thank you for your persistence and for your courage in following your dreams. Thank you for driving me in the early morning hours with the kids in the car so that I could do ministry, and I pray that the Lord will repay you richly. You have excelled in spite of it all, and I am so proud of you. You are a beautiful, blessed young lady, and the Lord will never forget you. You, Genesis and Syncere are engraved in the palm of His hands, and He is with you.

Brittany, thank you for lending me your laptop so that I could finish this book. Thank you for your courage, determination and independence as you pursue your goals. I pray that the Lord repay you doubly, for He is with you, and He will never leave or abandon you.

The hand of the Lord is on your life, and you are an inimitable, beautiful young lady. I am so proud of your achievements, for you refused to allow anything or anyone to distract you.

Destiny, thank you for your bravery, tenacity, discipline and commitment as you go after your dreams. You never gave up and have excelled. You are an exceptional, beautiful young lady, and I am so proud of you. May the Lord repay you richly, for He is with you and no weapon formed against you will ever prosper. May He give you peace. The hand of the Lord is on your life.

I love you all. Always remember that the Lord has promised never to leave or forsake you, and He is with each one of you and your children and your children's children for all generations to come. Call on the name of Jesus.

Thank you to my sweet grandchildren, Genesis and Syncere. God is with you. I love you.

I am especially grateful to my mother, Mary L. Holland, who passed in 2015. The lessons she taught will always be with me.

Additionally, I would like to express my sincerest appreciation to the following persons:

Yvette, my older sister, who passed some years ago, for your life and your example of courage, faith and godliness;

Tammy, my sister, for your support, friendship and for being there for me over the years in innumerable ways. May the Lord be with you;

Michael, my brother, for your support and care. Thank you for being there. May the Lord be with you;

Tony and Trever, my older brothers, for being there for me over the years. May the Lord be with you;

My nieces and nephews, Duane, Danielle, Erika, Brandon, Kevin, Michael, Jr. and Miles, Courtney, Temani and DJ, with prayers and love;

Andrew, thank you. May the Lord be with you and all of the Boynton family;

Jaqulyn Renee King, CEO/Founder of BWE, Inc. and Apostle Dr. Oscar Dowdell-Underwood, Overseer;

Lenise Young; Josephine Furiato; Jayshon and Colby Trower of Trower Music Group; Stephen and Thera Henry; Kisha Green; Georgian Court University, Lakewood, NJ; CreateSpace; Justin Q.

Young; True Servant Church; and every friend and family member who has shown support, thank you;

Every man, woman, child and family in need of Jesus Christ. May the Lord bless you and be with you. There is room at the cross.

Jesus Christ is Lord.

Luke 5:31-32

Jesus answered and said to them,
"Those who are well have no need of a physician,
but those who are sick.
I have not come to call the righteous,
but sinners, to repentance."

Prologue
"Tell it like it is"

Elder Maria Henderson's cell phone was on vibrate, but it rattled against the dresser in her New Jersey hotel room alerting her that there was a caller on the other line. She glanced at her thin, Quartz wristwatch that read 10:52 a.m. – only eight minutes before the start of the kickoff "To Jesus Christ, To Living Water" Women's Conference. Sister Veronica Hicks, a/k/a "Ronny," was scheduled to sing two Praise and Worship songs, and Elder Maria would be speaking to a packed conference room of mainly women who had come to hear the gospel of Jesus Christ from an admitted sinner saved by grace.

"Do you want me to get it?" Ronny asked.

She travelled with Elder Maria whenever the Elder had a speaking engagement outside of their home church, Holy Tabernacle, of Pennstown, New Jersey. The two women had not only become partners in ministry unashamed of the Good News and the foolishness of the Cross, they had become good friends who trusted one another with the private details of their personal lives.

"Yes, please," she replied.

Elder Maria poured mouthwash into its cap and then went into the bathroom and closed the door. In the private chambers of this simple rest room, she was taken back to that day, three and one half years ago, when she finally made the conscientious decision to call on the name of Jesus. Since then, her life had changed dramatically, and the day's Kickoff Conference celebrating the man from Galilee who told her everything she ever did was evidence of the Lord's blessing on her submission to His will. The Lord would have His way, and all Elder Maria had to do was trust Him.

Jesus had healed and delivered her brokenness, hurt, heartache and pain, and there was a new song in the Elder's mouth. Gone was the woman who found it difficult to trust anyone, even Jesus, because of the priority she gave to other "gods" in her life. Today, the delivered and anointed preacher of God's Word lived her life in complete submission to His will. He was the priority, number one, first, last and everything in between. He was worthy of it all, and Maria loved to testify about the Lord's goodness and unconditional love. What a blessing it was to be used by God for His glory.

"Look at where the Lord has brought you from," Elder Maria would preach. "Hallelujah! Give God some praise, you are destined to make it! If God be for you, who can be against you? God can do anything, He can deliver anyone from anything. I don't care what you've been through, Jesus died on the cross of Calvary for you, me and every sinner. I don't care who told you that you would never make it, who tried to block you or what spirit of infirmity may have kept you bound for 18 years. Don't give up. I know it gets hard sometimes, but He has ordained this moment in time for you. Yes, Jesus came to save the lost, and He alone is Lord. Say yes to Jesus, beloved, right now, right where you are."

Mother Wright of Holy Tabernacle Church used to tell Elder Maria that the Lord was calling her, and Elder Maria never really doubted, but she never truly imagined that His blessings would rain so abundantly on her life. After speaking at the anniversary service for her Pastor, Reverend Reginald D. Wright, Jr., Elder Maria was sought after by local clergy for speaking engagements at their churches. Her best friend, Neicy, felt led to share with her that she should write about her walk with Jesus, so Elder Maria completed her first novel, "To Jesus Christ, To Living Water." The documented spiritual journey with Jesus was in huge demand online and in bookstores nationally, and Elder Maria became widely sought after for conferences around the country. Thus, "To Jesus Christ, To Living Water" Women's Conferences were birthed with the blessing of Reverend Wright, glory to God.

2

"Maria, it's Rob," Ronny said, tapping on the closed bathroom door.

"Rob? Oh my God, I haven't spoken to him in months," Maria answered. She considered opening the door and talking to him, but she checked her watch again and decided she would have to call him back.

"We have to go downstairs. Please tell him I'll call him back," Elder Maria said.

"I tried that. He says he knows you'll probably think he's calling to start an argument with you, but he isn't. He wants to talk to you now, and it will only take a minute."

Ronny waited patiently on the other side of the bathroom door.

Elder Maria took a deep breath. She did not have time to speak to her ex-husband, and she really didn't want to. He had tried to damage her ministry enough. The last thing she needed to do before preaching was engage in another toxic conversation.

"I can't take the call right now, Ronny. I'll call him back."

Elder Maria prayed and asked the Lord for His strength and support, and then she walked out of the restroom, where Ronny stood waiting with the cell phone in her hand. She forced the phone into Elder Maria's hand with friendly abruptness and turned to walk out before she could refuse the call again.

"I'll see you downstairs," Ronny said. She headed towards the front door and walked out, closing the door behind her.

Elder Maria was left alone in the suite, and she could hear Rob's voice on the other line. Reluctantly, she lifted the phone to her ear, and with as much pleasantness as she could muster up said, "Rob, I can't talk right now. I have to call you back."

"Why can't you take my call? It's important. I'm not calling to argue. I need to talk to you right now......," said Rob. He sounded hurried and out of breath.

"Rob, the conference is starting. I'll call you back when it's over."

"Maria.....wait, just one second is all......."

"It's good to hear your voice, but I have to call you back. Goodbye, Rob."

She hung up the phone, turned it off, and placed it in her Python Leather designer handbag, which had been a gift from her

3

long-time best friend, Neicy, when she graduated Hampton Bible Institute. Elder Maria was not a diva or fashionista by any standard, she preferred shopping at Consignment Shops, but Neicy had insisted that Elder Maria deserved something better than her faux leather worn out purse she had been carrying for years.

"Girl, it's time to step up," Neicy had said when she presented the bag to Elder Maria.

She gathered her Bible and carrying case, which, ironically, Rob had purchased for her at Christmas two years ago. She knelt beside the king size hotel bed and prayed for her ex-husband.

"Lord, please be with Rob even now, and watch over him. Help me to pray for him as I ought, and as you reveal your will, teach and guide us both to obey you and lean not to our own understanding. Cover him, dear Father, in your blood, and bless him. You are our God, and it is nothing for you to help. Help us, Father, for we are called by your name. Grant your Holy Spirit to Rob, I pray, so that he may acknowledge you as his Lord and Savior. Open his eyes, Lord, and help him to see you, and crucify the flesh of his heart so that he may love and honor you with his whole heart, soul and mind, just as you ask in your own word. Grant that he would be everything that you have purposed Him to be, for you have plans for him, and he is your son. Be glorified, oh Lord. In Jesus' name, amen."

Elder Maria took another deep breath and checked the time on her wristwatch again before exiting the room. She was escorted to the first floor of the hotel by Neicy and Elder Nina Young, both leaders from Holy Tabernacle Church. The ladies took the elevator from their tenth floor suite to the main level, where the 11:00 a.m. brunch was being held. As they stepped off the elevator, Ronny could be heard singing an up-tempo praise and worship song in the hotel's main ballroom.

The ladies walked briskly as Neicy briefed Elder Maria on the status of the conference, which included the number of 375 attendees. Approximately 12 were from Holy Tabernacle Church.

"Praise God, the drummer showed, and Jerome, the usual piano player, is here," said Neicy.

"God is good," Elder Maria replied.

"All the time," Neicy and Elder Nina answered in unison.

The three ladies entered the conference room from a side door, and Elder Maria was escorted to a designated speaker's chair that faced the 400 or so chairs. Women of all ages and ethnicities had come, and the room was filled to capacity. Servers in black and white waited on guests, and the clinking of silverware and glasses sounded rhythmically with the stirring gospel music played by the keyboard player, drummer, bass player, guitar player, organist and trumpet player.

Elder Maria's teenage daughter and son, Genny and Papi, sat at a table upfront with their friends, and they appeared to be enjoying the worship music. Papi noticed his mother looking in their direction, and he tapped his sister, alerting her to sit up straight.

After Ronny finished singing, Neicy prayed, lifting up the name of Jesus Christ in at atmosphere that was already charged with the presence of the Lord. Neicy was also a seasoned gospel soloist who reminded many of Mahalia Jackson. When she sang a verse of their Pastor's favorite hymn, "Journey to Canaan,"[1] many women came forward and gave freewill offerings.[2]

Two Deacons collected the offerings and went to another room. Then, Elder Maria was introduced, and she prayed for God's blessing on the service and meal before the guests were invited up to the buffet tables. They dined on a wide selection of fish, chicken, beef and vegetarian dishes, along with bruleed French toast, eggs benedict, assorted fruits, custom omelets and soups before Maria was cued to the clear glass and marble podium, where she preached a message entitled ***"To Jesus Christ, To Living Water."***

"Preach!" "Hallelujah!" and "Amen!" were heard throughout Maria's sermon. Women wept and lifted their hands high in the air as the presence of the Holy Spirit blessed the room. Elder Maria expounded on **John 4** and shared her own testimony that she, too, was a sinner lost and apart from Jesus Christ. The living water that He gave satisfied the thirsty soul, and there was nothing that could compare with Jesus.

Maria stood at the podium and preached with a fire that was unique to her life experience, anointing and walk with Jesus Christ. She was a transparent vessel who shared with women her own struggle with placing a fleshly relationship before God. Her husband, she

5

would confess, had been her god, and it was not until she hit rock bottom that she cried out to the Lord for His help and went to Him for His guidance.

"This woman went back to the city she came from and told the men, the Bible says, about Jesus," Maria preached.

She was dressed in a long black skirt, tailored black jacket and white clerical collar. Her comfortable black heels gave her 5'10" frame an additional 1" in height. There was boldness about Maria's preaching style, a charisma where she did not shy away from the text. The anointing of God on her life was undeniable, and it wasn't that women were buying books or attending conferences to hear Maria – it was the God who was with Maria, and the God who Maria lifted up and gave all the glory to.

"This Samaritan lady didn't go back to the lifestyle the Lord delivered her from," she preached. "No, she went back to those people who may have known her before Jesus, and she had the faith and courage to witness about a man from Galilee. Can we do that? Can we go back to the people who knew us before we were saved and tell them about Jesus? Can we go back to the world, into the highways and hedges, and testify about Jesus Christ even though those same people are likely to look at us with doubt and suspicion? Who does this woman think she is? Jesus spoke to her for a few moments, and in those few moments, she recognized Him as the Christ. She didn't witness any of Jesus' miracles. She wasn't a part of Jesus' inner circle or core group of disciples when He raised Lazarus from the dead or when He walked on water. She didn't have the opportunity to put her hands in Jesus' side as Thomas. A few moments with Jesus was all it took for her to believe that Jesus was the Messiah whom the Old Testament prophets spoke about centuries earlier. How many women in here this afternoon only need a few moments with Jesus Christ?"

Many of the women in the ballroom, seated at round tables dressed in maroon linen tablecloths, stood and clapped their hands with praise and joy. Waiters and waitresses stood alongside the walls of the room, waiting for their cue from Elder Maria to serve the guests tall, long-stemmed flute glasses that had been engraved with the name of the conference. When the guests were seated, Maria continued.

"Jesus gave her a drink of water that satisfied her thirst, and we have all, at one time or another, been thirsty."

"Amen, Sister!" someone yelled from the room of women.

"Amen," Elder Maria continued. "There is more to this text than an immoral woman who can't keep a man, beloved. She had five husbands, and the man she was with now wasn't her husband. Praise God. How many other lovers have you had before Jesus? How many other gods did you lie with before you accepted Jesus as your Lord and Savior? How many times did He come knocking at the door of your heart, only to be turned away? We are all as this Samaritan woman, all in need of His grace, His deliverance, His blood, His mercy and His forgiveness. And the message of this text is not the Samaritan woman. No, it is the God *of* the Samaritan woman. What is God saying in the text? The God of Abraham, Isaac and Jacob, and the God of Moses, of King David, of Mary, of the Apostle Paul and of Lazarus. We spend so much time focusing on the woman in the text that we don't even see the grace of God that is blessing her as it is blessing all of us. It's not about me, and it's not about you – it is about Jesus."

The women in the main ballroom stood and lifted their hands to Jesus, blessing His holy name. Sister Ronny came back towards the podium with her microphone and sang with reverence a praise and worship hymn entitled *"That I Thirst Not:"*[3]

Give me this water, Lord
To thirst no more, I plea
Give me this water, Lord
Whereby my soul shall be free

That I may draw no longer
From wells that only run dry
That I may come no longer
To drink, and yet still die

Your precious water, Lord
That is thine own to give
Your precious fountain, Lord
Whereby my soul shall live

I want to drink from you
I am your daughter
You are the Christ, my Lord,
Lord, give my soul your water

Elder Maria gave the 15 or so servers the nod to begin serving the guests, and they each brought a cart of the long-stemmed flute glasses over to the tables. With care and precision, the servers handed out the engraved stemware to each guest in a smooth and synchronized flow that looked like it had been rehearsed to ensure perfection. The servers lifted the glasses from the carts and placed them before the guests in unison.

She asked the women in the Conference to stand, and every guest complied. Some women placed their handbags onto the tables as they moved their chairs back, and others had their handbags hung over the back of their chairs. The male servers assisted the older women in the room, including the Mothers of Holy Tabernacle Church. The musicians continued to play softly, and a server handed Elder Maria and Ronny their respective glasses.

"Praise the Lord, everybody," Elder Maria spoke.

"Praise the Lord!" the guests responded.

"We have come this afternoon to worship the Lord our God, Jesus Christ. Jesus Christ is Lord. He is the Messiah. Salvation is found in no one else, for there is no name under heaven by which any are saved but Jesus.[4] His name is above every other name, Amen. Every knee shall bow, and every tongue shall confess to the glory of God the Father that Jesus Christ is Lord.[5] As we lift up the name of the Lord Jesus Christ, let us lift up and raise our glasses in honor of Him."

There was a bustling in the room as each guest picked up her glass and raised it.

"Hallelujah. Dear Father, we just come to say thank You this afternoon for who you are. Thank You for being our Lord and Savior, our Alpha and Omega. Thank you for being with us, Oh God. We do this symbolically to toast to you, Lord, and to pray as two or three gathered in your name. The scriptures declare that you are among us,

and if we agree about anything we ask for, it will be done for us by you, our Father in heaven.[6] Dear Father, we stand on your word. We know that we shall receive what we ask for. You declared to us in your word that it is not your will for any to perish, but that we may have eternal life through your Son, Jesus. So, we pray, Father, for every life here today. Fill, we pray, each vessel with your holy spirit, Oh Lord. Sanctify us with your holy spirit that we may worship you, oh God, in spirit and in truth. Grant that we would no longer draw from wells of the world that leave us thirsty and hungry, unsatisfied and unfulfilled. Give us a holy hunger and thirst for you and your word, Oh God. We lift our glasses to honor you, our Lord and Savior, and we pray for this living water from on high. Let it be to us according to your word, Oh God, for just as this Samaritan woman asked you to give her this living water, so we have come to petition you. Give us this living water, dear Father, and we pray this in the matchless name of our Lord and Savior, who alone is God, Jesus Christ."

Elder Maria raised her glass to toast to heaven, and all of the women lifted their glasses as well.

"To Jesus Christ, To Living Water," Maria toasted.

The musicians continued playing as Elder Maria invited any woman who wanted to accept Jesus Christ as Lord and Savior to come to the altar and be saved.

"Hallelujah!" she sang. "Glory to God! Your precious fountain, Lord, whereby my soul shall live! Hallelujah! Praise the Lord. The altar is open."

Four young women of diverse backgrounds came forth. They were assisted by Elder Nina and Neicy, who walked with them from their tables to the front of the room where the altar of God was represented. The Mothers also came forth and prayed with the women.

Welcoming each with an embrace, Elder Maria said, "We would love to worship the Lord with you at Holy Tabernacle Church in Pennstown, which is my home church. Reverend Wright is our Senior Pastor, glory to God. We are praying with you that the Lord will fill you with a holy hunger for Him and reveal His purpose to each one of you. Be blessed with victory and abundant life in the name of Jesus.[7] Even as your soul prospers, be in good health.[8] Praise the Lord. Before you were formed in your mother's wombs, the Lord knew you.[9] He has plans for you.[10] The Lord be with you as you grow and develop into everything He has ordained and purposed for your life. The Lord fill you, amen, with His Holy Spirit. The Lord plant you and your family in a church home where you will be guided in the Lord with shepherds after the Lord's own heart who will lead you with knowledge and understanding,[11] in the name of Jesus."

As Maria was praying, a woman in the back of the conference room came towards the front of the room. She was holding a young boy, about two years of age. Neicy saw her approaching and looked at Elder Maria for some direction.

Mother Wright noticed the blank looks on their faces, and she said softly to Elder Maria, "There's always time for a soul to come to Jesus. The service isn't over yet. If you can't get past this, maybe you're not ready. This is about Jesus."

"Hallelujah," Elder Maria said, standing corrected.

It wouldn't have mattered anyway, Mother Wright was already turning to walk towards the young woman and bring her up front.

When they reached the altar, the young woman was visibly shaking with nervousness, and she stepped forward directly in front of Elder Maria. The toddler she carried was cute as a button, dressed in a blue shirt, white vest and white pants. The young woman, presumably his mother, removed the pacifier from his mouth, and when it appeared he would start crying, she lovingly rocked him in her arms.

It was an awkward and tense moment for these two women who shared a rocky past, but the Lord strengthened them both in that moment as they set aside their unfriendly history for the glory of Jesus Christ.

For some time, the young woman had resisted repeated urges to attend a worship service at Holy Tabernacle Church because she was told Elder Maria was one of the preachers there. She had only recently submitted to the Spirit of God that was leading her in this direction, and she was placing all of her confidence in Jesus. Besides, it wasn't about the preacher, as far as this young woman was concerned. It was about Jesus, and only He could judge her.

Elder Maria realized in that moment that the young woman before her was not a woman to be competed against. She was a soul who had come to the Lord for salvation, mercy, blood and forgiveness. It took a great deal of courage, humility and faith for this young woman to come that afternoon.

Elder Maria also understood that she was not a personal bodyguard hired to keep sinners from coming to Jesus, and it was not about her. Elder Maria was simply a vessel through whom Jesus flowed, and Jesus would have compassion and mercy on whomever He pleased.[12] His word declared that He would not refuse any who came to Him.[13] It *was* about Jesus, and Elder Maria remembered that her job was to preach the gospel of Jesus Christ and lift Jesus up. She had to bow before Him herself so that He could use her, and He would always give her the grace and anointing to do anything He asked. In this way, Christ would be glorified.

"I'm so sorry," the young woman said to Elder Maria with teary eyes, "please forgive me."

Elder Maria stood face to face with this young woman for the first time since she heard of her. She was very attractive, in modest dress, about 5'7" with her designer red heels. Her shoulder length hair was brushed back with a black and white checkered headband matching her black and white polka dot dress, and she wore a matte red lipstick that complimented her caramel skin tone.

"God bless you, daughter. The Lord be with you," Elder Maria said with sincerity.

She prayed with the young woman and her son, and then all of the women who had come to the altar were given a Bible from the Mothers of Holy Tabernacle Church.

The conference closed with Elder Maria giving the benediction[14], and then she greeted guests. Several women came forward and shared their testimonies of how Jesus had saved them from low self-esteem, abusive relationships, drugs and promiscuity. Elder Maria prayed with each woman, and they gave God glory for saving their souls.

"Never would have made it," one woman named Marian from East Orange, NJ, testified.

Another young lady, Lori, from Pleasantville, NJ, shared that she could always relate to the story of the Woman at the Well, and she was grateful that Jesus had given her another chance in spite of her past. She had been a dancer in a gentlemen's club.

Kim, a young woman of 28 years from New York, shared that she had been in an abusive relationship and had contemplated suicide. "Were it not for the Lord on my side," she testified.

Elder Maria greeted about 15 more young women, including her friend, Pam, who had been missing in action for months.

"Girl, it is so good to see you!" Pam spoke as she hugged Elder Maria. "Look at God!" Pam stepped back and took a good look at her friend, whom she hadn't seen in some time.

"God is good," Elder Maria replied, admiring her friend's wedding band.

"If I had known this much was going on at Holy Tabernacle, I would have been here. God is in this," Pam said with a youthful excitement and energy. She was as giddy as a child opening a present on his birthday when he didn't think he was going to get a gift.

"We tried to reach you, Pam. Where have you been?" Maria asked.

"Around," she answered evasively. "Oh, let me just tell you the truth, I can't lie to a woman of God," she chuckled. "Evan and I went to Las Vegas to get married. We didn't have enough money to pay for the big wedding I wanted, so we flew out and got married in one of those Elvis chapels."

Encouraging her friend, Maria replied, "Well, there's nothing wrong with that, Pam. People do it all the time, and God is with you."

"I know, and believe me, I'm grateful. We were looking for a house in Florida, but I just couldn't leave my parents here, so we came back. Evan started his own business, and we've been kind of busy with that. But, enough about me," Pam said, reaching to hold the hands of her friend, "I just wanted to come in and see for myself what the Lord has done. God is with you, Maria. He is just awesome! Look what He's done!"

Pam surveyed the conference room where He drew souls in to hear His word and be saved.

"Amen. Glory to God," Elder Maria answered, looking around the room with her.

"Well, I would love to stay, but I've got to run, and there are still more people waiting to see you, so I'll stay in touch. Oh, and Evan and I still haven't found a church, so……"

"So, why not come to Holy Tabernacle? God is in the house."

Agreeing, Pam replied, "I know He is. We'll see you next Sunday."

The two friends embraced, and then Pam walked off to greet a few other ladies she was acquainted with.

Elder Maria gave God glory for each of the other women who came forward. Each was delighted to share her encouraging testimony about Jesus Christ and how He had freed, delivered and saved her.

Towards the end of the line, Elder Maria's friends from East Borough, NJ, a suburb where she used to reside with her family several years ago, were next in line.

"It is so good to see you," said Caitlyn Jones, who was a former neighbor in the affluent suburb some thirty minutes away. Even though Elder Maria and her children had moved to Addington Park, their children remained good friends.

Caitlyn was dressed comfortably in a tan, khaki skirt with a crisp, white cotton shirt. The gold buttons at the wrist were undone as she had rolled the sleeves up, revealing three beautiful gold bangles on her left wrist.

"You too," Elder Maria replied.

The two women hugged and promised to stay in touch.

The last young woman, who was about 50 years of age, thanked the Lord for sending Elder Maria that day. She shared her testimony that she was married to her husband for thirty years, and he was a Pastor of a small church in North Carolina.

"I don't like to tell people who I am when I come to other churches or conferences. They tend to make an unnecessary fuss over you," the Pastor's wife said. "Please just call me Pastor Key. I'm here to personally say thank you. Thank you for allowing the Lord to use you, and thank you for sharing your story. None of us has a testimony without a test, but many of us want to preach and teach about things that we have not walked in and know nothing about. Thank you for saying yes to Jesus. He has anointed your ministry, and it is a blessing to so many women. God bless you. And please tell your Pastor, Reverend Wright, that I said hello. My husband and I have known the Wright family for years. Mother Wright was my mentor some years ago, glory to God."

"Praise God," Elder Maria said. "Mother Wright has been mentoring and helping me. She is such a class act, and she loves people. Thank God for her. Wait a minute, did you see Mother Wright? She was here earlier."

"Yes, I sure did. As a matter of fact, she and I were talking about getting together for dinner. We have a lot of catching up to do."

Pastor Key wore a short pixie haircut and a tailored suit jacket with a long, black skirt. She looked intently in Elder Maria's eyes, as if she were studying her. Pastor Key wore little makeup, just simple, sheer lip gloss and a plum colored blush that accentuated her rich, brown skin tone.

"I understand," Elder Maria replied. "Thank you so much for coming and blessing us with your presence, and thank you for your kind words. I'll be sure to tell Pastor Wright that you said hello."

Elder Maria embraced Pastor Key and then began to clear the podium of her loose papers.

"Elder," Pastor Key began. She needed a favor and hoped that Elder Maria would have time to accommodate her request.

"Yes," Elder Maria replied as she carefully folded and placed the papers inside the carrying case of her Bible.

"Well, I apologize, I have a friend who came in late, and she missed most of the service. They told her that you were out of books. Would you be kind enough to share your testimony briefly with her? That is, if you have a minute or two. I believe your message will encourage her, and she needs some help."

Pastor Key wasn't sure if Elder Maria would extend any more time or not, but she was hopeful.

"I would love to," Elder Maria replied. "There is always time to give God praise. Jesus saved me so that I may share His good news and let others know that Jesus can save them, too."

She guided the thankful Pastor to a table that had already been cleared by the servers, and the two women sat down. Just then, Neicy came over and whispered in Elder Maria's ear.

"Elder, I'm sorry to interrupt you, but it's Rob. He called on my phone. He says he has to talk to you. It's important. And we'll talk about *you know who* later. She left right after the service. Thank goodness you didn't let it distract you."

Maria refused the call but asked Neicy to tell him that she promised to call him right back. She then excused herself from Pastor Key and turned towards Neicy to whisper, "And, yes, we'll talk about her later, but glory to God, He will receive everyone who comes to Him."

Neicy softly replied, "Child, please, even the devil comes to church, but *okay*." She walked away with her cellphone at her ear.

"So, where is your friend?" Elder Maria asked, turning back towards Pastor Key who was seated to her left.

Pastor Key motioned for a young woman of about 30 years, who was standing near one of the exit doors, to come over to the table. "Confidentially, she is a member of our church, and she is called to ministry. Her husband divorced her, and she has been battling depression for several months. Your testimony speaks to her, Elder, it speaks to a lot of women."

"Glory to God," Elder Maria said.

"I'll be back, okay?" Pastor Key asked.

"Sure," Elder Maria said.

Pastor Key introduced the young minister, Christina Evans, to Elder Maria, and then she walked away to give the two some privacy.

"Thank you, Elder," Christina said, "I appreciate your time."

"Glory to God," Elder Maria said, "God is good. Pastor Key shared that you are in ministry. God bless you."

"Yes," the young and shy Christina answered. She pulled out her chair and sat down, clumsily straightening the seat underneath her. Once situated, she took her small black purse off her shoulder and placed it on the table with an unmistakable nervous energy.

The Holy Spirit spoke to Elder Maria at that moment and said, *"Tell it like it is."* Maria bowed her head in humble submission and declared, "Yes, Lord."

Noticing that Maria's head was lowered, Christina asked Elder Maria if she was okay.

"Amen, yes," she replied, lifting her head to look in Christina's eyes. "What's going on, Christina?"

"Well.........okay, let me just tell you the truth......I am confident that the Lord has called me into ministry, and when I shared this with my husband, he filed for divorce. I prayed through our marriage, but he still filed for divorce. Our marriage wasn't perfect, and I certainly wasn't. We were married for nine years, and we always worked through our problems. Divorce was never in either of our vocabularies. I just didn't, honestly, believe that the man I married would leave me over my commitment to and love for Jesus. Am I supposed to tell Jesus no? I'm sure you are going to ask me if he is saved. Well, I thought he was. He goes to church. He pays tithes. He reads the Bible. I don't know if he is jealous or what. I know that he isn't faithful to me, so maybe he is mad with God because God wants to use me. I am praying for him, Elder, and I'm praying for myself, too, but I'm struggling with this a bit."

Maria smiled. "Christina, none of us can be Jesus' disciples without taking up our cross and following Him.[15] His word says that we cannot love our family members more than Him.[16] Do you want to follow Jesus?"

The young woman sat up in her seat and answered unequivocally, "Yes."

"At the expense of losing relationships?"

Christina sat back in her seat and sighed. "I love Jesus. He saved my life. He saved my soul. He died for me. Yes, I want Jesus at the expense of losing any and everything and any and everybody. Yes."

"Well, sweetheart, get ready to be used by Him. He knows what He is doing. If your husband has confessed Jesus as Lord, he is a child of God, and God is working on him, too. We all make mistakes, none of us is perfect. Keep him in prayer and obey whatever the good Lord is telling you to do," Maria said tenderly.

Christina was appreciative of Maria's support, but she needed to be real about everything. She was tired of keeping up the image that she was alright, and others wouldn't expect that she, a leader in the church, would be going through anything. Christina was embarrassed to tell anyone that she was late to the conference due to a phone call from her ex-husband, who argued with her about God again. His position was that her "fanatical" faith had ruined their marriage, and now she was following some women from North Carolina to New Jersey to hear a woman speak to them about Jesus. She could hear about Jesus in North Carolina, her ex-husband attempted to reason. Christina argued that he had a problem with Jesus, not church, and she wanted to follow whatever Jesus was asking her to do with the support and blessing *of* her husband. Their disagreement lasted for over an hour and thirty minutes, and when the other women left their hotel room that morning to attend the conference, Christina stayed behind on the phone. When she finally came to the Conference, it was nearly over.

"Yes, I believe that, but can you just tell me how Jesus worked it out for you, please," Christina said. "I never had any issue following my husband, he is the head, and I respect his position. I want him to be the head – he is the man. I want to follow my husband as he follows Jesus, and everything was fine until Jesus *really* showed up. That means my husband has to lose his pride and allow Jesus to be the head of our family, including himself. Elder, I felt led to come today because I need someone to be real with me about this. Don't just quote scriptures from head knowledge, help me understand and apply the word. What did you pray? For your children, what did you pray? And how did God keep you from being bitter and resentful? Jesus can save anybody, so I know He can save my husband just as He saved me. When did you know Jesus was calling you? My husband and I were married in church. If he didn't know Jesus, I could understand, but he has been baptized, he prays, and he tells other people about Jesus."

With a gentle laughter and smile, Maria asked, "How much time do you have?"

"As much time as it takes," Christina replied. She sat back in her seat and looked with sincere interest in Maria's eyes.

Maria leaned forward and relaxed her hands on the table in front of her. "Amen. Well, then, glory to God, here is my testimony."

Chapter One

Maria

Like raindrops cascading from a windowpane, the tears running down Maria's face danced through the falling shower waters, one drop joining another drop and another drop joining another. So on, and so on, and so on the water skipped until it was difficult to tell where the tears began and where the pellets of water shooting from the showerhead ended. The bathroom was always Maria's favorite place to find recluse from stress and worry, a make do private getaway, an at home spa if you will where she sought refuge and opened up her heart and soul to the therapeutic cleansing ritual known to others as a simple shower, but to her a soul-cleansing purification rite. Here, Maria could be free, and she could expose the deepest longings of her heart to a God who was listening to and hearing her. Hearing her. Really hearing her.

Maria had found peace in the midst of chaos in a rectangular basin of water next to a commode. She was naked and open to Him, at liberty to give account of her soul's longings and desires. Maria cried out to him as King David, her soul panted after God as a deer for water brooks.[17]

She freely passed through the court of women in this temple; she took no notice of the sign in Greek prohibiting foreigners; she was a Samaritan woman at a well of water conversing with He whom she called Lord, and she was eager to go back and tell everyone of this man from Galilee who told her everything she ever did.[18]

Maria held an alabaster box in her damp hands, and she broke it at the master's feet, knelt before him, and wiped His feet with her shoulder-length hair. Jesus told the embittered religious leader that whatever she had done would be spoken of as a memorial of her,[19] and with joy, she immersed in the honor He had conferred upon her.

The shower curtain was the Old Testament veil behind which the priest went into the Holy of Holies to talk with God.[20] Here, every day was the Day of Atonement[21], and Maria stepped past the old curtain herself and entered into the presence of God through the blood of Jesus Christ, the new and living way.[22]   She was free and uninhibited, without condemnation and loved unconditionally. This was her sanctuary where living waters flowed in abundance. This was her pool of Bethesda where the angel stirred the water and she was first to step in and be made whole.[23]   She needed to talk to Jesus. There were some issues of blood that if she just touched the hem of His garment she would be free of. Yes, this daughter of Abraham was desperate for the power of Jesus Christ, and she pressed her way through the multitudes, having spent all she had to be next to her Messiah.[24]

"Merciful Father," she began to pray, *"in the name of your dear, beloved son Jesus Christ I pray. You promised in your word that you would never leave or forsake me. Keep me, Lord. I cry out to you because you are my God, my helper, my shield and my defense. I know that you always hear me when I pray, and I am grateful. Thank you for hearing me. Thank you for always being there and for being so good to me and my family. You always show up on time, and you are never late. I pray your will, my God, be done in my life. I need your help. Only you can do it, Jesus. I know that you know what I stand in need of before I come to you, and I am trusting in you with all of my heart, mind and soul. Hear my plea, Lord, for your own name sake. Don't pass me by, Lord. You are my help in the time of trouble, my redeemer and my strength. My defense is of you, Jesus. I don't know if I'm saying it right, but I'm speaking from my heart, Father, and I need your help. If you don't answer, I won't know what to do. I*

need you in a mighty way. I am desperate for you. In the name of Jesus, amen."

Chapter Two

Genny

A shy, precocious young girl of 12 years filled with concentration and innocence hurried to the front door of her mother's unfurnished home in Addington Park, NJ. Her family had just moved into this new neighborhood, and it was a far cry from the huge home in the suburbs she had not long ago shared with her dad, mom and little brother. Gone was the brick-faced Cape Cod on a quiet, tree-lined cul-de-sac, with huge, clean sidewalks ripe for hop scotch. April and Jade enjoyed double-dutch with her in front of the house and cold drinks in a never ending supply from whoever's mom brought them out first.

Genny had an ideal home and family just a few months ago. Everything was perfect. Dad worked and provided for them, and mom worked when she wanted to and took care of the home. Why parents break up and families separate was beyond the comprehension of her naiveté about life in the grown up world, but what Genny did understand was that her life had been great before the unexplained (to her satisfaction anyway) dissolution of marriage mom and dad agreed upon. Whatever happened to "til' death do us part?" Death didn't have to be death for it to be death. Her dad was still alive and breathing on his own. Death wasn't a cold, dead body in a hospital morgue; no, death was a 6'2" strong and perfectly healthy man who had checked out on her, her mother and her brother. Death wasn't 100 years away,

21

when you're aged and the doctors tell family members, "I'm sorry, there isn't anything else we can do."   No, death was now 47 years young and in the prime of his life, cheating his children out of their relationship with him and forcing their mother to relocate and make do without him.

Genny was angry with her father, as justifiably angry as any daughter would be with the sudden departure of the man she had looked up to her whole, young life. He had been her hero and her support, protecting her from the fierce and dangerous insects in her backyard, always ready with Neosporin when she was learning how to ride a bike and roller blade and cheering louder than anybody when she played basketball and made her free throws any percent of the time. She was safe with him, never afraid of the dark when she went to bed or the slightly ajar closet door that terrified her friend, April, when April had slept over.

"It's just a closet," Genny had said, but April was scared, so Genny shut it to help her feel more comfortable.

"How could he? How could any father and mother put their children through such unnecessary turmoil over a simple argument that as grownups, they should be able to resolve?" Genny wondered. *"What were they teaching us? If they couldn't work out their own little problems, how could they possibly advise their children to resolve their issues?"*

Divorce. And, it was so funny that they thought Genny didn't know. Genny knew. Papi knew. They wouldn't have had to pack and move, "just for a little while" mom lied, unless their mom and dad were divorcing, separating, or whatever they wanted to call it.

"I may be only 12," Genny thought, *"but I'm not stupid. Mom and dad were getting divorced."*

As Genny let herself in the front door of their new place to stay "just for a little while," her mother greeted her in a long, colorful robe and white towel wrapped around her head, styled like a Nubian Queen. Her mother's appearance lifted Genny's spirits for a moment as she saw on this tall, slender and beautiful woman a unique form and fashion evolving from an inanimate object. The 100% white cotton towel had been transformed into a gorgeous head wrap that other Nubian Queens would envy, and mom's light brown décolleté glistened through the opening of her covering with a few drops of water yet clinging to the skin.

Genny could see lions and tigers reverencing their native queen in the backdrop of lush, green homelands, and the earth laid down for its Nubian goddess and her children as they strolled powerfully, majestically across. Here, Genny was the Queen in Waiting, next in line for the royal throne, and their world never crumbled, faded away or disappeared. Dad was King if he wanted to be, and he defended his pride from breakups and intrusions. Their family stayed together and conquered enemies, lands, kingdoms and misfortune. Dads never left. They did whatever it took to keep their family together. That's how it would be when she grew up and ascended to the throne, and this imaginative journey briefly lessened the depression this sad change had imposed upon her. At least Genny still had the power to dream her way out of any situation, the power of her mind refusing to surrender to anything less than her absolute victory and her enemies' absolute defeat.

"Hi mom," Genny smiled.

Her mom came over and gave her a hug, which Genny always appreciated, but darn it, that hug was not going to take Genny's mind off of the divorce. As Genny thought about coming right out and asking her mom whether or not she and her dad had divorced, she hesitated, not wanting to put any more pressure on the one parent who was left and had stayed to be a parent. So Genny decided in her own mind that she would hold off for now and let it be. Besides, there was the smell of garlic bread coming from the kitchen, her favorite, and she would enjoy dinner tonight.

"Hi sweetheart, how was your day?"

"Good. Umm, something smells really good."

"I'm making your favorite Fettucine Alfredo and cheesy garlic bread."

"Yes! I'm starving," said Genny.

"Well, go cleanup for dinner, and we can dig right in."

Genny didn't pull away from her mother as quickly as she used to. She held tight for a moment and was sure her mother could feel her grip, but she didn't pull away either so Genny enjoyed the embrace. Then, just before it would have been awkward, Genny let go and turned to go into the bathroom where she washed her hands, fought back tears, and then returned to the dining room to play the part of the happy, non-confrontational, do what you're told, *"she's such a good girl"* girl her mom and dad would be proud of. This was not going to be easy. Genny could play that role with some motivation - allowance, a sleep over or a shopping trip courtesy of daddy dearest. Mom was different. She was no nonsense and about business. Well, Genny would come up with something. Since they forced her into this situation, it was all fair game. Game on.

Chapter Three
Papi

"Hooray, we won!" Papi shouted as he finished his assault on the bad guys who had tried to take down the world. Evil forces and sinister plots were in vain against the team of four superheroes Papi put together. Force fields, invisibility, super speed, shape shifting and teleportation topped the powers Papi's characters would possess if he had his way, and the lesser empowered villains were soundly and summarily defeated. Order was restored, and there was a peaceful calm over the city Papi imagined where law was upheld and criminals were brought before the bar of superhero justice.

Papi gathered up all of his favorite action figures and returned them to the wooden toy chest his dad had made for him last Christmas. It stood 4' tall by 4' wide and contained Frisbees, a broken tablet, a football, soccer ball, nun chucks, spy equipment and spy gear, three kites he loved to fly at dusk on the beach with his dad, playing cards, remote control cars, his school backpack, a few books and, what the ...... Genny's stupid glitter markers and pack of construction paper. What was her stuff doing in his toy chest? She knew how much he hated having her things mixed in with his. She probably did it on purpose to annoy him like she always did, but he would fix her. He looked deeper in the chest for something icky, like his hairy black widow spider or rubber python snake.

As he rummaged through what was at the bottom of his toy chest, he came across a photo of his family – dad, mom, Genny and him. A 4 x 6 color photograph of the real Fantastic Four[25] emerged through the broken water guns, play swords and long forgotten items

25

he had once treasured. Papi looked at the photo of his family and couldn't help but smile. He looked just like his dad - rich brown skin with almond shaped eyes and high, chiseled cheekbones. His mom had taken him to the same barbershop his dad went to, and they both sported short haircuts edged up real nice to frame the handsome features of their faces. His mom loved when he got a fresh cut, she would rub his little head and tell him how handsome he was. *"Man, its' cool and all,"* Papi thought, *"but not in public, mom, please."* He guessed dad didn't let her do that anymore because Papi never saw her rubbing his head, and dad stayed clean.

Mike Love had been his dad's barber since high school, and Papi was now, though only nine years old, an honorary member of an elite men's social club where his dad, Mr. Robert J. Henderson, was the boss. Everybody knew Mr. Robert J. (the "J" stood for "Just Me," his dad used to say) Henderson. Everywhere they went, he knew people. At the gym, in the supermarket, at school, on the street, on the courts, in the bank and at the airport. It didn't matter. It didn't even matter. He could go to the White House, and the President would say hello. That's how well-known Mr. Robert J. Henderson was. He was looked up to and respected by the whole town. The whole community loved him. He helped people. He worked hard. He would do anything for anybody - fix your flat tire, change the oil in your car, give you a ride or anything you needed. Once, Papi saw him giving a ride to Ms. Alston, an elderly neighbor who had lost her husband in a car accident and was living alone and without the care or support of her own two sons. That's the kind of man Mr. Robert J. Henderson was and the kind of man Papi looked up to. Whatever was going on with him and mom had to be something pretty serious for dad to leave. It couldn't be his fault, it just couldn't. Dad was always around, always there. It probably really was "just for a little while" like mom said. Maybe Genny needed to just chill.

In the photo, everyone was smiling, even mom. *"She was such a pretty lady,"* Papi thought. The most beautiful woman in the world, even more beautiful than Ms. Gregory, his first grade teacher. Ms. Gregory had style, too, but mom *was* style - effortless style and class. She knew how to put herself together without looking like she had spent a dime. In reality, she hadn't. She loved to shop at thrift shops, but Papi wouldn't be caught dead in one of those places. Dad either.

Mom didn't care. The fur trimmed, suede jacket she was wearing in the photograph had come from a thrift shop, and her matching necklace and earrings were on a clearance table at Lord & Taylor for a few dollars. She looked like The First Lady of The United States of America, and that made everyone else The First Family. You stepped up your game with Mrs. Robert J. Henderson, but mom was that quiet confidence that didn't pay any attention to what anyone else thought.

Mom's straight white teeth were flashing at the camera, and her big, brown eyes were bright and focused. Not like lately. Lately, mom had been pretending to be happy and cheerful, but c'mon, mom, your children know the difference. Besides, the camera wasn't lying, and a blind man could see the truth. Mom was at ease in the photo, seated behind her son with a genuine smile on her face. There was no pretension or phoniness. She was comfortable and secure with their dad in the picture, no pun intended. Mom was safe and at ease as much as her children were, and the relaxed muscles on her face and shoulders proved it.

What a completely different lady she was today. That picture had been taken about three years ago, and the family had intended to use it on Christmas cards for friends and relatives. Instead, it was distributed on social media pages with a "Merry Christmas" banner across the bottom of the page. So Papi had one of the extra prints in his collection of useful and useless items, and it would soon be time to sort through everything and decide which pile to put the picture in. For now, Papi would keep it as useful because he wanted to show his mom the difference in her persona. She would make up some kind of story, though, and convince him that she was fine, she was alright, it was just his imagination, but "thank you, baby, I appreciate you for caring."

Genny was smiling in the picture, too, a huge grin with chipped tooth, since fixed at the dentist, earned by her when she crashed her bike into a tree. Don't ask. Even Papi knew the tree was there. Genny smiled with confidence, too, and sat in front of their dad with legs crossed, hands clasped and eyes looking straight ahead into the camera. The breakup of mom and dad had probably hurt Genny the most. She adored their dad and wanted to show him off to the world. Papi was hurt, too, but there was a man inside of him that was willing to step up and assume the role of the man of the house. He didn't know exactly what that meant, he wasn't old enough to work and provide, but he learned from watching his dad. Mr. Robert J. Henderson had taught his son things that Genny, as a girl, he hadn't. Maybe it was just time for Papi to lead now that dad was gone. Mom would still be in charge, of course, but Papi could help if she let him. *"No, that would never work,"* Papi thought. Oh well, Papi would offer his assistance to his mother and let her say no. At least he would ask.

"Papi, come downstairs and eat!" Genny yelled.

"Be right there!" Papi yelled back, placing the photo back into the toy chest and grabbing the hairy spider he was looking for. He put the spider in his short pockets and went downstairs, walking faster as he got to the bottom of the staircase attracted to the delicious scent of garlic coming from the kitchen. Papi dropped the spider underneath the dining room table where Genny wouldn't miss it and went over to hug and distract his mom as she reached for plates from the cabinet.

"Hi mom. I love you," Papi said as he squeezed her tight.

"Hi Papi. I love, you too, sweetheart. Are you okay?"

"Yes, I just wanted to tell you I love you and the food smells de-e-e-e-licious."

"Well, good, eat up so we can have a little desert, okay?"

"Desert, too? Ummm, mom.........are you feeling alright?"

"Yes, what's that mean?" she asked, as she placed three white plates on the kitchen counter.

"Nothing."

Papi turned to check if Genny had went into the dining room yet, but she was sitting in front of the laptop in the living room, playing some stupid girl game. *"Why wasn't mom telling her to get off the computer?"*

He went into the dining room, heaven forbid if mom saw the spider first, and took the hairy insect from the floor, placing it instead on the chair Genny, and not mom, would sit in. Just as he finished, Genny came into the dining room and chose to sit in the chair he was going to sit in. Darn it! If he said anything, it would be too obvious.

"Mom, should we come get our plates?" Papi asked, purposely leading his mother.

"Yes, both of you can. You have two hands."

"Genius," Papi said to himself. *"Pure genius."*

Papi went into the kitchen first and took his plate, filled with fettucine noodles and Alfredo sauce, spinach and gooey, cheesy garlic bread. It looked so good, he wanted to eat it right then and there, but mom would have a fit, so he went into the dining room to sit in the empty chair without the spider. Mom would sit at the head of the table, so Genny had no choice.

He took his seat and waited anxiously for his big sister to come around to the other side of the table and find the little surprise he had for her. As Genny came into the dining room with her plate, she walked past her brother, smiling victoriously, and said, "I saw you put it there. You're so lame."

"Genny, that's not nice," said mom from the kitchen.

"Mom, he tried to scare me with his fake spider."

"Aw man," Papi said. He stood up from his chair feeling defeated and reached for the spider to remove it, but just then a little gurgling in his stomach and the onset of gas gave him hope. *"I'll get her after all,"* he thought.

"Okay, Genny, I'm sorry. You were right, I was trying to scare you. I see you're too smart for that, but let's see if you're smart enough to see this coming...."

With the skill of a sharp shooter, he aimed his little tushy perfectly in Genny's direction and released an explosion of gas that made his tummy feel better. There was no longer an aroma of garlic in the room, and the look on Genny's face was better than what he would have achieved with a spider anyway.

"Oh my God, you are so gross. Mom!" she yelled.

"Papi, excuse yourself when you have to pass gas. You know better than that. That is gross. You don't pass gas at the dinner table," Maria said while in the kitchen fixing her own plate.

"Yeah, around the food," Genny said. She covered her plate with one hand and with the other covered her nose.

"I'm sorry, mom. I'm sorry, Genny," he lied.

"He's not sorry, he meant to do it because he couldn't scare me with his dumb spider."

"I *am* sorry," he said again.

"I'm not eating in here with his nasty poot," Genny said. She took her plate and went back into the kitchen. "Mom, can I eat in here, please?"

"No, but you can wait a few minutes in here. Papi, you sit at the table and eat in your own little cloud of funk."

Genny laughed at her mom's comeback.

Papi laughed, too. He sat at the table and ate his food, pretending there was no smell in the room, but it was lingering. He laughed as he ate, and noodles were dangling from his mouth.

When their mother saw Papi's face, she laughed as well, and the whole atmosphere seemed to lighten up. He saw a smile of ease and contentment on his mom's face like the one in the picture, and although he had been chastised for his body's eruption, he was thankful that it brought back the old Mrs. Robert J. Henderson, even if only for a moment.

Chapter Four

Maria

Maria waited for her best friend, Neicy, at Geraldine's Soul Food Restaurant in renovated downtown Addington Park, New Jersey. The redesigned restaurant, now featuring a live, jazz band and over twenty main courses, drew a huge crowd, and there was a line of about 30 anxious people waiting outside. Maria was given the ok by the waitress to be seated although her party was not complete, but Maria was careful to order Neicy's favorite virgin strawberry daiquiri ahead of time to appease the waitress. She also slipped her a $10 bill as a tip in advance for making an exception. Maria didn't have the money she used to have to tip all night, and Neicy knew it, so she had better hurry.

The tables were full of unfamiliar faces. Couples sat in booths adorned with candle lit centerpieces, and Maria tried not to let her jealousy show.

"Who were they?" she wondered. *"How long had they been together? Were they married or just dating, and if just dating, was it their first time? Oh who cared,"* she thought, sipping her cranberry juice, and contemplating sipping Neicy's daiquiri if she didn't come soon. *"It probably wouldn't be long before they, too, were divorcing, and this night of intimacy, food and music will be a painful memory,"* Maria hoped, feverishly attempting to ease the heartache that was consuming her.

As much as she tried not to let it show before her children, she knew that on her best day, Genny and Papi could read her like a book. Of course they could, they only knew one side of her their whole lives: the loving, caring, compassionate and nurturing mom who managed the home, and manage, Maria could. She was a great wife and mom, cooking, cleaning, sewing, cheering, supporting, loving, instructing, teaching, guiding, praying over, praying over some more, basketball practices, karate classes, swim lessons, homework, reading, doctor's appointments, sleepovers, PTA functions, school board meetings, city council meetings, paying bills, staying at her husband's side in all of his business affairs, and raising two fantastic children who were well-mannered, intelligent and respectful. Maria held down the home while Rob was away handling business matters and generating income for his non-profit company that supported young men who were either high school students at risk or, on occasions, transitioning from prison to the workforce. He had a passion for these young men, probably because as a teenager, Rob had spent a few years in prison himself for drug possession. Maria was there, too, and though her mother had tried every way possible to discourage her from staying in a relationship with this teenager convicted of a crime and headed for trouble, Maria maintained her position and proved her mother and family wrong. After serving two and one half years at the tender age of 17, Rob came out a changed man. He never dealt drugs again.

Rob had been an "A" student at Addington Park High School, and he was gifted in football and basketball. His stint with the law cost him scholarship offers from Division I schools around the country, and according to Maria, his coach and teachers turned their backs on him. When Rob was arrested, his bail was set at $500,000. His family didn't have the money, so Maria begged the guidance counselor and teachers, who knew the kind of young man Rob was, to help out, but they said they couldn't. He was left in jail. He didn't talk to Maria much about what had happened, but Maria didn't need for him to. She wanted to be by his side because he was only selling drugs to get money so Maria could go to college with him for free, but no one cared for their side of the story.

Maria always knew the truth about Rob, and she had felt responsible for his dive into the hustle of drug dealing. He wanted to get in the game, make some quick cash, and get out with the help of his cousins who made a living selling cocaine. It was their 9 to 5. They got up in the morning and dressed for work, kissed their "wifeys" goodbye, and then they went out into the world to make a profit for their companies. They did what other white collar 9 to 5ers did, except someone somewhere signed a bill to say that this path of employment was not legal. As a result, Rob was sentenced to ten years in prison, but he served 2 1/2 years and was released. At 19 and a half years of age, he got down on one knee and proposed to the 19 year old Maria, and she said yes without any hesitation. They were married in a small, simple ceremony before a Justice of the Peace with only their family and closest friends. Maria's mother was mortified, and even when Maria told her mother why Rob had ventured into selling drugs, her mother refused to accept it as a valid reason to do anything. Financial aid, grants, scholarships, work study and loans were available to help with the costs of college, and the two of them would have to learn how to work for what they wanted. So they did.

Rob went to college and graduated with a Bachelor's Degree in Business Administration, and Maria graduated with a Degree in Political Science. The two continued to pair up for years in Corporate America and city politics, but Rob was a man's man, and he wanted to have his own. After a twelve year career in the corporate world, Rob abandoned his work and started the non-profit Robert J. Henderson Center for Young Men. Maria left city government, too, and joined him, only to discover that at 34 years of age, she was pregnant with their daughter, Genny, and their son, Papi was born three years later. Maria became a stay at home mom at her husband's insistence, and she devoted herself to helping him with his businesses. The work and money flowed for about ten years until Maria found herself staying up later and later to greet her husband when he came home at night. She knew he was seeing someone else, a woman always knows, and whenever she confronted him, he repeatedly denied it and assured her that she was the only one for him.

"Maybe the only one you are married to, but definitely not the only you are seeing," Maria had said.

Rob was a flirt. He had charm, charisma, a magnetic personality, and he was good in business, so he knew how to talk to people and get what he wanted. He had the ability to talk to you and make you feel like you were the only person in the world, and he could charm the wallets off of anybody. His magnetic personality had attracted and won over Maria. It was a sincere hold he had on her when they were young and in love, but as they grew up together, they grew apart.

Rob loved Maria, he cared deeply for her, but he admitted to himself that he was no longer in love, and it wasn't Maria's fault. She was a great wife, mother, business partner and support. At first he cheated just because he knew he could get away with it and Maria would never know, but he stayed in a relationship with a city employee because, truth be told, the young woman would soon be running for Mayor, and that move would help Rob's declining businesses that he was afraid to tell Maria about. He admitted to himself that it was a selfish and "punk ass" move, but he was willing to take the risk. Rob couldn't afford a scandal, so he served divorce papers on Maria, moved his things out of their home that he could no longer afford, and sold it for just below market value to gain some cash for him and for Maria to walk away with. Rob admitted to his closest friends that he had handled the situation terribly, and he confessed to taking advantage of Maria's vulnerability in the sale of the home she had come to love, but it was for a greater good, he tried to reason. He hoped that Maria would one day agree.

"Hey girl, why you sitting here staring into space?" asked Neicy, as she made her fabulously late appearance. The black, designer shoulder bag must have cost Neicy about $2,000. The two of them couldn't be more opposite, the clothes and accessories wore Neicy, but Maria wore the accessories and clothes. Maria wondered how much money her bff had spent on her navy suit jacket and tailored pants, but it wasn't Maria's money to budget, so she left it alone.

"Second Time Around Consignment Shop in nearby Shrewsbury Township would give that suit away for about $45, but Neicy had to have it off of a better rack, so let her spend the few hundred dollars she no doubt spent to get it. What am I doing?"

Maria thought. *"Always figuring out how much less I can have something for. Forgive me, Lord. I didn't mean it."*

"I'm not staring into space, I'm sitting here trying not to drink your drink," Maria laughed.

"Well," Neicy began, sitting in the booth across from her best friend whom she hadn't talked to since the divorce, "you can have some if you want some. I'll buy another one. You should have just drank it if you wanted it. This dinner is my treat anyway. I'm just glad you finally got out of the house. You've been like a hermit lately."

"That's alright, Neicy, I have money," Maria answered, ignoring her 'hermit' remark. "I'm not that broke."

"Maria, I didn't mean to imply that you are broke. Can I please treat my best friend in the whole world to dinner, please? That's all. I'm going to order another drink, I showed up late, and if you're still the same Maria, I know you probably threw the waitress some change to keep her happy. It's cool, girl, I got it."

The waitress returned to the booth and was instructed by Neicy to bring another daiquiri, so Maria sipped from the first one and settled back in the soft cushion seat to prepare to tell Neicy everything that had happened.

Neicy was a little crazy, but she was honest and real, and she could keep information private. She didn't run her mouth like Pam did, one of Maria's other friends from high school who was still around. You told Pam your business at your own risk. After Maria and Rob were married, Maria found out that Pam had told someone who told someone else that they were married because Maria was pregnant and trying to trap Rob. It was a ridiculous rumor that spread like wildfire, and when Maria never showed up nine months later with a baby, it was assumed that the rumor was true and that Maria had lied to trick Rob into marrying her. This was the silly drama Maria had to deal with whenever Pam was involved in intimate conversations, so Maria learned from her mistake the first time and never invited Pam to private conversations again. They were still friends, but Maria kept her at an arm's length.

"Okay, do your thing."

Neicy laughed. "Do my thing? Yes, I am gonna do my thing. You did your thing for years and was always taking care of a sista, so let me do my thing tonight. Is that alright?"

"Yes, girl, you got it. You are so crazy."

"I got this, okay," Neicy stated. "I can take care of my girl for once. Even if I couldn't take care of you for once, I would take care of you for once. I mean, Maria, you have been holding everything down for years. It's time you let somebody do something for you. You're going to wear yourself out trying to be superwoman for everybody else. What about you?"

"I'm good."

"You're good? Girl, please, you are talking to Neicy. You might be good to your mom and to your kids, but I know the deal. What about you?" Neicy asked again.

"I'm good, Neicy. I'm fine. I just needed to talk to you and be real with you because I can. Is that alright?"

"Of course."

Maria didn't know where to begin, she was embarrassed at her own nervousness. There was no reason for her to be, this was Neicy, one of the few people Maria could be open and honest with, but it was personal for Maria. It concerned her husband and children. At 17 it was cute to call your friend and tell her you and your boyfriend made out in the backseat of his car behind the high school. Were there cameras? Would anybody find out? Was there a chance the cameras had recorded his license plate? That was the big news of the day. Maria could talk about her menstrual cramps in gym class to Neicy without any hesitation, but this was her family. Her own family. Her children. *"Now,"* she thought, *"she knew exactly what her own mother had to go through with her."*

"Neicy........Rob and I aren't separated," Maria began.

"What? You two are getting back together?" Neicy asked, now more engaged in the conversation and leaning forward.

"No, we're not getting back together. That's not going to happen now. Rob and I are divorced."

"Rob and you are what?" Neicy asked, repeating what she heard in utter shock.

"Rob and I are divorced. He served me with divorce papers. I didn't fight him. If he doesn't want to be married to me anymore, he can go. I'm not going to beg him to stay. I felt guilty for years because of his incarceration, and I think he always resented me for it. I'm not going to put him in prison again. He's free to go. I think that is best."

Neicy reclined in her seat and thought carefully about what to say and how to say it, but for a moment, she was speechless.

"Maria, I....I'm sorry. If there's anything I can do to help you and the kids, you know you can call me. Wait....what about the kids? What kind of arrangement do you have? No wonder you haven't been coming out that much lately. I'm so sorry, how could you keep this from me? Are you okay?"

"It was amicable. We share custody. Genny and Papi stay with me, and he can come and see them whenever he wants. He has them every other weekend and for one month during the summer. We put that in the paperwork, but he knows he has complete access to them. He is a good father, and Genny and Papi aren't going to suffer for this. It will work out."

Maria was trying to comfort herself and fight back tears, but she wanted Neicy to comfort her. *"When would she offer some sound advice, some word of encouragement and hope?"* Maria thought. She was tired of soothing herself, and she wiped her eyes with the folded linen napkin set before her.

"Maria, if Genny and Papi live with you, why did you sell your home? Why didn't you stay in the house?"

"I think Rob was having money problems that he didn't want to talk to me about...."

"What do you mean, 'didn't want to talk to you about'? Maria, he's your husband. You're his wife. That is what husbands and wives do, they talk to each other about everything. It's called communication. Communication about the finances, the bills, the budget, the property. Wait, did he just up and sell the house without even asking you?"

"I don't care, Neicy."

"So he just up and sold the house without asking you."

"Well, technically, yes, but we got some money for it, and I walked away with 60% to his 40."

"So where is your money at?"

"I paid some legal bills, put some money in the kids' college funds, paid off all my bills and invested the rest. I'm going to buy a home, but I haven't found what I want yet, so I'll use one year to clear my mind. Neicy, I can't think straight. I can't see straight. I miss Rob so much."

Maria dabbed her eyes again.

"Maria, let's pray."

"I already prayed, Neicy. I pray all the time. God is not listening."

"Maria, let's pray. You don't need me to pray with you for God to listen, but He does say in His word that where two or three are gathered in His name, He is in the midst of them.[26] Please, let's pray. Right now. Right here."

"Alright," Maria agreed reluctantly.

They joined hands across the booth table, and Neicy began praying something, but Maria couldn't even hear what it was. She was trying to hear Neicy, but she didn't. Her mind had reverted to thoughts about Rob and how good he had been to her. Maria lost her husband, and she didn't even know why. He just walked out on her and their marriage. They could have worked it out, whatever it was, but he didn't even give her a chance. He was cold and cruel, almost wicked in how he left her all of a sudden, with no explanation, no rhyme or reason. Maria didn't want to pray. She didn't want to get her hopes crushed by God, too.

Out of the corner of her eye, Maria could see the waitress come within 20' of their table and then walk away, noticing Maria and Neicy both had their heads bowed in prayer.

"She must think we're crazy," Maria thought, *"sitting at this table praying to a God who doesn't listen about a man who doesn't care."*

Maria opened her eyes completely and looked at Neicy praying fervently, "In the name of Jesus!" on her behalf. It was cute, and Maria appreciated it because Neicy had such faith. She believed in God no matter what happened. Maria believed conditionally - if you help me God, I will believe in you. If you work this out, I will believe in you. What good was God if He didn't show Himself as God? He had to actually do something. Even Moses had said all He was doing was talking. Do something. Don't just talk.[27]

"In the name of Jesus!" Neicy prayed, and her voice got louder as guests at nearby tables looked to see who this evangelist was unashamed of the Gospel in a corner booth of a crowded soul food restaurant.

"Hallelujah, Jesus. We give your name praise, glory and honor, Lord, and we thank you in advance. Oh God, we give you glory in advance. Hallelujah! Bless your name!"

Neicy was gone. She had left the natural and was now operating in the spiritual realm, casting out devils and rebuking strongholds in the name of Jesus. It was cool, though, if it worked, amen, but if it didn't, at least God wouldn't be able to say that Maria hadn't tried Him. *"Therefore,"* Maria figured, *"it was His fault because she had called out to Him, but He didn't answer."*

"Maria, have faith!" Neicy shouted.

"Excuse me?"

Neicy opened her eyes and let go of her best friend's hands. "The Lord says have faith. You have to believe, Maria. Without faith, it is impossible to please God.[28] Have faith. He is an awesome God, He can do anything."

Maria was silent for a few minutes and thought, *"That must have been God. Neicy didn't know, or did she? Was this for real? God spoke through crazy behind Neicy to speak to me?"*

"God can use anybody, Maria," said Neicy.

"Okay, now this was getting weird," Maria thought.

"Maria, trust in Him. He's with you, and He's on your side. Go back to God and pray believing. If you ask in prayer and believe that you shall have it, it will be done for you.[29] But if you ask without believing, don't say you tried God and He didn't answer. He wants you to put your faith in Him. In Him, Maria, not in Rob."

Maria didn't say a word. She was afraid to. Neicy had went into some kind of mystical séance where she met and talked with the Spirit of God about Maria, and God answered. He never answered Maria like that, right away, Johnny on the Spot, but Maria would go back to Him in prayer and try to have faith like Neicy suggested.

"Neicy, I don't have the faith that you do. I want to. I want to believe God no matter what. I need to, but, I don't. That's the truth. I prayed and tried before, and nothing happened. Rob still left. He still walked out without any explanation, he still cheated and he still left me for another woman. I prayed and I was still served with divorce papers. I pray, Neicy. I pray as best I can. He's not listening. Go tell Him that. If I don't have faith like you or pray like you or say Hallelujah like you do, don't turn away from me. Hear me even when I don't have all the faith that I need to. It's faith that is bringing me to Him in the first place, even if it is as small as a mustard seed. It's still faith. And faith as small as a mustard seed, He says in His word, is enough."[30] *"There, Preacher, go tell Jesus that,"* Maria thought.

"He's still God. He's God no matter what. He's God if Rob stays, and He's God if Rob leaves. He's still God if Rob never comes back. He's still God, Maria, and He's still good."

"Neicy, you believe that because you're still happily married to your husband. You don't go through anything. I see your faith now, everything is in place for you, but what if Tony leaves you. Will you still be saying *'He's still God, Maria,'*" she asked in a mocking tone.

Maria didn't mean to, but Neicy was unbelievable. Her bills were paid, her house was in order, and she had just strutted in here wearing her wallet on her back trying to tell the budget queen of America about trusting in God no matter what.

"No, Maria, I believe that because it's true. You're in a tough spot right now, Maria, and it may be hard to see God in everything. I believe God because He's real, and He's alive. I go through, too, but I don't share everything because I already turned it over to Him, so I know that no matter what happens, it's going to be alright. Tony has cancer. I gave it to God, and I know it's going to be alright no matter what happens because God is still God. My mother is in Hospice Care, Maria. I wanted to tell you a few weeks ago, but I didn't want to burden you with my situation because of your and Rob's separation. That would have stressed you more. I gave that to God, and I know it's going to be alright whether she lives another 30 years or goes home to see the Lord tonight. He's God all the time, Maria, He's alpha and omega, the beginning and the end. We all go through storms in this lifetime, but He promises in His word that many are the afflictions of the righteous, but the Lord delivers him out of them all.[31]   God promises in His word that He will never leave or forsake us[32], and He tells us that in this lifetime we will have tribulations, but we are to take heart because He has already overcome the world.[33]   These things work for our good, and they produce endurance, perseverance, character and a hope in Him that does not disappoint.[34] God is a good God, and He doesn't mean us any harm. We are blessed to come to know Christ in the fellowship of His suffering[35], and in due season, we shall reap if we do not lose heart."[36]

"Okay, Neicy, you're right. It's not Sunday morning. I appreciate everything you said, I know you're only trying to help. I'm so sorry about Tony and your mother....."

"Why? Are they going to live forever? Am I? Are you? We are all going to go home to see Jesus one day. God is in control. I have to trust Him, Maria. Tony is my husband, but he is not my God. Rob is your husband....."

"Was," Maria interjected.

"Was, but he was not, is not and can never be your God. Trust in Jesus, Maria. He's still God."

The waitress returned to the table and asked if they were ready to order.

"I need another drink," said Maria. "This time, put some alcohol in it."

"Very funny," said Neicy. "I'll just have some living water, and please bring some for my friend here."

"Some what?" asked the waitress.

"Some living water."

The waitress was dumbfounded, but she went to the bar to check with the bartender about the order, and before she returned to say they didn't have it, Maria had taken the hint and made a mental note to call on Jesus again. This time, with faith and trust as Neicy suggested.

"Thanks, Neicy. You always know what to say."

"Don't thank me, sweetheart, thank Jesus. Glory to God."

"Yes, glory to God. Now, where is that darn waitress? I'm hungry!" said Maria.

"Yes, girl, they better come on and feed me, a sista is starving up in this place. I'm about to snatch those wings off of that table over there," she said, eyeing a plate of teriyaki glazed wings meant for other guests.

Maria laughed. Neicy was back. That mystical journey was over, and the crazy, real, and down for whatever bestie had returned and rejoined the party.

41

"Thanks, Neicy," said Maria again. "Thanks for everything. Is there anything I can do for you? I'm so sorry about your mom and Tony."

"You're welcome. Yes there is something you can do for me. Pray. Pray believing. And give God the glory. He's going to work it out."

Now that was the best friend Maria needed to talk to, glory to God.

"And come to church. Why haven't you been coming?" asked Neicy.

"I will. Neicy, I promise, I will. My head is a mess. I can't think straight, see straight....I don't know some days if I'm coming or going. I'm going to come. I pray at home, and Jesus knows my heart."

"Yes, he knows your heart. But faith comes by hearing, Maria, and hearing by the Word of God.[37] The Pastor preaches the Word every Sunday, and I am always encouraged to hold on and trust in Him no matter what it looks like. I am blessed every time I go to church and hear about others who trust in God, and they have far more problems than I do. We just finished a series on Sarah in Bible Study - what a woman! Past the age of childbearing, she trusted God to revive her dead womb and bless her with a son..."[38]

"I know the story...." Maria interrupted, but Neicy kept talking.

"She had to endure infidelity in her marriage, her husband's heart was not with her, he put her in harm's way, and after all that, the Lord says she is going to have a son with the same man, Abraham. Can you imagine? God tells a woman to stay in a marriage after her husband has his baby's mama living in the home and, therefore, lie down with him again so that she can get pregnant with a son God wants her to have. Did Sarah want to stay? God can do what He wants, and He can ask what He wants. He's God."

"Yeah, well, I don't know if I could do that, and I don't know why God wouldn't just bless Sarah or any other woman with a husband who is faithful. Why can't he just make men be faithful to women? You have to go through all this hell to come out with some deep revelation? It's not that deep. If He's God, and He can do anything, and He parted the waters for the Israelites to escape from

Egypt[39] and He called Lazarus forth from the grave[40], then do that. Grant that men would be faithful to their wives, in Jesus' name."

The two laughed.

"Maria, God will grant that you will be the best *you* can be. We're not perfect, but God is, and He will make you perfect enough so that the man who loves you loves you in spite of *your* imperfections. True love doesn't even look at flaws – it loves in spite of them, and it understands that there is also something perfectly imperfect about us all that someone else will have to love *us* in spite of. That's how God is. He loves us unconditionally – in spite of our sins. None of us are worthy of God's love."

"Okay, Neicy," Maria said. She didn't really want a lecture, but she knew once Neicy got started, she would drive her point home.

"Girl, don't hate on all men because of one experience. That's the problem with us, we hold all men accountable for the mistakes one man made. Rob cheated on you, ok. Tony has cheated on me, too, and I forgave him. Trust and believe, many a night I thought about putting something in his coffee, but I had to give it to God and allow Him to work it out however He wanted. I put Tony's behind out of the house. I threw some of his things out. But he prayed, and God showed me that he was truly sorry and had repented, so I forgave him. I am in such a better place, Maria. God loves me so much that Tony has the fear of God in Him now. If he messes around on me again, he messes around on my God, and that's gonna be his problem. God will take care of him. I don't have to do anything."

"Yeah, that sounds good, but are you happy? Do you trust him?"

"Maria, I am happy with myself. Yes, Tony makes me happy, but if Tony leaves, I am still happy. My happiness isn't based on him, and he knows it. I think that is what keeps him in line. I want him, but I don't need him. God keeps him in check. Please, girl, I plead the blood of Jesus over my marriage every morning. It's in God's hands. Whatever happens, God already knows, and He has already worked it out for my good. You give Rob too much power and authority in your life. You need to give that place of high honor you put Rob in over to Jesus. Put God first, and He will add everything. Your marriage is out of order because your priorities are. When is the last time you sat through a Sunday service? When was the last time your family came to church?"

"Are you judging me?" asked Maria, nearly upset with what she deemed were Neicy's high and mighty conclusions.

"No. Are you getting upset?"

"Girl, please. No."

"Yes you are. You asked me to come and talk to you. I came. I'm talking to you. I'm telling you the truth, and you don't want to hear it. So are we done here?"

"What the hell was her problem?" Maria wondered. "Are we done here?" she asked, repeating Neicy's question.

"Yes. Am I wasting my time, Maria? Are we done here? If you don't want to hear the truth, and you think I have an attitude or think that I think I am better than you for some silly reason, tell me now."

"Oh this child has lost her damn mind," Maria thought. She wanted to go off on her, but..... hold on. Maria knew the power of Neicy's Holy Ghost persuasion, and she would have to, out of respect for the truthfulness of Neicy's argument, listen to her, or to the God that was using her. As much as Maria hated to admit it, Neicy was on point.

Maria hesitated for a moment, and then said with assertiveness, "No, go ahead and say what you have to say. But then I'm going to say what I have to say."

"That's cool. You give Rob too much power. He's in God's place. Everything you said tonight was about Rob and how he hurt you, he left you, he served you with divorce papers, he cheated on you and he left you for another woman. God kept you, Maria. You were supposed to be out that night when Rob was arrested for selling drugs, remember? Your mother made you stay home. If you had went with Rob, your behind would have been in jail, too. God kept you from that. God kept you when you thought you were pregnant at 17, remember? We went to the doctor's office together, you were a nervous wreck. God was with you then. God made it possible for you to go to college and graduate with a Bachelor's Degree, to marry Rob and have two beautiful, healthy children, to have a good life, a good home, all your needs met, and you're in good health yourself. You've had some good days and some bad days, but Maria, it isn't over. Be grateful for what you do have. Thank God every day. Never give up on Him. He will never give up on you."

There was silence as Maria was forced, through the power of the Holy Spirit, to listen to and receive everything Neicy had said. There was a presence about them, an unexplainable, mystical, supernatural presence. Maria felt her mouth tingling, and she could not fight the power of the God who had sent Neicy to Geraldine's that night. God was real. He was listening.

"Maria," Neicy continued, "thank God for what you do have. I know you're hurt right now, but this, too, shall pass. I don't know why Rob left. He hurt you. But Jesus loves you so much, and He's waiting for you. Come back to Him now."

"I.........I will, Neicy. I mean, I am."

"Baby, we have to be grateful for the time we have here. We won't always be here, on this side. We are like flowers. We all have a set time that God has determined when we are scheduled to depart from this lifetime. You know those petunias I get every year for my garden? I love to look at them, Maria. I plant them, water them, fertilize them, and make sure they get enough sunlight, and they bloom and grow and keep the yard looking nice for the time that they are allotted – about six months. After their time is up, they die. So I have to enjoy them while they last. Now, all of them should last several months, and I do the best I can to take care of them, but what if somebody steps on them, or they are accidentally cut down when Tony mows the yard. I might think they died before their time. When is our time up? No sooner or later than when God has determined. Our days and times are in His hands.[41] The flowers are lent to me for a while, and then they die, just like we all do. We go home, Maria. Treasure every day you have here. Treasure your family, your children and your friends. But most of all, treasure the Creator who created all things, who gives and takes away. Whatever is God's will shall be done. He has a plan for you, Maria. It's not all being revealed right now, but His plans are for your good.[42] Trust in Him again. Yes, the Lord says, trust in Me. I am the Lord your God. Hallelujah, glory to God, oh bless His name, Jesus...."

Needing to stop Neicy before she got carried away, Maria interrupted and said, "Okay, Neicy. Thank you. Thank you so much, glory to God."

Continuing as if Maria hadn't said a word, Neicy said, "Hallelujah. Glory to God. We need to worship Him, a sham de le ba osa"," or something like that, speaking in tongues.[43]

"Oh Lord, she's gone again," Maria thought.

"Hallelujah! Praise the Lord," said Neicy.

The waitress returned and this time wasn't bothered by their prayer group at Geraldine's. She placed two tall glasses of water on the table, and Neicy lifted her glass to toast.

"To Jesus Christ, the physician of our souls, and to living water," said Neicy as she raised her glass to Maria's. "Oh my God, no one satisfies like Jesus."

"To Jesus Christ and to living water," said Maria.

The two tapped their glasses and drank in honor of the God who had brought them together for His glory. Neicy stood up from the table and raised her glass as the jazz band finished a song.

"To Jesus Christ and to Living Water, everybody up in this place. Hallelujah!"

A few women looked over and said "Hallelujah" with her.

"Hallelujah!" Neicy shouted again, dancing in the aisle by their seat.

Now some of the customers were looking at Neicy like she was crazy, and Maria could not have that, not after Neicy had just went before the throne of grace on her behalf. So Maria, against her more civil and ladylike judgment, got up from the table and joined Neicy, dancing before the Lord with all her might as King David.[44] The customers, at first turned off by their praise and worship on a Friday night, now applauded, and the band played an up-tempo gospel number that complimented the two. They may have thought the women were drunk, but there was something in the water and in the prayer that shattered every inhibition Maria had about letting herself go. She danced and clapped and shouted "Hallelujah" before the guests, mostly African American, who shouted "Hallelujah! Praise Him!" right along with them.

Praise and worship was a universal language that joined strangers drinking alcohol with wailing women drinking living water, all for the glory of God. The guests outside the front doors were looking through the glass windows between the lettering "Geraldine's" to see what the commotion was all about. One of the musicians in the band grabbed a tambourine and began to play it with all of his might, and two female background singers began to sing "Praise Him! Praise Him!" in perfect harmony that transcended the restaurant into a sanctuary filled with the highest praise. It was monumental.

Maria, too, had entered the supernatural realm of praise and worship, liberated by the powerful anointing that filled the atmosphere. The glory of God was in the house. Waiters and waitresses paused with trays on their shoulders, and couples seated in booths waiting for their food instead waited to see what God would do next.

Neicy shouted "Hallelujah, praise Him," without any reservation, and Maria, completely surrendered to her Lord and Savior, lifted her arms with a tear rolling down her right cheek. She was free, born again, and full of joy, unspeakable joy. Only Jesus could do this. Foot-stomping piano riffs, bass, guitar and drums charged the music to its crescendo, inviting every patron into the Holy of Holies without regard for race or gender. They rejoiced in the presence of the Almighty, exuberantly lifting their voices and clapping their hands. Then, as if on a perfectly rehearsed musical queue, the band slowed the music to its finale, and Maria and Neicy stopped dancing and took their seats, laughing, joyful, and full of the Holy Ghost. The restaurant burst into a thunderous applause with several couples giving the two women a standing ovation.

"Glory to God! Glory to God!" Neicy shouted.

Maria was busy fanning herself and speaking in an unintelligible language on this day of Pentecost, something that had only happened once in her life before.

The Maître' D came over to their table and thanked them, saying they would look into having a Gospel Band on Sundays, and Maria and Neicy were welcome to come back anytime.

"Of course, we will," said Neicy to the server, a young man who could not have been more than twenty five years old.

The two women were slightly out of breath. Maria took a few deep breaths, lifted a napkin to wipe her forehead, and shut her eyes to focus in on what she needed to say to her sister in Christ.

"Neicy......."

"Yes."

"…..I love you so much for this. Glory to God, Jesus is just what I needed."

"Yes, He is. To Jesus Christ, To Living Water," Neicy said, raising her glass to toast again.

"To Jesus Christ, To Living Water."

Chapter Five
Genny

Next month, Genny would be thirteen years old, and next year, she would be entering high school. Genny was looking forward to being a teenager and going to school with block class scheduling and pep rallies for the sports team. Addington Park had a reputation of being one of the best athletic schools in the state, and although their return to mom and dad's hometown was like a success story gone wrong, Genny was excited about playing basketball for Addington Park. Her dad had worked with her from the time she could pick up a ball and dribble, and Genny was skilled, just like her dad was. She was the starting point guard at East Borough Middle School and was averaging 18 points per game, five assists and seven rebounds. The Coach from East Borough High School had come to the games and asked about Genny, but honestly, Genny thought East Borough sucked. She didn't want to play organized sports there. She wanted to play where girls were stronger and could challenge her.

Genny never had the opportunity to go to sports camp, and she didn't need to. Her dad had coached her on every aspect of basketball - dribbling, passing, shooting, defensive stance, conditioning and form. She had been maintaining a 62% free throw percentage and 86% percentage from the foul line. She could hit three pointers with ease and several times scored at the buzzer to seal victory over an opposing school. She was the one her team and coach counted on in tight

49

situations, and although there was some degree of pressure, Genny loved the challenge, and she especially loved the high five her dad would give her at the end of every game. She had an air of confidence on the basketball court, having been molded into the image of her dad by the man himself, and he never liked to lose so Genny inherited that same swagger.

He used to tell her, *"Your opponent has already lost once you step on the court. It's a mental thing. You own the court. So own it. They see you coming. Don't give anything away. If they want it, they have to take it. If they take it, it's theirs. But you own it, so it can never be theirs. Maintain, Genny. Maintain the mental and the physical. You will win every time."*

That philosophy worked at East Borough, there really wasn't any competition in the district, but at Addington Park, those young men and women played basketball to survive, to stay out of jail, and to escape the ghetto. They had more passion and more reason to play. They went at it hard. Roughnecks from the hood suited up against privileged suburban children who ate dinner last night with mom and dad, knew nothing about the projects, gang banging or racial profiling and drove SUVs with legitimate tags. These same over privileged kids actually thought they could come in Addington Park's house and win a basketball game, too, stealing the dreams and hopes of the state's least likely to succeed? The young people from the inner city would never let that happen - Addington Park was too hungry. They wanted it bad, real bad, and they would never let anybody just walk into their house and take it from them, according to Genny's dad.

Conference titles and state championships were the norm for the city's athletes, and though it was true that the city was mostly known for the negative reports and stereotypes of crime, gang violence, shootings, drugs, corruption and poverty, there was a greater potential in the rebuilding of the city and the investment residents and business owners were willing to make to reclaim the town's rich heritage. That would mean better schools for the youth because everyone agreed that education was the most important and valuable tool every child had. So their move into the city was timed perfectly and was a great match for Genny and Papi who were groomed to excel academically and athletically.

East Borough had been easy. Genny was the only one who played hard, street basketball there. Her teammates used to tease her and say that she played like a boy. She had trained a few summers at the Boy's and Girl's Club in Addington Park with boys, and they were easy on her when she was younger, cute and in pigtails, but not once she became a solid player. No boy wanted to get clowned for letting a girl take him to the hoop or beat him down the court, so they blocked her shots, stole her passes, took her to the hoop and dunked on her every time they got the ball. Her dad put her in pickup games, assuring the young boys that Genny could play, and they cooperated with him because in Addington Park, Mr. Henderson was a legend and you didn't question him. However, they didn't take Genny seriously, even if she was Mr. Henderson's daughter, and she would run up and down the court for each eight minute quarter without ever touching the ball. She could be wide open, at the opposite end of the court, and no one would pass her the ball. If she by some miracle actually touched the ball on offense, her teammates screamed at her to pass it to them, so she did, almost afraid to disobey their order. Getting inside the paint for a shot was as much a possibility as her winning the lottery, so Genny stayed outside the perimeter of actual play, in three point zone. The boys trusted her to take the three point shots if they were desperate, and Genny usually made them, but since she wanted to get closer to the basket, their denial of her made her hungrier. Dad knew what he was doing. When Genny returned to East Borough with girls, she was so hungry for an inside shot that she nearly plowed down her defenders. She received many contested calls for blocks by coaches who screamed, "You gotta be kidding! That was an offensive foul!" Genny developed into a warrior on offense, she took no prisoners and showed no mercy, and that was exactly what her dad had been aiming for.

The boys she played with and against were like little Tarzans, beating their adolescent Tarzan chests in front of this little girl who threatened them with her three point shot and ambidextrous ball handling skills. They played harder against her than they did each other, having to prove to every player and spectator in the gym that these alpha males were the males and she was the female. Dad watched from the sidelines and never rescued his daughter from the slam dunks in her face and intercepted passes until one newcomer told him Genny played like a little girl and shouldn't be on the court. Robert J. Henderson, never one to back away from a challenge, put up $100 to have that man's 10 year old son play a one-on-one game against his eight year old daughter. Mr. Henderson's cousin, Walter, worked at the Club and held the money while Genny went at it for ten minutes against a boy who, though the same size as she was, could jump twice her size.

Genny was able to score two quick baskets on layups, faking and drawing the foul both times. The young boy's dad was livid from the sidelines while Mr. Henderson showed no emotion. The player's name was Chris Walker, and he blocked Genny's next shot attempt and went in for an uncontested layup. Chris Walker outplayed Genny for the next few baskets, scoring easily against her on shots inside the paint.

"Defense, Genny, defense!" her dad yelled from the side.

Genny got low and stayed on Chris like white on rice, nearly stealing the ball from him every time. He was a strong ball handler, however, taking the ball behind him and between his legs, impressing Genny with his fluidity and style. She was trying to believe, as her dad had always told her, *"this is your house,"* but Chris had moved in, changed the curtains and threw out the furniture. She didn't want to disappoint her dad, so she went up for a rebound, grabbed it, and dribbled back to three point range easily sinking a shot, "all net," her dad's favorite. She looked over at him on the sidelines, and he was clapping for her and beaming with pride.

"You gonna let a girl do that to you, man?" Chris' dad was yelling from the sidelines. "That's a mother f----- girl! Handle your business, man!"

"Whoa, hold up," said Mr. Henderson. "What's that supposed to mean? That's my daughter you're talking about."

Genny and Chris were shortly after escorted off the court by some of the spectators, who noticed the intensity of the yelling between the two fathers was likely to erupt into some kind of physical altercation. Walter gave each dad his $100 back and called the game. The unofficial score was 14 - 9, and Chris was ahead and would have probably won, but no one would ever know. It was likely for the best because this way each dad walked away with his pride intact and a story to tell about how he had to put his child on the court "to represent." Genny wasn't bothered by any of it. She earned the respect early on of the local basketball players, not just because she was Mr. Henderson's daughter, but because she held her own against the top ranked alpha male basketball player in Addington Park at the time.

So the return to this environment, where basketball was life or death, would force Genny to step her game up, and that was exactly what she wanted. She was happy about the move, but she would never let her mom and dad know. No, Genny would leave them to suffer for their decision and insensitivity until they apologized to her and Papi and reunited.

Mom made sure Genny received the best education possible throughout her whole life. She was brought up in private schools where advanced curriculums positioned Genny for talented and gifted programs at public schools when she transferred, so Genny was a double-sided threat, just like her dad had been. She listened to the stories her parents told others about Robert J. Henderson "back in the day" and how he used to take two and three people at a time to the hoop. He was a former standout point guard, 6' 2", who could dribble, shoot, pass, rebound and dunk. Her dad had been honest about his mistake at 17, but Genny thought the whole thing was romantic since he was trying to make money for the lady he loved to go to college. Of course, Grandma wasn't trying to hear any of it, and she was no fan of the former high school basketball star then or now. Genny was starting to agree with her grandmother, but her loyalty to her father would never cause her to take a public stand against him, so she kept her opinions to herself.

Of Pride and Prejudice[45] peeked from the open fuchsia bin positioned next to Genny's full sized bed, now covered with a rose and beige comforter, beige bed skirt and floral pillow shams in gold and pink. Genny hadn't had a chance yet to unpack the coordinating valances she had picked out while shopping with her mom a few years ago, but the beige mini blinds in the windows would suffice for now. Genny never read the complete book. Ms. Franklin, her Gifted and Talented English teacher, had given Genny the book to read, but she loved The Diary of Anne Frank.[46] It was not on Ms. Massey's reading list, so Genny read it anyway and planned to write a report for her Writing Class next year.

Genny loved to read, she always had her nose in a book, and she was grateful that her mom had instilled a love of reading in her at an early age. They used to take family trips to the bookstore, and Genny could sit there for hours and read through bestsellers in no time. Reading helped her to escape. That's where she learned to dream, to imagine, and to soar. Dad was right. It was mental. Reading encouraged her mind to soar, to travel around the world, and to enter into the palatial homes and mansions of main characters woven into storylines of intrigue, love, fiction and romance. Genny enjoyed a round-trip ticket to a far-away land every time she picked out a new book to read. She was a well-travelled pre-teen who had seen more places in her young years than most adults do in their entire lifetime. A Tree Grows In Brooklyn[47] took Genny to early 20th century Williamsburg; Kate Chopin's aggressive feminism in her work, The Awakening,[48] opened Genny's eyes to Louisiana in the 1800's; Alice Walker's The Color Purple[49] captured Genny's imagination of what life was like in the south circa 1930, and Emily Dickinson and Walt Whitman's poetry were like literary time machines that took Genny back to an earlier America when themes of life, death, spirituality and politics excited line length, meter and structure. Genny's favorite books, Incidents In The Life Of A Slave Girl, 1861[50] by the young woman, Harriet Ann Jacobs, herself and Maya Angelou's I Know Why The Caged Bird Sings[51], had already been unpacked and sat in the number one and two space in the top row of her wooden bookcase, respectively.

A New King James Version of The Holy Bible and Eugene Peterson's The Message[52], an easy to read version of The Bible, were on the second shelf. As Genny contemplated rearranging her books in order of her interest, she considered picking up The Bible and travelling to Jerusalem again. Genny had walked along the shores of Galilee, she heard Jesus pray in the Garden of Gethsemane, and she accompanied the Apostle John to the island of Patmos as he received instructions and visions. She saw Peter and the other disciples flee when Jesus was arrested, and she cried with his mother at His crucifixion. She heard the voice from heaven say, "This is My beloved Son in whom I am well pleased. Hear Him," and she, too, was at the Transfiguration with Peter, James and John where Jesus met and talked with Moses and Elijah. This was the power of her imagination, of course, whenever she read anything - she didn't just read words on a page, she envisioned herself in the text and the story came to life. She was a visual reader, and since she was too advanced to choose the books she read as a child that had pictures, she formed images and slide shows in her own mind through state-of-the-art graphic presentations courtesy of her brilliant intuition.

Instead of boarding her first-class flight and taking the much needed trip to Judea, Genny glanced at her cell phone on vibrate as a call from her dad came in.

"Ugghh," she said to herself. "Hello?" she answered, as if she didn't know who it was.

"Hi baby. How's everything with my favorite daughter?"

"I'm your only daughter, aren't I?" Genny wanted to say. She didn't feel like pretending everything was okay anymore. She wanted to ask him straight out. So she did.

"Daddy, are you and mom divorced?" Genny asked.

There was a few seconds of silence, and Genny listened closely to his breathing, detecting nervousness and uneasiness with the question.

"I knew it," she thought.

"Genny, what has your mom told you?" he asked.

"Here he goes, Mr. Robert J. Henderson, the 'J' stands for 'Just turn everything around,'" Genny thought.

"Nothing," Genny honestly replied.

"Baby girl, no matter what happens between me and your mother, it doesn't ever mean that I don't love you. I love you. I love Papi. I love your mom. No matter what happens...."

"Then why aren't you here?" Genny asked, refusing to sugarcoat anything to make him feel better about his own mistakes.

"Okay............we are just giving each other some space to work through our differences. We are going to try and work it out so that we can be together again........as a family, just like we have always been."

"Daddy, I don't believe you."

"I'm sorry, Genny. That's the truth."

"No it isn't. You and mom are divorced. You're not separated. You're divorced, and you left her for another woman. Why don't you just tell us the truth?"

This time the silence provided Genny with no breathing on the other end of the line. There was complete silence. She listened for some kind of clue, but there was nothing. She held the phone for a few seconds more before asking if he was there.

"Did your mom tell you that?"

"She didn't have to, Dad. We hear you guys arguing all the time. I hear mom crying on the phone and in her bedroom. She takes showers so she can cry and thinks we don't notice her red eyes when she comes out. She misses you, and so do we. But you don't appreciate *us* anymore. If you did, you would have never left, no matter what your differences were."

Genny was tearing up herself, and her voice was cracking. She didn't care anymore. She wanted to say what she wanted to say to him.

"Why can't you stay? Why can't you come back?"

"Genny, I'm so sorry. I would never do anything to hurt you, Papi or your mother. I love you all. I promise you, it is going to work out...."

"How? Are you coming home tonight? Is it true that you have another woman? Are you going to marry her and take care of her and her family? What about us? Can dads just do that?"

"Genny....."

"You lied. You lied to all of us."

"Genny, I'm here. I'm here for you...."

Genny was so upset that she hung up her phone and turned it off. It was a bold move for the young girl, but it also was a desperate cry for his help. She wished she could cuss and say a bad word like he did when he got upset. *"F---, S---, God d---."* There must have been some relief in it because he resorted to it whenever he and mom argued.

How could this man? How could he be so selfish and uncaring? How dare he call her up and call her his favorite daughter, like nothing had even happened. Like she was just supposed to accept this divorce and his lies and pretend again not to notice, not to be affected by anything they did, not to speak up because she should be grateful for a roof over her head, food in her stomach, and shoes on her feet. Yeah, you provide all that, Mr. Henderson, but what about love? What about family? What about staying together and being there for your children? Son of a bitch," she thought (she had heard her grandmother call him that). Genny thought it, she didn't say it, but it didn't make her feel any better.

"Maybe that only works for grownups."

She turned on the television set to fill the room with noise and locked the door so that neither Papi nor her grandmother, who was looking after them until their mom came home, could come in.

Genny tried calling April to talk, but her phone went right to the answering machine. As upset as Genny was, she refused to feel like she had been defeated, so she picked up her Bible, fell to her knees, and opened the book to whatever page it landed on and began to read.

The top of the page was **Habakkuk 2:1:** *"I will stand my watch and set myself on the rampart, and watch to see what he will say to me, and what I will answer when I am corrected."*

No, not that.

She closed the book and opened it again to whatever page it landed on and began to read.

The top of the page this time was **James 1:19:** *"So then, my beloved brethren, let every man be swift to hear, slow to speak, slow to wrath; for the wrath of man does not produce the righteousness of God."*

Aw, come on!

One last time, Genny closed the Bible and opened it again to whatever page it landed on and began to read.

The top of the page this last time was **Job 1:5:** *So it was, when the days of feasting had run their course, that Job would send and sanctify them, and he would rise early in the morning and offer burnt offerings according to the number of them all. For Job said, "It may be that my sons have sinned and cursed God in their hearts." Thus Job did regularly."*

Genny gave up. What was God trying to tell her? He didn't have anything to say about Mr. Henderson?

One more time, perhaps. Genny tried a fourth and absolutely last time, closing the Bible, saying a silent prayer, and opening it this time to **Psalm 20:1:** *"May the Lord answer you in the day of trouble; May the name of the God of Jacob defend you; May He send you help* *from the sanctuary, and strengthen you out of Zion; May He remember all your offerings, and accept your burnt sacrifice. Selah..."*

"*Yes, Lord,*" Genny prayed, "*defend me and mommy and Papi. Send help from your sanctuary. Answer us and remember us for your own namesake. In Jesus' name.*"

"*There,*" Genny thought. "*God would get him.*" She had read through the Bible before, and she remembered reading somewhere "Let vengeance be Mine, sayeth the Lord."[53]

Genny closed the Bible and returned it to the bookshelf. As she prepared for bed, she thought about her dad. "*Robert J. Henderson, the 'J' stood for 'Just Me.' Well, he's right, God, the 'J' does stand for 'Just Me,' because that's the only person he is thinking about - 'Just him.'*"

Chapter Six
Papi

"Daddy!" Papi screamed with joy, answering the telephone on its second ring as soon as he noticed it was his father.

"Hi Son! How are you doing?"

"I'm good, daddy. Daddy, when are you coming home?" Papi asked, excited to speak to the man who had never let him down before.

"I'll be home soon, Papi. How's school?" he asked, trying to swiftly change the subject and feel his son out.

"Good. We just started. I like my teacher, Ms. Charles. She's real nice, and she doesn't give us a lot of homework."

"That's good to hear, son. How's Genny?" he asked, needing to hear how things were with his daughter from her brother's perspective.

"She's good, dad. You know how she is."

"Yeah, but you are her brother, and I know she trusts you. Is she okay?"

"I guess, dad, I don't know. Do you want me to get her?"

"No, that's okay, just tell her I asked about her, please. How's your mom?"

"She's good."

"Is she home?"

"No, she went out with Ms. Neicy."

"........okay....is grandma with you and Genny?"

"Yes, do you want to speak with her?"

"No, that's alright. I'll talk to her later."

"Daddy, I've been practicing my nine point drills, can you come watch me like you used to, please. Please, daddy?"

"You've been practicing, huh. I would love to come see you. Matter of fact, I'll pick you up Friday after school and we can spend this weekend together, okay."

"You promise, daddy?" asked Papi, eagerly anticipating the time with his father.

"I promise. Now, I need you to do something for me. Has mom talked to you and Genny about us?"

"No.......well, not really....."

"Well, how?"

"She just said we would be here for a little while and that you were both trying to work some grown up things out."

"Is that all she said?" he asked.

"Yes."

"Are you sure, Papi?"

"Yes....well, *she* didn't say anything, but Genny said you and mom are divorced and not ever getting back together again."

"Did your mother tell Genny that?"

Frustrated, Papi answered, "Daddy, I don't know. I think Genny thinks you and mom are divorced. But even divorced people can be together again if they want to, right dad?" Papi was hopeful that his dad would say yes.

Mr. Henderson hesitated. He couldn't keep it up much longer. He loved his wife, he had been with her his entire life, but he had already signed the divorce papers and there was no looking back. He planned to marry Sophia Simmons, future Mayor of the City of Addington Park, to improve his businesses and political connections, and although he admitted that it was a completely selfish move on his part, he needed it. In fact, the sooner he went ahead and married his new wife, the sooner he could lose his guilt and be honest with everyone, including himself, that he was not coming home to Maria and his children.

Sophia Simmons was seventeen years younger than Mr. Henderson, about 5'5", shapely, cute and a new face in town. She had graduated from Penn State University and worked for the State of New Jersey before opening a thriving real estate office and serving as a City

Councilwoman for several years. She was a good connection for Mr. Henderson, in the know and among the state's professionals, business owners and politicians - just what Mr. Henderson needed to improve his failing enterprises. She ensured connections for him. He had invested most of his and Maria's savings in new businesses that promised a huge return on his money, but to his and every other investor's disappointment, tanked before the second year was through: a tattoo parlor on the corner of Main Street, one of the best locations for new businesses in the city; a waterpark on the city's redeveloped beachfront, which marketing executives researched and forecast huge profits by inasmuch as the demographics, income per capita and lifestyles of the city's residents were predicted to change drastically; and a ten story, chic condominium complex with oceanfront views, spiral staircases and complimentary doormen like the old days. Many complained that the condos were outrageously priced, and since it was rumored that organized crime had been involved, the city earned another negative report that frightened potential buyers. Simultaneously, the non-profit Robert J. Henderson Center for Young Men was facing resistance from residents who complained at City Hall that the young men who frequented the Center were attracting gang activity, drugs and shootings. True, there had been two shootings near the Center since he opened it, and one of the shootings did target one of his young protégés, but Mr. Henderson fought back at City Hall, arguing that the Center was one of the only places these young men could turn to that didn't judge them for their past mistakes and would offer them another chance.

Ms. Simmons heard the impassioned and strikingly handsome man speak on a few occasions, and she was interested in him, especially when they first met, and he told her that he and his wife were separated. It was just a little white lie at the time for Mr. Henderson, and he had only intended to spend one night with her out of lustful attraction and curiosity. When he lost his investments, however, and she shared confidentially that she would be running for Mayor (a race she would no doubt win against the unpopular incumbent), Mr. Henderson saw dollar signs again. He convinced himself that he had done all he could do and that he had been the best father and husband a man could possibly be. After sharing the story of his incarceration with Sophia, he became convinced by her perspective that his failure in business was all Maria's fault anyway. All he needed, Sophia seductively enchanted him, was a good woman by his side who could bring him up in the business world and not bring him down. He was a hustler himself, game recognizes game, and perhaps he shouldn't have been so easily ensnared by Sophia's deceptive charm, but he went willingly into the arms of another woman who guaranteed greener grass on the other side.

Mr. Henderson was vulnerable. Sophia overpowered him when he was down and out, and he became less interested in Maria and more interested in this future Mayor of Addington Park whose money talked and who wasn't too bad in bed either. Lying and cheating on his wife became easier once he was thoroughly convinced that all of the problems he ever had in his life were "her" fault, as Sophia would say, never mentioning Maria by name. If Rob mentioned Maria by name, Sophia would pout.

He fell hard, as Sophia introduced him to business executives and dignitaries from the city, county and state with whom he forged new relationships and explored creative, new ideas for successful ventures that excited the failed businessman and renewed a passion in him for living life at its finest. Sophia would toast to him aboard private yachts and first class flights to Italy, Croatia and Caya Coco, Cuba, Sophia's favorite vacation spot.

"I'm going on a business trip," he would tell Maria, who all along knew that her husband was having an affair. Whenever Maria confronted him, he would lie and turn the argument around to imply that she was insecure and always accusing him of cheating so he might as well.

Maria fought the battle with her husband for over a year, wearied emotionally and spiritually by his incessant lies, toxic behavior and verbal abuse. Maria prayed throughout the ordeal but became disheartened as her prayers fell on deaf ears and her husband continued his extramarital relationship in spite of his commitment to be committed to her and their children. After 27 years of marriage and 32 years of being together as a couple, their marriage ended in a county courtroom with a judge who knew nothing about them and two lawyers who both tried to portray the other as the reason for the split. Maria's only saving grace was that her husband actually defended her character before his own attorney. He was such a shrewd businessman that he timed the divorce after the sale of their marital home so that Maria wouldn't ask for it. Instead, she walked away with 60% of the closing price – $215,000.

She was an emotional wreck. Their marriage was over, and although she knew it had something to do with another woman, she didn't know who or why. Her best friend, Neicy, had been her support throughout the "separation", and she encouraged Maria to pray and come to church. Rob still left, however, so Maria neglected prayer for a while until recently, when she returned to her private sanctuary at home to lay it all on the altar before God.

Maria moved into a three bedroom rental home in North Addington Park, rented to her for a mere fraction of the asking price from one of Rob's many business associates who would take care of her and the kids as Rob asked, and although she had enough money to move somewhere else, she needed time to think and was happy to accept the offer, fooling herself into believing that Rob must have intended to reunite with her since he made sure to provide for them. She was heart-broken, but she didn't dare show it around her children, so she painstakingly tried to hide her tears in bathroom showers, middle of the night prayers and rides in the car to wherever New Jersey's Route 18 took her. This happened on and off for weeks, but Maria's dinner tonight at Geraldine's lifted her spirits, and there was healing and deliverance, wholeness in the Pool of Bethesda, and Maria, glory to God, was the first to jump in.

"Daddy, are you there?" asked Papi, who trusted in his dad no matter what anyone said or thought about him.

"Yes, son, I'm here. I'm always going to be here for you and Genny and mommy. You understand?"

"Yes.....but are you coming home daddy? And are you and mommy divorced like Genny said?"

"Papi, I will explain everything to you when I see you on Friday, okay?"

"Okay."

"I love you, Papi. I love you with all my heart."

"I love you, too. And I can't wait to see you Friday!" Papi shouted, not bothered by the uneasiness his questions had caused his father and interested only in spending the weekend with the father he loved and adored.

"See you Friday."

"And Genny, too?"

"And Genny, too."

"And mommy, too?"

"And mommy, too, sure....she can come if she wants."

"Yeah!!! Just like we used to do. Remember dad? Remember when we used to just get in the car and go for a ride, the four of us together. Can we do that again?"

"Sure, Papi, just like we used to. I'll see you Friday, okay?"

"Okay. Bye, daddy. Don't be late!"

"No, don't you be late. I'll see you at five."

"Ok. See you at five. Goodnight, daddy."

"Goodnight son."

Papi didn't have to end the call, it had already ended when he looked at the face of the phone to terminate the call. On the other side was a teary eyed father who still had a tenderness in his heart for his children, and who wondered for a brief moment if he had made a mistake. He held his head in his hands and then made two unanswered calls to his former wife's private cell phone number. Even if she was out with Neicy, as his son told him, she should still pick up that damn phone when he called. Rob still regarded himself as her man and knew that Maria's loyalty to him would never, not this soon anyway, pair her with another man. Jealous thoughts filled his mind as he pictured Maria in the arms of any other lover but himself.

Maria wasn't the vindictive type, she never held a grudge, and she had too much class to allow just anybody to get that close to her. Yes, they were divorced, but she was still his. He could do whatever he wanted, the other women didn't mean anything to him, but not Maria. *"No man will ever say that he had been with her unless he was her husband,"* thought Rob, still protecting, professing and providing. Maria was a good woman, quality and top notch. Rob had messed up, but he would never allow any man to mess up with her.

"What time was it?" he wondered. Rob glanced at the clock - 8:45 p.m. on a Friday night. *"They parted on good terms, why wouldn't she answer her phone? She always answered,"* he thought.

He tried a third time, and this time it went straight to the answering machine. *"So either she turned her phone off or it just died,"* he figured, preferring the latter explanation.

"Maria, it's me. Give me a call when you get this message."

Rob hoped that she was okay and assured himself that she was. After all, she was a grown woman. He experienced a warm, surge of guilt in the pit of his soul that though soothed by the soft lips of his future wife on his neck, did not go away. He almost didn't want Sophia as she reached for him. His time that night with her was more routine and robotic, not the rush of intense passion they usually enjoyed, but he pleasured Sophia thinking of Maria, who drifted into a deep sleep afterwards. The experience normally saw Rob holding his younger love in his arms until they both retired, but he couldn't sleep since talking to his son and daughter. So he lay in bed, looked upwards and thought things over.

In his mind, Rob reasoned, justified and explained everything away. Yes, he spent time with Sophia, and it was good while it lasted, but then it was over. He could get up from the bed with Sophia and erase the memory of what happened with a wash cloth and a bathroom sink. He had cheated on Maria many times during their marriage, but he always came home. He would stop on his way home and pick up roses and her favorite perfume "just because." Maria never suspected anything because he always showered her with gifts. The clandestine escapades of his were just a reminder to, oh yeah, stop by Nordstrom's on the way home and pick up a gift for the wife.

The affairs meant nothing to him because they meant nothing to him. It was sex and no more than that. Why didn't women understand that? He made it clear with the women he had cheated with that he was a married man who would never jeopardize his family and career over a few minutes in the bedroom with anyone. Yes, Lori and Janice were fine, so were Jeanine, Bridget, Sandy, Quianna, Ashley, Karen, Wanda, Debbie, Khadeejah and, what was that girl's name from the department store? They all had luscious lips and curvaceous hips, but the fact that he got it so easy with them saw Rob lose interest after he got it so easy. He had to work for Maria, she was a challenge, and that was an investment that he, divorced and all, would never lose.

Sophia was a business investment, too, but he didn't actually love her. He whispered those three words in the moment to keep her happy. Maria was the woman he took around his family and mother, she was the mother of his children, and she was the only one he trusted with everything he had. She was the complete woman for Rob. When he told Maria "I love you," he meant it. He did love her, then and now. As much as Sophia may have thought she had already learned her man, she didn't know anything about his heart. It was still with Maria and his children. His flesh, yes, joined with Sophia for temporary relief, but his heart would always be with his wife.

When he made love to Maria, he made love to her. He would please her and give her what *she* wanted. He wanted to. Pleasing Maria pleased him. Knowing that he had captured this strong woman other men wanted but never had turned him on something terrible. The key word in making love was love. Rob loved Maria, and Maria loved Rob. Lovemaking was truly lovemaking, and their marriage bed was undefiled. Best of all, Maria was pure, willing and all his.

He had sex with Sophia to please himself and *take* what he wanted.

Maria let her husband know that he was the man, and she played her role as the woman with superior ability. He hunted for her and had taken her captive as his prey. Her lovemaking with Rob was equally generous and mutually beneficial. She aimed to please him, and no one would recognize the demure and ladylike Mrs. Robert J. Henderson behind closed doors except Mr. Robert J. Henderson. No other man had been with his wife, he had taken her virginity, and she was fiercely loyal and committed to the husband she loved, adored and supported come hell or high water. She had confidence, passion, dreams, intelligence, beauty, loyalty, friendship, sexiness and a keen sense of nurturing with his children.

Why let all that go?

The truth for Rob was that Rob was broke. His manhood was defined for him by what he did, and lately, he wasn't doing much of anything. His manhood was an easy target for Sophia Simmons and her money and connections. He did what he believed he should do. He let Maria go so that he could reinvent himself. He had to. If he didn't take care of himself, how could he take care of anybody else? He did the right thing, he was sure of it. He had to do it, even if it meant divorcing his wife and manipulating her into believing that she was to blame.

As much as he was attracted to Sophia for the opportunities and connections she could make available to him, he equally despised her and would never come to love Sophia for the selfish part she had played in his desperate act to save himself at the expense of the only woman he had ever truly loved. Sophia was a pawn in his plan to reclaim his identity, and he had no respect for this woman who was responsible for his wife's heartache. So Rob played the part, intending to stay long enough to get back on his feet and then leave Sophia and return to Maria and his children when he was through. He trusted that Maria wouldn't remarry. He would blame whatever he thought of to end his second marriage on his second wife. He would beg Maria for forgiveness. Maria would always love him. Maria would take him back.

After asking God's forgiveness and playing all the angles in his mind, Rob was certain he would be forgiven. So he lay in bed and placed his muscular arms around Sophia's naked body only to become aroused again as her ample buttocks brushed against him. Round two, and any brief sense of accountability and guilt was gone, as this time, he surrendered to the pull of Sophia's powerful attraction and assured himself that God was a man, too, and He would just have to understand.

Chapter Seven

Maria

It was almost midnight when Maria walked in the front door of her home, and upon entering, she smiled at her mother and Papi fast asleep on the comfortable, plaid sectional that filled the living room completely. It almost looked out of place, too big for their much smaller living room here, but it was in very good condition so Maria held onto it. She could afford new furniture if she wanted, but it was a vintage piece that would stay in the family for a few more years before being put on the curb.

The television was still on, something Maria's mom would never have allowed when she was growing up. *"Something about grandparents and their grandchildren - they let them get away with anything."* On the mahogany coffee table was her mother's backgammon board game, chess pieces and checkers. Grandma insisted when she came over that Genny and Papi put away their "computerized games" and play the "board" games with her, which Genny humorously referred to as "bored" games. The children would always condescend to their grandmother's wishes, so they learned how to play backgammon and checkers, and Papi mastered the moves of pawns, bishops, rooks, knights, king and queen. Genny preferred saying "King me" to "Checkmate" so Grandma had to split her time between chess and checkers when she came over. Maria was the backgammon champion in the family, and she and her mother would compete to the delight of the children who cheered for Grandma to win, so Maria would feign defeat to amuse her children.

Maria put the games into their respective boxes and turned the television off, awakening her son, who kissed her and told her he loved her. She couldn't have asked for more.

Thank goodness, Papi had not forgotten to change into his pajamas. He was clad in red and blue Spiderman pj's, and Maria admired her son and treasured the time she would have with Papi as a young boy. She would teach him about women, honesty, manners and opening car doors. She would teach her son how to treat a woman so that he would respect women when he got older.

As Papi went upstairs to get into his own bed, Maria pulled her phone out of her purse and turned it back on. Three missed calls from Rob, and one message.

"Not tonight," she thought. *"I am feeling good, and I refuse to allow you, Mr. Henderson, to bring me down."*

She changed into her night clothes and grabbed a huge pillow from the hall closet. There was plenty of room on the sectional, so she made herself comfortable and drifted off to sleep, basking in the deliverance she enjoyed earlier at Geraldine's.

She hadn't been sleeping long before she heard her cell phone ringing. At first she thought she was dreaming, but the third and fourth time, she awoke and realized someone was actually calling her at - what time is it? - 5:11 a.m. Her mom was still fast asleep, and Maria picked up the phone to see that it was Rob calling.

"There must be something wrong," Maria hoped. *"Forgive me, Lord."*

"Hello?" Maria answered.

"What, you couldn't pick up your phone?" Rob asked with abrasiveness.

"Rob?" Maria asked, yawning.

"Who else?" he answered. He sounded like he had an attitude.

"Rob, what is wrong with you? It is 5:00 in the morning."

"You didn't get my message last night?"

Maria paused. His pubescent jealousy used to be cute when they were married, but she wasn't his wife anymore, and she certainly wasn't going to come off of this high with Jesus because he was probably in bed with another woman and trying to make himself feel better about it by accusing her of being with another man.

"I thought we were going to tell them together."

"Tell them together what?" Maria asked, having no idea of the conversation he had shared with their children last night.

"Tell them together that we are divorced."

"Yeah, so what's the problem?" she asked, yawning again.

"The problem is that Genny and Papi know already, and I didn't tell them."

"Rob, what do you think, they are stupid? If they do know already, they are smart enough to figure it out. I didn't tell them anything, but I am not going to cover for you. If they know, they know."

"Well, they know."

"Lord, Jesus....." she began

"Lord, Jesus? Didn't you get my message last night?" he asked again.

"Lord, Jesus. Please bless Rob. I don't know what he wants. I know he has cheated on me many times, and he is probably with someone right now. Bless them, Father. Bless him and bless her. In Jesus' name."

Rob was speechless. He used to be able to flip it on Maria and transfer his guilt to her, but Maria flipped it on him. He wasn't prepared for that.

"Goodnight Rob. Tell the whore you're with that I said she can have you."

Maria hung up the phone, turned it back off, and got down on her knees. She prayed for Rob and the new woman in his life, and she asked God to bless them. She didn't mean it, but at least it was a start. She really wanted to pray, *"Lord Jesus, please kill this son of a bitch and his ho. Please let him fall into a ditch. Please let someone come in his life and break his heart like he broke mine."* She wasn't there yet, and she didn't mean a word of what she had said to Rob. *"Bless him and bless her."* Please. This would take time. Maria could care less what happened to him, she only said that because Neicy had suggested that she do so. At least she could get the words out of her mouth. Well, Jesus was patient, He was just going to have to be with Maria.

The healing, however, had begun. Maria wasn't as angry as she used to be, and her attention was now focused on herself and her children instead of Rob. She knew what she had to do. Tomorrow, she would tell the children they were going to church. She was ready to do that. She would give it to God and trust Him to work it out. Yes, she would tell Genny and Papi that they were going to church. For them, for her and for Jesus. Praise the Lord.

Chapter Eight

Genny, Papi & Maria

"Why do we have to go to church?" Papi and Genny asked. They sat in the dining room with their mom, playing with their scrambled eggs and waffles that their grandmother had cooked before she left.

"Because I said so," Maria answered.

Maria ate a piece of rye toast with strawberry preserves and sipped her orange tea as her two children waited for her to give them a better explanation.

"Is dad coming?" asked Genny, with an air of sarcasm that could never fool Maria. It stung, almost, because Maria knew that Genny had said it out of her own pain.

"Genny and Papi, I have to tell you both something. Your dad and I are.....we are divorced. We did not separate for a little while. We divorced, and we are no longer married."

"Yeah, mom, we know," said Genny.

"Yeah..." Papi added.

"You know?"

"Yes," replied Genny.

"How?" asked Maria.

"How? Everybody knows, mom. You and daddy can't hide anything. You have been divorced for years. You guys were just living together."

"What?" asked Maria.

"You have been divorced for years, mom. Your marriage was over years ago. Everybody knows."

Maria was shocked. Had it been that obvious? She lowered her cup of tea and took a deep breath before speaking.

"Your dad and I love you both very much. It doesn't change anything. We love you, and our divorce had nothing to do with you. We should have been able to work it out, and I can't make everything make sense to you right now, but please trust me that we did the very best that we could do as grownups. And your dad will still be around for you, for karate, for school, for basketball, for everything you love to do because he loves you. And divorce does not ever change that."

"Can I go?" asked Genny.

"Yes," Maria answered, knowing that her words hadn't had much impact.

Genny got up from the table and went upstairs to her room, shutting the door.

Maria knew Genny would take it hard. Papi sat there eating his and Genny's food as if nothing had happened.

Maria had told them the truth. She made a conscious decision to bring her children to church. She prayed for Rob and his new woman. She was on the right track. Next Sunday, they would go to church and join and give themselves to Jesus. Then, everything would be in order, and God would heal her family. That was the best thing she could do for herself and her children. Yes, she was ready, and it was time.

Chapter Nine
Genny

On the 20th day of March, Genny became a young woman. It should have been one of the most memorable days of her life, one which she shared with her mother and had a mother/daughter talk about the birds and the bees, and which was more convenient for a 12 year old girl to use: tampons or feminine napkins. When Genny discovered the onset of her menstrual cycle that morning, she wanted to tell her mother. She wanted to be hugged and shown some kind of support and affection, but she decided against it. Genny would share this momentous occasion with her two girlfriends, Jade and April, who had already gotten their periods and who would suffice, for now.

It was Friday, thank God, and Genny had received her mother's blessing to attend a sleepover at Jade's East Borough home. She hadn't spoken to her father since their infamous telephone conversation when Genny hung up the phone on him, and neither she nor her dad said anything to mom, so Genny didn't volunteer any information. Instead, she would spend some much needed time with her two best friends with whom she could say any and everything she wanted.

"My dad is such a pain in the behind," she would tell them, *"he actually thought I didn't know he had divorced mom and left her for another woman."*

"That is so cruel," Genny imagined April would say.

"Yeah, some dads can be so mean," Genny imagined Jade would chime in.

"Aw, you got your period. Congratulations!" April would offer.

"Yeah, welcome to the club. It's really not that big of a deal," Jade would comment. *"And by the way, use the tampons. Pads are so embarrassing, I mean, I think you can notice them from behind. They feel so bulky and uncomfortable."*

As Genny went over their conversation in her head, she counted the hours remaining on the school clock at Addington Park Middle School. Not much longer, and April's mom would be picking Genny up and whisking her off to their five bedroom home in the suburbs, complete with fenced property, golden retriever and a dad. Genny thought April and her mom might be a little uncomfortable coming to her new neighborhood, but April's mom assured her that even though she was a blonde-haired, blue-eyed girl from East Borough, she would be alright.

Genny had transitioned to her new school without any major problems. Her grades had landed her in every Gifted and Talented Class the school had to offer, and she was excited to join the school's Reading Club and turn in writing assignments on the Book of the Month selected by the Club's Advisor, Mr. Engleton. He was the Gifted and Talented English Literature Teacher, and Genny was fond of his passion for literature and reading. An older gentleman of short stature, reading glasses, and a receding hair line, Mr. Engleton took a liking to Genny almost immediately and noticed, as watchful teachers do, her advanced learning and intellect. He recommended she join the Reading Club at the High School and gave her assignments from their AP Reading Lists. Genny had not yet read To Kill a Mockingbird[54] or Wuthering Heights[55], and she was excited to read One Hundred Years of Solitude[56] and Grendel[57]. Beloved[58] and The Glass Menagerie[59] were his recommendations, so Genny promised to read those as well. Six books on her list, and six reading assignments she would turn in before June 22nd, her last day of 8th grade and last day to turn in all work before the June 25th graduation ceremony.

Mr. Engleton thought it might be too much for her, but Genny assured him she would complete them, especially inasmuch as she had finished basketball season at East Borough and there was no Outdoor

Track & Field Team at Addington Park Middle School. The books, she promised him, would keep her busy and interested, so he happily complied, encouraging her with his comment, *"You can do anything you put your mind to, Genny."* Genny had heard that before from her mom and dad, but hearing it from a teacher who barely knew her inspired her in a way that moms and dads, who *have* to say it, didn't. She was encouraged. She was inspired, and she couldn't wait to start her first book.

At 3:30 p.m. promptly, Genny walked out the front of the school to a huge black Range Rover where Mrs. Caitlyn Jones and her daughter, April, stood out like two sore thumbs. Jade was visible through the slightly tinted rear windows with earphones on and a green and white East Borough sweatshirt.

"Ugggggh," Genny thought, *"I actually used to wear those colors,"* already expressing loyalty to her new school and future teammates. Next year Genny would try out for the girls' basketball team at Addington Park High School, where the school colors were blue and black, and she was glad that the windows were slightly tinted so that Jade could not be easily seen.

April and Jade spotted Genny and waved her over to the car, smiling, chewing gum and listening to rap music. As Genny approached the vehicle, Mrs. Jones got out of the car and came over to give Genny a hug. She was wearing blue jeans and a white, Oxford shirt, and her hair was pulled back into a ponytail. She wore sunglasses, even though there wasn't much sun, and she took them off to take a good look at her daughter's best friend who had been known by their family since the girls were in first grade.

"Aw, I'm so proud of you, Genny. So, so proud of you. How are you feeling?"

"They told her," Genny thought. "I'm fine, Mrs. Jones. How are you?"

"I'm good, sweetheart. How is mom and Papi?"

Genny noticed that Mrs. Jones didn't ask about her dad. "They're fine, thanks. Thank you for picking me up and letting me sleep over."

"Anytime, Genny. You are welcome to sleep over anytime. Do you have everything?"

"Yes, I do," Genny replied, heaving her heavy backpack onto her shoulders.

Caitlyn Jones took the backpack and placed it in the backseat of her Range Rover. Genny climbed in the backseat next to Jade, and Mrs. Jones got back in the driver's seat, pulling off onto West Niles Avenue towards Highway 524, turning left and driving thirty minutes back to East Borough. The girls shared small talk in the car about how much everyone missed Genny, and Genny responded with humble appreciation. They couldn't really talk like they would when Mrs. Jones left, so they kept their conversation generic and at a minimum.

When they pulled up to April's home at 26 Sea Gull Lane, the girls gathered all their belongings and hurried inside the house, past the freshly manicured lawn and up the white stone walkway lined with a spectacular array of green shrubbery cut into mini Christmas trees. A nativity scene adorned the front lawn and boasted of the family's bold faith in Jesus Christ, kept on the family's property long after Christmas at the insistence of the Mrs.

Caitlyn and her husband, David Jones, were not super religious by any means, but they did take April to Mass, and Genny and Jade had attended the service with them on a few prior occasions. They welcomed April's friends into their home and took advantage of every opportunity to speak to them about Jesus Christ, especially since neither Jade nor Genny were attending church services regularly anywhere.

"Dinner time is 6:00, girls," said Caitlyn Jones, who was happy to be hosting the sleepover tonight because it would make her own daughter happy.

Genny, April and Jade closed the door to April's room and plopped down on her queen size bed, laughing and carefree. April's bedroom was decorated in a soft beige and yellow, and sheer white lace panels dressed her windows with soft, whimsical femininity. A huge poster of the three girls taken on the boardwalk the prior summer had been autographed by each of them and still hung on the back of the door. Two chocolate brown bean bag chairs were neatly arranged at the foot of the bed, and both Genny and Jade took their respective places as the girls prepared to catch up on everything that had been happening with Genny.

"So," asked April, brunette hair dangling in her face, "what's it like not having your dad around anymore? I mean, that has to be so weird. He was always around."

"April!" Jade shouted.

"What? We can ask, can't we Genny?"

"I was going to tell you anyway. Jade, it's nothing, really," Genny replied.

"Okay, if you say so. We can ask with a little more sensitivity, April."

"Guys," Genny began, "….it's nothing, really. I was a little upset at first, but now I don't even care. He did leave mom for another woman, but I don't know who she is yet. I swear, when I find out..."

"Yeah," offered Jade, "when you find out, we are going to go and give her a piece of our minds."

"That's right," April agreed.

"It's just that....my dad is such a hypocrite. He is such a liar. He walks around like he's the King of the World, you know how he is, and he's always helping other people and he's Mr. All American, but he is such a hypocrite. He tries to help other young men be men, but how much of a man is he to leave his family? What kind of a man is that? How does he go and try to tell other young men how to be men and he can't even man up and take care of his own children?"

"Are you sure he is with another woman? Maybe that's not true," April said.

"It's true, April," said Jade, reclining in the bean bag with her feet up on the bed. She took the green and white East Borough sweat shirt off and had a white and green East Borough t-shirt on underneath.

"It's true," Genny echoed. "He can have her. He's coming today to pick up Papi. He's such a liar. He makes me sick."

"So what are you gonna do?" asked April.

"Yeah, and what about your mom and Papi? What are they gonna do?" Jade asked.

"They're not gonna do anything. My mom cries all the time and thinks we don't notice. Papi could care less, he thinks Robert J. Henderson is like a god, or something."

"Speaking of a god or something, why don't you ask your mom if you can stay to Sunday and to go mass with us?" asked April.

"No, I can't. She said we have to go to church on Sunday."

"Oh wow, what church are you going to?" asked April.

"Probably one of those churches in the hood," offered Jade. "If you do, I want to come. Those churches are fun. Me and my brother love to go with our grandmother. People run around and dance, they sing and play the best church music you would ever want to hear. And the preacher!"

"What church?" Genny asked. She was interested now that Jade had offered some insight.

"It's called First Baptist. You should hear my brother imitate the preacher. I'm telling you, hearing him is like being in church. Wait, let me call him," said Jade.

Jade's brother, Will, was the class clown. He always had jokes. He was 14 years old, tall, handsome and rugged. If he wasn't Jade's brother, Genny would probably have had some kind of silly crush on him, but since Jade was a good friend, it was just....weird. It would have been like having a crush on her own brother.

Will made everyone laugh with his imitations of teachers, their school principal, his mom, dad and even Jade's friends. He imitated Genny capturing the essence of what he thought was her personality: witty, intelligent, smart and lacking a sense of humor. So he told jokes to see her huge smile and hearty laugh, and Genny would always loosen up whenever he came around. Right now, Genny could use a good laugh, so why not.

"Okay hold on," Jade spoke into her cell phone, "I'm going to put you on speakerphone."

Jade placed her cell phone on the bed in the center of the three girls and coaxed her brother into doing his hilarious imitation of the Preacher they heard when they visited First Baptist Church in Addington Park a few months ago.

"Hey Genny, what's up girl?" asked Will on speakerphone.

"Hi Will. How are you?"

"Hi Will. How are you?" he repeated in a mocking, girly tone. "Girl, loosen up. No wonder my sister brought you back here. She told me you wanna hear me preach. Well," Will began in his best impersonating tone of a preacher with drawl and fire, "I'm about to preach. But, hah, I'm going to need you to do something for me. Dig, hah, dig in your pockets and bless, yes, Lord, I say bless the Lord with

an offering. Right now, hah, right now, in the name of Jesus, while there is an anointing of God in this place, hah. Hallelujah! Hah!" Will shouted.

Jade was falling out laughing on her bean bag, and April looked confused.

"Praise God," Will continued, "now who wants to hear the Right Reverend Will preach tonight?"

"Preach, Reverend!" Jade shouted. "Hallelujah!"

Shouting, Will continued. "Well, er uh, I'm about to preach on missing you. You know how it is to miss somebody? Hah. To miss somebody like we miss Sister Genny. But look at God. I said, can I get an Amen up in here, look at God. God brought Genny back to us. Even if only for a moment, he brought Sister Genny back to us so that we could tell her we miss her. So that we could spend a few minutes with her, hah. So that we could tell her we are thinking about her, and we thank God for her. Yes Lawdy, the Prodigal Daughter has come back to the nest. You see, God is good all the time. Amen?"

"Amen!" Jade shouted.

"Is anybody else in the house tonight?" he asked.

"C'mon, ya'll, say amen," Jade encouraged the girls.

"Amen," April and Genny hesitantly replied.

"Amen. Yes, amen. Amen, God is good all the time. Say it like you feel it. Praise Gawd. So we need to thank God anytime we get to see those we miss because we don't know when we are going to see them again. So Sis Genny, we just want to say, hah, like Moses in the wilderness, and like Joseph in the palace, and like Jesus before He went onto glory, Hallelujah, hah, and like Martin Luther King, Jr., we may not get there with you, but we as a people will get to the promised land, we are going into the heavenly Canaan, hah! Glory, glory, amen. Aaaaaahhhhhhhhh!" Will screamed. "Hah! Don't miss the ones you love while they are still here. When they go to heaven, you are gonna miss them enough. But while they are still here with you, glory to God, don't just miss them. Tell them you miss them, and let God do the rest. Glory to Gawd, Hallelujah, praise His holy name!"

Will paused, and then said, "Oh hold up, Jade, I got a call coming in. I'll call you back. Peace out."

He hung up, and the three girls burst with laughter.

"What is wrong with your brother?" Genny asked, laughing hysterically and holding her stomach. "Why is he screaming so much?"

"You know he isn't all the way there. Will is not right," said Jade.

"He is so funny," April added. "I never heard priests scream like that. Genny, are you okay? Do you need anything?" she asked, noticing Genny holding her stomach.

"Ummm, maybe I better use the bathroom," said Genny. "I'm okay, thanks."

"And you are not going to tell your mother?" asked Jade.

"No, not now. I'll tell her later."

Genny got up and went into the hall bathroom, laughing at Will's impersonation but thinking about what he had said. Comic relief was good medicine, but there was possibly some good advice in his routine. She did miss her father, but she was not going to be the first one to budge. She was as stubborn as the man himself, so she would just play this waiting game with him until he broke, which he would because guilt would eat at him until he made it right.

Genny knew how to deal with her father, but as she looked in the bathroom mirror, she had yet to see that the main person she would have to deal with was herself.

Chapter Ten
Papi

Maria heard a loud knock on the front door at 6:30 p.m. and knew it had to be Rob. She would never respond to a car honking outside, so Rob was trained to come to the door, knock and wait. Purposely, Maria made Rob wait outside the door for several minutes before greeting him. She wore no makeup, sweats, one of his old t-shirts that she had confiscated, and flip flops. Her hair was braided and covered with a silk scarf tied above her forehead in the humble style of Aunt Jemima, and there were no usual pearl or gold hoop earrings enhancing her lobes. Maria's healthy, long nails were unpainted, and she still wore her 14 karat gold wedding band on her left hand, holding on to the hope that their divorce was just a bad dream from which she and Rob would both awaken.

As she opened the door, Rob glanced at his ex-wife for the first time since their divorce hearing. She was both low maintenance and highly naturally beautiful to him, and her attempt to downplay her looks only attracted him to her more. His take on the situation was that she was playing hard to get and wanted him to pursue her. She was, after all, still wearing his ring, but he couldn't have been further from the truth.

"Hi," he said, standing in the doorway in his usual two piece suit, this time navy blue with pinstripes, and well-polished black shoes. His dark red necktie was slightly open, and there was a time when Maria would have grabbed him by his waist, kissed him, and then fastened his tie for him. He would grab her by her waist and tell her how much he loved her, and as they shared kisses and exchanged a tender "I love you," the kids would walk into the room and smile, pleased with their parents' display of affection. Maria noticed right away that there was no ring on Rob's left hand, but even when they were married, he didn't always wear it. His reason was that he couldn't work out at the gym with it on because it got in the way, and that was slightly true when he was at the gym, but more often than not it was because he had been with Sophia.

"Hi," Maria replied in an uninterested and nonchalant manner. "Papi was ready at 5:00."

"I'm sorry, Maria, I tried to call you and let you know I was running late, but my phone died and I didn't have my car charger. You're not angry with me, are you?" he asked.

"Papi, your dad is here," Maria spoke in a loud voice, turning to face the living room and blocking the entrance to her home with her body.

"Can I come in?" he asked.

"No. Papi will be right here," she replied, standing squarely in the doorway.

"How is Genny?" he asked, noticing that she had positioned herself so that he could not get past. He didn't want to upset Maria, so he took a step back and relaxed his hands in the pockets of his pants.

"She's fine."

"Is she here?"

"No."

"Where is she?"

"She's not here, Rob. She's with her friends. She is upset right now. You should talk to her."

"I tried talking to her. I called the other night, and she hung up the phone."

"Why?"

"You know why. She's upset."

"Well, do you care?"

"Of course I care. I wanted her to come for the weekend, too."

"Well, she'll be back tomorrow. And, I need Papi to be back before Sunday morning."

"Sunday morning? Where is he going?"

"He, Genny and I are going to church."

"Okay, alright, that's good. That's real good. Maria, you always were a great mother. I just want to tell you that I appreciate you, and I'm thankful that they have you. Thank you."

"Whatever."

Papi came to the door, excited to see his dad and oblivious to the "we're all mad at dad" stance that his mom and sister had taken against him. Papi ran to his father's open arms, and they shared a big hug for a few seconds, while his dad playfully ran his fingers through Papi's hair.

"It's time for a cut, lil' man. Tomorrow, we're going over to Sam's Place."

Sam's Place was the Barbershop where his personal barber, Mike Love, worked.

"Genny's not coming tonight, daddy. Can we go to the movies tonight, just me and you? Please?" Papi asked.

Rob knew better than to disappoint his son, especially with mama bear standing right there, so even though he had planned to cook a small dinner and watch a movie at home, he agreed to his son's request.

"Bye mom, see you Sunday morning!" Papi shouted, running to his dad's five year old silver Mercedes Benz, which his dad kept in showroom condition. He threw his army duffle bag in the back seat and climbed in, remembering to fasten his seatbelt.

"I'll see you Sunday morning, Maria. Thank you," Rob said, turning to go to his car.

Maria waved to her son and then shut the door without saying anything to Rob.

As Papi waved back to his mom, he noticed a black purse underneath the passenger seat. "Dad, can I take mom her pocketbook?"

"What?" Rob answered as he sat in the driver's seat and adjusted his expensive sunglasses.

"Mom forgot her pocketbook. Can I take it to her?" he asked again.

Rob turned and saw Sophia's black sequined purse under the passenger seat, which she must have forgotten after their last night together. They went to the Mayor's Ball in Addington Park, and she drove back that night because Rob had consumed one too many alcoholic beverages. Rob was never a drinker, but when he was out with Sophia he liked to enjoy himself, and he would have a few drinks with her to lighten his spirits. He only had a few glasses of Merlot, but the wine made him giddy and light-headed to the delight of Sophia, who was amused by the vulnerability of this 6'2" hunk of a man after drinking "a little" red wine.

"That's okay, son, I'll take care of it."

Papi and his father talked about school, karate, football and soccer as they drove 15 minutes to his rental townhome in Belmar, an oceanfront community of winter and summer rentals, townhomes, condominiums and single family homes. Papi and Genny loved coming to the Belmar beach with their dad, and even though the streetlights were on, Rob promised his son that they would fly his kites before heading to an 8:15 p.m. movie.

After eating cheeseburgers and onion rings on the boardwalk, father and son braved the cool weather and set up their kites on the sand. Once they unpacked their kites, Papi released his bright yellow rectangular kite into the ocean breeze as his dad let his bright blue triangular kite sail in the evening sky. The wind lifted the sturdy fabrics as Papi guided the kite in his young hands, tightening his grip as the wind current increased and struggling to maintain its' steadiness. His dad showed him how to adjust his grip as the strength of the wind changed, and in dad's big, strong hands, it looked easy. After a few tries, Papi was more successful, and he enjoyed the bending and bowing of his kite in the night air for about a half hour until his dad said it was time to head to the movie theatre.

The Community Theatre on a Friday usually meant a full house, and this night was no different. Rob paid for two tickets to see a two and one half hour action movie, and Papi promised that he would not fall asleep. At the end of the movie, Papi was wide awake, but his dad was exhausted.

"I can't wait until you're 17 so you can drive, son," Rob said in a playful tone.

"Me, too dad. I'll drive you wherever you want to go."

"I know you will. Right now we're gonna go home, and tomorrow we'll get that hair of yours cut."

85

"Thanks, dad, you're the best dad ever."

By the time Rob made it to his home, Papi was fast asleep in the backseat.

"Just like the old days," Rob thought, lifting his son out of the backseat and carrying him into his two bedroom townhome just five blocks from the beach. Rob had already prepared his second bedroom for his daughter to use when she came over, and he would sleep on the couch so that Papi could enjoy the first. Tonight, however, Papi would enjoy the larger bedroom since Genny decided to go with her friends. Although Rob agreed that he was wrong for the divorce, he didn't agree with his daughter's hanging up the phone on him. She's hurt, Rob understood that, but that still did not give her the right to be disrespectful. *"And, why hadn't Maria said anything to correct it?"* The more Rob thought about it, the more convinced he became that he was the victim, and they were both just overreacting.

He had resolved to give Genny and Maria some time until they both got over their anger and disappointment, and then he would try to have some kind of relationship with them. *"Yeah, that's it,"* Rob thought. *"That's what Sophia had suggested, and maybe Sophia was right."*

Rob answered his cellphone on the second ring as he noticed the call was from Sophia. He asked her to hold on for a moment so he could tuck his son into bed. Papi was snoring lightly, and after pulling the covers snug around him, Rob went back into the living room to sit on the couch and share his last conversation of the day with the woman he had not yet felt comfortable with bringing around his children.

"Hey baby, I missed you today," said Rob.

"I missed you, too. How was your day?" Sophia asked.

"Long and drawn out. I am exhausted. I picked up my son."

"What about your daughter?"

"She didn't come. She's upset or something and went with her friends."

"Are you okay with that?"

"What am I gonna do?"

"....true....I guess there isn't anything you can do."

"You know, Sophia. I am a good father. I am a good dad. I love my kids. My son loves me, I know he does, but my daughter is so angry with me right now, I don't know what to do."

"You should talk to her, Rob."

"I tried. She hung up the phone."

"She's a young girl, Rob. You're the parent. You have to be the parent."

"Yeah, that's right.....if her mother would talk to her as well I wouldn't be fighting this battle by myself."

"I'm sure she is doing the best she can do."

Rob didn't really want to talk about it to Sophia, but he had started this conversation, and he would finish it before going to sleep.

"Yeah, she is, I'm sure of that. Maria is a good mother, I can't take that from her. I'm a good dad, too. She can't take that from me. I don't know if she has said anything to Genny or not. I don't think so, but my daughter is a completely different person. Confrontational, angry...."

"Rob, what do you expect her to be like? She is, what, 11, 12 or 13 years old going through puberty, probably menstruating, mood swings, her mom and dad are not together anymore, she no longer lives in the home she grew up in, and she just changed schools and neighborhoods. You're not there anymore. Are you sure you did the right thing?"

Sophia didn't even remember how old his daughter was, and she was so casual about it. *"What, 11, 12 or 13 years old?"* Rob replayed in his mind. It agitated him a bit. Maria would have a fit if she ever heard any woman talking so casually about Genny's struggle. He and Maria could say whatever they wanted to, but no one else.

"Sophia wasn't actually supposed to offer her unsolicited opinion about Genny," Rob thought, with as much paternal instinct as his ex-wife's maternal, and he had to check Sophia on this. He was not in the mood to explain anything else.

"Sophia, my daughter is 12. Maria and I know what she is going through, and we will handle it, so let's stop *that* conversation. Now, as far as whether or not I did the right thing, I did the right thing for me. I am with you because *I* want to be with you. It has nothing to do with my daughter or my son."

"Okay, Rob, forgive me for saying anything about it. You brought it up."

"I did, you're right. I was just talking. If I do that, if I talk about my children with you, please don't say anything. Wait, I don't know what I am saying. What I'm saying, what I'm trying to say, Sophia, is that you are the only woman for me. I love you."

"Dad?" asked Papi, standing in the hallway just a few feet away.

"Papi?" asked Rob, stunned that his son was awake and standing near him, close enough to have heard everything he said.

"Sophia, I'll call you back." Rob hung up his cellphone and asked his son to come sit next to him on the couch.

"Dad, who is Sophia?" asked Papi. "Is that the woman you left mom for?"

"Son, come sit down. I'll explain everything."

Papi sat on the forest green couch near his dad and grabbed one of its three square pillows, willing to give his dad a chance to explain himself. *"He must have meant something else,"* Papi thought. He had to. Papi knew his dad. He was a good man, he didn't care what anybody said, and he was a great dad.

"Papi, your mother and I are divorced. That means we are no longer married. It does not mean that we love you or Genny any less."

"But who is Sophia? Do you love her like you said?"

"I....son, Miss Sophia is a friend of mine. I have friends, just like you have friends. She is just a friend. I don't love her like I love you or Genny or your mom."

"Did you and mommy get divorced so you could marry Miss Sophia?"

Rob didn't know what to say. He wanted to be truthful, but he needed to lie. He wasn't ready yet to tell his children that he might marry another woman.

"No, son," Rob lied.

"So why don't you and mommy just get married again?"

"Papi, I don't know what is going to happen. I love your mother very much. The only thing I can tell you now is that I don't know."

"If you asked mommy to marry you again, she would say yes. I know she would. She misses you, daddy. Genny says mommy misses you and cries all the time. Mommy thinks we don't know. Why don't you just buy another ring and ask her to marry you. Then we could be a family again."

"Papi, we're always going to be family. That will never change. I need you to trust me. Trust that I am doing the best job I can as a man, as a husband and as a dad. I will always be here for you and Genny, and for your mother, whether we get married again or not. I will always be here for all of you. Always. That will never change for anybody."

"Not even for Miss Sophia?"

"Especially not even for Miss Sophia. Miss Sophia is just a friend."

"But I heard you tell her that you love her."

"Son, I do love....I do care for my friends. Don't you?"

"Not really. I never told my friends that I love them."

Rob had patience with Papi because he knew Papi would love him no matter what he did, but he didn't want to lie to his son or mislead him.

"Papi, I love Miss Sophia as a friend. She will never have the love I have for your mother because she is not your mother. I love her as a friend. That's all. Do you understand?"

"Ummmmm, I guess. Okay dad, I'm going to go to sleep now. Laser tag tomorrow?"

"You got it!" Rob answered, happy to be able to change the subject. "I hope you've been practicing because I'm really good," he said playfully.

"Yeah, we'll see," answered Papi, yawning and rubbing his tired eyes.

"Go to bed, son. I love you."

"Good night daddy. I love you, too."

Papi hugged his dad and went back to the first, larger bedroom.

Rob was relieved that he told his son the truth – kind of. He picked up his cell phone to call Sophia back, but he noticed that he had not hung it up at all, and she was still on the call.

"Sophia?" Rob asked.

She hung up.

Chapter Eleven

Neicy

This was day seven of Neicy's seven-day fast for Maria. She had promised Maria last Friday night at Geraldine's that she would pray and fast for her until something happened. Something had to happen. Something always happened when Neicy prayed and fasted. God moved. She loved to commune with God and to draw closer to him.

Abstinence was an agreement between Neicy and her husband, Tony, and they both honored the other's spiritual needs during that time. The focus was on Jesus Christ and hearing from Him concerning His will. They were praying fervently concerning Tony's cancer and Neicy's mother.

Neicy was raised in the church as a young girl, and her mother had served at Holy Tabernacle Church as a Deaconess for as long as Neicy could remember. She taught Neicy to witness, evangelize and to never be ashamed of the Gospel of Jesus Christ.

Saved and singing in the church choir since the age of five, Neicy had a heavy baritone voice that could fill a room and needed no microphone. She reminded her Pastor, Pastor Reginald D. Wright, Jr., of Mahalia Jackson. She often sang solos on Sunday mornings in a church full of worshippers, mostly 45 years and older, and although the church definitely needed to do more to draw younger men and women, Neicy was grateful that their 72 year old Pastor had stayed true to the Word of God and refused to preach/teach/sing a different way just to get people in the pews.

Pastor Wright was a man of principle and integrity, and he did not compromise when it came to the Holy Bible. He believed that as long as he lifted up Jesus Christ and obeyed Him, God would do the rest.[60] This commitment to lifting up Jesus Christ in order that He would draw souls in kept the church flourishing for the 40 plus years that Pastor Wright served as Pastor. He had mentored dozens of young men and women in the faith, and families who joined Holy Tabernacle Church stayed. The environment was loving, nurturing, caring and non-judgmental. Pastor Wright taught the love of God, and he was sincere and firm. If there were records maintained for the retention rates of church members, as colleges and universities keep, Holy Tabernacle Church would rate among the best.

Neicy would call Maria tomorrow to see how she was doing, and she believed with all her heart that God had moved in a mighty way on Maria's behalf. Neicy had prayed morning, noon and night and called out Neicy's name and Rob's name. She didn't know the name of the other woman, but Neicy lifted her up in prayer, whoever she was. She had encouraged Maria to pray for Rob and his new interest, but she also had to be real and respect that Maria was still in pain and would need time to heal.

Maybe Maria was right, maybe it was easy for Neicy to say "just pray for them" because it wasn't Neicy's husband, marriage, family or divorce. Neicy's way of encouraging Maria, however, wasn't to promote her own faith in difficult situations but to promote God's ability and faithfulness. She didn't want to sound too preachy as she encouraged Maria through the Word, but that was exactly what *would* help anyone struggling to maintain his/her faith.

Neicy planned a surprise dinner for Tony tomorrow, steak and salmon, which she would prepare with fresh, herb-roasted vegetables and white wine. She had completely forgiven Tony for his past infidelity, and the temptation to contaminate his food had long since worn off. For desert, she would serve chocolate dipped strawberries with fresh whipped cream, and afterwards the two would make up for lost time.

It had been difficult completely surrendering to Tony again after he cheated on her, but Neicy had given it over to God, and God handled it for her. It used to consume her, just like it was consuming Maria, until she asked God to take it from her and give her peace either to stay in the marriage or His blessing and peace to leave. Neicy believed Tony when he asked for her forgiveness, and when he prayed on his knees at the altar in church, she knew he meant it. Only Jesus could have done that. What man bows himself to Jesus after he cheats on his wife and asks for Christ to forgive him and to touch his wife's heart to forgive him? That was Tony's prayer before God. Neicy took him back knowing that his marriage vow was not only to her, but to her God, and she was fine with that. Yes, she took him back, and yes, she completely surrendered to him again, respecting his intention to obey God and remain surrendered himself to their Lord and Savior, Jesus Christ. Most of all, she respected God's ability to keep Tony, and she prayed for her marriage in her daily prayers.

His good looks, nice body, money, big home and charm meant nothing to her if he wasn't obeying God, for without God, those things meant absolutely nothing to Neicy. She didn't need a husband without a God, she needed a God her husband would worship and honor. The only God for Neicy was Jesus Christ, and she trusted Him to do anything. He did it for her marriage, so he could do it for Maria and Rob, too.

Neicy turned the lamp off in her bedroom and knelt at the side of her bed to pray before going to sleep. Tony was just getting out of the shower and would be sleeping in the spare bedroom for the last night before the two would reconvene tomorrow.

"Goodnight, Neicy. I would come in there, but I'm naked, and you might not be able to control yourself."

Neicy laughed. "Hey, it's almost 11:00. If you don't fall asleep, you can technically come in here at 12:01."

"Neicy," Tony said, appearing in her doorway with a towel barely covering his lower torso, "I'm shocked at you. Do you want me to come in at 12:01?" he asked, sliding the towel back and forth across his lower torso and dancing suggestively.

"He was so sexy," Neicy thought, *"and he's all mine. Thank you, Jesus!"*

"Yes, if you're gonna dance like that!"

Tony laughed, covered himself completely, and decided he would leave his wife to wait until tomorrow when her anticipation would cause her to come to him. "Come see me in the morning."

"Oh my God, you come in here teasing me like that! Goodnight Tony," Neicy said.

"Goodnight, baby."

Tony turned with his back to Neicy, lowered his towel to expose his rear end, and turned his head to blow her a kiss.

"You are too much," she laughed.

"Yeah, I know. That's why you love me. Come see in the morning, girl. You know what's up."

Neicy laughed, and as Tony went into the spare bedroom and closed the door, she got back on her knees and prayed again.

"Father, thank you for blessing me with such a wonderful, God-fearing husband. Thank you for Tony, Jesus. Thank you for teaching me how to forgive him and love him again. Thank you for keeping him. Thank you for healing him, Father. You are still a healer, and we know that there is nothing impossible with you. Be glorified, almighty Father, in His life. Bless Him to love and thirst after you. You alone are God.

Thank you for my mother's health and life, and thank you for saving her soul. Yes, Lord, it is well with her soul, and for this, I am grateful. Thank you for working it out, dear God. Be glorified, I pray, for you are the physician of all physicians, and her times are in your hands. No one can call her home any sooner than you do. Grant that your healing virtue would be with her, I pray, Lord, and remember her, Jesus. She needs your help right now, Lord. Even now. Help, Jesus. You promised never to leave or forsake. Be with her, Lord, and may your presence bring comfort, encouragement and strength to her.

Please bless Maria to forgive her husband, Rob, and guide her, Father, as she seeks your face. Give her peace. Please, Lord, bless Rob with a desire for You. Bless him, Father, to seek your face and do your will for his family. Help him to be the man you have called him to be and to confess Jesus as Lord. Touch his heart. Bless this other woman he has left Maria for, Lord, I pray in Jesus' name, that she, too, may acknowledge Jesus Christ as Lord and Savior. Amen."

Chapter Twelve

Maria

Rob brought Papi home Sunday morning at 9:00 a.m. with his little arms full of shopping bags. He was a practical dad who had purchased boxer shorts, socks, undershirts and toiletries. Genny received a tasteful selection of undergarments and toiletries, and Maria, who knew Rob better than anyone, knew that Rob couldn't have possibly picked out everything on his own. Maria nearly flinched with rage at the thought of him inviting another woman into the private space of their daughter, but she tried to remain focused on going to church and giving her life to Jesus. She believed that her children would follow and had been up since 5:00 a.m. praying in the private sanctuary the kitchen and bathroom afforded her.

Genny, to Maria's surprise, was already dressed and ready to go when Papi came home, and she was in a better mood than she had been lately.

"Maybe," Maria thought, *"my prayers are working after all."*

When Rob dropped Papi off that morning, Genny came to the front door and talked with Rob for a few minutes. Maria didn't interfere in their conversation, and whatever transpired had lifted Genny's spirits. Thank goodness. The last thing Maria needed was to take Genny to church with an attitude, especially in front of all the older women who filled Holy Tabernacle Church. They would probably have something to say about "kids nowadays" and how "when we were young, my mother used to...." Maria was not the mother you could say just anything to about her children, so she straightened both Genny and Papi out at home before they left so that no one else would have to.

After eating an oatmeal breakfast with orange juice, Papi and Genny grabbed their jackets and new Holy Bibles that Maria had brought earlier in the week. The three left their apartment at 10:20 a.m. with plenty of time to get to the church. Holy Tabernacle was in the neighboring town of Pennstown and no more than ten minutes away. Maria would meet Neicy there, and Neicy was ecstatic when Maria called her the day before to tell her that she and the kids were coming.

"Oh my God!" Neicy shouted in the phone when Maria called her, "Thank God! Thank you, Jesus! Hallelujah!"

"Yes, we are coming to church tomorrow. Thank you for everything," Maria had said.

"Don't thank me. Thank God. Oh, God is awesome. Thank you Jesus!"

"Thank you, Jesus," Maria agreed.

"Maria, I have been praying and fasting for you all week. Praise God! I am so happy for you and the kids. Wait til' you get to know Jesus for yourself. He is so good. Oh, thank you, Jesus."

Maria and Neicy had shared a conversation for over an hour about Holy Tabernacle Church. Maria felt like she already knew the church leadership courtesy of Neicy's unbiased briefing, and she was looking forward to joining the church. She would be required to come forth during the altar call after the preacher's sermon and then complete some new member classes before receiving their right hand of fellowship and welcome as a full-fledged member. Alter that, she would be eligible to participate in any ministry she felt led to, and that ministry leader would reach out to her to talk about their work further. Genny and Papi could participate in their Youth Ministry and Youth Bible Study, which although in small number, was currently led by a dynamic and anointed Youth Ministry Leader, Minister James N. Barrington, who also doubled as their Praise and Worship Leader. Minister Barrington was a newcomer to the Church, and the Pastor believed that he would attract a younger population. He was all of 25 years, handsome, anointed and on fire. How Holy Tabernacle Church got him was beyond the comprehension of other local preachers, who regarded Holy Tabernacle as "the kind of church you go to when you get old and are ready to die." Minister Barrington, however, felt a strong calling to stay with the church in spite of what anyone else had to say about it, and he had responded to the call with obedience, willingness and joy.

Since Minister Barrington took over less than a year ago, five youths joined the Youth Choir. He started a Scholarship Fund for graduating seniors and a Counseling Program for young adults where they were given the opportunity to talk openly with him about anything. Neicy saw it as a good fit for Papi and Genny, and Maria agreed.

Their Women's Ministry was very active and involved in a host of community events and activities that might help Maria shift her attention from her own pain to her power through Christ to bless other women because of the pain she would, through Christ, overcome. Neicy had shared with Maria that she had several visions of her in a preaching ministry, and Maria was receptive, saying whatever the Lord's will is, let it be done. If that was what He wanted, Amen. Neicy was usually in the ballpark when it came to spiritual matters, so Maria did believe that there was some truth to what Neicy had said, but she wanted to have the kind of relationship with Jesus herself where His Holy Spirit would speak to her about her. Up to now, Neicy was a kind of middle man who went to the throne on her behalf, who interceded on her behalf and who prayed and fasted on her behalf. Maria was grateful. The night the two had spent at Geraldine's, however, impressed upon Maria's heart and mind that she needed to get to know this Jesus for herself so that when she prayed, He answered her - and not just Neicy.

At 10:35 a.m., Maria pulled into the church parking lot, which was already nearly full. As she and her children walked to the front door, she spotted Neicy and Tony's black Porsche next to the church van. Holy Tabernacle Church, Pastor Reginald D. Wright, Jr., Senior Pastor, was written in blue letters on the side of the white van which had been purchased two years ago through private donations and the members' offerings.

Other women, mostly older, were walking up to the front door, and Maria gave Genny and Papi another lookover to be sure everything was in place. Genny looked adorable in a long red and black dress that she wore on special occasions, and Papi was as handsome as ever in a black vest, starched white shirt and trousers. His shoes were polished, courtesy of his dad, and his hair was freshly cut and edged up, just the way mom liked it. Maria wore a lime green dress with an orange and cream silk scarf tied around her neck. Her knee high boots were a soft, black leather with straps tied in the back, the only thing she wore that hadn't come from a consignment shop. These boots were purchased from an online shoe vendor that offered unique styles of shoes and boots at moderate prices.

The two story church was situated on a corner, and a beautiful cross painted gold and white stood atop it. As Maria and her children entered the front door, they were greeted by two ushers who hugged and welcomed them. The ushers handed out envelopes for tithes and offerings, as well as a program for the day's service. Maria glanced through the program and saw Neicy's name listed for a solo. That would be a treat. Neicy was a great singer.

Maria looked around at the church and took note of all the changes it had underwent since she was last there about 20 years ago. Maria had visited other churches here and there, but she had never settled anywhere.

Addington Park had many different churches to choose from, there was a church on just about every other corner. She and Rob had been married in a quick ceremony before a Justice of the Peace, and they did attend church services after they were married. Neither, however, was fully committed, and the routine of going to church every Sunday and Bible Study every Thursday evening died out not long after, especially when Rob began working out in the gym on Sunday mornings.

"Well, I'm here now," Maria thought, *"and I will ask God for His forgiveness of my neglect of Him and dedicate myself to Him today. I need Jesus."*

Royal purple carpet covered the floor of the foyer and sanctuary, and stained glass windows decorated each side. A large, wooden organ and piano were to the right of the pulpit along with drums and sound equipment. Five microphones in their stands faced the congregation, and a few men and women stood in a circle next to them talking and appearing to be praying. Church mothers sat in the second row with gorgeous hats beautified with jewels and feathers. As Neicy said, there were not yet many younger people, but Maria believed that she had made the right decision for her children. Besides, as long as Jesus was there, everything would be alright.

"Hi babies," said a soft voice to Maria's left. She turned and spotted Neicy, who embraced Genny and Papi as if they were her own children.

"Hi Aunt Neicy!" Genny and Papi said together, thrilled to see their favorite Aunt.

"How ya'll doing? I miss you both so much. Gimme some sugar..."

Genny and Papi both kissed their Aunt on the cheek. Neicy wore a soft pink suit with a fuchsia pink flower pinned at her left shoulder. Her hair was brushed back into a neat bun, and small gold post earrings were in her ears. She looked completely different from the diva fashionista she presented herself as when the two hung out together.

"Hey Neicy."

"Good morning, Maria. God bless you. I'm so glad you came. God has so much in store for you," she said, still holding on to Genny and Papi.

"I believe that, Neicy. I can't wait to hear you sing."

"Glory to God. He can use me for whatever He wants. I'll probably sing *'Journey to Canaan'*, that's our Pastor's favorite song, and he is preaching today. I think everybody else is tired of hearing it, but he's the Pastor. I love singing the song, the Spirit moves in a new way every time we do it. Oh," she said turning to Genny and Papi, "we do have Youth Church downstairs at 11:30. They'll announce it. Minister Barrington is here today, so you two should go. You'll like him."

Maria nodded affirmatively as Genny and Papi looked at her for approval.

"Well, enjoy the service. I'll see you when it's over, I have to sit with the Praise and Worship Team today."

"Bye Aunt Neicy," said Genny.

"Bye Auntie," said Papi.

"See you two later. And be good in here so none of these mothers has to come over here and pluck you on the back of your neck." Neicy imitated a plucking motion with her hand, and the two laughed.

Neicy and Maria hugged, and then Neicy went upfront. Deacon Tony was seated upfront with other leaders. A mature woman in a white uniform asked everyone to stand for the scripture reading and prayer. She read from the book of Isaiah and prayed fervently for the will of God to be done in the church. "Hallelujahs" and "Praise the Lords" filled the sanctuary, and the musicians played softly behind her as she called on the name of Jesus. The church began to fill to capacity, and men and women clapped as the Mother completed her prayer "in the name of Jesus."

She was followed by their Praise and Worship team who sang an up-tempo praise song, "Thank you for the blood."[61]

Oh, precious Savior
Who gave His life for me
What an awesome Lord
Who died to set us free

His precious body
Raised above the ground
Love like no other
Turned my life around

The blood, the blood, the blood
Thank you for the blood
The blood, the blood, the blood
Thank you for the blood

Dear Heavenly Father
It pleased you to send Him
and bruise Your own son
to save my life from sin

All evil forces
At His name must flee
So grateful, Jesus
Oh, for Calvary

The blood, the blood, the blood
Thank you for the blood
The blood, the blood, the blood
Thank you for the blood

Their voices were in perfect harmony, and the members of the church moved with synchronicity, swaying to the left and to the right as the musicians played with more intensity, allowing the spirit to have its way and move as it pleased. Men and women danced in the aisles and gave sporadic offerings of money at the altar. Papi asked if he could give money, so Maria placed a $20 bill in his hand and told him to put it on the altar with the other bills.

"All this?" Papi asked.

"Yes, Papi. All that. The whole thing."

"Ok..."

Papi walked towards the front of the church, and the members smiled at him as he placed the bill carefully on the altar. The Mother who prayed motioned with her hand for him to come to her, and Papi went, thank goodness, without making any kind of scene. She put something in his hand, which Maria couldn't see, but when Papi came back to his seat near Maria, she saw that it was a business card with the name "Mother Theresa M. Wright." She was Pastor Wright's mother.

"What did she say to you, Papi?" asked Maria.

"Nothing. Well, she said for me to tell my mother and father to call her."

Maria took the card from her son and put it in her purse. *"What is this about?"* she wondered. She would call her as she asked, or see her after service.

"Genny, do you want to give an offering?" Maria asked.

"Ummmmm.......ok, I guess."

"Here, take this up there," said Maria, handing her daughter another $20 bill.

"Mom, we just gave the church $40.00, and we just got here."

"Yes, and?" Maria asked, thankful that the music was too loud for anyone around her to hear what they were saying.

Genny stood, but Maria told her to wipe the attitude off her face before she went anywhere, and she did.

Genny walked towards the front of the church and placed the bill on the altar. The Mother again motioned with her hand for Genny to come over. Genny walked towards her, and Mother Wright stood and gave Genny a hug. Maria noticed that Genny didn't let go, and after a moment another woman gave Genny tissue to wipe her eyes. The two women prayed right there with Genny as the music played on, and when they were finished, Genny returned to her seat as Mother Wright turned and looked at Maria.

"Am I supposed to go up there and see you, too?" Maria wondered.

Mother Wright sat back down, and Maria almost felt slighted.

"Genny, are you alright?" Maria asked.

"Yes, I'm fine," Genny said, sitting down.

"Did those two women pray with you?"

"Yes."

"Why were you crying, sweetheart?"

"It's nothing, mom."

Maria could see that her daughter didn't want to talk about whatever it was, and although she wanted to know what was going on in Genny's head, she was grateful that another Mother could reach her daughter the way Mother Wright had. Mother didn't even know Genny, and Genny responded to her.

Pastor Wright walked into the pulpit with three other ministers at his side. He knelt to pray and then sat down in a high backed chair that looked like it was fit for a King. It was covered with a royal purple fabric that to Maria's discerning eye for quality must have cost a fortune, and the covering on the arms of the chair was fastened together with huge, gold buttons. The pastor's chair was in the center of the pulpit, and the ministers sat at his side.

The choir finished their selection, and Neicy came forward to begin her solo. Her voice was heavy and rich, and she started the Pastor's favorite song acapella. Neicy didn't need the microphone, but it amplified her voice and filled the sanctuary. There was definitely some kind of presence, or anointing, when she sang. It was undeniable. You felt a kind of wind or breath that came upon you, and it was so thick in the atmosphere that Maria took a step back and exhaled. "Hallelujah", "thank you Jesus", and "praise the Lord" were heard in the pews as men and women stood on their feet and swayed back and forth in unison. Maria swayed back and forth with everyone else and was unable to maintain her composure as the other singers and musicians joined in with Neicy, who led *"Journey to Canaan"* like a professional. Reverend Wright stood behind the Pulpit and rocked with his church.

> *Grateful to be over*
> *Finally I'm in*
> *Egypt is past, now at last*
> *Promised Canaan*
>
> *He said that He would do it (yes, yes, yes)*
> *I know (yes, yes, yes)*
> *He'll do it (yes, yes, yes)*
> *Oh, Canaan*
>
> *Thankful to be over*
> *He has saved from sin*
> *My soul is free, eternally*
> *Oh, Canaan*
>
> *Thankful to have made it*
> *He has brought me in*
> *Precious His blood, unconditional love*
> *Oh, Canaan*[62]

The entire congregation was on its feet shouting, praising God and singing with Neicy. A few women were jumping in the pews, and the ushers came to them with tissues and folded cloths. One young woman was running around the church, and Maria noticed Papi laughing. She shot him a "you know better" look, and Papi lifted his Bible to cover his face. Genny was standing and clapping to the music.

"*Thank goodness,*" Maria thought, "*she is getting something out of this.*"

The pastor came to the microphone and asked for people to come to the altar right then as "the spirit is moving," and present any prayers to God that they needed. Genny, to Maria's surprise, went right up, and Papi, more out of curiosity than obedience to the Pastor's instruction, followed his sister.

"Thank you, Jesus," Maria said to herself, as she also went forth and knelt at the altar to pray. She was grateful. Her prayer earlier that morning was that her children would desire Jesus and come to know Him for themselves, and not because she was force-feeding them. *"Thank you, Jesus, for answering my prayer. Please be with my children, and my children's children for all generations forevermore. Cover them in your precious blood from the crowns of their heads to the soles of their feet. Lead, guide and protect them, Father, fill them with your Holy Spirit, and teach and instruct them in all thy ways,"* she prayed.

"The spirit of the Lord is in this place," said Pastor Wright. He was a tall, thin gentleman, very dignified in appearance, and well-groomed. He wore a white pastoral robe with a red and gold stole, and his voice was also lush and heavy. He sounded like a man. His voice had a calming, soothing effect, one you could trust and believe, and was yet powerful and authoritative. "God is here," he spoke with confidence and assurance. "Come now, brothers and sisters, lay your burdens at the altar. Jesus is here, Hallelujah."

"Hallelujah," men and women said.

About 70 men and women were at the altar as the musicians played softly. Maria couldn't see what was going on, she was kneeling and her head was in her hands.

"Please, don't let me cry here," she prayed. *"Not here, Jesus, in front of everybody."* She tried to hold back the tears, but they started, and she used her hands to wipe her face. Someone placed a tissue in her hand and a cloth over her back, and she took the tissue to wipe her eyes before Genny and Papi saw her.

When she stood on her feet and turned, she saw Mother Wright holding a box of tissue. Mother reached out to hug Maria, and Maria accepted the invitation. Mother Wright had a firm hold on Maria, and Maria lost it. She was broken. She held the tissues to her eyes so that her children wouldn't see the tears streaming down her face, and Mother Wright held her and said in her ear, "To God be the glory. To

God be the glory. He's got you, baby. He's got you and your children. God is good. Say yes to Him today, baby. He's calling you."

"Thank you," Maria managed to say, as Mother Wright released her hold. "Thank you so much."

"No, sweetheart. Thank Jesus. God bless you."

Mother Wright stepped away and attended to another woman who was kneeling and in tears. Pastor Wright stood at the pulpit and allowed the Spirit of the Lord to have its way. As Maria looked up, they made eye contact. The Pastor stared intently at her and then lifted his hand and spoke directly to her: "God is calling you, young lady. Don't leave today without saying yes. The hand of the Lord is on your life. What others meant for evil, He meant for good. You are precious, daughter. Say yes to Him today."

Maria was ready. She would join the church and give her life to Christ.

The service continued after everyone returned to their seats with announcements and another selection from the choir. Minister Barrington, the Youth Minister, asked for all the young people, 13 and under, to go downstairs with him for Children's Church. Papi and Genny stood and took their cue to leave.

"Now, we can have some church," said Pastor Wright to the amusement of the church members.

Pastor Wright asked everyone to stand for the reading of the Scriptures, and they opened their Bibles to **Luke 1:39-45**. Pastor Wright read the last verse, *"Blessed is she who believed; for there will be a fulfillment of those things which were told her from the Lord,"* two times.

"I had prepared another message for this morning, but I feel a pressing on my heart to speak from the Gospel of Luke this morning. I won't be long before you, we have already had church. Thank you, Sis Neicy, and all of our musicians and singers for taking us in. Glory to God. I believe that God has already preached today, and we are going to let His message resonate in our hearts. Amen."

Pastor Wright walked to the side of the pulpit and continued. "You know, when I was younger I used to hate when someone would tell me something, and I didn't believe it. Then it happened, and they would come back to me and say they told me so. I never liked to hear anybody tell me they told me something. *'I told you,'"* he said in a mocking tone. "If I told someone else something, and they didn't believe it, and then it happened, I also had to fight the urge to go to them and say *'I told you.'* Well, the topic of my sermon this morning, Saints of God, whether you or I want to hear it or not, is *'He told you.'* Let me say it again: *'He told you.'* Amen somebody."

"Amen," the congregation responded.

"Amen. He told you. Has God ever told you anything? If He has, you can trust what He says. God told Mary something, and she believed Him. He sent His angel, Gabriel, to Mary to tell her that she was going to bring forth a Son, Jesus, who would be called the Son of the Highest. Mary didn't know how this would happen because she had never been with a man, but the angel answered and said to her, *'The Holy Spirit will come upon you, and the power of the Highest will overshadow you; therefore, also, that Holy One who is to be born will be called the Son of God.'* Mary was a young girl, a virgin, engaged to a man she had never been intimate with. God would intervene in Mary's life and interrupt everything in order to bring His plans to pass. Has God ever interrupted your plans? Has He ever come in the midst of a marriage or relationship and asserted His will without asking you how you feel about it? He just steps in and requires our submission to His will, and He finds a pliable heart in this young woman who answers, *'Let it be to me according to your word.'*"

"Oh that we would answer God like Mary and respond with a *'Let it be to me according to your word.'* God doesn't see as man sees. He searches our hearts. He chose David over Saul because He saw that David was a man after God's own heart who would do according to all God asked. Oh, that God would search our hearts and find us willing and ready to do His will. When He sends someone to you who blesses you with His Word that You have been chosen by God, called by God, that there is greatness inside of you....Hallelujah....let us respond as Mary did. Search me, Lord. Say 'search me, Lord.'"

The members of the church repeated, "Search me, Lord."

"I'm not going to be before you long this morning, God has already shown up and spoken to us," Reverend Wright continued. "He has told us. Yes, He told you. Now, how will you respond?"

Reverend Wright lifted a glass of water from a table near the altar and drank for a moment before proceeding.

"When Mary and Elizabeth came together, the Bible says Elizabeth's babe leaped in her womb, and she was filled with the Holy Spirit. There are others you will connect with in this lifetime who will be genuinely happy for you as God calls your name and puts His plan for your life in motion. Elizabeth was older than Mary, praise God. Mary was blessed with another woman in the faith who would rejoice with her. No, there was no jealousy or envy between the two, they weren't competing for the attention and affection of one man for they each had her own relationship. Mary's engagement would be tested when Joseph found out that she was pregnant. He hadn't been with her, so there was no way possible that it was his child. Mary would have to go through something in order to give birth. We all have to go through something, saints, in order to get to the blessing God has for us. I wish I could tell you this morning that the blessing God has for you is going to be easy; I'd love to tell you that joy comes in the morning without a night of weeping that endureth,[63] but I wouldn't be telling you the truth. Say 'Amen' somebody."

"Amen!" a few women shouted.

"Elizabeth seems like she doesn't go through anything. She is married and with her husband, and there is no threat to their marriage so maybe it is just easy for Elizabeth to talk to Mary about faith and believing. Zacharias is declared mute by the angel for not believing the Word of God, but the Bible doesn't say that he wanted to divorce Elizabeth. Her marriage was intact, and Mary's was threatened. Have you ever, Saints of God, had a friend who talked to you about God and encouraged you to just hold on and have faith, and it seems like it's so easy for them to talk about it because they aren't going through the same situation you are. How do you know, Elizabeth? What have you been through?"

"Oh my God," Maria thought, wanting to slide down the pew and hide underneath. She wished she could disappear. *"Father, forgive me."*

"What, Elizabeth, have you been through?" Pastor Wright continued, taking his time. "What qualifies you to talk to me about faith and *'just believe?'* Well, the Bible says Elizabeth conceived a son in her old age, and she was called barren. Elizabeth waited a long time. In that day, having no children was seen as a curse, it meant that God was not with you. The person talking to you right now, though

106

she may look like she doesn't know what you are going through, knows all about it. Elizabeth waited for years. She knows all about it. Her husband had been made mute by God because of his unbelief in the Word, and here is Elizabeth with a husband who doesn't believe God for her. How does Elizabeth hold on? Her husband doubts that God is able, and he is the head of the family who should be leading her to Christ by faith, but none of us are perfect. Amen, but let me also tell you that God will do everything He promised to do whether or not your spouse believes in God. The Lord is able! He's God! He is sovereign and does whatever He pleases. Who among us is His maker or can ask Him what is He doing? Elizabeth is a woman who knows all about it. She has to trust and hold onto God when the mouth of her husband is shut! She can't talk to him about faith. Lord have mercy, have you ever been in a relationship with someone who doesn't believe God can do the miraculous? Have you ever been in a relationship with someone who doubts that God can heal you, fix it, make a way out of no way, bring it to pass, save a lost loved one, destroy every yoke because of His anointing, bring you out of poverty, raise you up to be the mighty man or woman of God He has purposed you to be! When the only one you can talk to at home is Jesus all by yourself, talk to Jesus all by yourself! If nobody else in this house believes, I believe. Lord, help me and my family to have faith and to trust you. Can I get an 'Amen'?"

"Amen!" some of the members declared.

"Praise God. Zacharias would not be able to say a word until after his son was born to Elizabeth. What a situation to be in, when you are in a marriage with a husband who is visited by God concerning you, but who does not believe the word God has spoken over your life. The Bible says that Zacharias told the Angel that he and his wife were too old. Elizabeth has to have faith in God *in spite of* her husband who is the head of her family! Mary, precious soul, I'm here to tell you Elizabeth knows all about it," he said with both force and tenderness. "The Bible doesn't say that Elizabeth told Mary what had happened with Zacharias. No, when Mary visited Elizabeth, Elizabeth gave God praise for Mary. She blessed Mary and rejoiced with her, and she didn't allow her own situation to stop her from praising God for what He was doing in Mary's life. Elizabeth, glory to God, was secure and content in the blessing God had for her."

Reverend Wright's voice became more intensified as he came to his conclusion, and several members of the church stood with him.

"I thank God today that we are a church of men and women who are content with what God has for us. I thank God that we are a church of mature Saints who can rejoice with one another when God moves in our lives. Aunts rejoice with nieces, mothers rejoice with daughters, fathers rejoice with sons, and heaven rejoices more over one sheep who is found than 99 who never strayed.[64] We rejoice with you today, daughter. Welcome home. Jesus knows all about it. Whatever you are going through, Jesus knows all about it. For we do not have a High Priest who cannot sympathize with our weaknesses. Let us now, therefore, come boldly to the throne of grace that we may obtain mercy and find grace to help in our time of need.[65] The altar is open, Saints. If you do not have a church home, our doors are open to you today. If you have never confessed Jesus Christ as Lord and Savior, come to Him today. Today, while there is yet time. It is no coincidence that you came today. This message was for you. God showed up and met you today. Come to Him, beloved........."

It was time. Maria came out of the pews and walked towards the front of the church. She saw Neicy with a huge grin on her face and hands lifted in the air. Deacon Tony, her husband, was standing with her, and Mother Wright was clapping. The entire congregation applauded as she approached the altar where the Pastor stood. A Deaconess came to her, held her hands, and prayed with her to receive Jesus Christ as Lord and Savior. She was then ushered into a back room where the New Member Ministry Leader, Sister Lori James, wrote down her contact information. She told Maria she would be reaching out to her during the week to discuss new membership classes, and she gave Maria a small gift bag with Holy Tabernacle Church pens, notepad and a pamphlet called *"God's Love"* that Reverend Wright had authored.

"I have two children downstairs," Maria said to Sister Lori.

"Praise God. Minister Barrington will be bringing them up. Wait, let's go see if he's back upstairs yet."

The two walked down a narrow hallway back to the sanctuary, and Maria spotted Genny and Papi at the altar. Maria walked towards them, and Pastor Wright asked her if she was the mother. Maria said yes, and Pastor Wright commended her for bringing her family to

Jesus. Both Genny and Papi were then led in the same backroom with Minister Barrington, and Maria followed.

"Good morning. I'm Minister Barrington," he said to Maria, extending his hand to shake hers.

"Good morning, Minister Barrington. I'm Maria Henderson."

"It is a pleasure to meet you, Mrs. Henderson."

"Ms.," Maria replied.

"*Ms.* Henderson. It is a pleasure to meet you. You have two wonderful children. You are blessed."

"Yes, I am, thank you."

"I was sharing with all the children downstairs that I was young myself when I joined. They both said they wanted to."

"Really?" she asked looking at Genny and Papi.

"Really, mom," said Genny.

"Yeah, mom, we like this church. Except if I had been running around, somebody would have told me to sit down," Papi replied.

Minister Barrington and Maria laughed, and she gave him her cell phone number to call if he needed to reach them.

"Thanks, Ms. Henderson. I'll be in touch. Our Children's Church is every Sunday at 11:30, and I do have a Counseling Ministry available for young adults and their parents if you ever want to come in and talk about anything."

"Where did you go to school?" Maria asked. She was interested in his background.

"I have a Bachelor's and a Master's Degree in Clinical Psychology from Rutgers University."

"Wow, that's a great school. I am impressed. And you are how old?"

"29."

"I've never seen you around, Minister Barrington. We've lived in Monmouth County for years. Where are you from, originally?"

"Newark."

"Praise the Lord. I've heard so many good things about you. Thank you for being here." Turning to her children, she asked, "What did you do this morning?"

"We talked about forgiveness," said Genny.

"And, what about it?"

"That Jesus forgave us for our sins so we should forgive others."

"Amen," said Minister Barrington, gathering his papers into a small briefcase.

"Yes," Maria began, "that is true. We should forgive others."

"Yeah, mom. We should forgive dad. Even if he did leave for Ms. Sophia," Papi said.

"Awkward," Genny thought. She looked at Papi to alert him that the question was inappropriate, and he lowered his head.

"What did you say, Papi?" Maria asked, lifting his head with her hand so that he would make eye contact with her.

".....mmmm.....nothing mom."

"I'll talk to you when we get home," Maria said. Then she turned to Minister Barrington and thanked him. "We'll see you next Sunday."

"Yes, see you next Sunday. Have a blessed week."

He left the family in the back room, and just as Maria was about to question her son, Neicy entered the room and instructed them to come back into the sanctuary for the benediction, and afterwards Neicy would take them out to celebrate. The kids were happy, and Maria was, too. She was not going to allow - for now - "Ms. Sophia's" name to interrupt the name above every other name, Jesus Christ. She would find out what she needed to know from Papi at home. The Word of the Lord that had been spoken to her that day confirmed that God *was* calling her. That was more important than anything else.

"Neicy," Maria asked.

"Yes."

"Did you talk to the Pastor about us?"

"No...........Oh, I get it. No, I didn't. That's all God, sweetheart. God knows. He's calling you, Maria. It's time to give Jesus His rightful place in your life. Number one. Before Rob. Before everybody."

"Yes, you're right. Well, what is Mother Wright's story?"

"Mother Wright doesn't have a story. These people aren't fake, Maria. They're not playing church. God is using them. Mother Wright is prophetic, she sees things. God shows her things, and if she said anything to you, trust me, God will confirm that word. Did she say anything?"

"She said the same thing you said."

"Well, there's your confirmation. Just get ready, Maria."

"Neicy....I appreciate your prayers and Mother Wright's word today very much. I do. But..........I want to hear from God for myself. You pray and get answers right away. Mother Wright sees things and speaks them to confirm what God told you. But, I want to hear from God myself. Won't He talk to me about me?"

"Of course He will, Maria. When you pray tonight, ask Him to fill you with His Holy Spirit for He says in **Luke 11** that He will give His Holy Spirit to us if we ask Him. He's calling you. He told you, just like Pastor Wright said. So when you pray, pray as Samuel who heard the Lord calling his name and said, 'Speak Lord, for your servant hears.'[66] Now He has your attention. Respond to Him, Maria. Say yes."

"I do."

"Well, praise God. You have just said 'I do' to a man who will never leave you. Jesus will never abandon you. I feel like throwing rice. It's like you just got married to the man of your dreams, and this time, there will be no divorce. Jesus loves you, and He is the best husband any woman could ever have. Yes, I have a husband, too, but Maria, Jesus is first. Jesus is my first love, my one and only true love. My husband will never have Jesus' place in my heart, soul and mind. When you put Jesus first, He will add all things. His word says seek first the kingdom of heaven, and these things will be added.[67] Get to know Jesus, Maria, and trust Him to add to your life. He will take care of you, Genny and Papi. He will take care of Rob and the other woman. I'm proud of you."

"Thank you, Neicy. Thank you for everything."

"Can we go eat?" Genny and Papi asked.

"Yes, let's go!" Neicy replied. She waved to her husband, Tony, who knew that meant he would have to see his wife later.

Leaving the sanctuary and walking towards the front entrance, members stopped them and complimented Neicy on her solo. They welcomed Maria and the kids to Holy Tabernacle. A handsome man hugged Neicy and told her how wonderful she sounded today. Neicy thanked him and introduced him, Elder Keith Daniels, to Maria. They shook hands, and he welcomed Maria to the church.

"We'll see you next week?" Elder Keith Daniels asked.

"Yes. I'm looking forward to coming back," Maria replied.

"We're looking forward to having you here. Have a blessed week."

That was just what Maria planned to do.

Chapter Thirteen
Genny

The rest of the school year went quickly. Genny finished all six books as she promised Mr. Engleton, and he was flabbergasted when she turned in six typed book reports the first week of June. She had been spending all of her time after school reading and writing, and it showed in her finished works, which he graded and returned with all A's.

She also met two girls, Joanne and Bria, at her new school. They were both on the Middle School Girls' Basketball Team. Joanne was 5'6" and played shooting guard, and Bria was the 5'8" power forward who could also dribble well. Tonya, their point guard, was only a 7th grader, so Genny wouldn't be playing with her next year.

The girls' basketball team at Addington Park Middle School finished their season 14-2, winning their Conference Championship. That meant success at the high school level because the high school team had finished their season 16-5, winning their Conference Championship and ending the season just shy of a State Title.

When the day of her graduation came, Genny was excited and eager to have both her mom and dad with her, even if it was only temporary. Mr. and Mrs. Henderson put their differences aside for the day, and this time it was their turn to pretend that everything was ok. It was funny to Genny, who knew, of course, the truth about her parents as they walked together and greeted teachers, administrators

113

and parents. They had planned to go out to dinner at the end of the 5 p.m. ceremony, and April and Jade were invited much to Genny's delight. It would make the evening less embarrassing and painful for Genny because mom and dad would be on their own best behavior in public.

"Now," Genny thought, *"they will know how I feel."*

After dining on Italian cuisine at Fernando's in nearby Bradley Beach, Mr. Henderson surprised his daughter with a white diamond necklace and heart pendant. He also gave her a $50 gift card to a local bookstore, which Genny appreciated more than the jewelry. *"That still didn't make up for his leaving,"* Genny thought, but she accepted the gifts from her dad with sincere appreciation. Genny wanted a relationship with her dad, not his money. At the same time, he handed Maria an envelope, which the kids knew was cash, and Maria put it into her pocketbook without opening it.

The evening ended as they left the restaurant and got in separate cars. Papi went with his dad, and Maria and the girls returned to her home for a sleepover.

Summer months passed quickly and saw Genny going to church, reading, writing book reports, and practicing basketball at the high school with Joanne, Bria and a few other girls who were there. All of the girls were impressed with Genny's ball handling skills and her aggressiveness on offense. The high school outdoor basketball courts had four full courts with girls using one and boys using the other three.

One Saturday morning, the courts were packed with basketball players, and there was a huge argument going on between two boys' teams. It got so heated that the players asked everyone to step off the courts for a few minutes so that the two feuding teams could compete against one another. The other boys' teams complied, and the girls had no choice.

Ten young men were left on the main full court. Two additional players joined in and offered to serve as the game referees. It was silly to the girls, who were used to them arguing and fussing about bad calls, walks, fouls, three second violations and double dribbles. This latest contest, however, requiring everyone on the courts to stop their games so that ten young men could have control of their court and the other three was ridiculous.

114

At first Genny paid no attention to them. She was fine sitting in the bleachers and talking with the other girls about the high school teachers and classes: the coach, Mr. Milton, was nice but stern, and he was known for running the girls hard and having one of the best defensive teams in the state; the upperclassmen were supportive of all athletes, so Genny would be fine; the lunches were okay, especially the chicken sandwiches, pasta selections and beef tacos; don't use the bathroom on the third floor, the windows didn't open and it smelled; if you get Ms. Graves for Algebra, ask to switch - she was a hard teacher and difficult to understand; if you get Mr. Zimmerman for Calculus, thank God - he was nice and knew how to break it down so that anyone could understand; don't look for trouble, and whatever you did, avoid Brenda and Rhonda Miller. They were twin sisters, now seniors, on the basketball team, who were great players but liked to fight. Their brothers, Kasheem and Dante, were members of a local gang who had finished high school but still came to the games to support their sisters. The whole family was trouble.

Just as Bria and Joanne were about to continue enlightening Genny, Genny noticed a tall, thin boy on the court dunk on two opposing players. The spectators went wild!

"Oh," Bria began, "that's Chris. He's a junior. He thinks he's sweet."

Genny took another look. "Is that Chris Walker?" she asked.

"Yes. You know him?" Bria asked.

"No. Well, not really. I used to practice with my dad at the Boys' Club, and I think I saw him there before."

"Oh, I bet you did. He lives in the Boys' Club. His dad is always pimping him, you know what I mean? He puts him in games against other people and bets money. He comes to all the games and cusses everybody out from the bleachers. They say he may be a little crazy, but he's harmless. His son is good, don't get me wrong, but he's cocky as I don't know what."

Joanne added, "Yes he is. He's too cocky for his own good. Last year, the boys won their conference title, and you would have thought they had won the State Championship and were going to Disney World. We had a parade through the city, and he was at the front of the float waving to the crowd like he was the Mayor or something."

"Will they give us a parade when we win the states?" Genny asked.

"Now that's the kind of attitude I want around me," said Joanne.

"Me, too," added Bria. "Yes, when we win *the states.* We've won our conference title for about the past ten years, and I guess they got tired of giving us any recognition other than a shout out from the principal during the morning announcements. They're used to us winning. It's crazy – the boys lose and their games are packed. We win, and ours are empty."

"Three freshmen against juniors and seniors. Can you imagine?" asked Joanne, daydreaming.

"Yes," Genny said, "I can. I want to win the state championship every year. I want to dominate this sport. When I graduate high school, I'm going to Rutgers or UConn to play. I'm going to major in English. What do you guys want to do when you finish high school?"

"Girl, we just graduated middle school. I don't know yet," said Bria.

"Well, I like the way Genny thinks. I want to win the states, too. Maybe then we'll get some support. But holdup, where did you get all this fire from? Not from East Borough. You had some kind of hard life that we don't know about?" Joanne joked.

"Why are you laughing? It's not that I had a hard life, it's that I want to have a good life. Don't you?" Genny took a drink of water from the bottle she brought with her, and when she finished, she put it back into her gym bag and out of the direct sunlight. A medium sized black spider was crawling on her bag, and she, now immune to the fear of creepy little creatures thanks to all the run-ins she had with her younger brother, flicked it away perfunctorily. The eight-legged insect flew in the air, but hung on its long, thin and nearly invisible web, and it flew back in her direction. Genny watched it as it returned, and this time, she picked up her empty water bottle to break the web so that the creature would fall to the ground. She was successful, and the spider crawled away, camouflaging itself in the thick and uncut grass.

"Aren't you going to kill it?" Joanne shrieked.

"No. It's just a stupid spider, and it's gone," Genny replied calmly.

Joanne, irritated by Genny's casual indifference to the annoying arachnid, jumped and slid over in her seat, completely destroying, in Genny's mind anyway, Joanne's self-concocted image of a tough girl from the hood. *"What tough girl from the hood who had any kind of hard life was fearful of a little spider?"*

"So," Joanne continued their main conversation, "I'm saying. You're so serious about what is going to happen four years from now. Let's get through our freshman year first."

"I agree with Genny, Joanne," said Bria who had been watching the basketball game. She didn't notice the spider until Joanne shrieked. "We can plan for the future. When I graduate, I want to go to college and start my own company."

"That's good. When you start your own company, I'll help you," Genny replied. "My dad owns a couple of businesses. You can do it."

"When you start your own company," Joanne began, "I'll fall out. Genny, you are filling her head."

"What are you saying, Joanne?" asked Bria, wondering if her friend didn't think she could do it.

"I'm saying she is filling your head. Let's just focus on this year. We haven't even finished the first day of high school, and we're out here talking about what we are going to do when we go to college. Can we just get through high school first?"

"Sure, but there is nothing wrong with dreaming and planning. I'm going to start for UConn. Or maybe I'll start for Rutgers," Genny stated.

Their conversation continued for a few minutes with Joanne trying to refocus them on being freshman in high school, but she couldn't speak to where Genny was or change her determination. Genny's life may not have been "hard" by Joanne's or Bria's standards, as they each lived in the poorer sections of the city, but Genny didn't need for her life to get any harder for her to realize that she wanted better. Going to church every Sunday was helping her a lot – every time she wanted to be mad and resent her parents, she would hear from the Pastor about how God was loving and forgiving. Her heart had softened towards her father, who she wanted to be angry with, but who, whether she liked it or not, she was learning to forgive and love in spite of what had happened. Genny was no longer angry with her mother because she realized that the divorce wasn't her mother's fault. Papi had shared with her that their dad was in love with a woman named "Sophia" and that their dad had left their mom for this mystery woman. Her relationship with her dad was still fractured, but she had gotten to the point where she would receive his phone calls.

"The high school girls' basketball team hasn't won a state title in years. They get close, but they don't win. They don't get the support that the boys do, even though they are winning most of the time. I know they have to be tired of that. All that hard work all season long to come up short. We are going to win the state championship our freshman year. Do you believe that?" Genny asked, weary of their lackluster visions of the future.

"Yeah, I do," replied Joanne.

"Me too," said Bria.

Genny paused before she asked her next question. "Would you guys like to come to church with me sometime?"

"What? Now you're trying to drag us off to church?" Joanne asked.

"Yeah, Genny, baby steps. Baby steps, girl, you are moving too fast," Bria chimed in.

"Okay, I'm sorry. We go every week to Holy Tabernacle Church in Pennstown. I like it. You can come whenever you feel like it, there's no rush."

"Holy Tabernacle?" Joanne asked. "No wonder you're the way you are. That is an old behind church. My grandmother used to go there. Why don't you go to one of those churches in Addington, there are plenty of them, and they have programs for young people. What do you do there? Fan yourself and sing old slave songs? 'Old Man River,'" Joanne sang, laughing.

"Joanne, you can be so ignorant," said Bria. "Why are you speaking negatively about anybody's church? At least she goes, and for your information, those 'old slave songs' helped our people get through struggles you, from the hood and all, know nothing about. They struggled for real. They didn't have the choices and freedoms we have today."

Genny was proud of Bria for speaking up, although she could handle herself intellectually with the best of them. She glanced at Bria and they locked eyes for a moment. Then Bria turned away so that her longtime friend, Joanne, would not think that she was forming an unsubstantiated allegiance with the new girl.

Bria and Joanne had been friends for years, and as much as Bria liked Genny and her renaissance thought process, Bria checked Joanne because she felt Joanne needed to be checked. That was what solidified their friendship. Bria could tell Joanne about herself, but Genny was trying to move too fast, and Bria would politely let her know.

"I'm not being ignorant, I'm just saying, if I have to go to church, I want to go to a church where there are things for young people. The older people have control of the church, and they do what they want. They sing the music they want, they have the preacher they want, they have the programs they want, and they preach the messages they want. There has to be something for young people, too. The preacher has to be able to speak to everybody. If he isn't speaking to me, then I'm not trying to hear any of it," said Joanne.

"You know, you asked me about what kind of hard life I had, but what kind of hard life did you have that you speak so bad about church? You should give it a try," said Genny.

Bria let out a long and deep breath. She was sure Genny meant well, but she didn't know Joanne well enough to push her buttons.

"Genny....we haven't known each other for very long," Joanne said.

"Lord, please, let this be painless," Bria spoke under her breath, knowing that Joanne was pushed to the edge and about to verbally assault Genny.

"I know church," Joanne said. "I was raised in church. I didn't just start going a few weeks ago. My mother lived in church, that's all she knew. Church on Sunday, church on Monday, church on Tuesday, church on Wednesday. Church on Thursday, Friday and Saturday. Church, church, church. And you know what church did for my mother? Nothing. Absolutely nothing. My mother was in the street doing what she had to do to make money to feed us. When she needed the church, they talked about her like a dog. We act like the church is the answer to everything, but sometimes, the church itself is the problem. Hell, the church had a problem with Jesus. You can't mistreat women and children and try to use God's word to justify what you're doing. All the preachers tried to do was curse my mother, but my mother is blessed and you can't curse her. No weapon formed against her or her children shall ever prosper. Jesus cursed the leaders in Matthew 23. God is a defender of widows, orphans and children. You don't know anything, novice. Church can kiss my black ass."

Joanne got up from the bleachers, grabbed her spare APHS blue and black t-shirt and walked off.

"Thank you, Jesus," Bria prayed, cupping her hands at her mouth. *"That could have went a lot worse."*

There was an awkward silence between Genny and Bria, and Genny didn't quite know how to recover. So she used the silence to watch the game that was going on and saw Chris Walker shoot a three pointer and miss.

"It's all in the wrist," Genny began. "He's either tired or just not as good as he thinks. If he believes the hype, he will set himself up for a bad fall."

"You are so weird, Genny," said Bria. "I love that about you."

"What's the deal with Joanne? I didn't mean to say anything wrong."

"You didn't," said Bria. "It's no secret. Her mom was a stripper in a nightclub downtown. She's really pretty."

"Is she still a stripper?" asked Genny.

"I don't think so. She has some kind of job now, I think at the Mall. She also goes to school at night."

"That's great. So what's the problem?" Genny asked.

"The problem is Joanne is embarrassed of her mom. Joanne used to live with her mom and dad. Her parents broke up, and her mom was left with no money, so she did what she had to do."

"Well, where is her dad?"

"I'm not sure. He got married to somebody and then his new wife left him. He tried to come back to Joanne's mom, but she wouldn't take him back. She said she'd rather strip. He was working for the city for a while, then he left again. Joanne doesn't really say a lot about it. She's hurt, you know. Or maybe you don't. East Borough is 'bourgeois.' Joanne is from the hood, Genny. Not the play hood you visit and try to claim street cred for because you survived two or three days. She was born in the hood, raised in the hood, and she lives in the projects. Her brother got arrested for selling drugs and is in jail. It tore his mom apart, he had just turned 18 and was dealing to help his family. The church dogged her mom. Some preacher made a living talking about her, preaching off of her tears, sweat and pain. She was one woman trying to raise two kids on her own without any support from their dad, and people dogged her out. No one said anything about Joanne's dad. You don't know anything about that, East Borough."

"Well, no church is perfect, and yes, there are false prophets, but we can't give up on Jesus because of people. God is still in control. If she knew so much herself, she would know that. So they don't go to church anymore?" Genny asked, feeling uneasy with the turn of the conversation.

"No, East Borough, they don't. What you don't know is that Joanne is hurt. She needs time to heal, and God will heal her. Joanne used to love going to church on Sundays with her mother. You know, her mom can sing gospel music like nobody else. She used to sing in churches around town and was working in the club at night. Who is anybody to judge, right? I went to church, too, and I'm all for it," Bria hesitated. "See, East Borough, around here people really go through stuff, but we come through. Joanne's mom is gonna be alright. And Joanne is gonna be alright. Her brother is gonna be alright. The life we live makes us stronger. You wanna win the state championship. That's wonderful. That's *your* dream. We wanna win the game of life. Not get shot on our way home by a stray bullet. Not get arrested for something we didn't do. Not get molested by anyone, not get pregnant and not have to go to another funeral for another gunshot victim. Survive. Live. Make it. You know what I'm saying?"

Genny didn't know what to say. She was hurt by her mom and dad's separation, but her story wasn't nearly as bad as Joanne's. Genny's mom wasn't stripping, and she didn't live in the projects. Her brother wasn't in jail. A church had not treated her mother badly, in fact, Holy Tabernacle had welcomed them with open arms. Minister Barrington's words during Youth Church were never truer: "Be thankful for what you have and for who you have. Somebody else didn't wake up this morning, and there are many who would love to be in your blessed shoes. Be grateful."

"Are you ready to go, Bria?" Genny asked. She had a lot of thinking to do.

"Yeah. Let's catch up to Joanne. She plays like she's mad, but she wants our company. Let's go."

The two girls got up from the bleachers and left the excitement of the basketball game that was still going on. Young men from the sidelines cheered and argued, reminding Genny of the day a few years ago when she had competed against Chris Walker. She contemplated telling Bria, but decided not to as she passed by the court and glanced in Chris' direction. He made eye contact with her for a second. He remembered her, too. He nodded as she walked by, and she managed a smile without Bria noticing.

Genny lifted her arm and shot an imaginary basketball, flicking her wrist and holding it in its' extended position, elbow straight, cocked in its chamber like her dad taught her and in perfect line with the basket. She looked at him quickly and then looked away, hoping he would take the hint.

Chapter Fourteen
Papi

Papi and his dad spent most of the summer together at the gym, the dojo and the Center for Young Men. Papi was his dad's apprentice, learning every facet of community relations, business, roundhouse kicks and bench pressing that he was shown. Mr. Henderson was a second degree black belt, and he insisted that his children learn martial arts at an early age. Papi was working towards his brown belt, and Genny had trained and earned hers. Although she lost interest once she fell in love with basketball, she would still train until she achieved second degree black belt rank if her dad had his way. Maria, herself a black belt, encouraged Genny to continue in martial arts, but when mom and dad couldn't agree on keeping their marriage together, Genny lost all interest in doing everything that they wanted her to do. She enjoyed basketball and was good at it, so as long as she played well, mom and dad would be pleased with her.

The time dad and son spent together was precious to Papi. He looked up to his dad and admired him for his work with the Center. Six young men came to the Center on Mondays, Tuesdays and Wednesdays from 9am to 5pm, just like they were going to work, for the city and state grant-funded summer program Mrs. Henderson had helped her husband build. It was Rob's vision, but Maria knew how to connect all the dots and present him with a tangible, finished product that he could present and promote. His visions and his desire to provide for his family were his sperm, and her ingenuity, love and support of him were her eggs. Once the two got together and talked over what he wanted to do, scheduling action items, due dates and implementation, there was fertilization, and Maria delivered strong, healthy babies every time. The Robert J. Henderson Center for Young Men was his strongest "son" in business to date.

Mr. Henderson and his wife always did well when they shared intercourse in business. It was when he tried to raise his "sons" on his own that he failed. The failed business investments were done without Maria's knowledge. She could sniff a bad deal from a mile away, but Mr. Henderson, who knew all the risks of each, was willing to take a chance. He wasn't a gambler, but he trusted his own judgment and had grown used to lying to Maria as he had been cheating on her so frequently. When he lost all his money, he couldn't bring himself to tell Maria because she would know that he had spent their money without consulting her. Not that she didn't trust him, she did, and she never questioned him, but this was all their savings. So he convinced himself that he was actually divorcing Maria for her own good, and this is what helped him to sleep at night. Besides, he planned to make it up to her anyway, so there was really nothing wrong, in his mind, with what he did.

Mr. Henderson was well connected in the community, so he would always have different people coming through to speak to the young men about life, education, young women, and being responsible young adults. He took them on different trips throughout the state to prisons and colleges; poverty-stricken neighborhoods and affluent suburbs; the unemployment office and corporations built by hard-working men and women; prostitution ridden cities and wedding ceremonies in beautiful churches. *"Make a decision,"* Mr. Henderson would tell the young men. He taught them about money, credit scores, how to buy a home and how to read the stock reports. They watched CNN and MSNBC and were required to write reports on current events and how they would deal with terrorism, Afghanistan, Iraq, international crises and a split Congress. The young men observed Mr. Henderson opening doors for ladies and shaking hands with businessmen. They accompanied him on his visits to City Hall, where he would meet with the city's leaders and discuss short- and long-term goals for the community. They also had to go with him to the car wash and help hand wash and detail his silver Mercedes, which the majority of the young men resented, but not one of them would dare question the hard-working legend who invested his time and money in their development. After the car was clean to Mr. Henderson's high standards, he had his young protégés walk back to the Center, a distance of about one-half mile. The summer interns, James, Jamarr, K'Shon, Marcus, Eric and Isaiah, all from Addington Park, didn't complain about the assignments they were given. They trusted their mentor and knew that there was a lesson to be learned, and all of the young men were willing to be groomed under the guidance of the City's finest.

The young men were privy to just about every aspect of Mr. Henderson other than his personal life. There was a picture of him, his wife and two children in his office at the Center, and although it was a fabrication of the truth, he presented to the young men a picture of uninterrupted family life. As far as they knew, he was a happily married man and a loving, doting father. Papi appreciated that his father had their photograph in his office where the whole world could see and admire his dad. He was, or at least was at one time, happily married to his mom, Maria, and he had always been a loving father, so the picture really wasn't a lie - it was just a representation of his life at an earlier time that he still treasured, just like Papi did. It was all good until the end of the summer, however, when the young men were in the office cleaning, and Marcus accidentally knocked the framed photograph off Mr. Henderson's desk. The glass nearly broke, and Marcus apologized to Mr. Henderson as he checked the frame to be sure it was intact before returning it to its place.

"You sure have a beautiful family, Mr. Henderson," said Marcus, ignoring the call vibrating from his cell phone in his pocket. *"Probably Paris again,"* he thought to himself. Paris was a cheerleader. She was pretty with long, muscular legs and long, black hair that she always wore back in a ponytail with a ribbon to match whatever clothes she was wearing.

"Thanks, Marcus. Family is the most important piece of your life. Girlfriends, Marcus....they come and go. You can get a girl anywhere. Girlfriends have no business calling you all day long when you are here taking care of your business. So, I'm going to need you to turn off your phone, leave it on my desk, and go get all the guys and

125

bring them in here, please. Also, tell Papi he can play his game and use his earphones."

Marcus knew better than to talk back, so he took his phone from his pocket, noticing the last call was, in fact, from Paris, and left it turned off on the boss' desk. He went and did as he was told, calling all the young men to Mr. Henderson's office for what was likely going to be another one of his pep talks to inspire, encourage and motivate them.

Papi readily complied with his father's instructions, and Marcus closed Papi's office door to be sure he wouldn't hear anything.

It took less than five minutes for all six young men to walk into Mr. Henderson's office, quiet and ready for their next lesson, and happy to have a break from the odd cleaning jobs they had been assigned.

"Isaiah, is all the trash out?" Mr. Henderson asked.

"Yes, sir," the young man replied.

"Young men," Mr. Henderson started (he always referred to them in group settings as 'young men'), "tell me about family. Anything you want to say, whatever you think. Tell me about family. Marcus, let's start with you."

The six young men stood in Mr. Henderson's small but meticulously neat corner office with plush tan carpet, tall glass windows overlooking the city's redeveloped business district, and an antique wooden desk and chair that looked like they had been purchased from a garage sale but refurbished because someone said the wood was quality. The office was simple, a few wall paintings of plants and architectural designs, but inviting with the flat screen television mounted on the wall, peach and white throw rugs and two matching chaise lounges in black.

Eric, a 6'0 14 year old who secretly preferred swimming to basketball and science to rap music, took a seat and thought about what his answer would be. He was at the Center because his grades were slipping, and although he was highly intelligent, he had lately been missing class assignments and homework following the death of his father. Eric wanted to be here - he needed to be.

Isaiah, a junior who had been expelled from school after two fights where he and K'Shon jumped a young man and broke his nose, took a seat on the other chaise lounge.

Mr. Henderson would sometimes motion for them to bring chairs in from one of the other offices, but this time he didn't so the other four young men stood.

"Family," Marcus started, "is where you come from. It's who you are. Your mom. Your dad, if he is around. Your brothers and sisters. Your grandmother. Family is who we are - yeah. That's what I would say."

"Anything else?" Mr. Henderson asked.

"Well, family keeps you grounded. It's where you come from, but family will always be there for you. Like you said, girlfriends come and go, but your family, they will always be there."

"Okay," Mr. Henderson replied, "now Eric, what about you? And pull your pants up. Didn't I tell you that before? Perception, young man."

Eric stood up, pulled his sagging blue jeans up with both hands, and scratched his head, taking a moment before he answered. He didn't know what this was all about or for, but he would answer something.

"I can come back to you. Do you need a minute?" Mr. Henderson asked, sensing Eric didn't have an answer ready.

"No, I'm good. I was just thinking of what I wanted to say. I would say that family is what Marcus said, you know, your family will always be there for you. But family members pass, you know, they die - we die. So we have to value our family members while they are here. Also, family has good and bad. Family can be there for you when no one else is, or family can turn their backs on you. When anybody other than your family turns their back on you, who cares. It doesn't even bother me. When my family - my blood - turns their back on me - that cuts deep. So family has advantages and disadvantages. Whoever treats you right and loves you unconditionally - that's family. That's family to me."

"Can I answer, Mr. Henderson?" K'Shon asked eagerly.

"Sure."

"Well," K'Shon began, "I agree with my man. We have to love our families while we have them. Family has advantages and disadvantages. Family ain't about girls. Family, real family, is about love, respect and healthy relationships. Always be there for you - yes. Love you unconditionally - yes. But family, good or bad, is family.

We can't choose our families. My family is my mother, my brother, my sisters, my grandmother and my cousins....everybody. We are always gonna have each other's back. We're all family."

"Okay," said Mr. Henderson, "I'm going to explain why I'm asking you this question in a minute. James, you're up."

James was the quiet one. He hadn't wanted to come to the Center for the summer, but he would be a senior next September, and this would look good on his high school transcript, so he said yes when his guidance counselor recommended it to him. His grades were ok, he liked school enough, but his detached personality, as they sometimes classified him, wasn't due to any abnormality or psychological disorder. James really was just ready to finish school and make a go at life on his own. He had been the man of his house for most of his life, for his mother, two younger brothers and younger sister. He worked and went to school, helping his mother with the bills. He had experienced a life that forced him to become a man before he was ready. The streets had been his mentor. James knew how to hustle. He knew how to make money, and he knew how to save money. He planned to enroll in the local community college and then start his own clothing apparel business for men and buy his family a house. He would propose to his girlfriend, Grace, after they finished college. They would get married on the beach. They would have three healthy children by his 32nd birthday, and he would retire a multi-millionaire at age 50. He thought a lot like Mr. Henderson, but he didn't tell anyone about his plans, not even his mentor. James didn't like to talk, he liked to make things happen. Mr. Henderson, educated in the streets himself, knew that James had something special, but he didn't force it out of him. He knew James would come to him when he was ready.

"I agree with everybody," James said. He folded his lean, muscular arms and stood up straight, about 6'0. He wore red, yellow and black plaid shorts that were belted at the waist with a black and white striped shirt that would have clashed on any of the other young men and gotten them laughed out of school. James, however, ahead of his time, had style and sophistication, and he could easily turn what would wear as a preppy private school uniform on them into a fashionable urban ensemble other young men could rock from the hood to their college campuses.

"That's it?" Mr. Henderson asked.

"Yes. Well, if I had to add anything, I would just say that family gives a man a purpose. A real man takes care of his family. He guards them, he protects them, he provides. It is a responsibility, you know. He can't just check in and check out when he wants to, leaving his wife and kids to rely on state programs to be their daddy. If it's cheaper to keep her, why break up your family? That's bad business. Some brothers take their families for granted, especially the mothers of their children. They think a woman can handle her role and his. She can, but when she does, she is overworked. She doesn't have time to be the woman she should be because she has to do both jobs. She wears the pants and the dress. She's in the kitchen, the bedroom and the boardroom. She suffers. She tries to be strong, all of our women do, but inside she suffers. Maybe she cries when no one else is listening, or she finds religion because the preacher tells her that Jesus can take care of all her needs. She looks for help, she wants it, but she doesn't want to have to ask for it. She *shouldn't* have to. A mother shouldn't have to go to the courts to force a man to take care of his children. We let our women down, and if God steps in to take our place, who can *we* turn to? The Bible says that a man who doesn't take care of his own is worse than an unbeliever.[68] So if God is involved, that man has to repent before God. Our women suffer, and they spend their entire lives nurturing us and caring for us so that we can be better. They put their own needs last for us. Our children suffer. Then after we run around and discover the grass isn't greener on the other side, and the side chick gets on our nerves, too, we want to go back home, and we expect our women to welcome us back with open arms, like nothing ever happened. As fathers – we young men - come off like punk ass bitches."

The other five young men looked at James in disbelief. He hardly ever said a word. Then, they looked at Mr. Henderson, who was leaning back in his chair behind his desk. Mr. Henderson knew that the stoic James was somewhat reserved, but whenever James had anything to say it was always powerful and full of wisdom. When James did speak up, everyone listened.

Mr. Henderson contemplated what he would say as the room went silent, thankful that the conversation had stirred some passion in the more often than not phlegmatic young man before him.

129

"Everything ok, James?" Mr. Henderson asked, feeling a sense of conviction in his conscience, but then shaking it off and ignoring the possibility of any prophetic truth intently or not meant for him.

"Yes, sir."

Mr. Henderson paused. He needed to bring them back in and make his own prophetic statement.

He sat up straight in his chair, rolled a pencil back and forth in the fingers of his right hand, and then placed it on his desk. He unloosened his tie and stood up to check the temperature on the central air system, which was located on the wall behind his desk. It was set at a cool 68 degrees, but it had just gotten warm in the room, and he could feel beads of sweat beginning to form at his brow.

"Anybody hot in here?"

"It is a little warm," Marcus said, covering for his mentor.

They all noticed that Mr. Henderson was uncomfortable with the turn of the conversation, and they all agreed that "yes, it is a little warm in here."

Mr. Henderson turned the digital thermostat down to 65 degrees, and when he had sat back down in his chair, he opened the drawer of his desk to take out a black hand towel, which he used to wipe his brow and head.

"You okay, Mr. Henderson?" Marcus asked. "Do you want cold water?"

"No, I'm good Marcus. I think I need to get the air checked in here. Would you make a mental note of that, Marcus, and remind me to reach out to Walter."

"Sure," Marcus replied.

Mr. Henderson reclined in his seat and then sat forward again, ready to continue the conversation now that he had taken a break to stall and think of something he could say that wouldn't be self-incriminating.

"I appreciate your answer, James. Real talk, some fathers do come off like punk ass bitches. James makes a great point, young men, often overlooked in our community. Family is a responsibility that many of us do take for granted. Taking the mothers of our children for granted? Yes. Hell yes. Why? If all a girl is to a brother is a booty call, he isn't going to take her seriously because he doesn't consider a booty call family. He will take the child seriously, that's

130

family, and be there for his son or daughter, but the booty call? How seriously do we take her? Was she just a jump off, do we love her, do we respect her, or do we question whether or not the child is ours and resent the fact that we slipped up that night, and now we blame her for it? We call our women bitches and hoes in music and on TV like those are their names. We are not even embarrassed, for the sake of our mothers, our sisters, our grandmothers and the women in our family who we do respect. Does another brother's blatant, public disrespect of our women mean anything to you? And then we got the nerve to get mad if someone 'disrespects' our mothers. We disrespect our own mothers. Or does that even bother us anymore?" Mr. Henderson asked.

The young men just looked at him, speechless.

"And this is my point with each one of you," he continued. "I was telling Marcus earlier, who can't keep the young ladies from calling him when he is here, that girlfriends come and go. My wife was my girlfriend when I was in high school. I knew she was the one. I knew what I wanted in life. I wasn't trying to have a bunch of girls out here with my seed. I wanted all my children to come from one woman - my wife. You feel me? Let me put it like this so you can understand. You've seen the homes and apartment buildings I've taken you to. Okay, well it's like this. A girlfriend is like an apartment you rent - it's good enough for the time being, you live there for a while, pay the rent, hopefully make it to the end of the lease term, but if it doesn't work out, you can't wait until the lease is over. If it's really bad, you will either break the lease without care or you will look for someone else to assume the lease so you can get out."

"A baby's mama is like a house you rent. It's better than an apartment, it's bigger, but you're still renting it. There's no real commitment. You live there, pay the cost, explore owning it with a lease to buy option, but if she starts trippin', it's just a lease with an option to buy. It's an option."

"Real talk, young men, a wife is like a home you have saved your hard-earned money for. You shopped around for the best home your money can buy. You worked, put your time in, put your money in the bank and saved every nickel and dime you earned. Once you find the house you want, you check it out, make an offer, negotiate the best terms for yourself, put up a down payment and close the deal. It's your investment, and you take care of it because it's yours. Your wife is the woman you make your family with. Family will mean everything to you because you put your time in it, your money, your heart and your love. You grind for your family - support your family, love, defend, protect and provide for. No matter what happens when you leave your home in the morning, no matter how your day goes, who likes you, who doesn't, who promotes you and who supports your business. No matter what, young men, trust me when I tell you, at the end of the day, family is all we have, however good or bad it is. As men, your wife is the only woman who is your baby's mother. When you love your wife, take care of her, support her dreams and back her up, she will take care of you and support your dreams. No drama. No nonsense. No mess."

Mr. Henderson leaned back in his chair and folded his hands behind his head, hoping his words meant something to them. He hoped he had said enough to support James' statements and yet get his own point across.

The photograph on his desk of him, Maria, Genny and Papi was staring him in the face, and feeling convicted for his hypocrisy, he looked outside the window instead at the parked cars and people walking briskly along the city sidewalks.

"That was deep, Mr. Henderson," remarked Isaiah. "I don't have anything else to say."

"I do," said Jamarr. "Sometimes it just doesn't work out between two people. They may have the, you know, physical connection, but nothing more. They may be young, and maybe they just made a mistake. They can be forgiven, it's not like we should be judging anybody. Who are we to judge? I know a whole lot of cats with kids by women they ain't married to. They are there for their kids, but they ain't married. That doesn't make them any less of a man than the next dude who does get married. If marriage was so great, I'm sayin', why do so many people get divorced? Then their kids get dragged into the middle of that, and *they* get messed up. At least if there was no marriage, both sides know what it is. Everybody knows what's up. So what do you do as a man then?"

"Stop making our women 'baby mamas,'" Mr. Henderson answered. "Put a ring on the finger of any lady you want to be serious enough with to make a baby with. Our women deserve more from us.

Strap up! And if it can't work out, you are still responsible to be there for your children. Child support is non-negotiable."

Isaiah sighed. He did not agree, and he was not convinced. "Mr. Henderson, have you ever watched those TV talk shows? These girls come on and swear up and down that the baby is the man's they brought on stage, and then the results come in and you hear *'You are not the father.'* Man, females are just as scandalous and wrong as we are, and no one forced them to do anything. How are they sleeping around with two or three dudes, sometimes more, at the same time, not knowing who their baby's father is? Then they got some of these brothers who catch feelings for these shorties all messed up when they find out that the kid ain't even theirs. It's not all on us."

The other young men nodded and supported Isaiah's statement.

"Isaiah, you're right. Some of these females are scandalous. Some of them are wrong. But I'm talking to you about you. I'm talking about what you do, and who you choose to lie down with. Some of those young women you see on TV who don't know who the father of their child is have more likely than not suffered some kind of sexual molestation in their youth that manifests itself in their promiscuity."

"Well, that's not our fault," Isaiah interrupted.

"Hold on, let me finish," said Mr. Henderson. "Our community doesn't talk about that or support the young women who have and who do suffer inside, as James so eloquently said. We don't deal with our own dirty laundry, and if our sister or cousin has been molested by a man in the family or the community, we don't help them. We just leave them to self-medicate, heal themselves and get over it. That's the sad truth. They want help, Isaiah, but they're too afraid and ashamed to ask for it, and they don't believe we would support them anyway. All some of our young women know is abuse by a man. So they relieve their pain by sleeping with different men and mistaking sexual intercourse for true love. *We* know what *we* are doing. We know how to manipulate a woman's feelings so that we can get what we want, and we know how to prey on weak women, especially those who are looking for love in all the wrong places. Sex don't mean nothing to us! We don't catch feelings over sex with a female we care nothing about! It's just sex. So what, we may or may not be the father of a child whose mother we care nothing about. We can do back flips on stage and run through the studio audience and wave the results in the face of that young woman because we care nothing about what we did," he said, waving a notebook in the air in imitation of what he was saying.

The young men laughed, and Mr. Henderson continued once they quieted down.

"It was sex, we told her we loved her to get the drawers, and after it's over, we look the same young woman in the face and call her a hoe. We are responsible for what we do, Isaiah. If the young lady doesn't mean anything to you, leave her alone. Don't play with her feelings. Don't pull your pants down. Don't lead her on, and don't blame her for your own inability to control your own actions. If it gets too hot, make sure you keep some protection on you. Respect yourself. You, young men, are responsible for what you do. You know now, and when you know better, you will do better. Don't walk out of here and say Mr. Robert J. Henderson didn't tell you nothing, because I have been telling you all along everything you need to know about young ladies. The main point, Isaiah, and every young man in this room, is that you are responsible for what you do."

The impassioned Mr. Henderson sat leaning forward in his chair.

"Well, what if I'm with her, and I just can't control myself. If she's gonna give it, I'm gonna take it, for sure," Isaiah continued.

This time Mr. Henderson sighed. "Ok, Isaiah, it's heated. She wants to and you want to. She's fine. She's bad. Sexy as hell. Nice body, top and bottom, shaped like an hourglass and wearing the perfume you love on her. Full lips, soft skin, smelling good, pretty face and long hair you can run your fingers through. How are you going to say no to that? In the moment, any young man might forget everything I just said."

"She fine like a super model?" Isaiah asked.

The other young men laughed.

"Now if a super model is down for a brother, I'm sorry, Mr. Henderson, I appreciate everything you're saying, and you know we respect you, but I would hit that. Oh, she would get it for real."

"Isaiah, you couldn't get a super model for fake," K'Shon said. He laughed, and the other young men snickered.

"Man, you couldn't get a super model if she was taking numbers and you was next in line. You better stick to those low budget females, those ghetto barbies you like who don't have any standards," K'Shon continued.

All the young men burst out laughing, and there was a near raucous in the room. Eric was rolling on the chaise lounge with one hand covering his mouth in an attempt to muffle his boisterous laughter, and Jamarr opened the office door, ran into the hallway, and then came back into the office with a huge Cheshire cat grin locked on his face.

"Oh, hold up! You got jokes, K'Shon? I know *you* ain't trying to say nothing. You're still foaming at the mouth over the last low budget female I passed on to you. Don't get embarrassed in here, man, I'll let everybody in here know what's up. Sloppy seconds mother f......" Isaiah remarked.

"Alright, enough," Mr. Henderson interrupted. He waited for their laughter to subside, and then he spoke again.

"Let's be serious about this. Be men. You see how we talk about women? We are still carrying out the doctrine of former slave owners, antagonistic towards our own women who have loved, raised and nurtured us, hating each other and making it easy for others to divide and conquer us based on our own self-hatred and internal gender and class discrimination. We have to write our own doctrine for our families and for our communities. *We* are responsible for our families. We can't blame women because we aren't men enough to be in our place. The man is the head. Listen, our families are stronger when we are in our rightful place as the head of the family. When we build stronger families, we build stronger communities. When we build stronger communities, we build a stronger state and a stronger country. Our communities break down when we, as men, break down and fail our mothers, our daughters, our baby's mothers, our wives and all our women."

Mr. Henderson had commanded their attention. Continuing, he said, "Your assignment for this week is to find out the percentage of two-parent homes in Addington Park vs the percentage of homes where a single mother is the head of the household. Go to the municipal offices downtown and ask someone for help, or research it on the internet. Then, do a two page, double-spaced and typed research paper on (1) any doctrine, law or philosophy concerning slavery in this country, which taught separation in our race and self-destruction, and (2) condoms. Everything is due next Tuesday, no exceptions, and no one will graduate from this summer program without completing this assignment. That goes for everybody."

He made eye contact with each young man in the room until he was certain that they would all complete their assignment.

"The point, young men, and especially you, Isaiah, is to protect yourselves. Respect yourselves. You are responsible for what you do. The young lady you choose to lie down with is not responsible for you. You are responsible for your futures, and the choice is your own. Nobody else has that much control or power over your decisions and choices, I don't care how fine she is. There are consequences to the decisions we make. Does everybody understand?"

The six young men were quiet.

"So what did you get out of our discussion today?" asked Mr. Henderson.

The six young men looked around at one another, and then motioned for Marcus, the usual spokesman of the group, to respond.

"Focus," said Marcus.

"Focus?" asked Mr. Henderson.

"Yes, focus. Focus on our futures. Don't get caught up with girls. Take care of business when it's time to take care of business. Be men. Take care of our families. Protect ourselves, and strap up. We are responsible for what we do. The girl is not."

"Alright, good, and always be grateful for what you do have. When you love a woman, you will make love to her body, her soul and her mind. If it's just sex, you will play with her mind, use her for her body and sell your own soul to be with her for three or four minutes," Mr. Henderson said. "You will always know the difference. Now, it's just about 5:00, so you can all go home. And, Isaiah, if you get that hot and bothered, take a magazine or your phone and go into the bathroom."

They all laughed.

"Okay, Mr. Henderson," Isaiah said, "you got jokes, too. It's all good. I'm just keeping it real."

Mr. Henderson stood up from his desk and went on in his speech as he walked in front of them towards the door. "When you

136

are married, you can get it whenever you want from your wife. She'll come to you. Trust me, she wants it just as much as you do. I'll walk you out."

They left Mr. Henderson's office, and Mr. Henderson checked in on his son, who enjoyed his own space in the small office next to his dad's, complete with an executive desk, chair, file cabinet and couch where he often took naps.

"Papi, I'm going downstairs to lock up. I'll be right back," said Mr. Henderson to his son, standing in the doorway to be sure Papi saw him.

When Papi saw his dad there, he removed the earphones and said "Okay."

Mr. Henderson walked the young men down the stairs to the front door, and as he shook each one's hand and saw them all out, he noticed a black Honda Accord parked directly across the street that looked like Sophia's. The windows were tinted like hers, but she knew better than to come to the Center during his business hours with the young men. As the front driver side door opened, he saw Sophia. She was wearing a long jacket cinched at the waist and higher than usual heels. Her hair was flowing down her shoulders, and she deposited some coins into the parking meter. She then waited briefly to cross the street until a tan four-door Cadillac yielded to her. Rob noticed the driver was a man who no doubt stopped to get a better look, and Sophia sashayed in front of him.

Rob's son was there, and he had not yet introduced Papi to Sophia. "Papi, stay upstairs in your office," Rob yelled. "I have to take care of some business, I'll be back up in a few minutes."

"Okay dad," Papi yelled back. He was getting tired anyway, so he reclined on the couch and dozed off.

"Hi Rob," she smiled, walking up to the door like she had received a VIP invitation. She had an unusual air of confidence that Rob, as good as she looked right now, wasn't welcoming of.

"Hey baby," Rob managed to answer, opening the door for her to come in. "What are you doing here?" Rob asked matter-of-factly, looking out the door and checking to be sure all six of the young men were walking away from the Center. They were already two city blocks down the street.

"What, aren't you happy to see me?" Sophia asked.

"That's not the point. I have the young men I'm working with. You know that. This is business."

"Well, you make it sound like you've got somebody else in here. I waited until they left, and I counted six."

"I do. My son is still upstairs. Are you checking up on me?"

Sophia took a deep breath, knowing that Rob was not yet comfortable introducing her to his son. Rob noticed, and he retracted a bit, grabbing her around the waist and kissing her gently on the lips. She guided his hands inside her jacket where he could feel only her brassiere and bare stomach.

"Did you come over here with no clothes on?" he asked, opening her jacket to reveal her curves and light blue satin bra. "Lord, have mercy."

"I'm sorry, I shouldn't have come. You're taking care of business," she said coyly, turning to pretend she was going to leave.

"Wait. Let me check on my son. Stay right here for a minute. Don't go anywhere."

Mr. Henderson ran up the stairs like a track star and into his son's makeshift office. Papi was snoring heavily.

He ran downstairs, grabbed Sophia by the hand, and took her upstairs into his office, closing the door of his son's office and his own.

The two kissed passionately, and Sophia allowed her love-sick lover to throw her jacket to the floor, pin her to the wall and ravage her body. *"Good for him,"* she thought. They hadn't been on the best terms for a few months since she overheard his conversation with his son about Maria, and she never told Rob that she had heard anything. She just made herself unavailable whenever he called or wanted to get together, and she returned his phone calls on her own terms. That drove him crazy, and she knew it. That would make him thirstier for her when they saw each other, and she would reap all the benefit.

"I missed you," Rob said, kissing her neck and shoulders.

"I missed you, too," Sophia answered. "Are you sure we can?" she asked, still baiting her lover.

"What do you mean?"

"I mean, are you sure we can - here? In your office? Maybe we shouldn't, your son is right next door."

Rob didn't want to talk anymore. He went to sit down in his office chair and allow Sophia to do whatever she wanted. She playfully situated herself underneath his desk, and in so doing noticed the photo of his family. Rob glanced at Sophia as she stared at the portrait, and he placed his hands on her face, kissed her, and promised her that she was the only woman for him. They grabbed and groped for one another, bumping against the desk, and the glass-framed family portrait fell onto the floor, shattering in small pieces. Neither acknowledged the damage that was done, and Rob reclined in his seat and closed his eyes to get the image out of his mind. An omen, perhaps, that he would never ignore on any other occasion, but there was a greater need for attention to his overwhelming fleshly desires.

A few blocks away, Marcus realized that he didn't have his cell phone. "Oh no, I hope Mr. Henderson is still there. I left my phone. I gotta call Paris back."

"Damn, man," said Isaiah, "you didn't listen to a thing he said, did you?"

"What? She is just a friend. I'm not trying to have a baby with her. We're hanging out tonight, that's all. I'll catch up to you guys later."

"Peace," they all replied. The young men shook hands at the corner, and Marcus ran back to the office building. To his surprise the front door was not locked. Mr. Henderson never left the front door of his Center unlocked. Marcus secured the deadbolt on the door and checked the first floor conference room and bathroom noticing nothing was out of place. He went upstairs and saw Papi's door was closed. Marcus peeked in and saw Papi fast asleep on the couch. *"Lil' Man had a long day,"* Marcus thought.

He closed the office door and walked to the corner office of Robert J. Henderson, Director, detecting the soft scent of either a woman's perfume or some kind of floral air freshener lingering in the air.

Marcus approached Mr. Henderson's closed office door suspiciously and knocked lightly. There was no answer, so he turned the door knob and opened it.

Chapter Fifteen
Maria

Maria enjoyed the summer months at Holy Tabernacle Church and looked forward to the worship services every Sunday. She had successfully completed her New Member classes and received the right hand of fellowship from the Pastor and leaders. Mother Wright welcomed her desire to participate in the Women's Ministry as an Event Liaison/Coordinator, and Maria would also start classes at the Bible Institute Pastor Wright and his leaders were part of in September.

Her children seemed to be fond of Minister Barrington, and they also anticipated Sunday mornings. Both completed their New Member classes, and both joined the Youth Choir under Minister Barrington's direction. For now, they were learning the songs, and Minister Barrington was patient. Papi had impressed everyone with his pitch perfect voice and three octave range. Maria had heard Papi hum tunes around the house before, but his gift was really apparent in the church, where some of the youth were shy about singing. Not Papi. Although he was usually positioned in the back of the Youth Choir when they sang, and he didn't have a microphone directly in front of him, his voice resonated and his diction was clear. As she looked on proudly from the pew, she often wished Rob would be there to see his son. His singing in church was important, too, just as much as karate, and Maria would invite him soon she promised herself, for Papi's sake.

Maria had shared a conversation with Papi following their first visit to Holy Tabernacle about the mystery woman, *"Sophia."* Papi told his mother that his dad told him *"Sophia"* was just a friend, and he loved her like he did all his friends. Papi also shared with Maria that whoever this woman was, his dad told him she would never take Maria's place.

"Typical," Maria thought to herself during their conversation, *"just a friend."* Maria was livid after her talk with Papi, but she didn't let it show. Her rage was thereafter diluted as she knelt in prayer and talked about it with God. She was real with Him. She needed to be. Maria talked to God that night like she was talking to Neicy.

"I put so much into this marriage. I am a good woman, and I know it. After all this time, to be so betrayed by my husband, and he is just walking around like we never took vows, like our marriage and children don't mean anything to him at all. It's like we ceased to exist to him. How does he get to just walk away with another woman? Do you honor that? Are you blessing what he is doing with her? How can you be okay with all this? We were married before you, Jesus."

That same night, Maria heard the Spirit of the Lord speak to her for the first time. It was a clear voice at her right ear, and when she heard it, she turned her head to be sure there was no one else in her bedroom. ***"Do not fear."***

Maria fell to her knees and called on the Lord for His help. She was trying to get over Rob, but her heart was broken, and she was still in pain. There was no cynicism this time and no slick remarks. She wanted to be healed. She wanted to be whole again. She wanted to forgive Rob and not care what he did with Sophia or anybody else. She wanted Jesus in her life as her Lord and Savior, her God, her husband and her best friend.

"Please forgive me, Jesus. Help me to forgive Rob and Sophia. Heal me, please, I can't live like this. I am so angry with him for walking out. I hate him. I am trying to forgive and forget, but I hate him so much I have thoughts about him where I hope something bad happens to him, and I know that isn't right. I heard your word about forgiveness, and I still hate him. You are my God, and I need

you in my life, please. Help me to move on, you have already shown that he isn't the one you want for me. You allowed him to walk out and divorce me. I know that you don't put more on us than we can bear, but I am coming to you and laying it all at your throne of grace, Father, because you are my God, and I am looking to you for help. Please order my steps in your word, Father, and take everything out of my life that you don't want for me. Create in me a clean heart and renew my mind, Father. Empty me of myself, and fill me with Your Holy Spirit so that I may fulfill Your Holy purpose for the life you have given me. Thank You for being my God, for loving me unconditionally, and for being with me every day of my life. You have always been there, Jesus, and I am grateful for you. Thank you for covering Genny and Papi, and thank you for a church home where we can hear your word from ministers who have a heart for you, who are submitted to you, and who obey you. Bless and keep me, Genny and Papi, Lord, I pray in the name of Jesus. Thank you. Amen."

During Maria's sleep that night, she heard the same still voice say ***"Do not fear. I am with you."*** She woke from her sleep and knelt at her bedside, thanking God for being her and her children's God. She prayed fervently for Rob, for his heart and that he would make Jesus Lord of his life. She prayed for his success and happiness and that God would bless him as he moved on in his life. She did want him to be happy, and she did love him enough to let him go, but to go so soon and then tell their son about this other woman was disrespectful. He actually told their son that he loved this woman. *"Didn't he still love her? How could he talk to their son about loving any other woman? Rob needed his ass beat,"* Maria shared with Jesus. She had to be honest with Him, He knew anyway. *"Rob needed his ass whooped. Forgive and forget, okay Jesus, but how is that justice? How does that make it right? You are a God of justice, too, and I am your daughter. How can you reward him with success and happiness after he leaves his family? Isn't there some kind of 'family first' creed up in heaven, too?"*

When Maria finished her prayer that night, every complaint she had was poured out to God. He was listening to her. *To her*, and she heard Him just like Neicy did and just like Mother Wright did. *"Well then, I am going to give you everything to listen to. Cast all your cares on Him for He cares for you?*[69] *Okay, here are all my cares, in the name of Jesus."*

There was silence when Maria finished, and she remained on her knees for about one hour to hear what the Spirit of the Lord would say to her. At 4:20 a.m., she climbed back in bed, pulled the covers snug around her body, and she laid there meditating on the Lord's words to her before falling asleep.

Maria didn't hear the voice again until the next Sunday morning as she was preparing to go to church. ***"Do not fear. I am with you. I have heard your cry."***

During the same Sunday service, Pastor Wright preached on **Isaiah 41:8-10:**

"But you, Israel, are My servant,
Jacob whom I have chosen,
The descendants of Abraham My friend.
You whom I have taken from the
ends of the earth,
and called from its farthest regions,
And said to you,
'You are My servant,
I have chosen you and have not cast you away;
Fear not, for I am with you,
Yes, I will help you,
I will uphold you with My righteous right hand.'"

The topic of his message was **"Chosen One, You're Not Alone."**

Maria sat nearly frozen and mesmerized as the Pastor expounded on the scripture, highlighting the goodness and mercy of a sovereign God who loved, cared for and protected His people. Pastor Wright was not with Maria that night when she prayed to God and asked for His help, and she hadn't spoken to him about the Holy Spirit speaking to her. God had heard Maria, and He was using Pastor Wright to confirm His word just like Neicy said. It was confirmation.

The Pastor shared that as a chosen vessel for the Lord, we must expect to have tribulations in this lifetime, but no matter what we were going through, we must trust that the Lord is with us. Israel was chosen by God, and the nation had suffered repeatedly throughout its history. Yet, the Lord had not cast Israel away or ever forsaken or abandoned her. Israel had suffered when she abandoned God and put other gods, idols, before the Lord. "Seek first the kingdom of heaven and all its righteousness," Pastor Wright preached, "and He will add all things to you.[70] The Lord spoke to Israel and told her to fear not, for He was with them."

Pastor Wright repeated **v. 10**: *"Fear not, for I am with you; Be not dismayed, for I am your God. I will strengthen you, Yes, I will help you, I will uphold you with My righteous right hand."*

"Jesus will help you," he preached. "He is with you. If God be for you, who can be against you?"[71]

Pastor Wright's heavy voice filled the church, and the members of Holy Tabernacle responded in choruses of "Amen, Preacher!" and "Preach, Pastor!" Maria, so grateful knowing that God had heard her cry, joined in and leaped from her seat when Pastor Wright said "You are chosen, daughter of Abraham. Chosen for greatness, and you have no need to fear. God is using you for His glory. Let Him have His way. He is with you. Others walked out, others left and went their own way, but Jesus will never leave or forsake you. Hallelujah!"

As Maria shouted "Hallelujah" with the other men and women in the church, the eyes of Pastor Wright were fixed on her. He then said, "Anything you put before God is an idol. Any man. God wants to be first in your life. He is using you for His glory, that you may know and believe Him, and understand that I am He, says the Lord. It will all work together for your good, but He must be first, and He will help you. Glory to God, there is greatness in your future. Let God have his way, daughter. There is a call of God on your life."

Maria sat back down, feeling a sense of conviction. She needed to hear it. *"In that small space of time, it was just her, the Pastor and God,"* she thought, *"and the Lord had spoken directly to her. The message was too tailor-made and undeniable."*

The other members were praising God, fanning themselves, and shouting Hallelujah. Whatever personal connection and transcendent moment in the spirit she had was unnoticed by them. As Maria received the Word from Pastor Wright that day, she experienced a presence about her, especially her mouth. There was a tingling to it unlike anything she had ever known, but she knew it was spiritual. She felt a wind about her body, most prominent at her arms, chest and belly. *"I am filling you with my Holy Spirit,"* the voice spoke to her in her right ear. Maria was excited and did not fear. She had entered a spiritual realm where she could clearly hear the Spirit of the Lord, and as the Spirit filled Maria, she no longer heard the Preacher but could see him at the Pulpit waving his hands, ushering the Church into the presence of the Lord, and encouraging everyone to call on the name of Jesus.

"The Lord is here," Pastor Wright said in a gentle and yet confident voice, "The Lord is here. Praise Him. Whatever you need, speak it into the atmosphere. He will do it."

Maria hadn't heard what he said. Some members went up to the altar and knelt, others knelt at their seats, and a few skeptics, she supposed, stayed where they were without responding. *"How could they not discern the spirit of God?"* she wondered. Maria knelt at her seat, bowed her head, and submitted to the numinous manifestation of the Lord's presence about her body. The musicians played softly, and Maria thanked the Lord for being her God and for being with her. She prayed again that the Lord would free her heart, soul and mind from her anger and use her for His glory, whatever He wanted to do. She surrendered control of herself to her Lord and allowed Him, in fact pleaded with Him, to have His way and do whatever He wanted to do. She was a willing vessel, a child of God, and her Father wanted her to give all of herself to Him. He needed to be first. Maria surrendered. She released the unforgiveness, anger, resentment and bitterness to the sweet anointing of the Lord and the soothing calm of the Holy Spirit that had forgiven, freed, healed and loved her unconditionally.

Maria underwent an inner change in the intimate experience she shared with Jesus. There was peace. By the time she returned from her mystical journey, which may have lasted about fifteen minutes, she felt a shawl around her shoulders and lifted her head to notice the ushers walking around the church with boxes of tissues. She hadn't remembered anyone putting a prayer shawl on her. Maria clasped the blue and white wool and silk garment in her fingers, as the fringes dangled loosely from her hands, and she rose with it draped over her shoulders and flowing freely across her body. Mother Wright approached her, lifting her hands in the air and shouting "Hallelujah!

Praise Him! Hallelujah!" Maria began to remove the shawl, but Mother Wright shook her head and motioned for her not to.

As she came close, she told Maria "Keep it, baby. It was mine, but I want you to have it. We have intercessory prayer every Thursday before Bible Study. Bring it with you when you come. Baby, you have to pray. Every Minister has to pray. I'll see you Thursday."

Mother Wright hugged Maria tightly and kissed her on the cheek.

"I'll be there," Maria said.

"Oh, I know you will," said Mother Wright, "I know you will, baby." She walked back to the front of the church where she was seated with the other Mothers.

The church announcements were then read by one of the Elders, and it was mentioned that the Bible Institute had three vacant spots to be filled for September classes. Maria had free time and was interested, so she took down the information and completed an online application at home. The school called her that week to schedule an informal interview with her, and she was accepted for admission. She would complete a two year study preparing her for Ministry, and she was happy to invest some of her savings into her own education and development.

Thursday evenings saw Maria going to Holy Tabernacle for Prayer and Bible Study. The sanctuary was not full for prayer, there were only about 10 people, including Maria. Mother Wright led them in prayer, and Maria was asked to pray over the children of the church. Although Maria wasn't as well-versed in scripture as the other prayer warriors were, she spoke from her heart and recited the verse from Proverbs that she was familiar with: *"Train up a child in the way in which he should go, and when he is old he will not depart from it."*[72] Their "Amens" encouraged her to "preach" but she stayed in her respective lane and asked the Lord to help every mother and father be the best parent they could be for their children. Surprisingly, she wasn't nervous at all, and after everyone prayed, they praised the Lord their God and hugged one another with sincerity and love.

Bible Study was taught by Elder Keith Daniels, a tall, handsome gentleman of about 55 years with well-groomed salt and pepper facial hair and a bald head. He was a rich brown complexion, lean and in good physical shape, and although on Sundays he dressed impeccably, on Thursday evenings he wore trousers, an Oxford shirt and comfortable looking brown loafers. He carried a black leather shoulder bag and was not accompanied by an Adjutant when he came into the sanctuary. A podium was brought onto the floor directly in front of the pews along with a small table, where the Elder neatly arranged his Bible, papers and bottled water. Maria loved to hear Pastor Wright, he was on point every time she heard him speak, and she hoped the good Elder could teach.

"Good evening everyone," Elder Daniels said.

"Good evening," everyone replied. Several members came in as Bible Study started, about 20 or so more.

"Praise the Lord everybody."

"Praise the Lord," they responded.

They prayed again before they started, and then Elder Daniels welcomed any new members to the group. Maria stood and introduced herself again, and he smiled and thanked God for sending her, encouraging her participation in class and to continue coming on Thursday evenings throughout the summer. There were no other new members, so he began his lesson advising everyone that he would be teaching on forgiveness for the next few weeks.

"Geeesch," Maria thought to herself, *"God will not let this go. Maybe because I haven't."* So she yielded herself to the lessons on God's forgiveness, and how we, forgiven by God, are responsible to forgive others.

Elder Daniels taught that forgiveness was not for the one who has hurt us, but for us. Forgiveness, he taught, frees us. It releases us so that we can be free. It may not change those whom we are praying for, but it will change us. Holding onto a grudge makes us bitter, and bitterness was like poison.

Nelson Mandela was quoted as saying, "As I walked out the door toward the gate that would lead to my freedom, I knew if I didn't leave my bitterness and hatred behind, I'd still be in prison." Elder Daniels looked at Maria as he taught and said, "Don't put *yourself* in jail."

Maya Angelou, he taught, was quoted as saying, "It's one of the greatest gifts you can give yourself, to forgive. Forgive everybody." Gandhi taught that the weak can never forgive, but that forgiveness was the attribute of the strong.

Elder Daniels taught that we never heal until we forgive, and we must let go so that we can move on with our lives.

For weeks, the message of forgiveness was taught. How many times, asked Peter? 70 x 7.[73] Bless those who persecute you and spitefully use you.[74] Vengeance is mine, sayeth the Lord.[75] Forgive, and you shall be forgiven.[76] Let not your heart be troubled, I have already overcome the world.[77] Greater is He in me than He who is in the world.[78] Forgive. He will help you to forgive, God is close to the contrite and broken-hearted.[79] Cast all your cares upon Him for He cares for you.[80]

"Alright, alright, alright!" Maria wanted to scream. She surrendered and prayed for His help, and He filled her with His Holy Spirit that helped her, taught her and comforted her. His Spirit led her into all truth, and over the summer months, she made progress. She had come a long way.

The Word of God was medicine to a heart poisoned by the bitterness and rage she felt towards her ex-husband. Jesus was the physician of her soul, and His Holy Spirit ministered to her effecting a cure that she had not been able to find anywhere else. Her health insurance was the faith that God had given her. She was admitted to His holy hospital, Holy Tabernacle Church, and his physicians, Pastor Wright and Elder Daniels, attended to her and ensured that she stayed on course with the prescribed treatment plan: The Word. A pain medicine free of any side-effects was given to her from the Chief of Physicians, Jesus Christ, and it soothed her every ache. The Nurses on Duty, Mother Wright and Neicy, took her vital signs and followed up with her to make sure the treatment was working and that Maria had not relapsed. Maria followed the Doctor's orders and allowed the Word to penetrate her heart. She read the Bible at home, attended therapy at Intercessory Prayer and Bible Study on Thursday evenings, and she went to all her check-ups on Sunday mornings. She wasn't the only patient. There were some emergency room visits of patients who came in for immediate help, some short-term and some long-term. Maria wanted to be whole, delivered and free, so she cried out for His help, submitted herself, and surrendered to His plan. *"Have your way, Jesus,"* she prayed.

Maria saw Rob during the summer as he came to pick up Genny and Papi on Fridays and bring them back Sunday mornings by

9am. She could honestly declare that he really didn't have the same effect on her that he used to. She was so into her newfound relationship with Jesus that she didn't really care.

"How are you, Rob?" she would ask when he came by on Friday nights.

"Are you feeling okay?" he would ask in response.

"Yes. How is everything at the Center?"

Nervously assuming that she must have heard about his tryst with Sophia *("Had Papi said anything?"* he wondered), Rob avoided talking about the Center at all and shifted, as he always would, the discussion back to Maria and the kids. Where was the new karate gi he bought for Papi? How were his grades? How did he like his teachers? Had Maria joined the PTA? Was she attending Board of Education meetings? Was Genny still practicing basketball? He would start taking her back to the Boy's and Girl's Club again so that she could get ready for competition at the high school level.

"Whatever," Maria thought. She knew he was trying to turn it around so that he could complain about something she did or didn't do, but she could care less, and that was progress. The medicine, Hallelujah, was working.

Maria continued to pray for Rob and "Sophia," and though prayer was working, Maria was still a woman wanting to know who this other woman was. Addington Park was a small town, and Mr. Henderson was well-known. Somebody had to know something.

On a Saturday afternoon in July, while shopping in an area supermarket, Maria was spotted by Pam McMillan, her gossiping friend from high school. When Pam shouted "Hey Miss Girl!" in her one-of-a-kind high-pitched voice, Maria knew who it was without even having to look.

"Hey girl, how are you doing?" Maria replied, turning in the direction of Pam's voice.

"Oh, it is so good to see you. Long time no see! Where have you been hiding?" Pam asked, leaving her shopping cart against the aisle to walk towards Maria and give her a friendly hug. They were in the produce aisle of the supermarket, and Pam's basket was full of leafy green vegetables, fresh fruit and bottled water.

"Nowhere. You sure are a healthy eater," Maria remarked, looking over the basket of healthy food and embarrassed that her cart didn't contain foods that were as health conscious.

"I'm detoxing. I'm on this ten day plan of green smoothies, fruit, bottled water and tea. I did it before and lost 12 pounds. I'm getting married in December," Pam said gleefully, flashing a mouth full of perfectly straight, white teeth.

"Oh my God! Congratulations, Pam, I am so happy for you. Are you and Evan getting married after all these years?" Maria asked.

Evan and Pam were an on again/off again item for years. He was about ten years older than Pam and a retired Naval Officer. Pam had joined the Coast Guard after college and met him while serving off the coast in Florida. Why she ended up back in Addington Park was beyond the comprehension of her friends, but Pam was caring for her elderly mother and father who did not want to leave their home. It made sense to Maria because she would do the same for her own mother.

"Yes, thank God. He wasn't ready before, but we've been through a lot together, and it's time. See my ring?"

Pam extended her left hand to show off a white gold cluster setting diamond ring. It was exquisite. The detail was just remarkable. The ring looked gorgeous on Pam's hand with her French manicure and diamond tennis bracelet.

"It's beautiful, Pam. God bless you and Evan," Maria said.

"Thank you, Maria," Pam replied, smiling. She pulled her hand back, and admired her ring. "I hope Evan and I can be like you and Rob. How many years has it been?"

"Oh Lord," Maria thought. It wasn't like she and Rob had advertised their divorce to anyone, but she really wasn't ready to talk about it with anyone, least of all Pam.

"Oh, it's been almost 25 years."

"What is your secret? I want my marriage to last that long."

"Well, what about your mom and dad? They've been together for years, too," Maria responded, wanting to change the subject.

"Yes, they have, but they're older. Where are they going to go?"

"I don't know," Maria answered, "but you should talk to them, especially your dad. What kept him with your mom for so many years?"

Pam laughed and looked over a stack of pink grapefruit before choosing two.

"You want one?" she asked.

"Sure," Maria said. She allowed Pam to choose one for her and then placed it on top of the oranges and pineapple she had already selected. Maria admired Pam's fit appearance. She was dressed in a blue sweat suit with white Nike sneakers, and her hair was tucked underneath a Nike baseball cap turned backwards.

"My dad would probably say it was my mother's cooking. I'll tell you a secret, Maria, I can't cook to save my life. I have been watching cooking channels and reading books to step up my game. If Evan relies on my cooking, we won't make it past the first year," she laughed.

"You're so crazy. Where is the wedding going to be?"

"Oh my God, girl, I'm so sorry. Would you and Rob please come? Can you make it? I would really love for you to be there. I'll mail the invitation to you. Where do you live?"

"Let me have your email, Pam. I think we may be away in December, so I will have to let you know. Is that alright?"

"Sure. We're planning a pretty big ceremony," she said proudly. "Everybody is going to be there. We don't have a church home right now, Evan wants to go to Florida, but I want something right here where my mom and dad can come. If it was up to Evan, we'd just as well have it at the Mayor's Office downtown. You know I work there, right? Yeah, girl, Evan pulled some strings and helped me to get work in the City Comptroller's Office. I see Rob come in and out from time to time. He is always doing things for his Center and working with the Mayor's Assistant. Word is she may be running for Mayor next year. You have a good man, Maria. I'll text you my email, okay?"

"Sure, Pam. Is Sophia still the Mayor's Assistant?" Maria asked, her woman's intuition alerting her that there was something more to this and something more nosy Pam was suggesting Maria needed to be aware of.

"No, I don't know anyone named Sophia. The Mayor's Assistant is Paulette Simmons. She's supposed to be running for Mayor next term. Pretty lady, nice figure. I hope she wins because I can't stand Mayor Bradley. All he did was make a lot of promises he couldn't keep and lose everybody's money. I invested money in the beachfront redevelopment. You know those new condominiums that were built on Beach Avenue? Millions of dollars were invested, and we have 20 units that remain unsold after two years. They are so ready to get him out of office, whoever runs will be a shoe in. Hell, I should run for office."

"Well, why don't you?"

"Girl, I'm just joking. I'll leave that to the politicians. She sure seems interested in the work Rob does, though."

"Okay," Maria thought to herself, *"this isn't the woman I'm looking for, so let me shut this down."*

"Yes, most politicians are, and they do support the work Rob does for the community. When they align themselves with Rob, they appear more community-oriented, and it boosts their image. Happens all the time, Pam. Well, I've got to get going. It was nice seeing you. Congratulations again."

"Aw, Maria, thank you so much," Pam said, giving her another hug.

Maria hadn't felt bad at all about lying to Pam because as far as Maria was concerned, it was none of Pam's business.

"You're welcome," Maria said, turning her cart in the other direction. "I'll text you my email."

"Okay," Maria replied. As she reached the end of the aisle, Maria turned around and thought she should share the information about Holy Tabernacle Church with Pam since she had said she and Evan didn't have a church home. Pam was inspecting some spinach.

"Pam, I'm sorry, I meant to share something with you," Maria said, pulling her cart alongside Pam's.

"Sure, Maria, what's up?"

"Well, I'd like to invite you and Evan to Holy Tabernacle Church. You said you don't have a church home right now. We have a wonderful Pastor, Pastor Wright, and the Word is anointed and powerful. He always preaches a relevant message on Sunday mornings. We have service at 11. Do you think you and Evan could make it one Sunday?"

"Holy Tabernacle Church? How old is the Pastor?"

"He is up there, about 70, I guess, but girl he can preach. He's real, genuine, he cares and he's anointed. He has wisdom and compassion. What difference does his age make?"

"Well, I'm just saying. Pastor Wright was preaching at that church when we were kids. My aunts go to that church. I know the Wright family. I'm just saying, maybe it's time for him to sit down and let somebody else preach. His style of preaching was good during the Civil Rights Movement, but it's a new day. I am not trying to hear anybody preach to me that we shall overcome someday."

Pam paused, noticing a surly look on Maria's face, and she innocently asked, "What?"

"I just thought I'd mention it to you," Maria answered sighing.

"Thank you, and I'm sorry, I hope I didn't offend you. If they stream the services, I promise to watch online first before I come."

"No, the services aren't online. You will get more out of it if you come in person anyway and see for yourself. The church is right here, it isn't miles away. Besides, Evan is a little older, he might like it," Maria said cautiously, avoiding the temptation to be sarcastic.

"Oh no, Maria, Evan is young at heart. He does not believe that we have to be struggling and broke just to prove we're Christians. He needs something progressive, something relevant and fresh. I will tell him, though. Thank you for thinking of us."

"You're welcome, Pam. The Word is what matters, and Pastor Wright can bring it. I hope we see you."

"I'll tell Evan and see what he says. Thank you for thinking of us. Look at God, He has you out here evangelizing and witnessing. Go head Jesus!"

They both laughed and hugged again. Then, Maria turned in the other direction, finished her shopping, and went home.

Chapter Sixteen
The Henderson Family

Just as soon as summer started, it was over. Genny and Papi went with their mother to the annual End of Summer barbecue at Aunt Neicy's house during Labor Day weekend, and afterwards their dad picked them up and finished their school shopping with them. It was fun for Genny when she was eight and nine years old, but since turning 13, she would much rather shop with April and Jade. Mr. Henderson didn't approve of most of the outfits Genny picked out. *"Since when were blue jeans prohibited? Every teenage girl has a decent pair of blue jeans in her closet,"* Genny mumbled under her breath.

"Dad, I am going to high school, not boarding school," Genny complained.

"I don't care where you are going. You're not wearing those tight jeans."

"They're not tight, Dad."

Well, they were and they weren't. Genny was becoming a young woman.

"If she isn't menstruating," her dad thought, *"she soon will be. Maria hadn't said anything, and she should know things like that."*

"Genny, how are you and your mom doing?" he asked.

"We're fine dad, what do you mean?"

"You can talk to her and you can talk to me about anything, sweetheart. You know that, right?"

"Yes."

Oblivious to her dad's innuendos, Genny did know that any argument with him was futile so she chose a long jean skirt instead and a different pair of blue jeans that he did approve of.

She needed a book bag and thesaurus, so they stopped at the bookstore before going back to their home, where Genny was fascinated with the endless selection of bestsellers, English Literature and fiction. Mr. Henderson supported her love for reading and anything else she was interested in, so he sat and read a newspaper while his daughter searched for the perfect books. She chose a short novel involving mystery, adventure and psychology, as well as poetry by Phillis Wheatley, reportedly one of the first African American women to be published. The paperback thesaurus was an easy choice as she had one before but misplaced it during their move. Finally, Genny chose a heavy-duty tan and green canvas book bag and put all three books inside after her dad paid for everything. Satisfied and confident she would do well, Genny left the bookstore with her dad and brother eager for Wednesday, September 8th, the first day of school, to come.

On Sunday morning, Genny and Papi went back home, as usual, at 9am. There was a Back to School Giveaway that day at church, and Genny had volunteered to help. As the kids ran up to the front door of their home with their shopping bags in tow, they were greeted by their mother, who waved them inside to eat breakfast. Rob came up to the door, and this time, Maria allowed him to come inside.

Once he was sure the kids were not within hearing distance, he asked Maria if she had noticed the change in Genny.

"Of course," she said.

"Did she get her period yet?" he asked.

"Yes."

"Oh, okay. I was just wondering. You didn't think you should tell me?" he asked.

"Rob, it's nothing. She has had it for a few months. She didn't tell me, I just kind of knew."

"Well, have you had a talk with her?"

"Yes, Rob, I have," Maria answered, knowing where he was going. "Genny is very mature. You know how she is. She's into books, schoolwork, and basketball. I trust her."

"I trust her, too, but she's going to high school, Maria, with young men."

"Well, what do you want to do Rob, confine her in a chastity belt?"

"No. Just keep an eye on her. I am going to be picking her and Papi up on Tuesdays after school until basketball season jumps off. I promised Genny I would take her back to the Boy's Club so she can practice."

"Okay, she'll love that. Did she tell you that she has been practicing with some of the girls from the high school team?"

"Yeah, I know, that's cool, high school girls and all, but I want her to keep her skills up."

Rob hesitated, admiring the coziness of the living room and family portrait that hung over the rich brown sectional. He had a smaller version of the same portrait in his office. The living room table had a few newspapers on it, and the grandfather clock bought for Maria's 40th birthday chimed lightly in the corner of the room. She was so happy when she woke up and saw it in their dining room. He remembered that morning like it was yesterday. The kids were just as excited. Maria hugged and kissed him and told him he was the best husband she could ever want. Even though the clock wasn't in the exact location of their home that she wanted it in, she didn't move it. She told him she would never move it.

That morning, he cooked Maria breakfast, and their family shared the meal together – as a family. They went out together to the movies, and then the kids spent the night with their grandmother. Maria morphed into the kitten he loved, and he reaped the fruit of his labor with Maria catering to his every need all night long. They were teenagers in love again, and he held her in his arms as a man holds a woman he loves and cherishes. He was her provider, her protector and her one and only man. She would do anything for him, and he would do anything for her. She loved him for who he was, before the businesses and the Center and before the money. She loved him and stood by his side when he was in prison, and she loved him in spite of what everybody else said about him, even her own family.

Maria had always been there for him, and he knew she would always be. She gave birth to his two children, enduring a combined 38 hours of labor with no epidural or pain medicine, and she raised them with the best love, care, and nurture any man could want for his children. Rob drove Maria to the hospital after her water broke with Genny and Papi, and he held her hand through both deliveries. He saw the look of excruciating pain on her face as she endured contractions that forced her fingernails to pierce the skin on his hand and cause bleeding above his knuckles. He didn't flinch or complain. His hands, after all, were hardened from years of martial arts, but the nurse saw the blood and offered some medical attention, which he refused. He gave Maria cups of ice and kissed her after Genny was born. Rob wiped sweat from his wife's brow with his other hand. He counted ten fingers and ten toes and kissed his daughter after the nurses cleaned her and lay her at Maria's breast. It was an experience that he would never forget. It formed an even stronger and deeper bond between him and Maria. He saw her vulnerability. Her need for him made him feel like a man, and he wanted to fulfill Maria and Genny's every need. He worked hard at his businesses to provide a comfortable living for his family, and his wife and daughter never failed to show their appreciation for him.

When Papi was born, Rob was ecstatic. Neither he nor Maria wanted to know the sex of the baby during the pregnancy, so when the baby was born, Rob immediately looked between the legs. "My son!" he cried. He hugged Maria and kissed her on the cheek before assisting Dr. Marino with cutting the umbilical cord. The nurses cleaned Papi and then placed him at Maria's breast. That time, Rob brought a camera, and he took a photo of his son and wife that he treasured and still had in his wallet. Then he held his son. The nurses smiled at him, Dr. Marino shook his hand, and Rob thanked them all for their help, recognizing his own vulnerability because he needed others to support and provide care for his wife and son.

Maria's labor, she said, was harder with Papi, who weighed 11 pounds when he was born and measured 26 inches long. "That's my boy!" Rob cried, when the nurses weighed and measured him. He was a proud father who called everyone in his contacts and shared the good news. The hospital room where Maria stayed for two days was full of floral arrangements, cards and "It's a boy!" balloons in blue.

When Maria came home, she found that Rob had painted the nursery a light blue color and finished the trim in off white. The white and gold crib Genny had used was no longer in the room. Rob had instead purchased a new one and accepted the salesperson's recommendation to accessorize the crib in plaid sheets, bed skirt, bumper, blanket and a mobile musical toy. He entrusted his cousin, Walter, with the wallpaper border, and when Rob checked the work before showing Maria the room, he was extremely pleased. She loved the new look for the nursery, and after placing Papi in the brand new premiere convertible crib, Maria held her husband tightly and thanked him for being the greatest husband and father in the world. She told him how much she appreciated him and apologized for having scratched his hand. He didn't care. The scratch left a mark on his hand that reminded him, every time he looked at it, of just how much she needed him, and he loved it.

Rob looked at his hand and saw the visual reminder, and he wanted to sit down and make himself at home. He heard Genny and Papi talking and laughing in the dining room, and the aroma of grits, smoked turkey bacon, scrambled eggs and black coffee danced its way into the living room, inviting Rob to stay and enjoy breakfast with his family. He wanted to be there for Maria and his children like he had always been, but Rob knew he had messed up. He was depending on Maria's good graces to forgive him when this was all over, and he knew she would. He was taking advantage of her, but it was for everyone's good. He just had to get the business back up. *"How selfish of me,"* he thought to himself, *"Maria could care less either way,"* but Rob needed that edge – for himself. As a man, he needed that, and he would help her to understand one day.

Rob looked at his ex-wife and appreciated her motherhood all the more as she cooked for his children without him, took them to church without him and was living life without him. She looked radiant in her red dress and black pumps. A single strand of pearls was around her neck with matching earrings, the set he purchased for her on their anniversary a few years ago.

"Didn't she miss him? Didn't she want to fix his tie or grab him around his waist? How selfish of me," Rob thought. *"I'm the one who brought another woman into this. Still, didn't Maria think of him*

at all? It was like she just moved on and they had never been husband and wife. Was she seeing someone?"

"Are you dating someone?" Rob asked softly.

"What?" Maria asked in reply, taken aback by his question.

"Are you dating someone, Maria?" Rob repeated, this time more confrontational.

Maria didn't answer, and she didn't have to. She just looked at Rob, and he could tell from the look in her eyes that his question was ludicrous. Maria wasn't dating anybody.

"There's something different about you. You look beautiful, you always do. There's just something different, I don't know what it is."

"I'm pregnant," Maria joked rubbing her stomach with her left hand.

"Don't play with me, girl," Rob replied with his eyes fixed on her belly.

After a few seconds of awkward silence, Rob looked straight in Maria's eyes to see if the animalistic attraction was still there. He thought he still noticed the spark and smiled at her, inviting her into his fantasy. Maria just looked at him. She knew what that look meant, and if they were still married, she would look back, send the kids outside and throw him on the sectional they had christened many a Sunday morning before. Or maybe she would lead him into the kitchen, his favorite room in the house, where she used to wear only an apron and stiletto heels to drive him crazy. Rob remembered, too, and he gently lifted her left hand from her stomach, kissed it and leaned in to give her a kiss on the lips. Maria allowed him to, it had been awhile since she had been with him, but as his lips touched hers, she was nearly repulsed, imagining him kissing Sophia the way he used to kiss her, touching her, holding her and making love to her. She kept her eyes open as he closed his, and her mouth was motionless. Just before he could French kiss her, Maria took a step back and wiped her lips with the back of her hand, unbothered by how upset she had made Rob feel. He looked hurt, and she didn't care.

Rob seemed to understand her hesitations. "Okay, Maria, if I did anything to hurt you, I apologize. I'm the same man you always loved. Nothing will ever change that. This situation is just temporary. Please trust me."

Maria didn't care. She wanted to argue with him and hurl a bunch of expletives in his face, but why? She didn't even care. *"Who is Sophia?"* she wanted to ask. *"What makes you think you can enjoy my love again, Mr. Henderson? What if I do decide to date someone? I'm not your wife anymore, I can date anyone I please. Get the hell out of my house."* She didn't even care. She had peace.

"Rob, thank you for being a great father to Genny and Papi. I appreciate you."

"You mean that?" he asked.

"Yes, with all my heart. Thank you."

"Thank you, Maria, for being a great mother to our children and for being a great wife. I'm trying to take care of everything."

"Okay, Rob," Maria said. She didn't even care.

Rob went into the dining room and kissed his children goodbye. Before he walked back into the living room, he loosened his tie and hoped Maria might straighten it like she used to. He returned to the living room, where Maria was standing in the same spot, and approached her to give her a hug, being sure to make eye contact with her. She looked into his eyes, and Rob stood in front of her, testing the waters again, hopeful that Maria might notice his tie and care again. Maria did see the tie, and she thought it was cute that he was looking for some attention, but she refused. Rob cleared his throat, told her he would talk to her later and walked out the front door to his silver Mercedes Benz still running in the driveway. He sat in the driver's seat, adjusted his sunglasses, and took a deep breath as he pulled out of the driveway and onto the street. His heart was heavy, and he felt choked up inside. He loved and missed the totality of his family.

Genny noticed her father's car as she left with her mother and Papi in their mom's Toyota. He was parked down the street, and he followed them to Holy Tabernacle Church. Genny asked her mom if she had invited him.

"No, but he's welcome to come if he wants to," Maria answered, aware that Rob was following them from a distance.

As Maria pulled into the parking lot, Genny noticed her dad's car drive past the church. *"I guess he's not coming,"* Genny said to herself.

Minister Barrington pulled into the parking lot at the same time, and he walked with the Hendersons to the front of Holy Tabernacle. Papi edged Genny out as the two raced to the door, and their mom didn't say anything. She was engrossed in her conversation with Minister Barrington as they walked from their parked cars to the walkway in front. He offered to carry Maria's Bible for her, and she obliged him, hardly noticing her children's friendly competition. They stopped in the middle of the walkway, greeting the members who were arriving, their conversation interrupted every now and again. When there was a break in the flow of Sunday morning worshippers, Minister Barrington shared that he wanted to work with Papi so that he could sing solos.

"Your son has a tremendous gift, Ms. Henderson. We would truly be blessed to have him sing a solo. I will work with him on the songs. I know he's young, but he is gifted. He can do it."

Maria was thrilled. She hugged Minister Barrington and thanked him for his confidence in Papi.

"Of course he can. Thank you so much," Maria said to Minister Barrington, releasing her hug.

"Praise God. He knew what He was doing when He brought you here, Ms. Henderson. I'm looking forward to working with him."

The two walked up the front steps, and Minister Barrington opened the door for Maria and held it for a few other women who were approaching.

The silver Mercedes Benz owned by Mr. Henderson was parked at the corner, and inside was an ex-husband watching the scene in front of Holy Tabernacle Church and jealous of the attention this man had shown his wife. Even more, Mr. Henderson was jealous of the responsiveness of his wife to Minister Barrington.

"Who is this cat?" Mr. Henderson wondered. He had never seen him before, and Mr. Robert J. Henderson knew everybody. He wanted to get out of his car and go into the church and confront him - who the hell did he think he was, hugging his wife in broad daylight, trying to use the church to prey on Maria?

"I should bust this mother f------- up," Rob thought. *"No wonder there was something different about Maria, she was seeing someone. How could she? She didn't even wait. It had only been a few months since their divorce. I can't believe she is carrying on like*

this. Next thing you know, she's gonna have the brother up in the house around their kids. Oh no, not around my son and daughter. Maria must have lost her mind."

The more Rob thought about it, the angrier he became. *"This was the ultimate betrayal,"* he said to himself.

Rob called Maria's cell phone, knowing it would go directly to the answering machine. It was 10:48 a.m.

"Yeah, Maria, it's me. You know, I confessed my heart to you this morning. I know I'm not perfect. I made mistakes, but I would never disrespect you publicly. You're going to church and acting like you're such a God-fearing lady right now, but please, I saw you with that brother this morning. Don't have him around my kids. You understand? Don't have him around my kids, Maria."

Rob hung up the phone and then sent her a text to make sure she got the message: *"Why are you disrespecting me? Keep him away from our kids."*

As soon as he sent his text, his phone rang. It was Sophia.

"Hello," he answered abruptly after the second ring.

"Hello. Boy, you sound like you woke up on the wrong side of the bed this morning," she said, noticing the anxiety in his voice. "Probably because you weren't with me," she giggled.

"Sophia, I'll call you back," he answered in an uninterested tone.

"What's wrong? Where are you?"

"I'll call you back."

Rob hung up and turned his phone off. He got out of his car and walked up to the church. Before he went in, he prayed that he would not have to kick this man's ass when he got inside.

Inside the foyer were several ushers and greeters wearing all white and holding communion trays.

"Good morning, welcome to Holy Tabernacle Church," said an older woman in white with a gold nametag that read "Usher."

"Good morning. Thank you," Rob said, as she offered him bread and wine. Another usher blessed the sacraments, and they anointed him with oil in the center of his forehead before he went inside the sanctuary.

Rob entered like a Ninja on a secret mission, avoiding eye contact with anyone and feigning an interest in the program he had been given. He sat in the last pew where he could leave when he was ready and scanned the place for Maria and his kids. He spotted them several pews ahead, and thankfully, they hadn't turned around to notice him. An older woman, no doubt one of the church Mothers, came before the church and started praying. When she was finished, several men came forward and prayed before everyone took communion together.

A woman's voice behind Mr. Henderson asked softly, "Mr. Henderson?"

Rob turned around and saw Mrs. Parker, Isaiah's mother. Immediately, he smiled and turned the magnetic personality and charm back on that the city's residents were accustomed to.

"Good morning, Mrs. Parker. How are you?"

Mrs. Parker was dressed in white with a gold nametag that also read "Usher."

"Blessed and highly favored. I thought that was you. Praise the Lord. We are so happy that you are joining us."

Rob was a little embarrassed. He was here to spy on his wife, not to become a member of the church.

"Mrs. Parker, I heard such good things about Holy Tabernacle, I wanted to come and see it for myself. You are doing a wonderful job. Can I talk to you outside for a minute?" he asked.

"Sure, in the foyer, okay?"

Rob got up and walked towards the double doors of the sanctuary that were now closed with ushers stationed at each like military soldiers protecting a fort. Before he walked outside, the musicians started playing, and he heard a male voice say "C'mon and praise the Lord, everybody. Oh c'mon, get up on your feet and give God some praise!"

Rob turned around before exiting the sanctuary and saw the man who was hugging his wife just a few moments ago. Rob did not let his anger show, but internally, he was boiling. A few church members walking into the sanctuary noticed him, and he shook hands with them before escorting Mrs. Parker to a corner of the foyer where they could talk privately.

"Mrs. Parker, I am looking for some young men to help me with the Center. Who is that young man singing?"

163

"Oh that's Minister Barrington. He is our new Praise and Worship leader. Yes, he is doing a fine job."

"Is he from around here?" Mr. Henderson asked.

"No, I believe he is from East Orange or Newark. I think he's from Newark, but I'm not sure. In any case, he would certainly be a fine addition to your Center. You're doing a wonderful job there. Thank you for helping me with Isaiah. He is so focused right now. He looks up to you. Thank you."

"You are more than welcome. Isaiah is an outstanding young man. Does he come to church with you, Mrs. Parker?"

"He does, most times. He said he wasn't feeling well this morning."

"Well, I'll speak to him about that. You have my word."

"Thank you, Mr. Henderson. Aren't you going to come back inside and join us?" she asked, noticing him looking out the front door.

"I'll be back. I have some things to take care of this morning, but you have been a big help. Is there anything I can do for you? Do you need anything?" he asked.

"No, I have Jesus, and He is all I need."

"Can I give you an offering for the church?" he asked, pulling out his wallet.

"Well, we will certainly accept whatever offering you would like to bless us with."

Rob pulled out $300 in crisp $100 bills and placed them in her hands. He hugged her, thanking her again for her assistance and then walked out the front door and back to his car.

Meanwhile, Maria, Genny and Papi were having a great time. Aunt Neicy sang, Pastor Wright preached, and a young man joined the church that day. The Back to School Giveaway was well attended. Genny helped distribute 50 backpacks full of school supplies to families in need.

After the service, Neicy accompanied Maria to her home for dinner. Maria hadn't spoken to her about everything that happened, and she was excited to finally be able to share with her best friend and spiritual advisor what had occurred over the past few weeks. There were so many people at Neicy's barbecue the day before, they didn't have time to talk.

Once inside the house, Genny and Papi went upstairs to change their clothes and enjoy the free time they would have since their mother would be preoccupied with their Aunt. Maria led Neicy into the dining room, and she wiped the dining room table and moved a vase of fresh flowers to the adjacent kitchen counter.

"Neicy, the Lord spoke to me," Maria said as she cleared the table.

"Are you serious?" Neicy asked, sitting down in the chair closest to the kitchen. She relaxed and took her expensive, designer heels off and placed them ever so carefully inside a new Black Tote Bag in the chair beside her.

Maria walked to the bottom of the stairs and said, "Genny and Papi, bring Aunt Neicy the ottoman from my room, please."

"I'm fine," Neicy insisted, stretching her legs underneath the dining room table.

"They can bring it down for you. It's no problem."

The pitter patter of feet could be heard in the upstairs hallway and then down the stairs. Neicy got up to be sure Genny and Papi were okay. She helped them bring the ottoman into the dining room where she sat comfortably and rested her feet atop the colorful tapestry, admiring the square piece of furnishing's intricate details atop its four shapely legs. Genny helped herself to a handful of green grapes inside a bowl on the kitchen counter, and she and her brother ran back upstairs.

"I've been wanting to talk to you about everything, Neicy. So much has been going on. I start the Bible Institute next week, I think I'm healed and free of the pain with Rob, I'm loving the Intercessory Prayer and Bible Study with Mother Wright, Minister Barrington asked if Papi could sing a solo, and Genny has her period. We haven't really talked, Neicy."

"Papi is going to sing a solo?" Neicy asked with excitement in her voice.

"Yes. Minister Barrington asked me this morning. He pulled up at the same time we did. We talked for a few minutes before the service started this morning, and I think it would be good for Papi. He and Genny like him. Papi's not afraid or nervous when he is in front of the church, and his voice is loud. Do you think he can do it?" Maria asked nervously, wanting Neicy's support and encouragement.

Besides, Neicy had been singing in church since she was a child, so she would know what Papi would be feeling.

"Of course, my baby can do anything, and Minister Barrington knows how to get the best out of those kids. You know I will help Papi with anything he needs. And Genny has her period? Oh my God, God bless her. How is she doing?"

"She's fine. What are we going to do, right. It's part of life. She has grown up so fast, I don't know where the time went. But you know what, Neicy, I have to honestly say, she is doing so much better today because of our going to church. She was so upset before."

"I'm sure she was. You know how much she loves her dad. Papi just goes with the flow. Well, Jesus is working on your children, too. Keep praying for them. So what did the Holy Spirit say to you? Tell me about it."

"Well," Maria began, "He said *'Do not fear,'* and *'I am with you.'* He also said He heard my cry, and He would help me. The first time it was in the middle of the night, and the second time it was on Sunday morning. I heard Him clearly, Neicy. When I went to church, during the service, I felt a presence all around me. There was like a wind, or a breath of air, and my mouth was tingling."

Neicy lifted up her hands and blessed God. "Maria, the Lord gave you His Holy Spirit. He is anointing you. You have the call. He has to prepare you for it. Hallelujah."

"It was so peaceful, Neicy. Pastor Wright was preaching, and he looked right at me and said that I should let the Lord use me for His glory, and that any man before Him was an idol. That meant Rob. He probably was an idol…."

"Probably?" Neicy interrupted. "Girl, you worshipped the ground that man walked on. Rob wasn't your husband, he was your god, and that's where the problem was. Pastor Wright was telling you the truth. Maria, I know you may not want to hear this, but Rob did you a favor."

Maria chopped cabbage for homemade coleslaw. She didn't want to hear that. She wanted to hear her best friend agree with her that Rob was wrong.

"I'm sorry, Maria," Neicy said.

"That's okay. You're right. Honestly, I don't really care anymore. I mean I care, but not like I used to. Do you know he was here this morning trying to come on to me? I almost wanted to, but when I thought about him and this woman, Sophia is her name, he made me sick to my stomach. There was no desire or attraction, and Rob and I used to go at it like rabbits."

Neicy laughed. "Girl, I know that's right. Tony can handle his business, too."

Maria paused for a moment before speaking. "You know, that used to be enough. We would argue and then make up, and it was all good. We would fuss and separate over something trivial, make up, and everything was okay. He could keep me happy in the bedroom, he always could, and for some women that's enough. I think he probably was cheating, then he would come home to me and make love to me, and in his mind, that was enough."

"I don't know, there's too many killer STD's to be playing Russian roulette with your life and your spouse's. Maybe some women will settle for that nonsense. That is all it takes, so they put up with their husband's infidelity. When I was 20 and in heat, maybe. At this age, girl, please. I love and respect myself too much. There has to be a stronger bond between us. We have to be connected spiritually, emotionally, professionally and mentally. I want to be able to have an intelligent conversation with him. I need to know that he will be by my side when I am going through something. Is he into me? Does he support my dreams? Is he a good father? Can he raise our son to be a responsible young man? Can he be a role model for our daughter? Does he respect and honor me? Does he put God first? I want him to worship Jesus and follow Jesus so that He can lead me. If the man isn't following Jesus, I don't care how good his performance in the bedroom is, at this point in my life, Maria, I won't follow him anywhere."

"Yeah, I agree with you. I'm over him. I'm really over him, thank God."

"Well now that you are, keep God first."

"I will."

"So, who is this Sophia?"

"I don't know who she is. Oh yeah, I saw Pam in the supermarket the other day. Did you know she and Evan are getting married in December?"

"I heard something about that. I'm happy for her."

"She said she works in the Comptroller's Office and always sees Rob coming in and out. She was hinting that the Mayor's Assistant, Paulette Simmons I think is her name, is really interested in Rob and his work."

"I don't know who she is, Maria. You know I don't keep up with who's who in this town anymore. So you don't know who Sophia is, right?"

"No."

"But you want to know, right?"

"Well, yes. I want to know who she is, what she does, what she looks like. I want to see this woman who Rob divorced me for. Oh, I forgot to mention to you, he told me that this situation is temporary. Can you believe that?"

"Your divorce is temporary?" Neicy asked.

"Yes, that's what he said."

"So how do you feel about that?"

"I feel like he has lost his mind."

"That's good. What man would divorce his wife and call it a temporary thing? That sounds like he plans to try and come back to you after he gets something that he wants from this Sophia. If that's the case, he is banking on you not going anywhere, being the faithful, ride or die chick that you have always been. The hell with that ride or die loyalty mess. You are dying to remain loyal to his ass, and he's doing whatever he wants to do with whoever he wants to do it with. *He's* not loyal. *He's* not ride or die. How the hell can he expect you to be loyal to him? He wants to have his cake and eat it, too, and then he tries to turn this around on you like you broke some *'thou shall not cease to be a ride or die chick'* commandment. Girl, please. He probably thinks you'll be here waiting for him, no matter what he does, like you have always been, Maria. Rob is a businessman. He's smart. Maybe she has money, and he's just using her. No, that couldn't be it. He's smart, but he isn't shallow. Rob loves you and his kids. He wouldn't sell his soul, would he? Maybe she can help with his businesses, you said that he lost money and didn't tell you what was going on."

"Could be. I don't know for sure."

"Maria, you are the wife. You need to know for sure concerning everything your husband does."

Maria was hoping that Neicy would get mad and go off on him, but she didn't, and that was just as well, so Maria changed the subject.

"I start my classes at the Hampton Bible Institute next week."

"Ok, that part of our conversation is over," Neicy said sarcastically. "Well, I am excited for you. God wants you. He recruited you," Neicy laughed.

Maria laughed, too, and put the chopped cabbage in the refrigerator. The steaks she would grill had been marinating since that morning, and she took them out along with two bottles of spring water.

"Here you go," she said, handing a bottle and glass to Neicy. "Yes, he recruited me, and I can't wait to start. Mother Wright is so encouraging. She believes that there is a call on my life, just like you do. She has been calling me 'Minister.' Can you imagine that?"

"Yes. You are a Minister. There is a call on your life."

"We'll see. Whatever the good Lord wants - He can use me for whatever He wants. It's just that it is all happening so quick."

"Trust God. It's His timing."

"His timing," Maria repeated. "Amen. The Bible Study has been going well. Sometimes Elder Daniels teaches. He's on point, too."

"Yes he is. That man can preach, and he's a good looking man. He's a widow, Maria. His wife passed three years ago, and he has been single ever since. It's not like he couldn't have any woman he wanted, there are a whole lot of ladies at Holy Tabernacle who would love to be the next Mrs. Daniels. He has a daughter who lives in New York. She's a School Principal."

"Wow, I'm sorry to hear about his wife. You would never know it, he is always so composed and dignified. He's so focused, he just comes into church, does what he has to do, and then leaves. Three years? He has got to be lonely. I don't know any man who could be without a woman for three years."

Defending Elder Daniels, Neicy said, "Well, he may just be waiting on God to send him the right woman just like we women wait on God to send us the right man. He is a good man. God will give patience, so be careful what you ask for." Then, she looked in Maria's eyes with a glimmer of hope and said, "You know, Maria, you're single. You could be the one he's waiting for."

"Neicy, I am not interested in Elder Daniels. Besides, I am not trying to jump back in a relationship with anybody. This time is good for me."

"Yes, and you need to heal. Well, you said you believe you are healed, right?" Neicy asked.

"Yes."

"Well, you will know for certain when you pray for him, and you mean it. *'God bless Rob,'* and you mean it. *'Lord, prosper the work of his hands,'* and you mean it. *'Grant him happiness with Sophia,'* and you mean it. You'll know when you pray for his happiness and you see him happy with someone else, and you're happy, too. You'll give God praise. Your prayers for him will be genuine, you won't just be praying to heap coals on his head, praying for his happiness but secretly hoping he is miserable. Are you there yet?"

Maria hesitated. "Close to it. Very close. I just want to get on with my life. He came on to me today, and it almost messed me up. We kissed, but there was nothing really there. I think I just let him have the kiss so I could see if there was any attraction. He gave me that look that he used to whenever he wanted to, you know, and he used to be able to swing that no matter how much we argued. Not this time. This time it is about Jesus. Jesus has become the standard. He is so sweet and caring. He is so tender and patient. He came to me as I was: lost, hurt, broken and humiliated. I was so fragmented, Neicy, broken in little pieces, and Jesus loved every piece of me and put me back together again."

Neicy smiled with admiration at her friend, and Maria smiled back.

"I never loved any man but Rob. He was the only love I ever knew, the only man I have ever been with. *He* was the standard. Rob was good to me, but Jesus loved me more than Rob ever could. Jesus never left me, even when I left Him. He provided for my soul. He protected my mind and my heart. He took me home to meet His Father, and He professed my name at His throne. He blesses me to have a relationship with Him, and He is always there. God is faithful. I don't deserve Him, Neicy, I am so unworthy. Thank God for the blood. Jesus forgave me for putting others before Him, He gave me a new heart, He opened my eyes so that I could see, and He taught me that as His daughter, I had no reason to fear."

"Girl, you better preach! Testify!"

"Hallelujah, He is good!" Maria testified.

The two women laughed and lifted their hands, praising their Lord and Savior in the kitchen and dining room of Maria's home.

"Hallelujah. If anyone had ever told me that I would be going to a Bible Institute, I would have laughed in their face. Me? Mrs. Robert J. Henderson? What need did I have of Jesus when there was already a man in my life who saved me? All the years and time invested in my marriage, in this commitment, just to end up with a divorce decree where he can walk off with someone else. I can't believe that I was so heartbroken and hurt over him. Amazing grace, I once was lost and now am found, was blind, and now I see. If it had not been for the Lord on our side, thank you Jesus. Can I get an Amen? It was good for me, Hallelujah!"

"Amen!" Neicy shouted. "Girl, you better preach! Hallelujah!"

"Hallelujah!" Maria finished. "Let the church say Amen."

"Amen!"

"Say Amen again!"

"Amen again!" Neicy finished.

"Praise the Lord everybody."

"Girl, I am so thankful to God right now. You sat in the house for weeks. *'No, I don't want to have lunch, Neicy.' 'No, I don't want to go anywhere, Neicy.'* You were wearing the same clothes for days. You hair was a hot mess, did you even comb it? I have never seen you look so disheveled, like you didn't even care for yourself. Maybe you fooled Genny and Papi, but not me, and definitely not your mother. She called me a few times to ask me to check on you, you know."

"My mother called you?"

"Yes, Maria. She was concerned about you. Not that she thought you were going off the deep end or anything, but we both were worried that you had sunken into a depression, which, honestly, would have been understandable. Do you think you were depressed?"

"Oh, I'm sure I was. My heart was so heavy. I know I didn't fool my mom, but I tried to mask it around the kids. Genny told me, however, that she and Papi knew we were divorced. Her exact words were that we had been divorced years ago and were just living together. I guess I was depressed, then. I would have did the break-up "cut all your hair off", but it would take too long to grow back."

Neicy laughed. "For real, girl! Today, you can just buy a short haircut if you want one."

"Thank God for Jesus," Maria continued. "When I pray, Neicy, I can tell Him everything. He hears, and He listens. I put my burdens down, and I don't pick them up again. I am so free today, so healed, delivered and whole. Jesus was everything me, Genny and Papi needed. He fixed everything."

Genny came downstairs and into the kitchen, apologizing for interrupting. "Mom, daddy is trying to reach you on your phone."

"Okay, sweetheart, thank you," Maria said. She went into the living room to retrieve her cell phone from her purse and walked back into the kitchen, turning it on and noticing several missed calls from Rob. There were a couple text messages as well, and when she read Rob's 10:48 a.m. irate text message, she paused.

Neicy noticed that something had to be wrong, so she asked Maria what was the matter.

"Read this," Maria said, handing her phone to Neicy.

Neicy read the text from Rob:

"Why are you disrespecting me? Keep him away from our kids."

"What is he talking about? This text is from this morning."

"I have no idea," Maria said.

"Well, what does he mean? Keep who away from your kids?"

"Neicy, I have no idea," Maria repeated.

Neicy sat up in her seat and put her feet on the floor. "Wait a minute. I bet I know what this is about. This morning when Tony and I came to church, there was a Mercedes parked at the corner. I could have sworn it was Rob's."

"Yes, it was. He picked up the kids this morning and followed us when we left."

"So who is he talking about?" Neicy asked.

"I don't know, Neicy…….. Oh, wait a minute. I think he means Minister Barrington. He and I talked in front of the church before we went inside. Rob could have seen us from where his car was parked if he was trying to see."

"This man has lost his mind," Neicy laughed heartily.

"All we did was talk," Maria spoke defensively. "Minister Barrington asked about Papi singing a solo, and we said hello to people as they were walking in."

"Maria, you don't have to explain anything to me," Neicy laughed. "You better explain that to *your husband.*"

"Girl, please. His silly jealousy was cute when we were kids, but we are both almost 50."

"Yes, not to mention the fact that he is the one who cheated on you and divorced you, and look at his guilt-ridden behind trying to turn it around and play the victim role. C'mon, Rob, you can do better than that," Neicy said, still laughing.

"That's God, Neicy. I let it go. I gave it to Jesus. It's not my burden anymore."

Neicy stopped laughing and stood up from her chair. She stretched her arms and then sat back down, lifting her legs to raise her feet on the ottoman again. "Maria, you are so right. Thank God you came to church and gave it to Jesus. Are you okay?"

"Yes, I'm fine. Hold on, let me listen to this message."

Maria listened to the earlier message from Rob, and then put her phone on speakerphone so that Neicy could hear. They listened to Rob's irate warning from earlier that day, and a second phone message where he issued another warning, and then a third where he asked Maria to call him as soon as she got the messages. The two women looked at each other and then burst out laughing. Neicy was in tears, and Maria handed her a couple napkins from the napkin holder on the kitchen counter.

"Girl, what did you do to this poor man?" Neicy laughed.

"It's God, Neicy."

"Yes, it is. Rob will be alright. I can't even believe what I'm hearing. After all the years that this man has been cheating on you, lying to you, now divorcing you for another woman, hiding his business affairs and money from you, selling your home from under you, then telling you to relax, he divorced you, but don't worry, it's only temporary, like that is supposed to make his infidelities okay, this man actually has the audacity to call you on Sunday morning before you go into the house of the Lord to threaten you. A Minister is talking to you about having his son sing in the church, who also, mind you, is teaching the Youth about the Lord each and every Sunday afternoon when he is nowhere to be found. Maria, Rob probably wishes he could catch you cheating on him. That would make him feel better about all the times he has cheated on you. Glory to God. Ain't this something?"

"Neicy, I don't care," Maria interrupted. "Rob can throw a temper tantrum all he wants. He was so comfortable cheating, lying and disrespecting our marriage, and part of that was my fault because I didn't want to know Jesus before. Jesus has always wanted to be my first love. I did put Rob before Him. Jesus is first, now, Neicy. He fixed my heart. I can pray for Rob and mean it. I pray for his happiness and could care less about his threats, guilt, anger and drama."

Neicy smiled at her best friend. What a transformation. This was the crying, snot-nosed grown woman who was boo hoo-ing at Geraldine's Soul Food Restaurant just a few months ago over the man who had so disrespected her and her children that Neicy, too, as sanctified and Holy Ghost filled as she may have been, was praying for Rob and didn't really mean it. Maria was right that night, though, when she said Rob wasn't Neicy's husband. It was easy for Neicy because *it was* Maria's family. Neicy truly wanted the best for her friend, and because the divorce had already been signed when she found out, the only thing she could do was pray.

"Thank you, Jesus," Neicy said. "Maria, you're going to be fine. God has plans for you. He will speak to you, and every time he does, do what he says. He is ordering your steps. Everything happens for a reason. Stay with Him, Maria. Go to school. Go to Bible Study and Prayer, and come every Sunday for our worship service. God has plans for your future, and He is with you. And pray for Rob."

The two women hugged, and then Maria's phone rang. It was Rob.

"Are you going to answer it?" Neicy asked.

"Sure. Hello?" Maria answered on the third ring.

There was silence for a second or two on the other end, and then Rob spoke.

"Maria, I've been calling you. I'm sorry if I did anything to hurt you, but I don't want anyone else around my kids."

Maria didn't say anything.

"Are you there?" he asked.

"Yes."

"I just wanted to tell you that."

Again, Maria didn't say anything. There was silence on the phone as Maria waited for Rob to say something, and he waited for her to respond.

"Rob, who is Sophia?" Maria asked, weary of holding it in any longer.

"What?" he asked.

"You know what. Who is Sophia?"

Rob was silent. *"Papi must have told her. That's okay, he couldn't be expected to keep his dad's affair a secret forever."*

"You told our son that you love Sophia. Who is she?" Maria asked.

After another few seconds of silence, Rob answered. "She is nobody, Maria. She doesn't – I mean she didn't mean anything. She is just a friend. I'm not seeing her anymore. Remember I told you this situation was temporary."

"Our divorce, to you, was temporary. The sale of our home was temporary. The break-up of our family was temporary. Is that what you're saying?"

"Well, yes and no......I'm taking care of things.......It's...I'm...."

"So why aren't you seeing Sophia anymore, Rob?"

"I just need to get some things in order. I'm doing this to help all of us."

"Rob, you're lying. I know you're lying, but I don't care. Whatever you're doing, you're doing it for yourself. You don't throw your family under the bus so you can get things back in order. I was your wife. Genny and Papi are your children. It wouldn't have mattered to me what you thought was wrong, and you know it. I've always loved you and stood by your side."

"Maria, you're still my wife."

"Rob, let's stop this, okay. Just stop it. You are delusional. I pray for your happiness with Sophia, but do not ever disrespect me and tell our son that you love her. You are disrespecting me, Rob. I don't appreciate your texts and phone calls demanding I call you back and telling me who you think should be around our children. I will bring whoever I want around our children whenever I want. If you weren't so busy spying on me this morning, you could have come to church with your children yourself and met Minister Barrington. The only reason I'm even telling you this is because he asked Papi to sing a solo in a few weeks, and you should be there to support him. He's good. His voice is amazing. Papi is just as good singing as he is in karate. I don't care who you date, you can see whomever you want, but you're still Papi's father, and he will always need you. Genny will always need you. I would never disrespect you before Papi or Genny, and you know that. Now, I'm going to hang up and finish having dinner with my family. Don't send me another text. Don't leave me another message. If you have any problems about how I am raising them, go tell Jesus all about it because I am raising them in the Lord. And Rob, I already forgave you. God bless you."

Maria hung up her phone and turned it off, putting it on the counter a good distance from the marinated steaks she had yet to grill.

"Are you hungry, Neicy?" Maria asked.

Neicy was in shock. This was a completely different woman. Maria had changed. The old wine was gone.

"New wine," Neicy said.

"You want a glass of wine?" Maria asked, not understanding what Neicy had said.

"No, girl, I said new wine. I'm going to call you that from now on. That shy and passive lady I knew before is gone. The righteous are bold as a lion, amen. Yes, I'm hungry. I'm starving."

"Good, help me get these steaks on the grill, please."

"You got it," Neicy said.

The two opened the screen doors in the dining room and walked outside into the fresh September air. Potted plants lined the small patio, and the soft tinkling of bells from a wind chime played melodically in the air. The well-manicured green lawn was routinely cared for by a landscaper, and leaves from the huge oak tree in the center of the property were cascading down, only to be lifted up again with the gentle wind that carried them in different directions. Maria turned on her gas grill and waited for it to reach the ideal temperature so that grill marks would pierce the steaks. As she did, she felt a soft wind brush across her body and the reminiscent tranquility of the Holy Spirit speak peace to her inner man.

"Neicy, did you feel that?" Maria asked.

"What?" Neicy asked, straightening the patio chairs.

"Never mind," Maria said. Maybe it was just her imagination, or she was supposing that every little instance of wind or air could be the visitation of the Lord. There was peace again, and a stillness that calmed her. Then the voice again at her right ear, ***"Do not fear."***

Maria told Neicy that she had to use the bathroom and would be right back. She asked Neicy to put the steaks on as soon as the grill was hot, and Neicy agreed.

Maria went inside and into her bedroom, closing the door and then kneeling at her bed. She felt a heaviness in her spirit that nearly forced her to her knees. Maria bowed low and prayed that the Lord would have His way. *"Yes, Lord. Have your way,"* she prayed. A presence was about her arms and hands, and she could feel the soft wind again about her mouth, head and ears. The presence remained about her entire body for several minutes, and then it was over. She grabbed the prayer shawl that Mother Wright suggested she use and covered her head with it, thanking Jesus for being her Lord and Savior and for saving her life. She worshipped Him and blessed His name. She prayed just to say thank you. She lifted up her children and prayed that He would be with them and their children, and their children's children for all generations forevermore. Maria thanked the Lord for Neicy and for her church, for Pastor Wright, Elder Daniels and all the members of the church. She thanked the Lord for Rob and prayed earnestly for his happiness with Sophia. She asked the Lord to forgive her of her sins and to bless her to be the best woman she could be for herself and for His glory. She laid prostrate before Him, with the covering over her head, and she thanked Him for being in her life. She reverenced Jesus as Mother Wright taught her and worshipped Him in spirit and in truth. She lay still for several minutes more until hearing a soft knock at her door.

"Mommy, Aunt Neicy said the steaks are ready." It was Papi.

"Okay," she said. "I'll be right down." Maria returned to her knees and blessed her Lord, Jesus Christ.

"I love you, Father. Thank you for loving me. Thank you for forgiving me of my sins and for giving me another chance. Thank you for being my God. Whatever you want, I am willing, Lord. Fill me with your Holy Spirit, Lord, teach and instruct me in all thy ways. Teach me your will. I'll do whatever you want me to do. I trust you, and I am so grateful to you. Bless Rob, Lord. Watch over him. Bless him so that he, too, bows before you. Bless Sophia, and be with her in all she does. Grant that she, too, would confess Jesus Christ as Lord. She is your daughter. Thank you. In Jesus' name, Amen."

She wiped her eyes and nose with tissue, changed into a white t-shirt and denim shorts, and returned to the patio with her family to have dinner. Neicy had finished the coleslaw, and a salad of fresh spinach, arugula, carrots, tomatoes and olive oil was neatly dressed and in a glass bowl.

"Everything looks so nice. Neicy, the steaks look delicious. Thank you," Maria said, sitting down as Neicy had taken over and was plating their meal.

"Genny, will you say grace, please?" Maria asked once Neicy was done.

"Yes ma'am."

Neicy served Maria and leaned in close to ask if she was okay.

"Yes, I just needed a few minutes."

"You were gone for a half hour."

"Really?"

"Yes. It must have been a good few minutes, though," Neicy laughed.

"Yes, it was. Thank you so much, Neicy. I don't know what I would do without you."

"Yeah, Aunt Neicy, if you weren't here, the steaks might have burned," Papi said.

Neicy took her seat, and Maria motioned for Genny to start.

"Dear God, thank you for this food that we are about to receive. Thank you for Aunt Neicy and mom who prepared it. Thank you for watching over us and for blessing us with a church. Please forgive us of our sins, and help us to forgive others so that we don't

block any blessings you have for us. And please forgive daddy, and bless him to look to you. In Jesus' name, Amen."

"Amen," they all said.

Maria smiled at Genny, and Genny smiled back. Genny prayed, and she meant it. Jesus did fix everything, glory to God.

Marcia L. Boynton

Chapter Seventeen

Genny

Addington Park High School, Home of the Championship Blue Knights, was a beautiful, four story concrete and glass building situated in North Addington Park, just minutes from the Atlantic Ocean. The athletic field in the back of the school overlooked a small lake, atop which railroad tracks of north and southbound trains could be heard rattling as they passed by. The "better" neighborhoods boasted gorgeous Victorian homes with views of President's Lake, but typical remnants of urban blight disproportionately affected the poorer neighborhoods and inner city where businesses and homes had been earlier abandoned, defaced or altogether destroyed. Several city blocks had yet to be redeveloped, but there had been and were still sincere efforts by politicians and businessmen, including Mr. Henderson, to revitalize potential industry and build upon the city's infrastructure. Stereotypical social and economic conditions, albeit not as bad as media reports suggested but existent nonetheless, presented the city's youth with fewer options than their suburban peers. Gangs attracted young, black males who may have been looking for a sense of brotherhood and family, and who, frankly, could use the money from drugs to help their single parent households. The usual high crime rates, poverty, unemployment and fragmented families, along with suspected political corruption, could be relieved by either the liquor stores on every other corner or the churches. The solution for the God-fearing parents who thrived no matter their circumstances, and who knew that Addington Park was a great town with great leaders working to restore confidence of the residents in their leadership, was education.

The Abbott School District had produced great young men and women who prospered in spite of the odds against them. The city's athletes were the elite of the state, true, but Ivy League schools and U.S. Marines recruited as well as Division One football, basketball and track programs. Alumni dinners and local chapters of fraternities and sororities welcomed home successful medical doctors, educators, surgeons, attorneys, chemists, philanthropists, businessmen and women, television personalities, publishers, U.S. Army, Navy, Air Force and Marine Officers, bestselling authors, award-winning actors, government leaders, multi-lingual Officers of the United Nations, entrepreneurs, inventors and internationally acclaimed musicians, to name a few. They came home to speak to the city's youth and to encourage students to finish school, go to college and never give up on their dreams. They thanked their high school teachers and guidance counselors for not giving up on them, and they inspired the next generation to believe in themselves and work hard for what they wanted. Their less publicized successes and achievements were overshadowed by a frequency of titillating negative reports, which always managed to make the evening news and front page of local newspapers, and which only further deteriorated the image of the city.

During the first week of school, an assembly was held to welcome back Duane Brownlee, a 30 year young APHS graduate who was a well-respected computer genius and up and coming software design mogul.

"Use the stones that have been thrown at you to build your empire," he spoke confidently and passionately during his early morning speech. "Don't hate your haters. Use them to your advantage."

Mr. Brownlee's revolutionary technologies and designs were completely re-defining word processing through voice activation. He had been approached by a leading software giant for sale of his company and was now in negotiations. His visit to the school was flanked with media coverage, politicians, parents and the legendary Robert J. Henderson. His Center for Young Men helped promote the event. Mr. Henderson was always welcome at the school, and he sat as a dignitary along with the school's administration and city officials on that solemn Friday morning. After greetings, flag salute and introductions, Mr. Brownlee was welcomed to the podium by the Superintendent of Schools, Mrs. Gina DiGregorio, an attractive, mature woman who school officials respected for her staunch support of their out-of-the-box initiatives.

As Mr. Brownlee arose from his chair and walked towards the podium in the center of the stage, he shook the hands of each and every official and politician, which took several minutes. The students didn't seem to care that this would only further prolong the assembly. They continued their applause and cheered for the young man who looked like them and who knew their struggle up close and personal. Once he adjusted his hand-held microphone, he insisted that a chair be brought so that he could sit on the floor directly in front of the rows of students, and this only further endeared the speaker of the hour to his young listeners. The students gave Mr. Brownlee a standing ovation, and he joked, "I haven't said anything yet. I hope everyone gets something out of what I have to say this morning."

A chair was brought out as Mr. Brownlee requested, and he began his speech at 10:42 a.m. with a time limit of 18 minutes.

"Good morning. I'm going to share my story with you today to encourage everyone here. I am from Addington Park, I grew up in the projects here, and I love this city and this school."

There were cheers and applause again, as if someone had been holding a queue card that said "Applause!"

"I didn't graduate high school, I dropped out and finished my G.E.D. I walked the stage here 11 years ago as a 19 year old who had been arrested twice for selling drugs. If I got arrested one more time, they were going to send me away – three strikes and you're out. That was my wake up call. I was always good with computers. They just came easy to me, but no one believed that I would make it at a school like M.I.T., Carnegie Mellon or Purdue. My grades were good, and my teachers supported me, but I wasn't applying myself completely. Can I keep it real with everyone this morning?"

"Yes! Please do!" the students shouted.

"Well, alright then. I sold drugs. Selling drugs was quick money, but the consequences could affect you for the rest of your life. Spending the rest of my life in jail was not a choice I was willing to make. Everybody has a hustle, a vision, a dream. My dream at one time was making money. When I was arrested for making money illegally, my dream changed."

There was laughter in the assembly.

"My dream became vision. For me, my dream was something that I wanted to do, and I didn't really see how I was going to make it happen, but I knew that I *could* make it happen. For me, my vision was also something that I wanted to do, but the difference was I could see clearly *how* to make it happen. You have to believe in your own dreams and visions. You have to see your vision and dream your dream in the midst of any struggles you may be going through. That's why you have them. They help you to see beyond your present circumstances. Okay, we may not have any money today, but I see myself owning my own home in five years. Maybe I'm living in the hood right now, but I see myself owning and leasing million dollar property in fifteen years. My plan to get there is to finish my education and know that I can do anything I set my mind to. Having a dream, a vision, an idea of where you are going in life, and having a plan to execute that dream and vision, will help you to be successful. If I hadn't wanted to do better after my second arrest, my life would easily have been lost. I might not be here with you today. I was looking at two options: jail or the grave. No sir."

There was applause again.

"If you don't believe in yourself, no one else will. Your parents and the teachers here will give you all the tools that you need to be successful in life. Appreciate them. I was not accepted to any of the schools I applied to, and there were many who believed that I would either end up in jail or dead. To them, Duane Brownlee was a statistic, an accident waiting to happen. That was unacceptable to me. I refuse to be defined by someone else's prejudices and pre-conceived notions that suggest I should only aspire to go so far. When all the Ivy League schools I applied to denied my application, I researched what books they required their students to read, and I read every one of them. I made friends on social media with students who attended classes there, and they shared their professors' syllabuses with me. I visited the schools and went to the lectures and pretended to be a student. There were about 400 students in the lecture halls, so the professors didn't even know who I was. I wanted to learn. Once I got the syllabuses, I did the work on my own. With my grades, SAT scores, GED and record, none of the colleges I applied to accepted me, so I had to be creative. Necessity is the mother of invention."

Again, there was applause.

"I partnered with one of the students I had come to know, and together we formed 'GFI Software.' His name is Brad Youngerman, and he couldn't be here today, but he is one of the most down to earth men you will ever want to meet. He sends his regards."

"So, 'GFI' simply stands for 'Go for It.' Whatever your dream is, go for it. You can do it. My college applications were rejected so much, my mother got tired of me trying to go to school, but she kept telling me to go for it, and that is my recommendation to you today. Today, my partner and I are in negotiations with one of the largest software companies in the world for the sale of our technology, and I am proud to say that I am a bona fide student of the top ranked engineering university in the United States."

Everyone in the assembly stood and applauded. When their applause quieted down, he continued.

"I have the teachers of this high school, Addington Park, to thank. I have my mother to thank. I have my guidance counselor and every school official to thank. They never gave up on me, and they will never give up on you, but don't give up on yourself. You don't have to sell drugs, brothers, to make money. Drugs can get your life and freedom taken. Education, young men and young ladies, is the greatest gift you can give to yourself, and no one can ever take that from you."

The school officials and administrators stood and applauded again. Every dignitary in the auditorium was on his/her feet cheering, and their standing ovation was accompanied by the students' cries of "GFI!" "GFI!" "GFI!"

"Whatever it is you want to do," Mr. Brownlee continued once the ovation and cries were dulled, "whatever your passion is, no matter how many rejection letters and no matter how many times you think your dreams are being stepped on by someone who is seated across a table from you, go for it. That thing that wakes you up in the morning, and that vision that won't let you sleep at night. You know what it is. What are you going to do about it? How are you going to make it happen?"

"Go for it!" the combined assembly of 250 freshmen, sophomores, juniors and seniors shouted.

"Yes!" Mr. Brownlee responded. "Go for it! You can do it!"

Mr. Brownlee returned to his seat with the school officials, and Mrs. DiGregorio returned to the podium to thank him for coming and to dismiss all teachers and students. They were all asked to return to their classrooms, but nearly everyone stalled and delayed in obvious attempts to get in any of the photos the news reporters were taking. Genny had been seated with her science class just a few rows from the front, and her dad was shaking hands and passing out business cards in the immediate vicinity of Mr. Brownlee. A cameraman gathered a few people with Mr. Brownlee, and he snapped several photos before leaving from the side exit door. Another cameraman appeared to ask Mrs. DiGregorio for students to take a photo, and she motioned with her hand for Ms. Shelly, Genny's science teacher, to come forth with a few. Without being asked, Genny went forward.

"What were they going to do?" she figured. *"My dad is practically the Mayor."*

Mr. Henderson spotted his daughter, and he called her name to be sure no one interfered with her effort.

As Genny approached her dad, an attractive woman in a dark green suit walked over to him. Genny stopped where she was, just a few feet away from him, and he spoke with the woman for a second. She looked in Genny's direction and smiled, stepping forward to introduce herself, but her dad pulled the woman back by the hand. They talked again, and then the woman stepped back into the crowd of people who were gathered around.

"Hi, Genny. C'mon in close, they want to take another picture," her dad said.

Genny and the other students who had been called forward were positioned before Mrs. DiGregorio, Mr. Brownlee, Mr. Henderson, and a few other school officials. Mrs. DiGregorio asked the woman who had been speaking with Genny's dad to join them as she had attended the assembly on behalf of the Mayor's Office.

"How can we take this photo without the Mayor's Office?" asked Superintendent DiGregorio, looking around for Ms. Simmons. "Where is Ms. Simmons?"

"I'm right here," Ms. Simmons answered, stepping forward again. "Of course, it would be my pleasure."

She joined the entourage and stood between Mr. Brownlee and Mr. Henderson, and the photographer for the *Addington Park Reader* took several pictures. He also asked to have a few moments with Ms. Simmons regarding the mayoral race next year, but she declined, stating that the hour was for the children, not politics.

"That's why we need you in the Mayor's Office next year, Ms. Simmons," said Superintendent DiGregorio. "You'll have our full support."

Genny and the other students were instructed to return to their classes, and as Genny was walking out the assembly, she turned to wave to her dad. She saw Ms. Simmons engaged in conversation with her dad again.

"If it was innocent," Genny thought, *"he would have introduced me to her."*

The Vice Principal then approached Mr. Henderson, and he appeared to be just talking politics and business like everyone else, so Genny dismissed her suspicions.

The school year got off to a quick start, and it wasn't long before Genny had mastered her block scheduling and classroom assignments. She was attending practice at the Boys' and Girls' Club with her dad on Tuesdays after school, and he agreed to train Bria and Joanne as well. The girls ran suicides for 20 minutes and laps around the gym for another 20. Then, they played in a full court game with boys, who ran at top speed up and down the court, ensuring the girls' conditioning. Joanne and Bria were exhausted. They both wanted to sit down on the sidelines, but Mr. Henderson refused their request and insisted that they now practice their foul shots, tired and all. Joanne was bent over breathing heavily, and Bria walked around the court with her hands on her hips. They both missed more than half their shots, and Mr. Henderson had them run laps for another ten minutes.

Genny, trained and conditioned, made 8/10 of her foul shots, but Mr. Henderson penalized her for not making at least nine, and she was forced to run laps along with her teammates.

"Your dad doesn't ease up," Joanne said while running.

Genny didn't talk. She knew she had to save her energy for the final five minutes of suicides. Sure enough, as they finished their laps, Mr. Henderson told them to go line up. He blew his whistle, and Genny was off and in the lead as Joanne and Bria dragged behind and breathed heavily.

"You're out of shape, ladies," said Mr. Henderson. "Conditioning is everything. Addington Park lost a couple seniors last year, and the top teams in the Conference are going to be coming for you. Your biggest competitors are top heavy, and we are bringing in three freshmen. All of you will make the Varsity team. You are good players, but you have to be in good condition, and you have to be able to make your foul shots. Most of your fouls are going to come when you are going in for layups, so you can't afford to be tired. We are going to run every week, and once the season starts in November, you will be able to run and shoot without gasping for air. I will see to that."

This would conclude their weekly practice, but Mr. Henderson gave them drills to practice at home to improve their ball handling. Genny was used to running, but Mr. Henderson didn't let up on his daughter – in fact, he expected more from her than anyone else. To Joanne and Bria, nothing Genny did was good enough, but Genny knew that her dad pushed her to get the best out of her, and she was content.

This was their routine for weeks until a Thursday evening in mid-October when Mr. Henderson arranged a three-on-three game between the girls and three teenage boys from a travelling basketball team.

"We're playing against boys?" Joanne asked. She sounded petrified.

"Yes, it will help us to be better and stronger players," Genny answered.

"Are they going to take it easy on us?" Joanne asked.

"No," Genny said, "and you don't want them to. We can handle our own. Joanne and Bria, you're both strong shooters, I'll get the ball to you. We play man-to-man. Stay with your man, and 'D' him up. We're girls, we're already at a disadvantage, but we will play them tight."

"We're going to lose," Bria said with a sullen directness that made it clear she had no confidence.

"We're going to do the best we can," Genny replied. "We're going to make our shots and draw fouls. We're going to run with them and play solid defense. If we do lose, we lose swinging. Let's go."

"Ain't no 'if', we are going to lose," Bria repeated.

Mr. Henderson was already seated in the stands. He would not get involved or interfere, unless it was absolutely necessary. This would be Joanne and Bria's first game against boys, and he assured them before the game started that it was just practice. Genny just shook her head, she knew her dad was a fierce competitor who hated to lose even "practice" games.

Their opponents entered the gym dressed in blue and yellow jerseys over their t-shirts. Two of them were only about 5'10, but the third was about 6'4".

"Who's going to guard him?" Joanne asked.

"You are," Genny insisted.

"What is the point of this?" Joanne complained. "They are going to kill us."

Mr. Henderson sensed Joanne's fear, and he called her over to the stands to have a pep talk with her.

"Joanne, you're a great defensive player. He's tall, but he has no left hand. Play to his left side. He has another weakness. You should be able to spot it before the second quarter, and I'm going to call you over again and ask you what it is, okay. So play your game, and you'll be fine. He's just a basketball player."

Just then Chris Walker and a few of the players from the high school boys' team walked in the gymnasium. Rhonda and Brenda Miller, senior girls on the basketball team, also walked in with their brothers, Dante and Kasheem.

"Oh my God!" Joanne said. "What is this? Why are we on display?"

Bria didn't want to look, she was already nervous, and Genny could care less. Genny was used to being a spectacle in the Boys' Club.

"Why is your dad embarrassing us?" Bria asked.

"Would you two just stop. It's just practice. Nobody here is sweatin' us that bad," Genny said.

A whistle blew, and Chris Walker and Paul Carpenter, both players on the APHS boys' team, came onto the floor to serve as the game referees.

"What is this?" Joanne asked, still complaining.

The girls went onto the floor and tossed a coin for possession. They won, and Genny would bring the ball up. The boys had to stay in a zone defense for the first half, but they could play man-to-man during the second half of the game. The girls could play defense however they wanted, so they chose to play man-to-man.

Genny sank a couple of three pointers early on with ease as none of the boys came out of their tight zone defense. Joanne sank a three pointer, and the girls finished the first quarter with a 12-8 lead.

Joanne saw that her 6'4" opponent was weak on the left side, but she hadn't yet determined what the other weakness was. Mr. Henderson made eye contact with her after the first quarter, but she looked away, and he knew she hadn't figured it out yet. He sat comfortably in the bleachers without coaching or saying a word. He wanted to see how the three girls would play together.

As the second quarter started, the boys appeared to be playing with a little more aggression. They came out a little on their zone defense and blocked Joanne's shot attempts. The boys were quick getting down the court, and even with their conditioning, the girls could not keep up. The score went from 12-8, girls, to 24-12, boys. Then the boys relaxed again, easing up on defense, and Genny sank two three-pointers to close the gap to 24-18. The second quarter ended, as the boys passed the ball to one another without taking a shot at the basket. It was obvious they were teasing the girls. They played like the Harlem Globetrotters, and any time one of the girls tried to steal the ball, their opponent would take the ball between his legs or around his back, exciting laughter from the onlookers who were amused.

189

Halftime was eight minutes, and Mr. Henderson did not coach. Joanne still hadn't figured out what the other weakness of her opponent was. She didn't want to play anymore, but Genny and Bria convinced her to just finish the game. They might be losing, but they were not going to quit.

"She's supposed to be so hard," Genny thought to herself.

When the game resumed, the boys played man-to-man defense, and they stole the ball, blocked shots, dunked, intercepted passes and went up to the basket strong, like they were playing against grown men. There were no calls for offensive fouls, even though the girls were knocked onto the floor as the players took them to the hoop, and Chris just smiled at them when they looked to him for support. A few times, Genny saw him trying to hide his laughter as their shots were not only blocked, but the boys actually grabbed the basketball and threw it into the bleachers. One of the players blocked Joanne's shot and then passed the ball to his teammate who kicked it into the stands like he was a soccer player taking a goal shot. The onlookers were hysterical, and Chris and Paul both fell onto the floor laughing nonstop with hilarity. They both rolled around, screaming with boisterous merriment, and when Paul got up, he walked over to the sidelines to get a cup of water. As he drank from the cup, he spit out water, still engaged in his hearty amusement. The girls were forced to wait a few minutes for him to calm down before the game could resume.

At the end of the third quarter, the score was 56-20.

"This is a massacre," Joanne said. "Can we please stop? They're humiliating us."

"We're not stopping," Genny said.

"What is the point of this? Boys are better than us? What are we supposed to be getting out of this? All I'm getting is discouraged," Joanne continued complaining.

Genny and Bria ignored her. They returned to the court to finish the game.

The fourth quarter went quick, and the boys did not let up. They played man-to-man defense again, and it was hopeless. Joanne walked off the court, but Genny and Bria stayed and took the beating. The boys showed no mercy, and the gym was transformed into a slam dunk and alley-oop competition as Genny and Bria, try as they might, were no match for these teenage boys who played and looked like they had been recruited from a professional league. With sixty seconds to go in the game, the boys retreated into their zone defense and allowed Genny to get one more three-pointer off, which she missed. Joanne came back onto the court, and the buzzer sounded. The players shook hands, and the boys grabbed their belongings and left the gym. A few people who had been seated in the stands went onto the floor and began shooting around.

"Good game," Mr. Henderson said as the girls walked over to him.

"Good game? Are you serious?" Bria asked.

"Yes, I am. You ran with them the entire time, and you played solid defense. Nice job. Let's go, I'll drop you all off at home."

"Mr. Henderson, with all due respect, what was this about?" Joanne asked.

"I'll explain later, Joanne. Did you see what your man's other weakness was?" he asked.

"Yes, but not until the end of the game," she admitted. "He telegraphs his passes."

"Good, Joanne. That's exactly right. A player who telegraphs his or her passes is a Godsend. That player is handing over the game to you. You just have to be hungry enough to take it, and I didn't see that hunger in your eyes today. Don't ever talk yourself out of the game. In any case, you did great, and I'm proud of each one of you."

From the corner of his eye, Mr. Henderson noticed two twin girls walking up to them. "Do you know them?" he asked.

"Yes, they are seniors on the basketball team," Joanne answered.

"Hi girls," Mr. Henderson said, turning to face the twins, Brenda and Rhonda Miller.

"Hello," said Brenda. Then, she fixed her eyes on Bria and said, "What's up, you could have asked us to play."

"It was just a freshman practice. We're trying to get ready for the season," Bria answered.

"Well, when is the next practice? We want to play," said Brenda.

"Girls, I'm Mr. Henderson. How are you?" he asked, extending his hand to shake theirs. They just looked at him.

"We're fine, Mr. Henderson....Oh my God, are you Mr. Robert Henderson who owns the Center downtown?" Brenda asked.

"Yes, how are you?" he asked again, with his hand still extended.

"Dante! Kasheem! Come over here! This is that man we were telling you about," Brenda yelled.

Rhonda shook his hand.

Dante and Kasheem, their brothers, came over with pants sagging and open bottles in brown paper bags. They brought with them the smell of marijuana, and they tested Mr. Henderson's patience and provoked his ire as soon as they strolled nonchalantly over, taking their time, and drinking without respect to where they were or who they were talking to.

Mr. Henderson inhaled and let out a deep breath from his nose, and he told the girls to go have a seat. They all did as they were told, except for Brenda and Rhonda Miller.

"This is Mr. Robert J. Henderson," Brenda said to her brothers.

"Hey, what's up man? I know a couple of brothers who've been through your place. My man Jamarr is there now, and you know, I just want to say thank you for what you're trying to do. Clean the streets up. Give us some alternatives to drugs and gangs. That's what's up," said one of the young men, slobbering over his words.

"It's nice to meet all of you," Mr. Henderson said. "I appreciate that, young man."

"Aw, man, you ain't gotta be so formal. I'm D, and this is my brother Kasheem," Dante, the older brother said.

"Alright, D, Kasheem," Mr. Henderson replied. "Well, I've got to get the girls back home, but I'll see you around. Take it easy."

"Whoa, hold up, Mr. Henderson," D replied, "you see, we heard a lot about you, and we just wanted to ask you to do us a small favor. We know you're a legend and all."

"Alright, young man, what's that?" Mr. Henderson asked.

"Well, you see, Jamarr ain't really down with us no more, so we need you to back up off him a little, you feel me?" D asked. He and Kasheem looked at one another.

"Excuse me, young man?" Mr. Henderson asked.

"I said, we need you to back up off him," Dante said forcefully. "He ain't down with us no more, and he was always down until he started hanging around your Center getting his head filled with all kinds of nonsense. Do I have to explain it anymore?" D asked.

He was about 5'10", sloppy, young and ignorant. His eyes were red, he had been smoking and drinking, and Mr. Henderson was not going to get into any kind of altercation with him or anyone else over helping anybody. He did a ten count in his mind and reminded himself that this young man was someone's son, just like the other young men at his Center, and just like he, himself, had been years ago.

To avoid the impending argument he knew would occur if he volleyed needlessly with Dante, Mr. Henderson answered, "Okay, D, no problem," and he turned and walked away.

"Yo, D, that fool is trying to play us. Did you hear the way he said that?" Kasheem asked his older brother.

"Mr. Henderson! Mr. Henderson!" Dante yelled.

Mr. Henderson kept walking away. He told the girls to get their things and go quickly to his car outside. In an instant, Mr. Henderson felt the barrel of a handgun at his back.

"Don't move. I will shoot you right here in front of everybody," he heard Dante say in his left ear.

Dante was breathing heavily, and the cocktail of alcohol and marijuana had clearly clouded the young man's senses and rationale. He stood behind Mr. Henderson with a gun in one hand and a brown paper bag in the other. Dante handed his brown paper bag to Kasheem, who tilted the bottle inside at his mouth and drank from it until it was empty.

"Dante, you better think carefully about what you're doing," Mr. Henderson said slowly while standing completely still. "You don't know me, son."

Kasheem, Rhonda and Brenda gathered around Mr. Henderson so that no one could see what was going on, but no one in the gym was paying attention. Brenda and Rhonda were reluctant, but they had to go along with their brothers.

Genny, Joanne and Bria were walking towards the front door.

"Son? Oh, you're everybody's daddy out here, huh. Don't try to play me. I don't want to have to shoot you, but you are messing with my money. Leave Jamarr alone. You play savior to anybody else you want to, but Jamarr don't need to be saved by you. I'm his daddy. He can't leave this shit, and if you try to talk him out of it, you're gonna get him killed, too. So leave Jamarr alone and nobody will get hurt. You got that old man?" D asked.

"This young man has the wrong one," Mr. Henderson said to himself. *"This young fool must be out of his mind."* Mr. Henderson was from the streets, he served time in jail, and he was not a punk by any standards. He was a second degree black belt, and he knew how to disarm a seasoned fighter of a weapon. He didn't have much time to make a decision, but he was not going to allow this young man and his wannabe thug brother and sisters to threaten his life. He didn't say a word. He just stood there with the barrel of the gun in his back, contemplating his next move and waiting for the right moment to defend himself.

"Yeah, that's what I thought," D said, pulling the gun away.

The two boys laughed, but Rhonda and Brenda scolded their brothers, telling them to stop being so stupid and go home.

Mr. Henderson turned around slowly and looked Dante in his eyes. He leaned in towards him, smelling the alcohol on his breath. Dante's clothes were hanging off his slim frame, and he couldn't have weighed more than 170 pounds. A gold chain and cross around his neck antithetically adorned the young man whose cheek was tattooed in black with gang insignia. The Christian pendant had been reduced to mere form and fashion, and although his tattoo and cross were diametrically opposed to each other, they represented a duplicity in the nature of many. That benefit of the doubt would grant Dante some leniency in Mr. Henderson's mind, but he also recognized that this young man had, cross on his neck and all, just threatened his life. Mr. Henderson lifted the gold cross in his hands and then looked Dante directly in his eyes again.

For a few seconds, there was a standoff between the two. Dante wasn't used to anyone standing up to him, especially when he had just pulled out his weapon, but Mr. Henderson didn't budge. They looked like two opponents before a boxing match - Dante with his corner man and trainers egging him on and convincing him that he could take down the Champ, and Robert J. Henderson in the center of the ring with nothing to back him up but his reputation and former championship belt.

Mr. Henderson stood there like a professional fighter, face to face with the next lightweight who was being paid to think he could actually win against him, engaged in psychological warfare to break the spirit of his opponent before the bell sounded. The stare alone induced fear into Dante, and as Mr. Henderson maintained his piercing gaze, tight jaw and tight lip, the smell of marijuana and alcohol was now predictably replaced with the smell of fear. Dante was now mentally defeated, and he stood there as easy prey. Dante stood as an overly confident hyena before a powerful lion, king of the jungle, who was set to pounce on him.

The small handgun was slightly visible in the front pocket of Dante's hoodie, and Mr. Henderson planned a simple move to finish taking Dante down without serious injury. He head butted Dante with force, knocking the young man backwards and drawing his hands upwards, and at that moment Mr. Henderson confiscated the weapon. Then, he swept Dante off his feet, and Dante fell backwards onto the floor, hitting the back of his head against the hard gymnasium floor. By now, everyone in the gym was looking, and the girls turned around. Genny ran towards her father.

"No, Genny, go back!" her dad yelled.

She ignored his warning and ran forward to stand directly in front of her father as Kasheem, Rhonda and Brenda looked on in shock. Dante appeared to be unconscious.

"D, wake up! Wake up!" Kasheem yelled. "What did you do to my brother?!"

"Dante, get up! We told you to stop being so stupid!" Brenda and Rhonda yelled.

Mr. Henderson had the gun in his hand, and he put it into his back pocket. He grabbed Genny by her arm and moved her behind him. Just then, the Club's Security Guard came into the gymnasium.

"Everything okay, Mr. Henderson?" the guard asked, seeing him standing over Dante Miller, a notorious gang member and drug dealer. The gymnasium fell completely silent.

"Yes. Everything is okay, right Kasheem?" Mr. Henderson asked.

"Yeah. Yeah, we're cool. My brother had a little too much to drink, that's all." Kasheem answered.

"We're good here," Mr. Henderson said.

"Okay," the security guard replied. He returned to the other side of the Club, where young people were playing pool and table tennis.

Kasheem and his sisters picked up their brother from off the floor and escorted him to the stands. After a few minutes, he woke up and checked furiously for his handgun on his person.

"I'm going to keep it, Dante," Mr. Henderson said. "Now, I don't want any trouble out of either of you, but if you come back looking for trouble, I guarantee you, you will find it."

Mr. Henderson left the club, reprimanding his daughter for not heeding his voice, and as he did so, Brenda, Rhonda, Joanne and Bria all looked at Genny with newfound respect.

The car ride to Joanne and Bria's homes was silent, and Mr. Henderson apologized to the girls for the trouble. They told him there was no need to apologize, and they thanked him for keeping them safe. Bria explained that Rhonda and Brenda were actually pretty nice girls, once you got to know them, and it was their brothers who caused trouble whenever they showed up at the games. The high school had banned them from attending, and Mr. Henderson vowed to speak to the Club's officials and be sure they were banned from the Boys' Club as well.

Once he dropped Joanne, Bria and Genny off, he decided to go to the police station and turn in the gun, which he would say he found.

When Mr. Henderson pulled up in the municipal parking lot, he observed four police cars with flashing lights and sirens leave hurriedly and travel down Hubert Avenue, the same street as the Boys' Club. Sergeant Johnson, a childhood friend of his, came out of the department, and Mr. Henderson asked him what was going on. The Sergeant told him that there had just been a shooting on Hubert Avenue outside the Boys' Club. Rival gangs had shot and wounded two youth. It didn't look good.

Mr. Henderson decided against turning in the gun. He spoke with the Sergeant for some time in front of the police department about gang activity and the need for better parenting, schools and education. Not long after, several police officers hurried inside the department, and the report came back in that two youth, Dante and Kasheem Miller, had been shot and critically wounded. They were transported to the area hospital, and officers had been dispatched to the Club and hospital to try and obtain witness statements.

The next morning, the local TV station reported that Dante Miller, 23, of Addington Park, NJ, had been shot and killed in gang related violence by rival gang members outside of what was supposed to be a safe haven for the city's youth, the Boys' and Girls' Club. His brother, Kasheem Miller, 20, also of Addington Park, was in critical condition at an area hospital. The news story featured family members, including twin sisters Brenda and Rhonda Miller, who were crying hysterically and pleading for young people to stop the violence.

Mr. Henderson's telephone rang off the hook, and he avoided most of the calls until he saw his daughter's number.

"Daddy, are you okay?" Genny asked.

"Of course, sweetheart. How are you?"

"Daddy, did you hear? Dante is dead. He was shot last night in front of the Boys' Club. Kasheem is in critical condition. Oh my God, daddy, Brenda and Rhonda were on the TV news this morning. Are you okay, daddy? I'm so glad you're okay. Thank God."

"Genny, I'm fine. Are you alright?"

"Yes."

"Genny, don't ever disobey me when I tell you to do something, okay. I'm grateful that nothing happened to you or me last night, but don't ever disobey me when I tell you to do something. Anything could have happened. I'm a man, I can take care of myself. I'm trained to do this. Please, anytime I ask you to do something, just do what I ask. Okay?"

"Yes, daddy. I'm sorry. I wasn't thinking, it all happened so fast, and all I could think of was you. I'm sorry."

"Sweetheart, it's okay. I'm just grateful you're alright. I'm sorry about your friends."

"Daddy, they're not my friends. I don't even really know Brenda and Rhonda. They catch a bad rap because of their brothers."

"You didn't practice with them over the summer?"

"No, Joanne and Bria told me to stay away from them because they are trouble, and look what happened."

"Yes, I did, but they also were trying to get their brothers to stop."

"Dad, please don't try to play hero to them. Please."

"You don't want me to help?"

"Dad, I want you to be my dad, to be here for me."

Rob paused. "Okay, I can do that. I will do that. I promise you. I love you, Genny. Is your mother up yet?"

"Of course. I had to tell her what happened. I didn't tell her about everything at the Boys' Club, just that they had tried to get loud with you, and she didn't even flinch. She said you were the wrong one to mess with, and you know how to take care of yourself. Then, she laughed and said she would have loved to be a fly on the wall."

"Is that what she said?"

"Yes, those were her exact words."

"Alright, thanks for letting me know. I'll talk to your mother later on. And Genny......."

"Yes?" Genny asked.

"I love you. I would lose it if anything happened to you. Please, always, always without exception do what I ask you to do. Can you do that for me, daughter?"

"Yes, dad, I can. And I love you, too. Thank you for protecting us."

Father and daughter hung up the phone. It was unfortunate that it took such extreme circumstances to restore their communication and relationship, but the violence also helped them to appreciate that time was precious. So Genny happily committed to spending time with her dad and Papi on the weekends.

The shooting was front page news for a few days, and the city imposed a 7pm curfew for all youth, which lasted one week. It quieted the tension in the city and allowed the police and sheriff's office to scour the neighborhoods for leads. It was commonly accepted, however, that even if there had been an eyewitness that night, no one would come forward. The only lead the police had was a black Jeep fleeing the scene, and black Jeeps were a dime a dozen in and around Addington Park.

Dante's funeral was held at a small, Baptist church in Addington Park at 4pm the following Wednesday. It was well attended, and Genny, Joanne and Bria were present with the other members of the APHS Girls' Basketball Team to show their support. The Miller family sat in the first row of seats on the right, and after the girls viewed Dante's lifeless body in the black coffin adorned with orange, purple, white, and (ironically) pink roses, they embraced Brenda and Rhonda. Gone was the bravado and toughness, and in its place was a "please help us" look in the eyes of two deer caught in headlights struggling to hold back tears. This bitter reminder of how powerless they were against the "sovereign will of a God who had called His son home," as the Reverend eulogized, broke the arrogance of the twins. Their heads were low, their voices were soft, and dressed in black dresses and low pumps, their resemblance was unmistakably female. They even sat with their legs crossed. Rhonda's hair was in soft pin curls, and Brenda had pinned her long dreads atop her head. The fear in their eyes was masked with their muffled "We're good, thanks," remarks, but Genny could smell fear, having been trained under the auspices of her father to detect the same for years.

Their Aunt and several other members of the family, presumably, hugged the girls and thanked them for coming. None of the other family members appeared to be visibly upset, Joanne remarked as they took their seats several rows back, but Bria offered that their family was so familiar with death, maybe they had become immune to it.

The service lasted a little more than one hour, and few people showed any emotion until there was a final viewing of Dante's body at the conclusion. Brenda and Rhonda, who appeared to be trying to maintain their strength and composure, both cried hysterically and hugged their brother's coffin until several ushers attended to them and helped them to their seats. That was the catalyst for the entire family, and finally, they eased up and allowed their tears to flow. There were no longer any attempts to remain strong and hard – death had come knocking, and it took Dante, as notorious and powerful on the streets as he may have been, home.

The Miller girls didn't come to school for several days after the funeral, and when they returned, there was a complete change in them both. They seemed withdrawn to some of the other students, but to the girls on the basketball team, they were simply humbled. Ashes to ashes and dust to dust was a solemn reminder that there was a God in heaven who was in control, and neither twin wanted to bury another relative again anytime soon, so each privately vowed to the other to change her ways.

The Miller family found little consolation in the residents of the neighborhood for many felt that Dante's violent end, considering his choice of lifestyle, was inevitable. The mixed opinions only further divided their community.

It didn't take long for school to return to normal. Grief counselors, curfews and police presence died down. It was amazing how soon after the funeral was over, Dante seemed to have been forgotten. Kasheem was still in the hospital with a bullet lodged in his spine, and the report was that he suffered paralysis and would be confined to a wheelchair for the rest of his life.

Basketball tryouts were scheduled the following week. After two grueling days, the roster of varsity basketball players was posted on the door to the Athletic Director's office. Genny waited with Joanne and Bria behind the upperclassmen on that November afternoon, and they were all delighted to see their names in bold letters. Genny Henderson, freshman, would start as the point guard; Joanne Hicks would start as shooting guard; and Brianna Mitchell was selected to start as power forward. Rhonda Miller and Brenda Miller were the other two starting players, but Coach Milton knew of the incident at the Boys' and Girls' Club in October, so he suspended them for the first five games. Brenda quit the team, but Rhonda stayed.

The girls' first scrimmage was scheduled for November 16th, and it was an easy, unofficial win. Coach Milton was impressed with the conditioning of the girls, and he thanked Mr. Henderson, who attended with Maria and Papi, for his support and assistance.

Their season officially started, and they were now expected to come to practices every day after school. The laps around the gym and suicides came easy to the three, and Joanne finally appreciated the method to Mr. Henderson's madness. The girls' first home game in an empty gymnasium was on November 19th, and they won easily, 52 – 29. After their game, the boys were scheduled to play, and the gymnasium filled up with high school students and visitors from both teams. When the fans weren't rooting for their favorite players, they were cheering with the cheerleaders, whose boisterous chants filled the gymnasium and brought the games to life.

"Why don't we have cheerleaders?" Genny asked. She sat in the bleachers with her family, Joanne and Bria.

"Girls don't get cheerleaders, Genny," Joanne answered.

Although the Henderson Family noticed the disparity in attendance between the girls and boys games, they didn't say anything.

When Brenda Miller recognized Genny's dad, she and her sister, Rhonda, came over to him and apologized for the incident at the Club in October. He told them it wasn't necessary, but they insisted, and Rhonda nearly broke down. Mrs. Henderson hugged the girls, and Rhonda and Brenda both told Genny how lucky she was to have her mother and father. The twins' mother had passed, they hadn't seen their dad in years, and they and their brothers had been staying with their aunt and her boyfriend. Mr. Henderson, always the community-minded man, listened to their story and had a brilliant idea. He offered to host a Thanksgiving Day Dinner at his Center for the Miller family. He and Maria used to host different community events there, and as long as she would agree to help, they could pull it together in one week. Brenda and Rhonda weren't really receptive to the idea, however, because they didn't like the whole "community" feel, which made them feel like charity. So he discussed different options with Maria to somehow make it happen, knowing that she would not refuse an opportunity to be a blessing to others during her favorite time of year.

"We need to do something," Mr. Henderson said. He was manipulating her, but his intentions were good.

It was decided that they would host a Thanksgiving Dinner for the Homeless at 4 pm, and the Miller family along with the young men Mr. Henderson worked with at his Center would be asked to come and assist at the event.

"That's great," Maria said. "It would help them to be a blessing to others who are less fortunate than they are."

"Lord, please give me the strength to do this," Maria prayed silently. *"Have your way. I know he is playing games, but have your way, Lord. In Jesus' name."*

Mr. Henderson gave his ex-wife full reign and authority to work the event however she saw fit. This would ensure her participation, but he also did so to keep tabs on her.

They were both excited to be working on an event at the Center again. Maria knew exactly what she would cook, who she would call for help, and how she would arrange the first floor of the Center to accommodate the anticipated guests. Mr. Henderson had some money in the budget for his non-profit to purchase supplies, and he readily handed over the organization's credit card so that Maria could go shopping and get whatever was needed. Joanne and Bria offered to help, and Genny was thrilled to have her mother and father again, just like it used to be.

The Henderson family got ready to leave during the fourth quarter of the boys' game. The score was 58-31, APHS down 27 points.

"We have to do something to get people to come to our games," Genny said.

"Don't worry about people coming, Genny. Focus on playing well," said Mr. Henderson.

"I know, but it doesn't make any sense that people come out to see the boys lose. We win, and no one supports us. There has to be something we can do," Genny said.

"Do you think you will play any better if people are in these bleachers?" he asked.

Genny paused.

"Just play your game. Don't worry about who comes and who doesn't come. Your mother and I support you. Your coaches and your teammates support you. That's all you need."

Rolling her eyes, Genny thought, *"That's such a typical parental answer."*

Just then, the crowd went wild for Chris Walker who dunked on an opposing player. He hung on the rim for a second and then released his grip, landing squarely on his feet with a huge grin on his face. His teammates high-fived him as the referee blew his whistle and called a foul on the defendant.

"Shooting one!" the referee yelled above the crowd.

"Did you see that?" Genny asked.

"Yes, I did," said Mr. Henderson.

"The boys are losing by almost 30 points. Chris dunks, and the crowd goes crazy. That's all it takes? I bet if I dunked in a game, people would come and support *us*."

Her dad, mom, brother, Joanne and Bria all laughed.

"I'm serious. I think I'm going to dunk in one of our games," Genny repeated.

Everyone continued laughing. *"You can laugh all you want to,"* Genny thought, *"but I am going to dunk in one of our games. That will get people to support us."*

"C'mon, let's go home," Mr. Henderson said.

They said goodbye to the other girls on the team and left the gymnasium. Both Mr. and Mrs. Henderson's cars were parked just in front of the school, and Mrs. Henderson would be dropping off Joanne and Bria. The girls climbed into their mother's mid-size Toyota, and Mr. and Mrs. Henderson talked briefly before he went to his parked car, just a few feet away, alone. His cell phone had been on vibrate, and there were several missed calls from Sophia.

As Maria pulled off in her car, Rob sat in the driver's seat and watched his family. If they were together, he would take them out to dinner to celebrate the start of the season. He missed his family, and there was a longing in his soul to go after the blue Toyota that was fading in the distance in front of other vehicles. To compensate for his guilt, he reminded and convinced himself that *"this situation is just temporary."* He still needed to take care of some business with Sophia. The deadline for submission of mayoral candidates was March, just a few months away, and he would need her in his corner so she could approve some city contracts for his businesses. So Rob returned Sophia's call and promised instead to stop by her oceanfront condominium on Beach Avenue and spend some time with her.

For Maria and Genny, who were starting to believe that their dad might be changing after all, there was a lot of work to do in the next week. Mom's to do list would include shop, cook, invite, promote, arrange staff and stay within the budget. Genny's to do list would include learn how to fly in the air like Mike, learn how to dunk, learn how to hang on the rim and be the first girl in the history of Addington Park High School girls' basketball to dunk on her opponent during a high school basketball game.

"I'm going to dunk on somebody," Genny said to Joanne and Bria. The three were seated in the back, and Papi was dozing off in the front passenger seat.

Joanne and Bria laughed again.

"Okay, Genny, dare to dream," Joanne said.

"Well, you know I like the way Genny thinks, Joanne," said Bria, "so if you want to dunk on somebody, we'll both help you."

The girls laughed together at what they thought the look on everyone's faces would be if they actually pulled this off, and Genny asked them not to speak of it to anyone. She wanted it to be a surprise when they did this in a game. They were all sworn to secrecy, and Genny was responsible for putting everything together and making it happen.

After Maria dropped Joanne and Bria off, Maria drove her children home. She carried Papi, who had dozed off on the ride home, into their house, and Genny ran inside and searched the internet for sites that would teach her how, at just 5'8", she could, in fact, dunk the ball. She turned the lamp off in her room and sat on her bed with the light from her laptop radiating a small fluorescent glow. Genny delved into a facet of the sport dominated by young men. Although she didn't find one site where women were represented, she was convinced and determined. She didn't have six to eight months as one site suggested, so she prayed that the Lord would help her within two months. Then, Genny fell asleep staring into the computer screen, dreaming of the cheerleaders and support her school, coaches and team would receive once she soared above the rim like Jordan.

Chapter Eighteen
The Henderson Family

Maria had solicited a few friends to help her at the Thanksgiving Day Dinner for the Homeless. Neicy and Tony would meet her there as well as Pam, Evan and Denise (another friend from high school who was also a social worker). Denise was an excellent cook, and Pam would prove to be a personable hostess. The Miller family respectfully declined the invitation but had sent some deserts. Mother Wright had graciously offered to provide her famous homemade sweet potato pie and bread pudding, and several of the women from Holy Tabernacle offered to volunteer serving guests and help with clean up. Rob arranged for a couple of his friends to come, so there were plenty of hands on deck, and the word was out that his Center would be serving dinner. Local shelters notified their residents, and the turnout was expected to be about 40 persons.

Maria gave instructions to Genny, Joanne and Bria for table and chair setup as well as holiday place settings and centerpieces - gold faux pumpkins neatly arranged with pinecones and burlap leaves. The orange, brown and green décor was a festive display of wreaths, acorns and leaves along with scented candles in wrought iron sconces Maria had purchased from a garage sale last year. They adorned the walls of the Center's foyer, and the two small wooden end tables were paired with hurricane lamps, vases and stemware filled with nuts and ivory pillar candles. Four folding tables dressed with bone linen tablecloths were rented and arranged in the Center's foyer for adults. Ten chairs with padded seat cushions tied in the rear surrounded each table. The first floor conference room was set up with two long tables and eighteen folding chairs for young people. Classic R&B music played softly, and every now and then one of the adults would turn up the music and say *"That's my jam!"*

"Do you think it's too much, maybe too elegant?" Denise asked Maria.

"No, not at all. We show the same love and attention to all our guests. Every person who walks in this door tonight is a human being who is worthy of our respect, and everyone is to be treated with dignity."

"Girl, don't get Maria preaching," Neicy interrupted as she walked into the foyer and surveyed the decorations. "Maria can preach, now. She got that burnin'.'"

The three ladies laughed. Pam entered the foyer and commented that everything looked beautiful. She thanked Maria for her care and attention.

"Ladies," Neicy began, "let's pray before we start. It's only 3:15, we have some time."

"Okay, that's a great idea," Maria said. She asked for everyone to come into the foyer, and they all gathered inside and formed a circle, bowing their heads in prayer. Neicy and Maria would lead the prayer, and as they began, Rob and a few of his friends came into the front door.

"Hey, look who's here! It's the man himself," said Pam. "Long time no see."

Rob surveyed the atmosphere of his Center that had been completely transformed. The vision in his mind was now manifest. Maria had such a flair for details, she completely encapsulated his words and birthed yet again his vision with such effortless ease that Rob nearly regretted abandoning his family. Maria was holding hands with their children and was there because he asked her to be. She was doing this because he pleaded for her support. She had arranged, cooked, designed and committed 110 percent to his vision again because he had manipulated her into doing this for his benefit. The social media pages and local newspaper promoted the event as:

"Robert J. Henderson Center for Young Men Serves the Community at 1st Annual Thanksgiving Day Dinner"

This event would make Robert J. Henderson look good, and Rob, deep down inside, knew it. It was good press for him, and he needed to keep up his positive image, even at Maria's expense. She would do whatever he asked, but he knew how to use her to get what he wanted without her knowing that he was just using her.

Rob wanted to smile and encourage everyone else at the Center, but there was a heavy presence about his soul that made him uncomfortable in his own skin. A large, oval framed mirror hung on the wall as you came into the foyer, and as many times before as he came in and out of his Center, he never took notice of that mirror like he did now. The presence about him forced him to look at his reflection, and for the first time, he could see his egomaniacal haughtiness, pride, avarice and cowardice staring back at him. They were an inner ugly breaking the surface of his external good looks, charisma and expensive clothes. *"Could anyone see the real me?"* Rob wondered.

"Aren't you going to join us?" Maria asked.

"Yes, sure. Everything looks so nice in here. You did a great job. Thank you, everybody. Thank you for what you did," he answered.

"We appreciate what you are doing here, Rob. Thank you," Denise answered.

Rob joined the circle and took the hand of Maria on his right and Genny and Papi on his left. His friends joined in, and Maria and Neicy prayed.

Neicy thanked the Lord for blessing them to be a blessing to others. She thanked the Lord for everyone who had come and supported the dinner in any way, and she prayed that He would bless those who were coming that they might see Jesus in all of this.

Maria prayed the Lord's blessing on every soul, and she thanked Him for using them to minister to others. She thanked the

Lord for her family and then asked if everyone in the circle could thank God for one thing that they were grateful for. Each person spoke briefly, and by the time it was Rob's turn, he was silent. Maria looked at him and thought she saw a tear coming down his cheek. He said he was thankful for his wife, Maria, and his children, and he asked God to help him to be the best man he could be, in the name of Jesus. They lifted their heads and hugged one another, and although no one else may have noticed anything different about Rob, Maria knew that something was changing.

The music was turned up a little louder, and the ladies returned to the back office room where tables of food, cornucopias of edible goodness, were set up buffet style with burners.

The conference room for young people was turned into "a man cave" as Rob and his friends took over the room, and one of the men hooked up a flat screen television to watch the NFL pre-game shows.

"Oh Lord, no they didn't," Pam said. She noticed that Evan had made himself comfortable, too.

"Oh, let them be men," Neicy said. "We got this."

"Neicy, did you hear what Rob said?" Maria asked.

"Yes, of course."

"What do you think?" Maria asked.

"What do *you* think?" Neicy returned the question.

"I looked at him when he was praying. I think he was tearing."

"God is working on him. Let the Lord have his way."

"Amen."

The first guests arrived at 3:50 p.m. Denise was the perfect hostess, greeting the guests and making them feel welcome. She served tea and coffee and gave her card to help provide any additional services the guests might need. Rob shook hands and shared his own testimony with the guests to encourage them. Mike Love, Rob's personal barber, offered to give complimentary haircuts and shaves to the men at his shop during the week.

At 4:20 p.m., just as the sun was beginning to set, the announcement was made that dinner was ready to be served. They had about 30 guests, and any additional people who came would be welcome to have dinner when they showed up.

Sister Ramona, one of the volunteers from Holy Tabernacle, was chosen to pray again over the food. Then, the guests were asked to come up by table, and the ladies served huge helpings of roasted turkey, turkey gravy, cabbage, cornbread dressing, candied yams, mashed potatoes, garlic string beans, lima beans, collard greens, baked ham with pineapple, baked macaroni and cheese, seafood salad, rice, black eyed peas, smothered steak, corn pudding, potato salad and cranberry sauce. Bottles of fresh, spring water were in coolers of ice along with apple cider. Pam prepared pitchers of fresh squeezed lemonade.

The guests were all served, and several came up for seconds. The desert table was full of assorted pies, one pineapple upside down cake, one rum cake, bread pudding, rice pudding, banana pudding and peach cobbler.

Rob came into the foyer with Mike Love and his friends, and he asked Maria and the ladies to come from the back office and into the foyer for a few minutes. He wanted to personally thank each and every one of them for their help and support.

As the ladies joined the men, Rob and Maria's wedding song came on. Neicy and Pam clapped and coaxed the couple to dance, and Genny and Papi were delighted that their mother and father were together again in a positive, family environment. Rob asked Maria for a dance, and she agreed to the delight of their children.

Pam and Evan were in a loving embrace in the corner of the room, and Rob invited them to come onto the floor.

At the same time, Sophia was out front looking for a parking space. She hadn't officially been invited to the dinner, Rob had explained that it was business and he had to handle it himself, but she wanted to bring a ham she had cooked and a red velvet cake she purchased from a bakery the day before. There were hardly any parking spaces, so it must have been a good turnout for Rob, and she knew that would make him happy. She wouldn't stay long as she had promised her mother and father she would come to Pennsylvania that evening to visit. Rob was invited, and he promised that he would try to leave early so that he could make the drive there with her. It was only an hour away, and the time on her dashboard said 5:26. They could leave as late as 7:30 and still be fine.

She found a parking space nearly three blocks away. Before she got out of her car, she poured herself a cup of wine from the Merlot bottle she had packed for her parents. The third cup of wine that afternoon was soothing going down, and she needed it. A small glass of Hennessey Sophia drank earlier had given her some courage, but she was nervous about coming. The last time she showed up at the Center to surprise Rob, he made it worth her while, but he needed so much prompting that Sophia was questioning how genuine his feelings were for her.

Sophia checked her lipstick in the rearview mirror and tossed her shoulder-length hair. Then she took a breath mint from her purse and let it rest on her tongue. Satisfied with her appearance, she got out of the car and opened the back door to get the food.

A car with loud rap music pulled up and parked in the space behind her car, and Sophia turned to see about five young men inside. Recognizing them as the young men from the Center Rob always spoke about, she was glad to finally be able to meet them in person. Rob had told her about each one of them, and she felt like she already knew them. *"Isaiah, K'Shon, James, Jamarr, Eric and……. Marcus. Yeah, those are their names,"* she thought.

The young men got out of the car, and one of them came over to her, noticing that she had packages to carry, and offered to help.

"Here, let me help you with that. How do you do?" he extended his hand.

Sophia looked at the 6'0 tall, slender young man standing in front of her. He was either Marcus, James or Isaiah. He wore neat trousers with dress shoes, was well-groomed and had rushed ahead of everyone else to help her. He couldn't be James - James was the stylish one. From what Rob said, Marcus was his right hand man and the one the others looked up to, but this young man seemed too natural with his approach.

"Isaiah?" Sophia guessed.

"Yes, that's me. How do you know my name?"

"Hi, I'm Ms. Simmons. I'm a friend of Mr. Henderson's. I work in the Mayor's office, and he told me all about you. He told me about all of you. There are six, right?"

Five young men had exited the parked car behind her. They looked like players on a basketball team who were dressed nice because their coach told them to.

"Yes," Isaiah said. "James may show up later. He's still with his family."

"Well, it's nice to meet the five of you."

The young men shook her hand and greeted her respectfully, and Isaiah took the packages from her hands.

"I guess we're all going to the Center, huh?" she asked.

"That's right," Isaiah replied. "So you work in the Mayor's office?"

"Yes, I'm the Mayor's Assistant."

"That's cool," Isaiah replied, "after you." He allowed Sophia to walk ahead of him and couldn't help noticing her shapely figure underneath her fitted Shearling Coat that accentuated her small waist and rested flirtatiously on her curvaceous hips.

"Damn!" he said to his friends.

Marcus kept staring at Ms. Simmons, and when she turned her head to cross the street, he looked at her from the side and instantly recalled who she was.

"Yo, I mean, excuse me, what did you say your name was again?" Marcus asked.

Sophia turned to him and said, "Ms. Simmons. Do you know me?" she asked, noticing him staring at her.

"I know I've seen you before," he answered.

"Maybe it was at the high school. I was there recently for a speaker event. Duane Brownlee, the software designer. Were you there?"

"No, it's not that. You said you're a friend of Mr. Henderson's, right?" he asked.

"Well, yes, but this feels like you're interrogating me," she said playfully.

"Yeah, Marcus, what's up with that?" Isaiah asked.

Marcus knew who she was. This was the woman who was in Mr. Henderson's office during the summer. He had only told James and Isaiah about what he saw: Mr. Henderson reclined in his seat with some woman, who did not look like the wife in the picture, on her knees before him. His hands were pulling her hair, and Marcus got a quick look at her from the side. She was a lighter complexion than the woman in the photo. Marcus had closed the door quick and ran downstairs, letting himself unheard out the front door. When he called Isaiah that night to tell him, Isaiah cared less.

"He's a man, he works hard, and he's got a chick on the side, so what," was Isaiah's reply. In Isaiah's opinion, Mr. Henderson was entitled to that.

James, however, was less forgiving, calling their mentor fake and a hypocrite. He would, however, get everything he needed out of Mr. Henderson, including a letter of recommendation for college and the mention of this community service on his transcript. Did it change James' opinion of him? Yes. As their summer program came to an end, James' loss of respect for Mr. Henderson was demonstrated in his showing up late and not returning phone calls. Mr. Henderson asked the other young men if James was alright, and Marcus lied, covering up for him and blaming his behavior on some problems he was having at home. James was still awarded a Certificate of Completion at the end of the summer program, and he did come to the informal ceremony at the Center to receive it. He shook Mr. Henderson's hand and then left early, without joining him and the other young men for a young minister who was scheduled to appear and talk about, of all things, *"Living Your Sermon – How Your Life Should Resemble the Message You Preach."* The other young men all told James that the speaker was incredible, but he couldn't really receive it due to the hypocrisy Mr. Henderson continued to flaunt in front of them. James was convinced that Mr. Henderson held them to a higher moral standard than he, himself, maintained, and James was not one who you could front with. He kept it real, and in so doing, kept his distance, calling on Mr. Henderson only when and if he needed him.

"Nothing, I'm sorry, I guess it was at the school," he lied.

When they came to the Center, they stopped short as Sophia paused and looked inside. She saw Rob with his hand around the waist of "her," and the couple was in front of the room smiling, laughing and making a toast of some kind. Sophia stepped back, and all the young men except Isaiah went inside without noticing what it was that caused Sophia to stop so abruptly. They were engrossed in their own conversation, laughing and excited to be going inside to eat some hearty, home cooked food.

"Are you ok?" Isaiah asked. He paused behind her on the sidewalk in front of the Center.

"Yes, I'm fine. You know what, why don't you just take those things inside. I forgot something. I'll bring it back."

212

"Are you sure? You don't look too good. What's wrong?" Isaiah asked.

"Isaiah, thank you so much for your help. I'm fine."

"Well, you don't look fine. I mean, you look fine," he said bumbling over his words. "You're fine. You know you're fine. What am I saying? I'm saying, let me take these things inside, and then I'll walk you to your car. It's already dark out, and you shouldn't be walking on these streets by yourself. Can't you come inside and say hello?"

"No, I'd rather not, but I'll wait outside for you."

Sophia took a step back from the glass window and positioned herself against the neighboring red brick front building. From the angle where she stood, she could still see inside.

Isaiah hurried in and was greeted by Maria and Rob, who hugged him and appeared to be scolding him for showing up so late. Maria pointed him in the direction of a back room where he should take the packages, and Rob continued talking to his guests, who were shaking his hand. Sophia figured that the two children by their side must be Genny and Papi, and they looked like a happy family celebrating Thanksgiving together.

"I can't do this anymore," Sophia said to herself. She turned and walked away, and Isaiah hurried out the front door to walk with her.

"I'm sorry if I took too long. I haven't seen Mrs. Henderson in a while."

"Mrs. Henderson?" Sophia thought.

Sophia was quiet and walked quickly to her car. Isaiah was struggling to keep up. She looked upset, and he didn't know what to say to her, so he was quiet. When they got to her car, she fumbled for her keys and in so doing dropped them onto the street. Isaiah picked them up for her and opened her car door. She plopped down inside and cupped her face in her hands. He noticed the open wine bottle in the passenger seat and empty cup.

"Were you drinking and driving Ms. Simmons?" Isaiah asked.

"Isaiah, please, are you a cop now?" she asked. She poured herself another cup of wine and drank it without stopping.

"I can drive you home," he offered.

"I don't need you to drive me home. I don't need you to do anything for me, thank you."

"Ms. Simmons," Isaiah said, noticing that she was trying to turn her ignition on without realizing that there was no key *in* the ignition, "please get up. I will drive you. You are a little tipsy."

"I'm fine."

"No, you aren't. Please let me drive you. I have a license."

"You do? Who gave you a license?" she asked laughing. "Did Mr. Henderson give you a driver's license?" Then she took the bottle of Merlot and drank from it. Isaiah tried to pull it away, but she pushed his hand and drank several gulps before getting out of the car and spilling some on her coat.

"You see what you made me do, Isaiah?" she asked. She looked him in the eyes, and she was beautiful to him, tipsy and all. Her eyes were slightly red, and her full lips dripped with wine. She was intoxicating, and for a moment he thought about what any man with a woman that fine would think about. He shook off the temptation and walked to the other side of the car to open the door for her.

"You're such a gentleman, Isaiah. Did Rob teach you that?" she asked.

He ignored her, and after closing her door, walked over to the driver's side, climbed in and started the car. Pulling off, he asked "Where are we going?"

Sophia was hardly coherent, so he opened the glove compartment and pulled out her registration. Her name read Paulette Sophia Simmons, 1210 Oceanfront Condominiums, Beach Avenue, Addington Park. That was only 5 minutes away, so when he got Sophia back to her place, he would call one of his boys to come and pick him up. He also noticed her date of birth and figuring the subtraction, she was only 30 years old. Mr. Henderson was 17 years her senior. *"Damn!"* he thought to himself.

Isaiah parked Ms. Simmons' car in the parking garage of her condominium complex, and she told him she would introduce him to the security guard as her brother. They walked past the front desk and went to the elevators, going up to the 4th floor where her two bedroom, two bath luxury condominium with a sprawling ocean view was situated.

214

"Wow, this is beautiful," Isaiah said as he helped Ms. Simmons inside. "I've never been in here before. Mr. Henderson takes us to beautiful homes, but he never brought us here."

"I don't know why not," Sophia answered, "he has a key. He could bring you here anytime."

Sophia took off her coat and was wearing a form-fitting blue dress with blue heels that had straps tied around her ankles. He was trying not to notice, but "*Damn*," he thought, "*she was bad.*"

"Do you know Mrs. Henderson?" Isaiah asked, needing to change the subject so that he could focus on something else.

"Are you uncomfortable here, Isaiah?" Sophia asked, completely ignoring his question. *She* needed to change the subject. "You don't have to be uncomfortable with me, I'm not going to bite you. Come sit down."

Sophia sat down on the loveseat in her living room rather than the larger couch. There was a beautiful black grand piano in the middle of the room, and he instead went to sit down on the piano bench.

"Do you play?" she asked.

"Yes, I can play a little," he said.

"What do you mean, *'a little'*? Either you can play or you can't. Well, play a little for me. Would you do that, Isaiah?" she asked.

Isaiah sat down and played some basic chords for a few minutes. She was so out of it, she wasn't really paying attention, and that was just as well. He needed to leave.

Standing up and adjusting his coat, he said, "Ms. Simmons, I'm going to be heading out. I'm glad you made it back safe....Ms. Simmons? Ms. Simmons?" he asked.

She didn't respond.

"Ms. Simmons?"

Isaiah walked over to her. She was snoring lightly on the loveseat. "Ms. Simmons?" he asked.

"Yes," she answered groggily.

"Ms. Simmons, I'm going to be leaving now, okay? Are you okay? Do you need anything before I go?"

"No, thank you. Well, wait. Could you go into the bedroom and just grab a blanket for me off the bed, please."

"Okay, sure."

He found his way down the long corridor into a bedroom where there was a huge queen size canopy bed in heavy cherry wood. A matching night stand was on each side of the bed, and a bedside bench was at the foot with a silk red negligee folded neatly on top. Isaiah lifted the negligee and admired it for a moment along with the rest of the bedroom, which to him looked like the chambers of a Queen. Gold and purple curtains tied back with sheer bone panels gracefully decorated the windows, and a beautiful crystal chandelier hung from the ceiling. The carpet was so thick, Isaiah thought he was sinking into it with every step he took.

The only blanket Isaiah saw was the one on the bed, which was tucked in tight at every corner. There were about ten pillows – neck rolls, heart-shaped, and square-shaped with fringe borders and tassels completing the elegant palace feel of her private boudoir. He pulled the blanket off, also pulling the sheets with it, so he tried to fix the sheets as they were. As he did so, he heard someone come into the room, and he turned and saw Sophia standing in the doorway.

"Ms. Simmons?" he asked.

She walked over to him and turned around, lifting her shoulder length hair with one hand and pulling it over her right shoulder.

"Would you unzip my dress, please?"

Isaiah paused. He didn't move. Sensing his nervous energy, she repeated the question.

"Ms. Simmons, I don't think….."

"Isaiah, I can't do it myself. If you're uncomfortable, it's fine. Can you just unzip it a little, please? I can do the rest."

Isaiah took a deep breath and with two shaking hands, he unzipped the back of her dress as far as it would go, to the middle of her back. He saw a pink lace bra on soft, delicate skin that looked like it had never been touched.

Sophia turned to face him and asked if he was okay. Isaiah cleared his throat and assured her that he was, but she knew better.

"Have you ever been with a woman, Isaiah?"

"Um, sure."

"A woman, Isaiah. Not a girl. There's a difference. And I'm sure that a handsome young man like yourself could have whoever he wants."

Isaiah's breathing pattern was changing, and he turned away from Sophia to avoid eye contact.

"Ms. Simmons," he said nervously, "I'm going to go now. You're a friend of Mr. Henderson's, and he is a friend of mine. I can't do anything to jeopardize my relationship with him. You are a beautiful lady," he said, still looking away, "and if the circumstances were different, I would love to spend some time with you. I'm sorry, I can't. I won't."

"Okay," Sophia said. She stepped out of her dress with nothing but her pink bra, thong and heels. "I'll show you out, Isaiah. I'm sorry."

"That's okay. It's cool," Isaiah said. He breathed a sigh of relief and turned around to see Sophia walking out of the bedroom and down the long corridor. *"Oh my God,"* he said to himself. She was about 5'8" with her heels on, and her long, caramel-colored legs were perfectly tone. Her calves popped like two rocks, and her quadriceps pulsated with each step. *"Damn!"* he said under his breath. She was a perfect hour glass. Isaiah stood in the same spot, mesmerized, and completely intoxicated by her.

Sophia peered around the corner and startled Isaiah, asking him if he was alright. A small grin appeared on her face.

When he didn't answer, she said "I'm sorry. Isaiah, the front door is open. You can walk out, I won't bother you."

Isaiah turned around again, facing the huge bay windows with a clear, panoramic view of the Atlantic Ocean. He was convinced that if he just walked out of the condominium, without looking at Sophia, he would be okay. He walked quickly down the long corridor and into the living room, where the front door was open and Sophia was standing next to it. He tried not to look, but his eyes had a mind of their own and his lower body a brain. Her lace bra was so thin, he could see through it. Her stomach was flat and tone, boasting a gold hoop naval ring. She resembled a prize thoroughbred. A thin gold necklace was around her neck, and Isaiah noticed that there was no wedding ring on her finger. She was wearing a thin pearl bracelet on her left wrist, and the pearl studs in her ears looked like they completed a set.

"Goodnight, Isaiah," Sophia said.

"Is she so confident I will leave?" Isaiah asked himself. He reminded himself that this was a grown woman, not the young girls he was used to and could easily manipulate to get what he wanted. *"She knows what she is doing,"* Isaiah thought. *"She got me up here pretending to be drunk and now here she is half naked in front of me, and she's saying goodnight. This woman has game."*

"Goodnight," Isaiah said, walking to the door.

"I'm not playing this game with you," he said to himself. He knew better. He played girls, they didn't play him. He got as far as the entranceway, pausing for a moment, and then he closed the door softly with his right hand. He stood next to Sophia and turned to her, allured by her beauty and the intoxicating aroma of her feminine scent. She made eye contact with him, and he leaned in to give her a kiss. The wine on her lips was sweet and the perfume on her neck inviting. He kissed the silky smooth skin of her neck and shoulders, and she held him tightly.

"Well, if she's gonna give it to me," he said to himself, justifying what he was about to do next.

Isaiah was a man, too, and he knew that her being a "friend" of Mr. Henderson's meant more than that. Just the way she said it implied that their relationship included benefits. Besides, a woman this fine? How could any man be just friends with her? Mr. Henderson did have a wife, so he couldn't really say anything, but Sophia hardly knew Isaiah. She had already given him a private strip tease. He knew he could get the lap dance, and he didn't even have to flash any money. The alcohol may have clouded her judgment, somewhat, but this was too easy. He would play her game, but his plan was to handle the business and put her to sleep. Then, he would leave, but he had to know what was up.

"Ms. Simmons, doesn't Mr. Henderson make you happy?" he asked. He continued kissing her shoulders and neck, not wanting to spoil the mood, but needing to hear something from her to convince him that he wasn't committing a gross act of disloyalty to his mentor.

"You don't need to be so formal with me. Rob has a wife. I am single. I can do what I want."

Sophia was tracing her long nails into the curve of Isaiah's spine. She had a point there.

"Well, you don't know me at all. Why me?" he asked.

"Isaiah, I know all about you. Rob told me about you. I've always wanted to meet you, but whenever I would come around the Center, he would ask me to leave."

"Oh really?"

"Yes. I'm a grown woman, Isaiah. I can do whatever I want. You're a grown man, and so can you."

"I'm not grown yet," Isaiah said.

"Oh, yes you are," Sophia replied, pressing her body into his and arousing him even more.

Entranced by her seduction and completely captivated by her spell, Isaiah took her by the hand into the private chamber of her bedroom and laid her gently on the bed. He would stay for the next hour, fascinated by the game she was playing with him and enjoying every moment with the flirtatiously intoxicating Paulette S. Simmons, the "S" stands for "Sophia."

Back at the Center, Pam and Neicy were interrogating Marcus and the other young men.

"Where is she?" Pam asked. "Why couldn't she come in?"

"I don't know," Marcus said. "She gave Isaiah the food and then he went to walk her to her car."

"That's not like her. She knows she has to keep her appearances at these events. That is just downright rude," said Pam.

Pam went to ask Maria about the invitation to the Mayor's office, and she told her that the Assistant, Paulette Simmons, had stopped by but didn't come in.

"Well, that's okay, it is Thanksgiving. Maybe she had other stops to make. At least she dropped something off."

Not satisfied, Pam went to ask Rob about the invitation. He was in the temporary "man cave" watching the game with all of the men.

"Rob, can I see you for a minute?" Pam asked.

"Sure." Rob got up from his seat and the room full of men cheering and insulting the two teams who were playing to the delight of fans everywhere. He was wearing a Giants jersey and blue jeans, a much different look from his suits and ties, but he was still incredibly striking in appearance.

"What's up?" he asked, joining Pam in the hallway. The music was playing, and a couple of the women could be heard saying "That's my jam!" as another classic R&B song came on.

"The Mayor's office came by and dropped off some food. They didn't stay. Didn't you extend an invitation?" Pam asked. She was nosy and suspicious, and Rob knew it, so he didn't engage her.

"Of course, we did, and that's great. Is that all you wanted to know, Pam?" he asked.

"Yes, I just think it was rude of Ms. Simmons not to come inside and join us. She represents the Mayor's office, you know, and the guests here could take that as a slight. This is not a drive-thru community event."

"Ms. Simmons came by?" he asked.

"Yes."

Avoiding her prying, he said, "Well, you're right, she should have come in. That sends a bad message. Thanks, Pam, I'll take care of it."

"Oh, okay. I'm just saying."

Just then Marcus walked into the hallway. He looked at Mr. Henderson and then rolled his eyes and looked away.

"Marcus, are you okay?" Mr. Henderson asked.

"Yup. I think we're going to leave now. Thanks for having us."

"Okay, if you have to. Excuse me, Pam, I need to say goodnight to everyone. Thanks for the heads up."

"Sure," Pam answered. She returned to the foyer where Maria and the other women were clearing off the tables.

"Um, James didn't make it," Marcus said. "He had to be with his family. Everyone else is here except for Isaiah. He walked Ms. Simmons to her car over an hour ago and hasn't come back."

Mr. Henderson took a deep breath and then exhaled through his nose. Marcus knew what that meant. Mr. Henderson was upset and thinking of what to say.

"What's wrong, Mr. Henderson? Can't Isaiah walk Ms. Simmons to her car?"

"Marcus, what are you trying to say?" Mr. Henderson asked.

"Nothing, you look like you're upset about that is all."

Rob refused to discuss it further. He shook Marcus' hand and said goodnight. The other young men came into the hallway and thanked Mr. Henderson for the dinner.

Rob went upstairs into his office and called Sophia from his cell phone. There was no answer. He called two more times, but there was still no answer. He went downstairs and told everyone that he was leaving and would be right back. As he went into the office where the food and women were, he overheard Pam telling Neicy and Maria that Paulette Simmons had dropped off some food and did not come in, and that Isaiah had walked her to her car over an hour ago but had not come back. Pam looked on her phone on the City website and there saw photos and a roster of city employees. She exclaimed that "Paulette Simmons" was "Paulette S. Simmons." That "S" had to stand for "Sophia," and this had to be the woman Rob was seeing.

Rob paused in the hallway, and he did not know what to say. He bumped against a table, knocking over a vase, and Maria came into the hallway, seeing him slouched over and trying to pick up the vase and return it to the table without being heard.

"You brought that woman here?" Maria asked.

"Maria, it's not what you think. I didn't bring anybody. I didn't invite her."

"Is that who Sophia is, Rob? Paulette S. Simmons, the Assistant to the Mayor of this City? The 'S' stands for Sophia? I should have known that you would call her by another name. Her 'S' stands for something just like your 'J' stands for something. Maybe the 'S' is for 'slut,' and the 'J' is for 'jackass.' Is she the one you left me and your children for?"

Maria didn't look angry. That would have made it easier for Rob. He could deal with her being upset and cussing him out. He knew how to deflect and diffuse Maria's temperaments, but she didn't look angry at all. She looked hurt and disappointed, and he knew that it was because of him. He didn't know how to turn that around on her. A surge of guilt rushed over him, and he was at a loss of words.

"You invited her here, Rob, as if she's a part of our family? Have you lost your mind?" she asked.

"Maria, it's not what you think. I promise you. It's not what you think."

He picked up the vase and returned it to the table, stepping forward to hold her hand and try to salvage whatever he could of their fragile relationship.

"Please go, Rob. Just go. Get out. Go," Maria said calmly.

"Maria, please," Rob said, "I promise you…"

"Get your hands off of me. Don't touch me!" Maria screamed. "I am so sick and tired of your lies."

Neicy and Pam came out of the office and stared at the couple. Humiliated, Rob turned and walked into the room where the men were, assuring them that everything was ok, and it was time to leave. They all gathered their things and left, one by one, until there was no one remaining except Maria and her children, Neicy, Pam and Denise.

None of the ladies said a word as they cleaned up. Maria assured them that she was okay, and when they had finished, all of the ladies took a few trays of food to their cars parked right in front of the Center. Maria locked up, and she and her kids went home.

Rob drove over to Sophia's condominium and parked his car in the garage next to hers. He walked up to the fourth story condominium and let himself in. He surveyed the condo, and nothing looked out of place.

"Sophia! Sophia!" he yelled, as he walked through each room.

There were no dishes or glasses on any of the coffee tables, and the second bedroom looked untouched. It was almost 7:30 p.m., nearly too late to go to her parents' house, and that was just as well because he didn't really feel up to it. He walked into Sophia's bedroom where she was lying under the covers fast asleep. Rob lifted the covers to see that she had a nightgown on, and he smelled her breath, which smelled like wine.

"She probably had too much to drink," he thought to himself, *"and fell asleep."*

222

Her dress was draped across a chair by her vanity, and her shoes were underneath.

Confident that nothing out of the ordinary had happened, Rob kissed Sophia softly on the cheek and went into the first bathroom to relieve himself. As he lifted the toilet seat, he saw a telltale sign that another man had been there: on the sink countertop was a used, wet washcloth thrown haphazardly on top of the neatly folded hand towels she always kept for him.

Chapter Nineteen

Maria

There were only three members at the Intercessory Prayer Group on the following Thursday evening: Mother Wright, Maria and Denise. Mother Wright didn't mind, quoting the Scripture that said where two or three were gathered in the name of Jesus, He was right there in the midst of them.[81]

The Bible Study for that night had been cancelled, and Mother Wright insisted that one of the Deacons open the church for their Intercessory Prayer. The leadership knew better than to question or oppose the Pastor's Mother, so Deacon Tony came over to open and close the church. He prayed with the three women, and once they finished their prayer, Mother Wright asked to see Maria privately for a few minutes. Everyone else left the sanctuary, and Deacon Tony agreed to wait for as long as they needed him to in the Church Office.

"How are you doing, baby?" said Mother Wright as she and Maria sat down in the first pew of the Sanctuary.

"I'm blessed and highly favored," Maria said, repeating the phrase Mother Wright so often used.

"Hallelujah. Isn't God good?" Mother Wright asked.

Mother Wright was comfortably dressed in a pair of blue jeans with a white turtleneck and black sweater. There was little makeup on the face before Maria, some 85 years Reverend Wright bragged, and hardly a flaw or blemish that would warrant the use of any. Mother's skin was the color of brown sugar, a cocoa brown that needed no foundation. She stood only about 5'3" tall, but even when she was seated there was a tall, godly presence about her that commanded respect. Her hair was slightly thin in the crown area, but it was styled with big, loose curls that to a less discerning eye would hardly be apparent.

"Yes, all the time," answered Maria.

"Amen. You're getting it. How are your classes going?"

"I love them, Mother. Right now we're studying The Life and Times of Jesus Christ, and I have another class on The Life of David. I love the Word and the assignments. The teachers are thorough and easy to understand."

"Praise God. Listen, we're having a Women's Day service in March, and I would like your help in organizing it since you are the Liaison for the Women's Ministry. Can you help out?"

"Of course, Mother. I would love to."

"Oh, thank you so much," Mother said, lifting and folding her hands as if she was about to pray. "Hallelujah. We always have a blessed time. I'll be working with you on the speaker and invitation letters for the other churches, but what I really want to talk to you about is something else the Lord put on my heart. Listen," she began, turning towards Maria to look directly at her. "We all have steps that the Lord has ordained for us to walk in, lanes that we are anointed to stay in. Have you ever heard the expression 'stay in your lane'?"

"Yes."

"You are on a path right now with Jesus, Maria, and He has put you on my heart for a reason. As soon as you start living for Jesus, you better believe the devil is going to try and put some distractions in your lane, in your path, to distract you and try to get you to give up in your faith. Jesus was tempted in the wilderness by the enemy, and the enemy's purpose was to take Jesus off the path of humiliation and suffering. '*Jesus didn't have to suffer,*' the enemy tried to reason with Him. '*He was God. He could turn the stones into bread if He wanted to. He could have all the kingdoms of the earth if He would get out of His lane and into the devil's. If He did things the devil's way.*' [82] You see, Maria, that expression, 'stay in your lane,' isn't always a negative expression. No, it is meant for our good. I believe the Lord has sent me here tonight to give you this very word: Stay in your lane. Don't be frustrated about anything that is going on around you, on the left or on the right. You have a high calling on your life, and the Lord is with you. He is going to use you here in a mighty way, but there will be obstacles in your path. Pray always, Maria.[83] Keep your focus on Jesus, and look ahead, not behind or around you. Pray for your enemies, yes, most especially, pray for your enemies. The wrath of your enemies will give God praise.[84] Don't let it consume you, whatever you're going through. Pray and praise God through it." Mother Wright stopped abruptly. "Ride or die? Who's driving that man's car?"

Maria was puzzled, and her expression clearly showed that to Mother Wright.

"You know who I'm talking about," Mother Wright said. She placed her right hand on her hip, almost daring Maria to feign any ignorance.

Maria appreciated the maternal approach and smiled. "Well, I honestly don't know, Mother."

Mother Wright relaxed in her seat, and placed both of her hands on her knees. "Praise God, you're being honest with me, but let me share something with you. Don't ride in that man's car. He's not letting Jesus drive right now. If we ride without Jesus, we might as well die - we can't do nothing or go nowhere without Him. Stay in your own lane with Jesus, and let Jesus take the wheel and direct your path. When that man gives up the wheel to Jesus, and he will, God will steer him into what He has for him."

Mother sat back in her seat and folded her hands across her lap. "Thank you, Jesus. Bless your name."

"Thank you, Mother, I receive everything you said. Thank you so much."

Maria leaned over and gave Mother a hug, and as she did, she felt Mother Wright hold her tightly and ask her if there was anything she wanted to talk about. Maria leaned back and said yes, sharing with her in confidence what had been going on with her and Rob. She told Mother that she had found out who the woman was he divorced her for, and although she wanted to be angry and upset, she wasn't any longer. She was hurt, yes, but she had given it to God and was trusting Him completely for whatever His will was.

"Amen. He is a son, and God is working on him. He will never leave or forsake His own.[85] Pray for him, Maria. Pray for the other woman. And, keep yourself and your children covered in prayer. Until he gives Jesus the wheel, he's going to be driving all over the place looking for something loose, fast and easy to make him happy for the moment. You know what I'm saying."

Then, Mother looked directly at Maria and said "As long as he's in his flesh and driving the car himself, he'll make stops at every other street corner looking for some temporary satisfaction. When he makes Jesus Lord, and he will, that car will stay parked where it belongs. But not until then. Pray, Maria. This too shall pass."

The two women sat in the empty sanctuary in silence for a few awkward moments before Maria replied, "Thank you, Mother. I appreciate what you're saying, but I don't really care where he parks his car anymore. He already divorced me, and I did the best I could do."

Mother Wright smiled. "Yes, I am sure you did. But, have you forgiven him, Maria? And, would you wait for him while God works on him?"

Without any hesitation, Maria replied, "Yes, I have forgiven him, and yes, I am praying for him." Then, Maria paused and thought for a moment. Mother Wright knew she was searching for an answer, so she took a mint from her purse and offered one to Maria as if to fill in the silence between the two, which was only amplified by the huge sanctuary in which they sat. As Mother unwrapped the mint, Maria answered.

"Wait for him? For what? I will do what God wants, but I'm not sure I'm willing to accept that God wants me to wait for him. Is that what you're saying God is telling me? Rob committed adultery, and even God says in His word that adultery is grounds for divorce.[86] He's still seeing this other woman and lying to me about it. I deserve someone who loves, respects and honors me. With all due respect, Mother, I'm a good woman, and I know it."

Tenderly, Mother replied, "Maria, you wouldn't be waiting by yourself. The good Lord has work for you to do, and you will be a blessing to many souls. Your hands would be so full of the Lord's work that you would hardly notice the time that goes by."

Mother placed Maria's hands in hers and prayed silently. Maria saw Mother's lips moving, but she did not hear what she prayed. Continuing, Mother said, "You see, with the Lord, a day is like a thousand years, and a thousand years are like a day.[87] He'll keep you in perfect peace while you wait, and while you wait, trust Him. Now for your other point, yes he sinned against you and God. Yes, adultery is grounds for divorce. But baby, and don't take this the wrong way, we were all adulterers before we received Jesus Christ as Lord and Savior, and that means you, too. We were all cheating on Him with something or somebody. We weren't faithful to Jesus ourselves."

Maria shifted her seat and took a deep breath. She wasn't saying she was perfect, just that she had been faithful to her commitment in the marriage and expected the same in return from her husband who took the same vow. Mother noticed but ignored her and kept right on talking.

"We all have sinned and fallen short of His glory.[88] Jesus forgave you, and you have to forgive."[89]

"Mother," Maria respectfully interrupted, "He is forgiven. However, he isn't even sorry or repentant about what he has done. God forgives us, yes, and we are all sinners, but He wants us to repent. That means to change what we do and to change our minds about what we do. Even Jesus preached 'Repent for the Kingdom of heaven is at hand.' Rob needs help that I can't give him through forgiving him. He divorced me, and that was his choice. He needs Jesus, and that is also his choice to make."

Mother paused. "Forgiving your husband is for you as much as it is for him. Forgiving him heals you. Has he apologized to you, Maria?"

"Well, kind of, but it doesn't matter what he says, because he still continues doing whatever he wants. So if you, with all due respect, are here to tell me that God told you that I should just wait and be miserable with a man who, if he loved *me* and respected *me* would never have divorced me but would have honored *me*," she spoke with passion, "I'm sorry, I don't believe that."

"Baby, I understand, but this isn't about you. God is working on him, and when He is finished, that man will come forth like pure gold. He's working on him just like He's working on you. God doesn't want any of us to be miserable, He wants us to trust and obey. Maria, I'm going to say this again – you must pray. It brings you closer to God, and He will give you the grace to do what He is asking you to do. That man is going to spend time waiting for *you*. Trust in Jesus. He doesn't have any choice *but* to wait because now, Jesus is the head of your life, so that man has to come back correct if he wants you back," Mother spoke.

She paused for a moment in prayer and then continued speaking. "Hallelujah, he wants his family back, yes, glory to God, and he has and is going about it the wrong way, but God knows *your* heart, too. The good Lord wants to give this to you in His way and in His time. You wanted you husband when others told you no. God gave you what you thought you wanted so that you could see it wasn't what you needed. You still love him, Maria."

Maria looked in shock at Mother.

She placed her hand in Maria's again, and tenderly spoke. "We can't keep nothing a secret from Jesus, baby. But, if you choose to take him back, and it is your choice, God will give him back in His way and in His time. *Both* of you will wait, and God will be glorified. You see, God is going to drive that man's car and take over, even if He has to knock him out of the driver's seat, just like he did the Apostle Paul.[90] Hallelujah!" Mother stood and lifted her hands in the air, praising and blessing God.

Maria must have had her autobiography on her forehead because Mother had just read her like a book. *"Everything she spoke,"* Maria admitted to herself, *"was the truth."* Maria was embarrassed to admit to Neicy that she still loved Rob, and there were times when she was upset with herself about it. She had forgiven Rob, and part of her wanted to just go on with her life without him, but the forgiveness aspect of the Christian equation had made her heart pliable, and she was clay in the potter's hand[91] who turned her heart in whatever direction He pleased.[92] Maria didn't promise God that she would take Rob back, she had just been praying for him, that he would accept Christ as Lord and Savior. That didn't bind her to any further obligation, as far as Maria was concerned, however much she did, yes, still love him. She would always love him, they had been married for most of their lives, and they had two children together. They took vows together that they may as well not have taken because they didn't mean anything to him. Maria's only expectation from Rob was that he be faithful to her as she had always been to him. Disloyalty was a non-negotiable. Was that asking too much?

After a minute or so, Mother sat back down and spoke again. "Maria, the two of you were married, yes, but Jesus was not Lord."

Maria stared ahead in disbelief. It was as if Mother was reading her every thought.

Mother Wright continued, "God won't bless a relationship that He is not in. We can't be unevenly yoked. When he bows before Jesus Christ, and he will, God will move in a mighty way, and it will be your choice to take him back or not. But, Maria, be thankful that Jesus was patient with you, too, when you weren't loyal or faithful or committed. You said yes to Jesus and yes to His will. If you really meant that, be willing to do this His way. It's out of your hands, baby. God is in control. He knows what He is doing, and right now, Jesus is driving *your* car. He's going to drive it wherever He wants, for the steps of a good man *and* a good woman are ordered by the Lord.[93] Let Him, baby. All you have to do is ride with Jesus. Pray, trust in the Lord, and stay in your own lane."

Maria sat and stared at Mother, wanting to hear more, something different, anything than what she had just been told. God sure had a sense of humor. Wasn't He paying attention to what was going on? Well, who was she to complain about anything Jesus wanted to do? Jesus had been good to her. He saved her life. He forgave her of her sin. He healed her of her pain. He delivered and set her free. She was now in a Bible Institute, and He had plans for her and her children. He was working on Rob. God was in control. He loved her unconditionally, and He shed His blood to freely pardon her. He blessed her and her children. Genny was free of her anger, and she and Papi were in church and singing in the Youth Choir. He was patient with her when she hadn't put Jesus first either. She would trust God and pray as Mother said, and when God confirmed His word, she would wholeheartedly commit to it.

"Thank you, Mother. I'm sorry if I sounded ungrateful. I appreciate your time and everything Jesus has done for me. I'm grateful to you for your wisdom and care. Thank you."

"Glory to God. You're welcome. Well, I guess we better get going. God bless you, sweetheart, Deacon Tony is going to drop me off."

"Okay, I'll get him from the office," Maria said.

As Maria stood to walk out of the sanctuary, Mother said, "Don't worry, Maria, the Lord will confirm His word. Amen."

"Amen," Maria said.

Upon opening the door to exit the sanctuary, Maria heard Mother mumble "Ride or die. Hmmmppphhh," under her breath.

Deacon Tony was seated at the desk and talking on his cellphone as Maria approached the Church Office.

"Hold on, Neicy," he said, taking his cellphone away from his ear to address Maria as she walked into the office. "Hey, Maria. Are you finished already?"

"Yes. Hi Neicy!" Maria said, shouting loud enough so that Neicy could hear her over the phone.

"She said hi," Tony said to Maria, getting up from his seat and coming around the desk to turn out the office light.

"Please tell her I'll talk to her later, as soon as I get home," Maria said.

"She heard you," Tony laughed.

"And, Tony, you look good. You look like you gained some weight. How are you feeling?" Maria asked.

"Blessed. God is good all the time. Must be all that Thanksgiving food we had at your place."

"Yes, thanks to Neicy. Your wife throws down!"

"Yup, that's one of the reasons I married her. When are we going to see you and the kids over again for dinner?"

"Any time. Just let me know, and you know we'll be there," Maria said.

Tony locked the office door, and they walked down the hallway and into the sanctuary where Mother was waiting. The three left the sanctuary together once Tony set the alarm, and Maria drove back to her house where her mother was watching Genny and Papi.

"How was choir rehearsal?" Ms. Wilson asked as Maria came in.

"It was good, mom. Hopefully, you will be feeling better next week and can make it," Maria said as she set her pocketbook and keys

231

on the dining room table. She didn't bother correcting her mother, who often forgot anything that was said to her. Prayer, bible study, worship service, choir rehearsal, women's ministry meeting; it didn't make a difference, she knew that Holy Tabernacle was the place where Maria would be.

There was an open bottle of Robitussin on the kitchen counter, and Maria placed her hand on her mother's forehead. "You don't have a temperature, thank goodness," Maria said smiling and then giving her 70 year young mother a hug.

"Oh no?" her mother asked, tickled by her daughter's attempt to play mother to her.

"How are you feeling, mom?"

"Pretty good. I'm so glad that you and the kids are going back to church. Thank you, Jesus."

Mrs. Wilson had raised her only daughter in church. She and her husband, Melvin, were faithful members of Faith Fellowship Baptist Church in Red Bank, NJ, some 20 minutes away from Addington Park. The Church was undergoing a lot of turmoil in leadership when the Wilson family was attending services there due to one scandal or another. One of the pastors had allegedly fathered a child with a choir member, and another was under internal scrutiny for financial impropriety with church funds. The talk and rumors never bothered Mr. or Mrs. Wilson, they were staunch supporters of the Church no matter what. When the choir member gave birth to a son, however, the boy was the spitting image of the pastor, Reverend Herb Daniels. The mother refused to leave the Church, and she continued to attend services with her son to the ire of the Daniels family who believed the woman was only coming to provoke them. It upset Mr. and Mrs. Wilson that the Daniels' family ostracized the mother and her son, and Mr. Wilson voiced his opinion to the male leadership of Faith Fellowship, only to be himself ostracized for supporting "this Jezebel harlot woman," as the church male leadership viciously personified her. For weeks the sermons from the altar blamed women for everything from Adam's fall in the garden to Moses' intermarriage. Samson's defeat in battle was because of Delilah, and the divided Kingdom was caused, they said, by Solomon's many wives. The male preachers were relentless and unforgiving in their condemnation of the great whore Babylon in Revelation, the pain of

232

childbearing because of Eve, and the adulterous woman throughout the Book of Proverbs. David's weakness was women, and it was the fault of women. Bathsheba had no business bathing where the King could see her. The Samaritan woman at the well had five husbands and was living a loose life. Women had demons that needed to be cast out, according to one sermon, after all Mary Magdalene had seven. If women dressed modestly and were quiet, submissive and kept their mouths and everything else closed, the holy, upstanding men of God in the Bible would not have suffered so and been distracted. The Word of God had been so twisted and tortured to appease the guilty conscience of Pastor Daniels that several of the members left. The Wilsons, however, stayed, until one Sunday when a visiting Pastor came and spoke of the prophet Nathan's rebuke to King David. King David had killed a man, Uriah, in battle in order to take his wife, Bathsheba, and the Lord was displeased.[94] The visiting Pastor spoke of the lustful spirit of King David that caused him, not the woman, to murder a man so that he might satisfy his own carnal desires, and the prophet Nathan let King David know that he was the man responsible.

Melvin Wilson was on his feet throughout the sermon saying "Preach" and "Tell it!" before the disgruntled looks of the church leadership, and Pastor Daniels, apparently convicted, fell to his knees at his seat in the pulpit. Melvin knew that Pastor Daniels was convicted, and he rejoiced in the Lord who had sent a messenger to proclaim the truth.

In those days, things were swept under the rug and kept secret. Young girls who got pregnant were sent away to live with their relatives out of state. This young girl's family refused to ship her off, and it threatened the control that Faith Fellowship had, so they retaliated by trying to make this young girl's life miserable. When the son was born and brought to church, everyone knew that it was Pastor Daniel's son. He looked exactly like the 45 year young Reverend, and the young mother had just turned 18.

The following Sunday, Pastor Daniels was no longer seated in the pulpit, and a few short weeks later, he reportedly resigned from Faith Fellowship. Mr. and Mrs. Wilson were among the few families who stayed, and shortly after Mr. Wilson passed from complications following a surgical procedure. A small funeral service was held at Faith Fellowship, but the Pastor who was scheduled to perform the service didn't show. He was allegedly loyal to Pastor Daniels and in the camp of the Church leadership who had ostracized Melvin Wilson. The families waited for an hour and a half for one of the new Elders to come and perform the service. Mrs. Wilson was persuaded to leave Faith Fellowship by the other family members who were outraged that the Church had shown blatant disrespect to Melvin, and that was the last time she attended services there. Maria was 14 years old at the time.

After that, they visited churches, finally settling at Second Baptist Church where Mrs. Wilson was a regular and active member. The Church was pastored by a young man from Harlem, New York, just 34 years old, who reminded the congregation of Reverend Dr. Martin Luther King, Jr. He was a graduate of Columbia University who held his Ph.D. in Theology from Boston College, and he preached on themes of social justice in many of his sermons. The Reverend Dr. Joshua B. Kipling and his wife, Pastor Michelle Kipling, attracted a much younger congregation, and the church greatly expanded in the first few years under their pastoral leadership. The average age of their members was 44, according to church records, and an influx of 20 somethings came in droves to Second Baptist Church to hear this young preacher who was on fire for the Lord preach racial and gender equality, equal employment opportunities, affirmative action and fair housing. He was a lifetime member of the NAACP who partnered with other area ministers to support those politicians who adequately and effectively addressed the social issues important to the young, working poor.

The music changed from the traditional hymns to more contemporary gospel music with trumpets, saxophones and an upright bass. Praise dancers worshipped the Lord joyously, but there were some longtime members who complained that it was too much change too soon. The Church grew steadily, but longtime members continued to voice their disapproval, and many of them left. The Pastor was not concerned, stating that you simply cannot please everybody, and the only somebody he wanted to please was Jesus. His uncompromising stance only won over more of the area's residents, and after about five years, the Church had expanded so much that they needed to build an addition onto the property.

Today, the property of Second Baptist includes a 3,000 seat sanctuary, one Food Pantry, one Preschool, an accredited K-8 private, Christian Academy, low-income housing townhomes, and a Community Development Corporation with a library and computer lab headed by the Pastor's son, Joshua B. Kipling, II. Second Baptist Church became a blueprint for other startup churches, and the Pastor became well-respected as a mentor to other young men in the faith. The church was Bible-based and progressive, but Maria, according to her mother "an old soul," preferred a more traditional church setting. It was no surprise when she joined Holy Tabernacle with her husband, Robert J. Henderson, and Mrs. Wilson was just thankful that the two had finally settled where they believed the Lord had called them to be.

"Mom, I love it. I love Second Baptist, too, don't get me wrong, but I feel like this is home for me and the kids."

"Baby, you have to go where you are led. I don't take it personal," she said laughing. "That's God's decision for you, and He knows best."

"Do you want to stay over tonight? You can have my room, I'll sleep on the couch."

"Um.....yes, I will take you up on that offer. Yes. I'm going to go lie down right now, my legs feel a little cramped. I'll see you in the morning."

"Thanks, mom," Maria said.

Mrs. Wilson left the kitchen and went upstairs into Maria's bedroom, shutting the door behind her.

As soon as Genny and Papi were asleep, Maria called Neicy as promised, and the two talked for nearly an hour about a Girls' Night Out that Pam wanted to have with the two of them. At first Maria declined, but then she reconsidered once Neicy told her she thought it was a good idea and would help Maria to have some time to just enjoy herself. All Maria did, Neicy reminded her, was go to church, Bible Study, Intercessory Prayer and the Bible Institute. Pam wanted to plan the Girls' Night Out, insisting that if it was left to Neicy and/or Maria, their night out would find them celebrating at the local library.

"Girl, you are kind of a bookworm, and you could use a night out. Why not?" Neicy asked.

After each and every valid protest Maria offered was swiftly rebutted and overruled, Maria agreed with Neicy that they would have the Girls' Night Out on Friday, and Pam could plan it as long as she agreed to let Maria arrange one to follow it.

They called Pam on a three-way call, and Pam consented. She would pick up the girls Friday night at 6 p.m., and their only hint about where they were going was to look their best.

On Friday night, at exactly 6:00 p.m., Pam and Neicy pulled up at Maria's home. The kids were with Rob for the weekend, and fortunately, there was no altercation between the two of them when he showed up. He arrived on time at 5:00 p.m., and the kids ran out of the house to see him. They had no idea what had transpired the previous Thursday, and Maria would not tell them.

"Where are we going?" Maria asked, climbing in the back seat of Pam's white Chrysler.

"It's a surprise," Pam answered, "but I promise you, you are going to love it and forget all about 'this bitch' (Pam's new nickname for Sophia)."

"Just relax, Maria. Get ready to have some fun!" Neicy said, sitting in the front passenger seat.

"Okay, if you say so," Maria replied. "This reminds me of when we were teenagers."

The three laughed, and they talked about high school memories for the one hour drive to, as it turned out, Atlantic City. It was good conversation for Maria, who had only been conversing lately about King David and the religious leaders of Jesus' day. She had to admit that she did need a break, and she stopped fighting the urge to check the internet for the Latin, Greek and Hebrew and instead enjoy the Ebonics they spoke as they recalled high school sayings and phrases. Pam stationed her phone to old school rap, and they talked and laughed while the music played in the background.

At 7:25 p.m., the ladies pulled up in front of a hotel on the boardwalk, and before they got out of the car, Pam assured Maria that she would have a great time. "I've been here a few times before, and the show never fails. I'm telling you, you are in for a long overdue treat."

Neicy was laughing, and she got out of the car and held Maria's hand as the two walked into the Hotel behind Pam. Gamblers played an array of games on tables immediately inside. Waitresses in uniforms Maria would only wear in the privacy of her bedroom served patrons drinks.

"I hope this isn't what I'm thinking," Maria thought to herself.

"Neicy," Maria whispered as they waited in line to get into the show, "is this a strip show?"

Neicy held Maria's hand tighter, and said "Do not fear." She burst out laughing, and Pam joined her.

"Oh my God. It is a strip show," Maria said, this time a little louder. "I can't do this."

"See, Neicy, that's why I didn't want to bring the librarian. What would you prefer to do, Maria, go to the bookstore tonight?" Pam asked with sarcasm.

"First time, huh?" one of the women in line said to Maria.

Maria just looked at the mature woman standing next to her, and then she looked back at Neicy and Pam, who were both laughing. "I can't believe you brought me here. You know I'm studying the Word, Neicy."

Neicy rolled her eyes. "Maria, we are not committing any sin. We are here to have fun. We brought you here so you can relax and loosen up."

"Why do I need to loosen up? You're the one who told me I should pray and come to church, and I am, and now you have me out here at a strip show?"

"Look, if you don't want to come in, Maria, you can sit at the bar or go play blackjack at one of the tables. Or, you can go and sit in Pam's car. We did this for you. Robert J. Henderson is not the only man on the planet, and this night was planned for you so that you can remember that. God is not going to strike you down because you are enjoying yourself for one night. You're not going home with any of these men. This is not Sodom and Gomorrah. We are going to go in, sit at a table, eat, have a non-alcoholic drink, watch the 'professional dancers' *(emphasis added)*, and then we are going home. Tony knows I am here, okay. You could say thank you."

Pam snapped her fingers in a sister girl, "she told you," sort of way and stared straight ahead.

As they came to the door, Pam asked Maria if she was coming in. Pam was footing the bill. Maria was surrounded by women who were anxious to get inside and holding up the line wasn't making any of them happier. She agreed to go in, and if it really bothered her she would just sit in the lounge areas further back from the stage or leave altogether.

The room was full of 30 or so round tables and chairs tastefully styled with beige table coverings and folded "All-Male Revue" placards as centerpieces. The walls were full of mirrors to give the impression of a larger-sized room. Women of all ages, ethnicities and sizes were seated as bare-chested waiters in tight black pants served drinks.

"That's the lounge area," Pam said, pointing to an open room in the back with booths and media screens hanging from the ceiling. "You can watch the show from back there if you don't want to be a part of the action, or if you're late and can't get a good seat. My recommendation is that both of you keep your seats, and keep your eyes open. Don't blink!" she laughed.

The host seated them at a table in the center of the room, about three tables from the stage, which gave them a perfect, full view. An empty chair was in the center of the stage, and the women at the first row of tables were cheering, laughing and waving bills.

"You see those girls? If you two don't relax and stop acting like tourists, I'm going to go sit up there with them," Pam spoke to Neicy and Maria. "Evan knows I am here, too, and he doesn't mind. I have my fun, and I go home, and we go to church, too. It's about balance. That's what was wrong with the religious leaders of Jesus' day. They spent so much time studying the law that they missed what the law was all about, so please, don't get all Bible with me. Balance, Maria. It's okay to have fun sometime."

When the waiter finally came to take their order, the ladies ordered a trio of appetizers and non-alcoholic drinks. A popular, classic R&B song came on, and it got a lot of the women up to dance. Pam and Neicy sang along, and even Maria had to ease up and admit, "That's my jam!" There was a good mix of classic R&B, hip-hop and house music. A popular club song played, and nearly every woman either stood and danced at her table or sat and rocked to the house beat. As soon as the food and drinks were served, it was time for the show to start.

A handsome tall gentleman came to the stage dressed in a black cowboy hat, no shirt, and tight blue jeans with the rear cut out. He wore ankle high cowboy boots with spurs.

"I can't look," Maria said, covering her eyes with her hands.

"Don't do that!" Pam warned. "That only makes them come over to you, and you are not going to embarrass me."

Maria removed her hands and pretended to be watching as "Ride 'em Cowboy" danced for several minutes onstage. Maria looked at her food and sipped her drink, pretending an interest in the male dancer as he jumped off the stage and began walking around the tables within a few feet of where they sat. Pam was screaming and waving bills, and Neicy was laughing and enjoying herself. The dancer leaned over the next table to grab a few bills from the cleavage of a customer with his mouth, and Maria turned to see his round buttocks exposed from the opening in his jeans. She wanted to enjoy herself and relax like the girls said she should, but she was not comfortable, and she couldn't hide it.

"I'll be right back, I just have to use the Ladies' Room," Maria said. Neither Pam nor Neicy was listening. They were enjoying the show at the next table.

Maria got up and turned to go to the Ladies Room marked in the corner of the room. As she was walking away, she heard the cries and screams of women get louder, and then a hand grabbed her arm and turned her around.

"Ride 'em Cowboy" was standing directly in front of her, dancing and flexing his biceps and making a wave motion with his stomach muscles and back. He stood about 6' tall with dark brown skin that glistened under the lights and looked like it had been anointed with oil. He took his cowboy hat off and put it on Maria's head, and then he lifted her hands to caress the top of his bald head. Pam and Neicy were screaming and laughing hysterically, probably at the frightened and uneasy look on Maria's face.

"Oh my God," she thought.

She was paralyzed with nervousness, but she did caress his head slowly, which only seemed to excite him. Then, he grabbed a chair and sat down, inviting her to sit with him. Maria refused and turned to walk away, but he pulled her close to him and straddled her on his lap. Pam and Neicy were now standing and screaming. There were tears in Pam's eyes, she was laughing so hard. His whole performance with Maria lasted about two minutes, and then he walked around the table in Pam's direction.

Pam tipped him a $20 bill, and he grabbed her by the hand and took her onstage as she screamed "Giddy up! Giddy up!" The DJ turned down the song that was playing and encouraged everyone in the room to shout "Giddy up!" along with Pam. The women stood and cheered, and Pam sat on the lap of the dancer in the center of the stage waving one hand in the air and mocking the form of a professional jockey. The room burst with screams, cheers and applause.

That was the last thing a nearly out of breath Maria remembered seeing before she went out to the lounge area where no one was seated. Instead of staying there to watch Pam's show on the media screens, Maria went over to the bar and ordered a glass of ginger ale so that she wouldn't look so aloof. The bartender acknowledged Maria while taking the order of a party of five, so she waited patiently for her turn. Another young woman came and sat next to Maria, and she glanced at Maria and smiled.

"I know you. Aren't you Robert Henderson's wife?"

Maria looked at the young woman sitting next to her. She looked like a dancer, with thigh-high black patent leather boots, winter white leggings that fit her like a glove, and a ruffled collar black jacket, reminiscent of the Artist Prince, that tied at her tiny waistline. Her surgically enhanced breasts were nearly pouring over her jacket, and a thin gold necklace dangled loosely around her neck. She wore a bright red-orange lipstick and simple eye makeup with an artistic black cat eye, long, false eyelashes and contour makeup enhancing her high cheekbones and giving her pretty face a lift. Her hair was in an asymmetrical bob, dark brown with blonde highlights. Maria knew her as well, the face was familiar, but she couldn't recall her name.

"Yes, I am. I'm sorry, I'm terrible with names," Maria answered embarrassingly.

"That's okay. My stage name is Pebbles, but my real name is Veronica Hicks. We went to school together, I was a year under you and Rob."

"Oh yeah, how are you?" Maria asked. "Oh my God, it's been a long time."

240

"Yes," Veronica smiled, "it has. It's always nice to see good people from school. You were always cool. Rob was cool, too. How is he doing?"

Maria could barely hear her over the screams, so she leaned in closer and spoke. "He's good, thanks. No complaints, you know."

"I should say thank you. He takes my daughter to basketball practice with your daughter."

"Oh, I knew it. I'm so sorry, Veronica, or should I call you Pebbles?"

"Ronny is fine," she answered with a smile.

"Your daughter is Joanne Hicks. She's really good."

The bartender came over and took their orders, but Ronny insisted that the drink be put on her tab.

"Are you working tonight?" Maria asked.

"No, tonight is the All-Male Revue. The hotel does this one Friday a month. I have a few friends who are dancing tonight, so I just came for support." Pausing, Ronny took a deep breath and said, "Please don't judge me. I take care of my daughter the best way I can."

"Ronny, I wasn't going to say anything. Who am I to judge anybody?"

"Yeah, like I said, you were always cool. So what do you do?" Ronny was more comfortable with the conversation now, grateful that Maria wouldn't be judgmental of her for her line of work.

"Well, right now I'm not working, but I am in school."

"That's good. Care to talk about it?"

"Since you're interested, okay. I'm studying the Bible."

"The Bible?" Ronny asked curiously.

"Yes," Maria answered. "Please don't judge *me*. I may do some work in ministry at my church."

Ronny was at ease with Maria, and she turned in her seat to face her. "Who am I to judge anyone? What church do you go to, if you don't mind my asking?"

"Holy Tabernacle Church." Maria was prepared to hear the usual *"oh that's a church for old people"* reply, but she resisted the temptation to be on the defensive.

"I've heard a lot of good things about Holy Tabernacle and the pastor, Reverend Wright. I need to get back to church – used to go a lot back in the day. ....things change."

Ronny took a few napkins and placed them in front of her. The bartender brought over their drinks, and for a minute, the two ladies sat without saying anything.

"Ronny," Maria said, letting her guard down, "if you don't mind.....we would love to see you at Holy Tabernacle. Our service is at 11 am every Sunday. Reverend Wright is still the Pastor."

"Are you some kind of preacher there?" Ronny asked.

"No. I just love the word, and I love Jesus."

"I know you do. You're sitting at the bar, and there are fine ass black men all around you. You just walked away from the top dancer in the show to come over here and talk about Jesus with a sinful woman like me. Jesus doesn't have to worry about you."

Maria took a sip of her ginger ale, and then gave glory to God.

Ronny was intrigued. "I love Him, too. I love him because He doesn't judge me. I can call on Him right now, and He won't look down on me."

"Ronny, we're all sinners. I'm a sinner, saved by grace, and Jesus came for sinners like you and me and everybody else. He is no respecter of persons. God is love. Why don't you just come back?" Maria asked.

"Maria, I miss the Church. I feel like I can talk to you," she said, looking directly into Maria's eyes. "You're sitting at a bar in an All-Male Revue, and I saw you with Ride 'em Cowboy. You weren't comfortable, but you were real. That's why he came after you. Do you know how many other women he passes up when he dances? Women throw money at his feet, and he walks right past them. Now that other women see that, they'll all be pretending to be uncomfortable and uninterested just to get a dance with him. He knows the truth. He chose you because you were real, and, that's how God is. That's why he chose David, because he saw David's heart, that David was sincere and real. He chose Peter because Peter was real. So, I came over here to talk to you because I believe that you will keep it real with me. God knows what he is doing, glory to God, even in a room full of half-naked men and screaming women."

"I don't get what you're trying to say."

"Well, I want to share my story with you. I've been needing to talk to someone about my experience with the church for so long."

Ronny shared with Maria how she had been a member of a church for years, and she felt persecuted and ostracized after her son was arrested for selling drugs and her husband left her for another woman. She stayed at the church, and when she was about to be evicted, she started dancing in local clubs to make the money that she needed to pay her bills and keep her home. When the church found out, the members persecuted her relentlessly and ostracized her and her daughter. She soon after left the church and had been visiting other houses of worship, but she hadn't trusted any were where God wanted to plant her. Ronny said that she had forgiven them for the whole experience and had moved on with her life. The missing piece was that Ronny wanted a church home for herself and for her daughter, Joanne.

"You may not be a preacher now, but you will be one day. It's all over you, Maria. You know, God *is* love. Do you love me enough to welcome me and my daughter into your church without judging me for the work I do?"

Maria sat in silence for a moment, thinking of how to answer the question.

"Yes," Maria answered. "I'm not your judge. The Lord wants us to come to Him as we are, and God loves each and every one of us."

"Okay, I'll come as I am. But what if I don't want to quit the work that I do. Do you love me enough to welcome me and my daughter into your church without being critical of me for the work I do?"

"Ronny, when you enter into a relationship with Jesus, a real relationship with Jesus, He wants your heart. He will accept all of us as we are, and we are to come to Him as we are. He loves us unconditionally," Maria answered with gentleness and compassion.

"Well, if he loves me unconditionally, He'll love me whether I change work or not, won't He?"

"I am not your judge. He loves you unconditionally, yes. He wants your heart. When you give your heart to Him, Ronny, you will want to do whatever He wants you to do, and He will help you. Your desires will change. He gives us His Holy Spirit to help us, and we never come out of the presence of Jesus unchanged. Jesus also says in His word that if we love Him, we will obey Him. Do you want to keep dancing for some reason?"

"Not really. I've been dancing because it helped pay the bills when my husband left. It kept food on the table. God *made* a way, and I make good money. If there's a better way, I'll take it, but I haven't seen a better way so far."

Ronny took another sip of her drink. She was looking for an answer and hoped that Maria might be able to help her.

"Ronny, God is the way. I'm not going to front with you. My husband and I are divorced. Rob left me for another woman. Genny took it hard, and I didn't tell her – she and our son, Papi, already knew. I was angry and bitter. The anger was consuming me, and if I hadn't given it to Jesus, I would still be upset. It was consuming me, Ronny. I put on a front and tried to act like it didn't bother me, but it did, and I got tired of always being so strong. I hated Rob. If he was on fire, I wouldn't have spit on him. All it did was make me miserable. So, I prayed and prayed and prayed some more. The Lord led me to Holy Tabernacle, and now the joy of the Lord is my strength. The pastor preaches the Word. It is the Word that saves us, that heals, delivers, fixes us up and puts us back together again. The members have always made me feel welcome and at home, like I am family, but the main thing is that Jesus is in the house. It's about Jesus and His Kingdom. It's not about who else is there, and to be honest, I could really care less what people think because people aren't perfect, no church is perfect, but God doesn't fail. There's nothing wrong with Jesus. As long as Jesus is in the Church, and He is the head of the Church, glory to God. As long as I am in God's Will, glory to God. Today, Jesus is first in my life. Jesus is my husband. Rob doesn't even compare. So can you make it on Sunday?" Maria asked. "We would love to have you and Joanne."

"Maybe. I'll think about it. Let's exchange numbers."

As they exchanged information, Maria added, "Since you sing, you should think about joining the choir. Neicy sings. She's here with Pam up front."

Ronny laughed. "I know, I saw the two of them. Pam is a regular here. She's so funny."

"Well, the next time we hang out, you have to join us."

"That sounds like it might be fun, Maria. Thank you."

The room erupted with cheers and applause as another dancer, about 6'5" with deep brown skin, came onstage with a shield and javelin. He was wearing a black loin cloth. The dancer looked like a professional body builder with a mass of muscles bulging in his shoulders, arms, chest, back, abs and legs.

"Even his muscles have muscles," Maria said.

Ronny laughed.

The waiters were walking through the room with buckets of what looked like white stones, and they handed out a few stones to women who dropped bills in the buckets.

"Who is that?" Maria asked Ronny.

"That is Goliath, and that is also my cue to get up. You may want to go back to your table with Neicy and Pam. This is going to be good."

Ronny stood up from the bar and placed her large pocketbook over her shoulder. She drank the last of her margarita and noticed Maria's uneasiness about going back into the room.

"Girl, it's alright. C'mon, I'll sit with you guys, if that's ok."

"Sure, the more the merrier," Maria answered, happy that she would not be walking back to her seat alone.

The two ladies walked back into the room towards the seats by Neicy and Pam, and Ronny motioned for one of the waiters to come over to their table.

Maria introduced Ronny to Neicy and Pam, but there was no need to. Both Neicy and Pam remembered exactly who Ronny was.

"Hey girl, good to see you," Pam said, reaching over to hug Ronny.

"Hi," Neicy said, "you are looking good, girl."

"You too. You all look like you are still seniors in high school," Ronny responded. She sat in the empty seat next to Neicy and offered to get some stones for the ladies from the waiter, Jeff, who she advised was a friend of hers.

"What are we supposed to do with the stones?" Maria asked, clueless.

The other three ladies laughed.

"Haven't you ever heard of the story of David and Goliath?" Pam asked.

"Yes, of course I have," Maria answered.

"Well," Pam began, "whoever can hit Goliath with one of these stones gets a free dance with him. They go by tables, so wait for the signal."

The waiter came over and offered a stone to Ronny, but she politely directed him to give the stone to Maria.

"Lord, forgive me, please. Please forgive me," Maria prayed to herself as she received the plastic, white stone from the waiter and sank down in her seat, hoping the massive hulk-like man on stage wouldn't see her.

Goliath spotted the demure and discreet lady in front of the room, and he walked offstage towards the table where the ladies were seated. Maria put her hands over her eyes, and there was laughter and screams as he approached her with his shield in one hand and javelin in the other. Ronny had a sly grin on her face, and she directed Goliath to go over to Maria.

He stopped directly in front of Maria's seat, and she opened her eyes to see him standing directly in front of her. Then, she put her hands over her eyes again and sunk down in her seat, to the delight and amusement of the ladies who had brought her out that evening. The screams heightened when Goliath removed his loin cloth and covered himself with his shield. He dropped the soft fabric in Maria's lap and danced around the table, teasing the women by playfully lowering and raising it. He removed Maria's hands from her eyes with one hand and placed her hands on his shield. The entire room thundered with cheers and applause, and women screamed for Maria to let down his guard. Maria kept it in place for him with her hands shaking as he danced and teased for a few minutes, and then he took ownership of the metal covering again and went to another table where bills were waving furiously.

Maria started to laugh with the other ladies as Goliath walked away, his huge, freshly waxed glutes shining underneath the ceiling lights and rippling with each step he took.

"Damn!" Maria said out loud.

The ladies at the table laughed as Maria held the loin cloth in her lap. Ronny told her that it was a souvenir for her to keep. Looking in Neicy's direction, Ronny spoke in a soft voice, "I knew that would do the trick. You owe me $100."

Neicy slipped Ronny the money under the table. She was grateful to and responded, "Here you go. It was worth every dime."

When Pam and Neicy had arranged for their night out at the All-Male Revue, Neicy complained that she didn't think any of the men would be able to get a rise out of Maria. Maria had, after all, been with Rob her entire life, and she stood by his side through all his infidelities. So, Pam reached out to Ronny, and Ronny agreed to coax her dancer friends to cater to Maria that night. Neicy didn't think that would work either, but Ronny insisted, and the bet was placed at $100. Ronny was confident her dancer friend, Goliath, would serve well to remind Maria that she was still a beautiful, desirable woman.

"If any of you say anything about tonight, I will deny it," Maria said.

They all laughed. The rest of the evening was spent admiring the likes of Five-O, a dancer dressed as a police officer who would frisk and arrest the naughtiest girl in the place. A bride-to-be at another table, surrounded by her girlfriends, won the honors; Uncle Sam, a dancer dressed in a tall red, white and blue hat who would recruit the best dancer into his performance onstage. It was a tie between two women, one in her 20's and the other pushing 60 and full of personality. The audience voted for the winner, and the slower, but more entertaining, senior won; and The Geek, a dancer with large eyeglasses dressed like a nerdy college student, who some women booed. He danced onstage without rhythm and tripped when he walked. Then, he walked around the room and tried to get a lady to dance with him, but some of the women had been tricked into believing that he was included in the show as a joke. When a young lady finally agreed to dance with him, he took her onstage and disrobed, revealing himself to be just as impressive as the other dancers.

At the end of the 90 minute show, dinner and drinks, the ladies said goodnight to Ronny, promising to stay in touch and spend another night out with her again soon. They went to Pam's car and back to Maria's house where they talked and laughed for most of the night before falling asleep in the living room.

Maria went upstairs to say a prayer in the privacy of her own bedroom, and she thanked the Lord for Neicy and Pam who had taken her to the hotel. There she met and talked with Ronny, a soul who needed Jesus. Maria may have been a bookworm who was uncomfortable during their Girls' Night Out at a "professional male dancers" Revue, but she was comfortable speaking about Jesus to a sinful woman there who recognized her family's need for a Savior, and for this, Maria gave God much praise. She was grateful for the opportunity to witness to Ronny and looked forward to planning their next Girls' Night Out, which would be Maria's choice and would, to Pam's chagrin or not, be at Holy Tabernacle Church for Intercessory Prayer and Bible Study.

"Lord, have your way," Maria prayed, *"in Jesus' name."*

Chapter Twenty

Robert J. Henderson and Paulette S. Simmons

Rob and Sophia had been arguing non-stop since Thanksgiving night. Sophia swore up and down that Isaiah had only walked her upstairs and then left. The washcloth on the bathroom counter had been used to try and clean the wine off her Shearling Coat, Sophia explained, and it was no big deal.

"Why are you acting so insecure," she told him, "you know that you are the only man for me."

Rob didn't believe her at all, but he also didn't believe that Isaiah was anyone Sophia would be interested in. After a heated argument Thursday night, which spoiled their plans to go to her parent's home in Pennsylvania, and another argument on Friday, Saturday and Sunday, Rob became convinced, somewhat, that her story may have been true. Rob had called Isaiah to thank him for taking Sophia home, and Isaiah was as calm as a feather. Rob didn't detect anything in his conversation with Isaiah that suggested anything had went on that night, so he dismissed his suspicions and then got upset with himself. He was the player. He needed to turn the tables in his own advantage and project his frustrations onto Sophia. So he started an argument with her on Monday about her showing up at the Center during business hours – hadn't he made that clear? She took the bait and predictably fussed with him about his ingratitude for the items she had bought, and she complained that she wasn't even able to go see her mother and father. Hadn't she made it clear to him that their plans for Thanksgiving would include a trip to Pennsylvania? How could he be so insensitive and self-centered? Rob made a mountain out of the mole hill, portrayed himself as the victim, and walked out of Sophia's condominium until she, he decided, would pursue him. It was callow, but it made Rob feel better, and in his mind, he needed to teach her a lesson and always maintain the upper hand.

Sophia, out of spite and revenge, continued her relationship with Isaiah until the end of the year. Isaiah was in it for the sex and nothing more, refusing to become emotionally or otherwise connected to this young woman who was playing Mr. Henderson as much as Mr. Henderson was playing her.

"If she's gonna give it to me, I'm going to take it," Isaiah would say to himself, and he hadn't made Sophia any promises.

She invited Isaiah over late Friday evenings when she knew Rob was picking up his children from "her" house. Rob truthfully insisted that there was nothing going on between him and his ex-wife, and that all they were doing on Thanksgiving at the Center was thanking their guests for coming and their volunteers for helping. Besides, he attempted to persuade her, Maria had moved on with her life and was into other ventures.

Sophia found his tone to be defensive of "her," and that caused another argument. Sophia was fed up playing the other woman. Her position was that Rob was divorced, so there was no reason why she should still be a secret. Rob didn't want her coming around the Center, she had never been introduced to his children, and the few friends of his who she did meet were told that Sophia was "a friend." Meanwhile, "she" was still being hailed as "Mrs." Henderson. Sophia believed that Rob should have never gotten divorced because he acted like he was still married, and her imagination began to take a toll. She supposed that Rob was doing more on his weekends than just spending time with his children. She would never know the truth, so she made herself feel better about the whole situation by engrossing herself in Isaiah's youthful energies in the bedroom that satisfied her temporarily and helped her forget about Rob. She didn't pursue Rob as he thought she would, and it was probably his carnal appetite that caused him to give in sooner than she did. Their make-up sessions were intense, but

250

Sophia found herself resenting her lover as he pleasured himself at her expense. When she missed her monthly cycle in December, she scheduled a visit to her doctor in Pennsylvania who confirmed what she already knew. Sophia was pregnant.

She believed the baby had to be Rob's. She used protection with Isaiah except for one or two times, and then Isaiah used self-control. She would tell Isaiah, and he would likely deny the possibility of his being the father. Then she would tell Rob the news, and he would hopefully be happy about it and want to get married sooner.

Sophia called Isaiah right away. He sounded indifferent, but he did offer a sincere congratulations.

"Mr. Henderson will be a great father. He's so into his kids," Isaiah responded.

"You're not mad?" Sophia asked.

"No, not at all. We both knew what it was, and I'm not a snitch. Are you sure there's no chance it could be mine?" Isaiah asked cautiously.

"I'm sure."

Relieved he replied, "Yeah, me too. I didn't slip. So, I guess this means we really won't be seeing each other any more now, huh?"

"Well, we can still be friends, Isaiah."

"Listen to you – *'we can still be friends, Isaiah,'*" he said mockingly. "It's cool. I was getting tired of sneaking in and out of your condo, but girl, you were worth it. If things change with you and Mr. Henderson, give me a call."

"Okay Isaiah, I will."

"And good luck with everything. I'll see you around."

Sophia and Isaiah hung up the phone. Just like that, their relationship was severed. Now, she just had to tell Rob.

When Sophia invited Rob over for dinner one Monday evening in early January, she told him that she needed to talk to him about plans for the Mayor's race. He came over with a bottle of wine and a dozen long-stemmed red roses. He needed Sophia under his thumb again as there were only a few weeks left before the March deadline of candidates. It was apparent to Sophia now, clearer than ever before, that he was just using her. Before she took another step with him in politics, she needed to clear the air with him as it pertained to their personal lives.

The two sat down in the living room before a luxurious marble fireplace mantel and shared what ordinarily would be a romantic dinner of rosemary rack of lamb with roasted potatoes and carrots. Rob appreciated the atmosphere and meal, but Sophia faked her way through it until an opportune time in the conversation when she could tell him he was going to be a father again.

Rob reclined in the off-white leather sofa facing the fireplace. A classic R&B slow jam was playing lightly on the surround system, and he was singing along. It was lightly snowing outside, and Sophia's 8' lighted Christmas tree was positioned by the large windows overlooking the waves crashing against the beach. Clear bulbs, silver and gold garland, crystal ornaments and a five point star atop the tree looked both beautifully festive and mood-inducing, and there were still a few wrapped presents underneath. When Sophia went to pick up one of the gifts, thinking now was as good a time as any, Rob was surprised and happy.

"For me?" he asked, as she brought a small, wrapped box to him.

"Yes. Open it," she said, sitting down on the couch beside him.

"I thought we were finished exchanging gifts," he said before giving her a kiss on the cheek.

"We are, but I wanted to give you something special," Sophia answered.

Rob carefully unwrapped the silver paper and white ribbon. He shook the box, and then took the lid off. Inside was a piece of paper, which he curiously unfolded. He read the first paragraph on the letterhead of Sophia's OB/GYN, Dr. Melinda N. Barry, Women's Care, Inc.:

Congratulations on your pregnancy. Women's Care, Inc. believes that prenatal care is very important, and we look forward to caring for you and your baby throughout your pregnancy. Thank you for choosing our office for your obstetrical care.

Sophia waited for a reaction from Rob, but he just sat beside her with a blank look on his face. The energy between the two of them shifted and became tense. Rob took a deep breath and then exhaled through his nostrils. Sophia thought she could hear his heart beating through his shirt. He re-read the words on the paper thinking that there had to be some kind of mistake.

Congratulations on your pregnancy. Pregnancy. Prenatal care. You and your baby.

"No," he was telling himself.

He put the paper down on the couch beside him and stood up to pace in the living room, almost forgetting that Sophia was sitting on the couch awaiting his joyous and proud response.

"When did you get that?" Rob finally asked. He stood with his hands folded across his chest and a look of disappointment.

Noticing his unhappy demeanor, Sophia stood up herself and went to hug Rob. He took a step back from her.

"What's wrong?" Sophia asked.

Rob repeated his question.

"I went to my doctor on Friday. I didn't want to call you over the weekend while you were with your kids. Aren't you happy, Rob?" Sophia asked.

"Whose is it?" Rob bluntly asked.

"What?" Sophia asked, startled by his question.

Repeating his question with as much bluntness, he asked again, "Whose is it? I know you were seeing someone else, Sophia. That washcloth on the bathroom sink? That was my M-O when I was younger. I know what men do, Sophia, don't try to play me. I knew it."

"Rob, I already explained everything to you. I'm not going to explain again." Sophia went back to the couch and sat down. She put the letter inside the box and closed it. "I'm not running for Mayor as an unmarried, pregnant woman. We have to plan the wedding for March or April, before I start showing."

"Plan the wedding? I'm not ready to get married. I'm not ready to have another child."

Sophia took a deep breath. She sat back in the couch and tuned Rob out as he complained for several minutes about what their options were: she didn't have to keep the baby; it wasn't a good time, she had the mayor's race to be focused on; she should just concentrate on winning the mayor's seat, and then they would see what happened; hadn't she been on birth control; she never got pregnant before; she must have been seeing someone else; he didn't believe he was the father; he wasn't planning a wedding right now; he hoped she wasn't doing this to try and trap him; he would give her the money to take care of it.

Unable to any longer listen to his suggestions for what she should do with the unborn child in her body, and angry that he wasn't supportive at all, Sophia sat forward in the couch and told him stop talking and listen.

"Rob, all you are trying to do is start another argument, turn everything around so that you can be some kind of victim, and then run from your responsibilities the same way you ran from your wife and kids. You are a coward. Go ahead and run. I don't care. I'm keeping my baby. It's my decision, not yours," she said determinedly.

Rob wasn't appreciative of Sophia's tone with him, and her defiant stance at his suggestions only triggered his innate self-preservation mode.

"Sophia you're 30 years old, you have plenty of time to have kids. You keep the baby all you want, but don't try to pin it on me. I'm not claiming anything until there is a DNA test. We've been seeing each other for a few years, and you've never gotten pregnant before. Hell, there were plenty of times when *you should have been* pregnant, as much as we used to go at it. It doesn't make sense to me. Well, weren't you taking your birth control? It worked every other time, so how are you pregnant now? Or I should I say *by who* are you pregnant now, because you never got pregnant by me before. And for your information, I didn't run from any responsibilities. I'm still taking care of Maria and my kids, and I always will. They will always be a part of my life."

Rob had said Maria's name purposely because he knew that it would anger Sophia.

Fed up, and rising to the challenge, Sophia threw Maria's name back at Rob. She responded, "Whatever, Rob. Take care of Maria and your kids. Go back to them for all I care. Leave me and your child just like you left Maria and your other children, coward. I'm pregnant now because I'm pregnant now. Go ahead and run. I don't care what you do. It's my decision."

"And it's my decision, too," Rob shot right back. "I don't want to get married right now. I don't want another kid right now. Why can't you run for Mayor without being married? This town is full of single mothers who don't let being single stop them from doing what they want to do, and they don't live in a fancy condominium like you with a good job, money, connections and two parents. Whatever it costs, I'll take care of it. I'm out."

He began walking towards the dining room where his coat was draped over one of the chairs. Sophia stood up from the couch and followed him.

"Now hold on, Rob, let me tell you something. Rob, I don't need your money," she said angrily. "That's right, I have a fancy condominium that I worked for and paid for, and I don't apologize for that to anybody. I drive a nice car, I have good credit and I pay my bills on time. Yes, I have both of my parents, and yes I do have connections through my job that I worked my ass off for as a woman in a man's world. Whatever I have, I went to school for and worked hard to get it. I stay on my grind just like you do. Who the hell do I owe an apology to? And, who the hell are *you* to talk to *me* about connections and money? That's all you are concerned about, Rob. That's what fuels your fire and gets you going every morning. That's why you need me in the Mayor's office. That's not your passion, that's your hustle, and do you honestly think I don't know your hustle? You need me in the Mayor's office to connect you with the people you wish you *were* connected with, and you know *Sophia* can make things happen at City Hall. You're one to talk about what happened before. Before, you wanted to get married, and I was the only woman for you. As long as everything is going well with me at City Hall, you are happy. Now, you are unhappy because I'm pregnant. So what you're saying is, if I keep the baby, we don't get married? Well, if we don't get married, I'm not running for office. You're right, I am only 30, and I can run for office anytime I want. That's my decision, and that's the way it's going to be. You don't get your way this time, Rob. Not this time. Not with my body, not with my career, and not with my decisions for my life. You can be out."

Sensing he had lost ground, Rob decided against continuing another argument with Sophia, and he simply replied, "I'll talk to you later." Besides, he knew that as a man it was useless to argue with a woman. Women didn't let it go until they had made all their points, and women didn't lose arguments. Rob learned that while being married to Maria and while growing up with two sisters who both lived out of state but stayed in touch with him. He shared with them that he and Maria were getting divorced, but he hadn't told them about his extramarital affairs. As far as his side of the family knew, Maria was to blame.

He leaned in to kiss Sophia, but she pulled away, so he put his coat on. He tried a second time to give her a kiss, but she turned away from him and walked back to the couch. Sophia picked up the box with the congratulatory letter in it and held it in her hands. Rob hardly noticed as he walked to the front door, opened it and left. He went to the parking garage and got inside his Mercedes Benz. He needed to clear his head. He was not getting married right now, that was a non-negotiable. He didn't want another child, and his hunch was that the child was not even his. Besides, she should have been taking her pills or whatever it was that she used. He wanted the city contracts, and Sophia would easily win the election if she just listened to him and ran. She could push them through and get some things done.

Weighing all his options, Rob concluded that Sophia would still run for office because he would talk her into it. He would promise to get married once the baby was born and he was sure that he was the father. That might work.

He checked his phone to see if Maria had by any chance returned any of his calls. Her number did not appear on the log. He dialed her cell phone number again only to reach her answering machine. She had been avoiding his calls for weeks, and the few times that he did speak with her, it was about Genny's basketball games or Papi's karate practices. If Rob tried to engage her in any other conversation, Maria would hurry him off the phone without giving him a chance to even say "I'm sorry."

He would have to tell Maria about Sophia's pregnancy before she heard it somewhere else. He owed her that much respect. When she did hear, that would likely be the deal breaker for Maria, as forgiving and tenderhearted as she was. If Maria couldn't forgive him for that, he might have to marry Sophia, and he wasn't even sure anymore that marrying Sophia was what he wanted. If he could just figure out a way to have his cake and eat it too, everything would be fine. Now that Sophia was pregnant, however, he felt cornered and out of control, and that was not a good position for any alpha male to be in.

"Maria, it's me. I've reached out to you a few times. Give me a call."

Rob started the engine of his car and drove off into the light snow. He would go home and plan his next move.

As his car pulled out of the parking lot, Sophia stood on the balcony of her condominium four stories above, watching her lover run off into the night, and she was planning what *she* would do next. The final decision had been made - she was having her baby. That was a non-negotiable. This would be her first child, and Sophia wanted Rob to be there for her. She was upset that he didn't even ask how she was feeling. The other non-negotiable for Sophia was that if she and Rob did not marry, she would not run for office. The press would have a field day with her and her morals, and they would find out that Robert J. Henderson was the father anyway. Then, they would pry into their relationship and crucify her as the mistress or other woman who he left "her" for. That would ultimately hurt both Sophia and Rob, she figured. She would not subject herself and her unborn child to the scrutiny of the media, and her conservative Roman Catholic parents would wholeheartedly object.

She went back inside of her condominium to escape the 20 degree cold, which dropped whenever a gust of wind, or "the hawk" as some people called it, whipped in her direction. There was an untouched black forest cake in a glass cake dome and decorative pedestal that Rob had purchased for her from Neiman Marcus. It was one of two gifts that he brought over to her on Christmas day after spending time with his children. The other was a pair of diamond earrings she had admired and told him about a few months ago, and she was thrilled when he remembered the exact pair and presented them to her.

Sophia checked her phone for messages, and she had missed her mother's call. She would tell her parents later rather than sooner, or at least not until she started to show.

After rinsing the dinner dishes and putting them in the dishwasher, Sophia cut herself a small piece of cake and headed into her bedroom, still pondering what she would do. She could run for office and then just let the press know that it was Rob's child, and if they persecuted her, the PR staff could spin that in her favor. He would be there for her, she would talk him into it. After all, he needed her in the office to help him. Or, she could do both without him, let the press know that it was his child, and when he wasn't by her side, he would self-destruct and ruin his own businesses and reputation. What would "she" do when "she" found out that Rob had fathered another child? Sophia wanted to be a fly on the wall when the news was told to "her."

Following careful consideration, and concluding that her health was more important than anything else, Sophia decided that she would take care of herself and her baby, enjoy a stress-free pregnancy, and if Rob couldn't be there for her when she needed him, the hell with him. She would raise her child and continue her bid for politics in four years without him. That might work.

Chapter Twenty One
The Henderson Family

After enjoying a Thursday night at Holy Tabernacle Church with Pam, Neicy and Ronny, Maria saw the rest of the year pass quickly. Pam hadn't wanted to come to an "Intercessory Prayer Group" and "Bible Study" as their featured Girls' Night Out, but she had promised her friends and so kept her word.

The ladies arrived on time, and Mother Wright welcomed Pam and Ronny with open arms. She gravitated towards Ronny, who came as she was, dressed suggestively in skin-tight black leggings, knee-high fur boots, and a fitted, cropped fuchsia pink sweater that cupped her enhanced breasts. Her hair was long and curly, and she also wore a bright pink lipstick and big, gold hoop earrings. It almost looked like Ronny had dressed that way on purpose and was daring the church to say something to her. There were only two people there besides them, however, and Mother Wright seemed incurious of Ronny's attire. Mother hugged everyone, thanked the ladies for coming, and started the prayer group with her commentary that people were always asking the church to pray for them. The church would call a prayer meeting, but few people showed up.

"Thank God that all of you have come into the house of the Lord tonight," Mother said. "Two or three is all it takes. God bless you."

Pam's participation was mainly as a spectator. She was polite and respectful, but Maria and Neicy could both see that she hadn't taken to the more conservative style of prayer, corporate worship and Bible Study, and that was just as well. Elder Daniels taught the Bible Study class on faith, and as Maria, Mother Wright and Neicy enjoyed the teaching and supported Elder Daniels' message with "Amens" and "Hallelujahs", Pam sat disinterested and checking her cell phone several times during the hour. Ronny was quiet during the lesson, but when the class finished and Elder Daniels' asked if anyone had any comments, she raised her hand and shared her gratitude and comment that the message was right on time.

When the ladies left that night, Pam promised to be back in touch with them to schedule another night out, but Maria hadn't heard from her since.

Ronny came to prayer once more, but she wasn't able to stay for Bible Study, she stated, because of her work schedule. Mother asked Maria to befriend Ronny and keep in touch with her, so Maria agreed. A couple messages were left on Ronny's cell phone just to let her know that she was in everyone's prayers, but Maria hadn't heard back from Ronny either.

Rob called a few times after Thanksgiving, but Maria was avoiding his calls and trying to just stay in her lane and focus on her children and Bible Studies. Rob and Maria still sat together at Genny's basketball games and Papi's karate practices, and they did exchange small talk, but Maria was almost on "e" with the whole situation. There was really nothing left to say.

Meanwhile, Genny had developed into a fiercely aggressive ball player, and she was a natural leader on the court with the other four starting players, running the offense and encouraging her teammates to get low on defense. Maria and Rob communicated about Genny with ease.

The girls' basketball team was undefeated at the end of the year, and the local paper now frequented both the girls' and the boys' games. The story of three freshman players from APHS dishing out defeats by margins of 20 plus points was newsworthy. They were, after all, competing against older and more seasoned opponents who seemed to crack under pressure when confronted by these underclassmen who weren't intimidated at all by their older competitors.

Mr. Henderson taught the girls that the reputations of the other teams didn't matter. When their opponents stepped in the gym, he didn't care who they were, their past accolades went out the door. It was a level playing field, and APHS would play to dominate. Genny had that fire and aggression in her eyes already, and Joanne and Bria soon after obtained it. Rhonda Miller was a well-rounded player who could be counted on to block shots, score and play solid defense, but it was apparent to everyone that she missed the dynamic of her twin sister on the court. Rhonda resisted adjusting to the three new freshman early on, and Coach Milton demanded she make an attitude adjustment quick or sit the bench.

"The court, ladies, is no place for your personal issues. Leave the issues at home. We are here to play basketball. If you don't want to play, you are free to go. If you are here to play, we play this game my way."

His unyielding disciplinarian approach, regardless of the fact that they were girls, was no issue for Genny – she was used to it from her dad. Mr. Henderson loved it. He would sit in the stands grateful that Coach Milton shared the same approach and passion.

Morgan Huntley, a returning junior who played at center, rounded out the starting five. She was 5'11" and a good rebounder, somewhat shy and reserved, but after a few games, it was like the caterpillar had blossomed into a butterfly and accepted her calling. Morgan stepped out of the background and into the forefront of the team's defensive strategies, blocking shots, limiting her opponents' infiltration in the paint, and out jumping other girls underneath the basket to snatch the majority of rebounds.

"This is the most complete team we have had in many seasons," Coach Milton told the girls, "but that doesn't mean we don't have to fight every time we get on the court. Every time! Do not take these wins for granted, and don't ever assume that any other team is going to just bow down and hand you a win. We play hard every game, even against those teams we know are an easy win."

That philosophy was identical to Rob's, so the two men got along great, and they both had the girls' best interest at heart.

Ronny did make it to a couple basketball games to watch her daughter, Joanne, who was becoming one heck of a power house in her own right. Joanne was quick on offense, and she and Genny would often run fast breaks together, passing the ball between themselves until one took the layup. Bria's mom came as well, and the families sat together in the stands and supported the girls with chants as if they were the cheerleading team.

Papi would soon be testing for his brown belt, and Rob was working with him throughout the week. One of Rob's partners was interested in purchasing a space nearby for a karate school, and he needed another Instructor. Rob asked Maria what she thought about him partnering with the friend, and Maria supported the idea. She honestly believed that it was an outstanding suggestion. So Rob's calls now weren't only concerning Genny and Papi, who were both fine and he knew it, but concerning his newest business venture for which he needed Maria's input and expertise. His strategically placed confidence and trust in Maria used to excite her passion for him and his work, but she was focusing more now on her own work with the church. Rob never had to compete for Maria's time with anything before, but the King of Kings had moved in, and Maria's heart and mind were under new management.

She was working feverishly on her assignments for Hampton Bible Institute, and she had fallen in love with the task of researching the Hebrew and Greek meanings of Bible verses. The Institute closed during the week of Thanksgiving and again for a winter break in December/January, and Maria was happy to spend the time over the breaks reading, researching and writing. When Rob asked the kids what their mother wanted for Christmas, they told their dad that she would probably appreciate a Bible since she read it all the time. Rob visited a local Christian Bookstore and accepted the sales associate's recommendation that an engraved NKJV Study Bible was the best way to go. It wasn't priced high at all, so he also purchased accessories including an engraved leather cover and carrying case, notebooks, book marks, Bible tabs, book lights, pens and highlighters. The store was having a Buy One, Get the 2nd Half Off sale, so he purchased the second for himself. The best way for him to communicate with Maria, he figured, would be to communicate with her about what she was most interested in.

262

When he went by Maria's home on Christmas day bearing gifts, he knew their kids supposed that they were probably the usual video games and gift cards. Maria was genuinely happy when she opened her gift, and she even gave him a hug. She was cautious about putting her trust in him, however, so she just continued to pray for him as Mother had told her to. Her gift for him was a new frame for the family portrait in his office, which he had forgotten about, but which Papi had mentioned to his mother. When Rob opened the gift, he felt convicted, but he was relieved when Papi explained that he saw the broken frame and wanted his dad to have another so that he could keep their family photo on his office desk.

Genny and Papi chose two silk neckties, which their dad promised to wear to his most important business meetings, and Maria also gave him a 24 carat gold necklace with a gold cross.

"Mom doesn't want jewelry," Genny and Papi insisted when their dad asked them.

"Are you sure she wouldn't rather have a diamond necklace or a new watch?" he asked.

"Absolutely not," they insisted. "Mom would appreciate the best Study Bible you can get."

The kids were right. Maria eagerly flipped through the pages of her NKJV Study Bible and was thrilled to see study and culture notes, word studies, a concordance, full-color maps, a digital download with purchase and a brief synopsis of each book of the Bible.[95] She and her mother noted the quality of the Bible and how easy to understand and organized it was.

Rob was grateful to make her happy.

"The little things," he thought to himself. *"All I had to do all this time was spend a few dollars on a Bible?"* Even with the accessories, he spent under $300, and that was less than what he had spent on Sophia.

The family went their separate ways on New Years' – Rob spent the night with Sophia in New York City, and Maria and the kids went to a New Years' Service at Holy Tabernacle until 12:30 a.m. Reverend Wright, Mother Wright and Elder Daniels led the congregation as they welcomed the New Year in prayer, praise, worship and thanksgiving. Mother asked Maria to pray for families during the service, and she was nervous but happy to participate.

Reverend Wright thanked Maria after she prayed, and he encouraged her to remain faithful to the Lord who was "preparing her to be used for His glory," and she should "keep her eyes on the prize, Jesus Christ, and not be distracted by any man."

His sermon that night was on **Joshua 24:15**

> *"And if it seems evil to you to serve the Lord,*
> *choose for yourselves this day whom you will serve,*
> *whether the gods which your fathers served that were on the other side*
> *of the River, or the gods of the Amorites, in whose land you dwell.*
> *But as for me and my house, we will serve the Lord."*

And **Matthew 7:13**

> *"Enter by the narrow gate; for wide is the gate and broad is the way*
> *that leads to destruction, and there are many who go by in it."*

His New Year's sermon topic was ***"The Choice to Cross Over,"*** and the good Reverend preached for thirty minutes on Joshua's address to the Israelites and the choice we all face in deciding whether to serve Jesus or not.

"Choose you whom ye will serve, now the matter is laid plainly before you." Joshua "resolves to do this, whatever others did. Those that are bound for heaven must be willing to swim against the stream. They must not do as the most do, but as the best do....They must come off from all confidence in their own sufficiency...." Reverend Wright quoted from Matthew Henry.[96]

Reverend Wright preached that the best choice anyone could make for the New Year would be the choice to serve Jesus Christ and to serve Him in His own way. No longer, he declared, would the Lord allow the people to straddle the fence as it pertained to their service of the Lord.

"We drive," Reverend Wright preached taking his time, dressed in a black suit and clerical collar and walking on the floor of the sanctuary before his members and guests, "in fancy cars today. I remember when I was a young man that if a young man drove a nice car, he would have a better chance with the young ladies. All a young man needed in my day was a Cadillac."

The members and guests laughed.

"Well, today, I guess the car of choice is a Mercedes or some fancy sports car. Ladies will love it if you pull up at their home in a nice car and take them out to a movie and dinner in a nice car. The young man, you know, he looks like he's got himself together, and he's going somewhere. Well, my brothers and sisters, I want to ask about the car the man is driving. I want to ask you about the car the woman is driving. And, I want to ask who is driving the car? Where is it going? A young lady would look real good, you know, in her man's expensive car. The girl's parents might appreciate the young man if he comes in an expensive car. We'd prefer that, wouldn't we? He *should* drive a nice car. But, ask yourselves if you would rather get in a $100,000 automobile going down a broad highway to hell or a beat up, old car entering through a narrow gate to joy, peace, happiness, abundant life and eternal life, destiny and salvation."

Several members of the church stood and said, "Preach!"

"You have come too far to turn back, daughter. God has brought you from a mighty long way, son. He has seen your every tear and heard your every cry. Every one of us has to make a decision in this lifetime, and that decision is whether we are going to serve Jesus Christ or not. If the man has already driven off, and he isn't letting Jesus take the wheel, he is headed for destruction. Pray for him, yes, but wait on the Lord to give you a clear answer and direction, for He looks down from heaven on all mankind to see if there are any who understand, any who seek God.[97] There are times, saints, when God will allow things to happen in our lives so that we will seek Him, and perhaps reach out for Him and find Him, though He is not far from any one of us.[98] The good Lord will never leave or forsake His own, and every disobedient child of God in a car driving on his own will hear from heaven sooner or later and be asked to hand over the keys to Jesus, for it is not the will of God that any man should perish. But, daughter, you are not called to be unevenly yoked with anybody, and until he bows down and humbles himself before God, he is driving in a lane that you are called to stay out of. Stay, Hallelujah, in your own lane! If it is God's will, He will do it in a perfect way. It is in His hands, amen. Well, you may ask, what do I do in the meantime? Pray and continue to seek Him. Let me encourage you with a few scriptures:

1. Show me Your ways, O Lord; Teach me Your paths;[99]
2. For this is God, Our God forever and ever; He will be our guide Even to death;[100]
3. Trust in the Lord with all your heart, And lean not on your own understanding; In all your ways acknowledge Him, and He shall direct your paths;[101]
4. If any of you lacks wisdom, let him ask of God, who gives to all liberally and without reproach, and it will be given to him.[102]

Now, when you hear from the Lord concerning what His will is for you, and He will answer for He is a rewarder of those who diligently seek Him,[103] be sure that you are willing to obey what it is He speaks to you. It would be a travesty to call on Him, receive an answer, and then choose to disobey His voice."[104]

"Amen" Elder Daniels said, standing up from his seat. "Preach, Reverend."

Reverend Wright continued, and his authoritative voice was raised as he emphasized the choice every child of God is faced with.

"The choice to cross over, saints, via the narrow gate is yours to make. Joy is straight ahead; abundant life is straight ahead; salvation is straight ahead; healing and deliverance is straight ahead. A faithful God who will never leave or abandon you, who died on the Cross of Calvary and shed His blood for your sins, begs the question tonight: whom will you and your family serve? Let it be, dear Father, help us Oh Lord, to decide tonight, going into the New Year, to declare with sincerity, authority and power, that 'as for me and my house, we will serve the Lord.' He will give you the grace to choose to cross over, Saints, and the Lord be with you, in Jesus' name. Call on the name of Jesus, beloved. The altar is open for prayer."

Minister Barrington and the praise and worship team were summoned to sing their rendition of the Hymn "Closer to You, Jesus."[105]

Closer to You, Jesus
My soul does long to be
Nearer to You, Savior
Nearer, Lord, to thee

Alas to the world
My soul does bid farewell
Free from death and danger
And from all flames of hell

Bliss and joy are mine
Oh what joy divine
Grace and mercy, holy blood
Christ, alone for me

Safely in His arms
From eternal harms
Blessed Son, please help my soul draw
Closer, Lord, to thee

Nearly the entire church joined in and sang the moving hymn, and the atmosphere was filled with the glory of the Lord. Members and guests knelt in prayer and called on the name of the Lord. Maria and her children went to the altar to kneel and pray, and while they were there, Papi fell asleep. Though Maria had made Genny and Papi take naps before they left, it had been a long day. Neicy joked that he was "slain in the spirit."[106]

Maria prayed at the altar for herself and everyone she knew, and she knew her prayers had been heard. She asked the Lord to help her get out of His way with Rob, and when she finished casting all her cares upon Him, she resolved to stand still and let the Lord fight her battle.[107] She also resolved that as Joshua, she and her children would serve Jesus Christ and allow Him to have His way and do whatever He wanted.

"Lord, please give me the strength to do your will. Thank you for being the head of my life and my house, and thank you for confirming your word tonight. Thank you for forgiving me of my sins, and thank you, Father, for blessing me to forgive others as you have forgiven me. I am but a sinner saved by your abundant grace and can only declare were it not for the Lord on my side. You are welcome to have control, and I submit to you. Let it be to me according to your word, I pray, in Jesus' name."

When Maria and her children returned home from the service, she turned on her phone and saw that there was no message from Rob that night. He called once or twice a week after the New Year, and he was used to Maria not picking up her phone, but when he found out from Sophia that she was pregnant, he knew he would have to face the inevitable and tell Maria the truth immediately. Maria would probably think that he had only given her the Study Bible on Christmas Day so that he could soften her up before he dropped the bomb, but he would have to assume that risk. He respected Maria and would protect her from the backlash his infidelity would likely cause all of them, and he would be the one to tell her before she heard it from anyone else.

One Thursday afternoon in January, Rob went to see his personal barber, Mike Love, at Sam's Place in Addington Park. He needed to be real with his best friend, who told it like it was. Mike Love insisted that Rob be honest and forthright with Maria, even if he did suspect the baby was not his.

"C'mon, man, you're talking about Maria – your wife. She held it down for you for years. You don't do your wife like that, man. You owe it to her to tell her the truth. Stop trying to punk out, and don't look at me to back you up, because if Maria asks me, I will tell her the truth myself."

Mike Love placed a black barber's cape on Rob as he sat in Mike Love's VIP chair. He was the proud owner of Sam's Place, a staple in the community for almost 20 years.

"Aw, c'mon man, you would do that?" Rob asked.

"Without any hesitation," Mike Love answered. He had known Rob and Maria since high school and was Rob's best man at their wedding. "Maria's a good girl. I hope this doesn't have anything to do with money. Please don't tell me you sold your wife and kids for the lure of some money."

"Hell naw," Rob lied. "I'm taking care of some things. I'm going to get Maria back, believe that."

"I hope so," Mike Love replied, "because Pam is always coming in and out of here, and you know she can't keep her mouth shut. She told me that she, your wife and Neicy hung out in Atlantic City at a strip show, and the strippers were feelin' Maria."

Mike Love picked up his clippers, but Rob turned in the chair before he could start cutting.

"Hold on, man. What are you talking about?"

Mike Love put the clippers down. "Pam. You know she's always talking."

"I know who she is," Rob answered. He was upset, and it showed. "Pam told you what about Maria?"

"Yeah, I know," Mike Love paused, "you still love Maria." Mike Love was not really shocked that what he had said *would* bother Rob. "You can't put your double standards on her anymore, Rob. You divorced her. What do you expect her to do? She can't go out with her girlfriends and have a good time?"

Mike Love knew he had a small window of opportunity to speak truthfully to his friend, so he continued to check his friend and confront him in love.

"That's right. Pam, Neicy and your wife went down to Atlantic City to a strip show, and the dancers were all over Maria. That's the word from your girl. And, she's also been talking and telling everybody that you're running around with that woman from City Hall because she's about to be the Mayor. So, this *is* about money. Why don't you just tape a For Sale sign on your behind and stay bent over."

Rob looked angrily at Mike Love, but Mike Love didn't care, and he kept right on going.

"Why are you upset about some strippers with Maria when you're on the block prostituting yourself? You just ditch your family? That's a sorry, coward ass, bitch ass move, and yet, you're trying to teach other young men how to be men. I bet they don't even respect you. When are you gonna stop frontin'? Don't try to fool me, man. You know you can't serve two masters, bruh, but that's your problem. You believe you are your own master. But you sold your family so that you could be the husband of the next Mayor, and I know that you are only doing this because that would put your new wife in a position to help you with your businesses. C'mon, man, game recognizes game. Be straight up about yours, don't lie to a brother."

Mike Love never wasted his words, and Rob knew that if he sat in Mike Love's chair, he would get real talk from his friend.

Rob replied, "Maria may have went down to Atlantic City. She can go. But if nosy behind Pam came back and told you some lie about strippers being all over my wife, I know for a fact, Jack, that she told you a lie straight from hell."

Rob was visibly upset. He started to remove the cape from around his neck.

"Okay, man, calm down. You still want me to tighten you up?" Mike asked.

"Naw. I'll come back later."

Rob grabbed his jacket from off the coat rack and left the shop. When he got in his car, he called his cousin, Walter, to get a second opinion, and Walter suggested that he deny it until it was proven that the baby was his – why stir the pot if you didn't have to? Rob appreciated the other point of view, and it did give him something to think about. However, he concluded that he would, out of respect for Maria, tell her the truth as soon as possible. He finally got his chance in the middle of January when she returned his call, softened perhaps by his recent purchase for her, and agreeing that yes, she did have time to talk.

"How are you, Rob?" Maria asked.

She almost sounded like her old self, but Rob wasn't comfortable playing with her emotions any more or taking her for granted. She was doing the Lord's work, and even though he wasn't an avid churchgoer or a saint by any means, he did, in his own way, respect God.

"I'm good, Maria. How are you?"

"Great, thanks for asking."

"Do you need anything else for your Bible classes?" Rob asked, needing to take his time.

"No, thank you so much. I love the Study Bible."

"Maria, I have something important that I need to talk to you about. Please hear me out."

"Okay," she responded carefully. Maria sensed nervousness in his voice, and she knew that whatever it was, it meant some kind of trouble for him.

Rob took his time explaining everything to Maria. He apologized to her for hurting her and breaking up their family, and he

270

admitted to the affair with Sophia that had been going on for over two years.

"I'm so sorry, Maria, if I hurt you and our children. My intentions were and have always been to provide for our family."

Maria listened to Rob on the other end of the call, and she was reminded of Mother Wright who asked if he had apologized to her yet. *"Well, yes, he has, but there is more to this story,"* she discerned.

"Rob, what's wrong?" Maria asked. "Please don't try to butter me up or sugar coat what it is that you need to say. Are you okay? What's going on?"

Nervously, Rob fumbled over his words until he finally got the courage to come out and say it. "Sophia......she is pregnant."

Maria was speechless. On the other end of the line, she closed her eyes and took several deep breaths. She had been standing in her kitchen contemplating what to cook for dinner, but his words cut to her core, and she went into the living room and sat on the couch, sinking into the pillows with her head in her right hand and the phone in her left. She dropped the phone on the couch and sat there, again completely on "e," with nothing in her reserve tank, completely numb. She had nothing to say. No curse words, no "this bitch," no "how could you?" There was nothing left in her at all. Rob could be heard on the phone talking, but Maria didn't need to listen anymore.

She was hurt in her heart. She had prayed, she was going to Bible Study, she had surrendered her life to Jesus, her children were in church, and she was doing the work that was required of her in the Bible Institute. She was passing her classes with high marks. What more did Jesus want from her? She was praying. Hell, she prayed all the time.

Maria concluded that she was not what Rob needed, and Rob was not what she needed. Rob needed Jesus, and Maria needed to move so that Rob could call on Jesus instead of calling on her. Rob would never change, and Maria was unwilling to keep going around this merry-go-round of heartache and disappointment.

"Rob," she said as she picked up the phone and interrupted him saying whatever he was saying, "I can't help you. I know that now. I think I have just been in God's way."

"What are you talking about?" Rob asked. "Did you hear anything I said?"

"I heard you."

"Maria, I said I don't believe the baby is mine. I know she was with someone else. I know that probably sounds like I'm just trying to get out of this, and you may think I'm lying, but I know she was with someone else."

"Well, Rob, was she with you? Did *you* sleep with her?" Maria asked. She would not allow him to deny his own involvement.

"Maria......." Rob started, pausing again.

"Did you sleep with her?" Maria asked again, sounding like she was an attorney on direct examination of a witness.

Rob didn't want to answer. He didn't want to actually say that he had; that would mean that he was admitting to it. If Maria just knew it without him saying it, he wouldn't feel so guilty and responsible.

"Are you going to answer the question, Rob? It's a yes or a no."

"Maria," he began, dodging the question, "It's not mine. I'm telling you the truth. It's not mine. I needed to tell you before this gets out. She may be running for Mayor."

Rob wanted to duck. He was afraid of what Maria would say to him, but at least he told her the truth. It was out now. He braced himself on the other end of the line, and he was in utter disbelief when he heard the sound of laughter.

Shocked, Rob asked, "You think this is funny?"

Still laughing, Maria replied, "Oh, Rob. When you can tell me that you slept with her, call me back, and we can talk. Ok?" She hung up the phone before he could say anything.

Rob called right back and continued evading the question, until finally, as if under continuous examination by a good attorney, he had to admit that yes, he had slept with Sophia. Yes, he admitted, there was a chance that the baby could be his, but he knew that it wasn't. He didn't tell Maria about his washcloth theory. The wet, used washcloth still hinging on Rob's mind hadn't been introduced into evidence, thank goodness, but Rob countered that he knew Sophia had been sleeping with other "men." He said "men" in the plural to defame Sophia's character, deflect attention from himself, and hopefully convince Maria that he was actually innocent and had been himself taken advantage of. Clothed with strength and dignity, Maria personified the Proverbs 31[108] woman and laughed without fear of the days to come.

"Rob, I'm going to get out of the way. I'm not angry with you, and I don't wish you or Sophia any harm. I'm not mad at all. I pray for you and Sophia, Rob, each and every day, and I want you to be happy. I will pray for your unborn child. But what I will not do is stand in the way of what God is doing in your life, and I am not going to fight with you about anything. The next time you want to talk to someone about this, call on Jesus. I can't help you, Rob," she said patiently. "I don't have all the answers, but Jesus does. Call on Jesus, Rob. Cast your cares upon Him. Seek His face. He has the help and the answers you need. I am grateful for the Bible you brought me, but you should go and buy one for yourself."

"I didn't call to have Bible Study, Maria. I'm trying to have a serious conversation with you," Rob answered with frustration.

"Okay, Rob, hear *me* out. I don't have what you need – Jesus does. Please be here to pick up the kids on the weekends, they are looking forward to seeing you. Thank you for telling me. God bless you."

"I'm not talking about Jesus, I'm talking about a baby that I know is not mine," Rob replied with more frustration.

"Goodbye, Rob."

Maria hung up the phone, and a flabbergasted Robert J. Henderson remained on the line for a few minutes wondering what had just happened and what he would do next.

The next morning, Maria called Neicy to confide in her.

"She's what?" Neicy asked.

"She's pregnant. Rob said he doesn't think the baby is his," Maria answered.

"Oh, Maria....I'm so sorry...."

"Why?" Maria interrupted. "He's been carrying on an affair with her for over two years. This was bound to happen sooner or later."

"Yes, but if they've been seeing each other for over two years, why hasn't she ever gotten pregnant before?" Neicy asked suspiciously. "I'm just saying. C'mon, Maria, this doesn't make any sense."

"Rob said that she might be running for Mayor, so maybe she did it purposely to trap him and force his hand."

"Yeah, that sounds about right. Or, the baby may really be someone else's. Can you believe this? We're almost 50 years old, and women are still getting pregnant to try and trap men into marriage? This is so immature. How old is this woman?"

"What difference does that make? Rob is 47, so he's just as bad."

"Well, from her photo, she looks pretty young, no more than 35, I would say. Forgive me, Maria, but you and Rob divorced months ago, and he didn't put a ring on her finger yet. I think she *is* trying to trap him. Either that, or the baby is really not his. So what did Rob say he was going to do?" Neicy asked.

Maria didn't care. "Well, I didn't really give him a chance to say anything else. I told him that he needed Jesus. I told him I would get out of the way and let God do whatever it is He wants to do. So, I am giving this entire matter over to Him."

Neicy was silent for a minute and thinking. Maria could be heard on the other end of the line cooking like nothing was wrong at all.

"Maria, I think that would be best. God is in control. Let go and let God."

Agreeing, Maria answered, "Yes."

"Does Pam know?" Neicy asked. "You know she will run her mouth all over town."

"I don't know, she works down there, but I haven't heard from her since our Girls' Night Out at Holy Tabernacle. I could care less who she runs her mouth to."

"Oh, she'll be alright," Neicy said with laughter. "You know, she and Evan are supposed to be getting married, but the last time I talked to her, she said they were going to Florida for a small wedding. I'll reach out to her and see how she is. If she catches wind of the latest news with 'this bitch,' she will go off."

Maria and Neicy both laughed, and Maria was grateful that the conversation took a lighter turn.

"Well, I have some good news to share with you, Maria," Neicy said.

"What? Are *you* pregnant?" Maria asked jokingly.

Laughing, Neicy responded, "Girl, please, ain't nothing going on over here. I contributed one young man to humanity, and that's it. Matter of fact, Tony, Jr. will be coming up this summer."

Tony, Jr. was Neicy and Tony's only child. They didn't speak of him much because Tony, Jr. was an openly bisexual man who was bitter about his experience growing up in the church. His parents had sought the help of Reverend Wright to pray that the Lord would deliver him from feminine tendencies and bisexuality. Tony, Jr. believed that God was love, and God created him and didn't make a mistake. Therefore, who were his parents or the Church to judge? They were heterosexual, and they were sinners, too, he argued. Heterosexuals needed the blood of Jesus just like everybody else did. He did date women, and to appease his parents, he eventually married a young girl from Holy Tabernacle. When he continued dating men, however, Neicy and Tony believed that their son was rebelling against God, and their differences caused a major split in their family. Their daughter-in-law divorced him, and Tony, Jr. left New Jersey and relocated to Atlanta.

"That's great news, Neicy. How long has it been since you saw him?"

Neicy explained that though it had been about seven years since they saw him in person, she did speak with him by phone.

"Wow, praise the Lord. I'm so happy for you and Tony," Maria replied.

"Well, thanks, but that's not the only good news. The best news, Maria, is that we just found out that Tony's cancer is in remission. Thank you, Jesus!"

Maria screamed in the phone, and she gave glory to God. "Hallelujah!" she yelled. "Praise the Lord!"

The two women were both crying and full of joy, exceeding joy, as they glorified God for His goodness and mercy on Tony.

"He is still a healer, Hallelujah!" Neicy exclaimed. "God still answers prayers. Maria, we have been praying and fasting, fasting and praying, and laying before God since we found out he had cancer. God answers prayers. He didn't answer us right away, not when we first cried out to Him, but He answered. The doctors are shocked. They have no answer. Tony was Stage three. They say that there is no medical explanation for what happened, and Tony's doctor, a Jewish man, said 'glory to God.' Can you believe it? Hallelujah!" Neicy was sniffling and crying through her words, and Maria was crying with her.

"Neicy, I am so happy for you. If anybody deserves a miracle of God right now, it's you and Tony. You are so giving, so loving, so concerned about everybody else, even when you are going through your own pain. You never complain. You're always there for everybody else. I praise God for you and Tony, and I am so happy for you. God is good all the time, Hallelujah!"

The two ladies remained on the line for another hour, praising God and giving Him glory for the things He had done. They were both witnesses to the power of the living God, and the testimony strengthened Maria's faith in the Lord. What need was there for either of them to fear? God could do anything, and He was worthy of all the praise.

"Maria, don't give up on what you are praying for. Whatever it is. You don't have to tell me, I don't need to know. I'm going to get out of *your* way. Draw closer to Him, Maria, and He will draw even closer to you.[109] God can do it."

"Amen. Let's go out and celebrate! We have to, Neicy. Friday night, my treat, me, you and Tony – we can go anywhere you want. Is that alright with you?" Maria asked.

"Sure, we'd love to. I'll see where Tony wants to go and let you know early Friday."

"Sounds good. God bless you, Neicy. Give Tony my love, please."

"I will. Talk to you Friday."

On Friday morning, Maria called Neicy to confirm their dinner plans, but she reached her answering machine. She called again early in the afternoon and again reached her answering machine, so she called Tony's cell. When he answered, Maria began by praising the Lord for Tony and telling him that she was happy for him and Neicy. Tony stopped Maria abruptly and told her thank you, but Neicy's mom had passed, and they were at the hospice facility. He would have Neicy call Maria back.

The following week, January 28th, a Home Going Celebration was held for Deaconess Crystal Savannah Gray, age 83 years of East Brunswick, NJ, a widow. She was survived by daughters, Neicy (Tony) and Shannell (Calvin) and grandchildren Tony, Jr., David, Vanessa and Dawn, and a host of nieces, nephews, cousins, relatives and friends. Reverend Wright requested that all clergy and leaders be present, without exception.

The church leadership and family endeavored to maintain the wishes of their deceased and keep the service as joyful as possible. Neicy's mother had emphasized that she did not want a sad, somber funeral. She insisted that they celebrate her life and her going home to rest eternally with her Lord and Savior, Jesus Christ.

"I don't want no sad songs at my funeral," she had told her daughters when she was moved into hospice care. "Ain't no reason to cry. I'm going home to be with Jesus. Just make sure that *you* make it in so I don't have to cry when I don't see you."

The weather that Friday morning was partly cloudy and overcast. Family and friends filled the sanctuary, and the church leadership worked as a well-oiled machine to ensure a smooth flow in the service. Ushers, greeters, hospitality and the Mothers welcomed each and every person who came into the sanctuary. Members of the Women's Ministry volunteered to help as setup, servers and cleanup for the repast, and just about every church member brought a dish or gave an offering to help out. The church kitchen was overflowing with food. Joanne and Pam came early and offered to assist, but the Women's Ministry had everything covered.

The service started with a visiting Psalmist, Keyara Oliver, who sang a stirring hymn, "Home with My Lord,"[110] which Deaconess Gray had requested. The worship moved most of the family to tears.

> *Thank God, He saved me to make it*
> *By the grace of the king*
> *I'm home*
> *Rejoice and sing!*

Marcia L. Boynton

Thank God, He chose me to make it
By my Savior's blood
I'm safe
In heaven above

Home, eternal home
Cryeth no more for me
With my Lord and Savior
My soul eternally free

Home, eternal home
Jesus prepared for me
With my Lord and Savior
Glory, glory!

He paid the price
And washed my sins
Forever in His blood

He prepared a mansion
Where my soul shall live
Hallelujah! Oh, what love!

My garments are new
Earthly tent is no more
Rejoice in the King,
What are you crying for?

He called my name
And it is time
With Abraham, Isaac and Jacob
We all shall dine

He hasn't left
Your hearts alone
Rejoice in the Lord,
He has called me home

Hallelujah!
Oh glory!
Home with the Lord.

All of the family members fought back tears as they came up to give their remarks about their mother, who had dropped out of high school when she was pregnant with her oldest daughter and who returned two years later to finish. Their mother didn't have a college education, but everyone knew that she had a Ph.D. in the Word of God. She raised her children in church and taught Sunday school for nearly 30 years. Neicy's mother mentored many young women in the faith, and she was looked up to for her wisdom, care and love of the Gospel. Many of the same young women she mentored went on to serve in various roles in ministry around the world. Some were able to attend, but those who could not sent Resolution Letters and/or cards. There were so many Resolution Letters, the family didn't have enough time to read them all, so they asked that the letters be acknowledged instead.

Reverend Wright performed the eulogy, and he preached on **John 16:16-22 – *"Joy, Unspeakable Joy."*** Maria had never heard the Pastor speak with such compassion, authority, love and fire. How a servant of God turned the loss of a mother into a joyous occasion and reason to celebrate was probably taught in Homiletics 101, but Reverend Wright completely lifted the spirits of the family through his smooth, oratorical skill focusing the family and friends on the ability of Jesus to comfort them. He also had a "sho' nuff" anointing, as the seasoned Saints said, as well as an authentic compassion that blessed everyone to know that he felt their pain. He had, after all, known Deaconess Gray since she joined Holy Tabernacle. She was family, but Reverend Wright assured the family and friends that Jesus felt their pain just as He wept when He came to Lazarus' grave.[111] His heart went out to a widow whose only son had died, and Jesus touched the bier and said to the young boy, "Arise."[112] Jesus loved Deaconess Gray just as much as He loved Lazarus, and He was moved with compassion just as much as he was for the widow, for He gave His own life on the cross of Calvary that Deaconess Gray should not die, but live eternally.

Jesus gave parting words to his disciples in John 16, but He told them and us that He will see us again. In this, we must rejoice.

"Deaconess Gray believed in Jesus, and though she passed on, she will live.[113] It wasn't possible that Jesus should be held by the pains of death.[114] He freed us from sin and the grave, and death has no power or authority over the blood of Jesus. Our joy, beloved, is that we will see Jesus again, and glory to God, we will see Deaconess Gray again."

The good Reverend expounded on his text for about 20 minutes. He shared that her body in the mahogany wood casket was but an earthly tent[115], and there was reason to celebrate and rejoice in her life for she knew Jesus, and her spirit had just returned home.

"We shall all go home one day," he preached. "Thank God she knew Jesus as Lord and Savior."

"Amens" and "Hallelujahs" filled the sanctuary.

As the Reverend finished his eulogy, Minister Barrington and the praise and worship team sang a medley in concert form of up tempo gospel tunes that were favorites of Deaconess Gray. Neicy belted out the last song, a spirit-filled "Journey to Canaan," and the tears running down her cheeks, she said, were tears of joy, unspeakable joy.

Neicy testified that she and her family had watched their mother's condition deteriorate, and she was moved to hospice care just a few months ago. She was grateful to God because He called her mother home to eternal rest, and her mother was no longer in pain. Neicy's family and friends, including Maria, stood and lifted their hands to bless the Lord as Neicy didn't just sing, she worshipped. She worshipped as the praise and worship team sang background vocals, and Neicy was full of the spirit. Reverend Wright and all of the ministers stood in the pulpit, and he motioned for everyone to sing with her. There wasn't a seated person in the house. The musicians continued playing when Neicy finished, and the church erupted into high praise with worshippers dancing in the aisles and before the altar. Ushers attended to the worshippers, and the mothers stationed near the immediate family members embraced them and offered tissues. Deacon Tony played a tambourine with the musicians, and he and Neicy danced together before the church. Their son, Tony, Jr., was also seated up front with dark sunglasses on, and he stood and lifted his hands. Joanne and Pam were a few rows back, standing and worshipping the Lord. And Rob, who came in a few minutes late and sat with Maria and the kids, stood respectfully as Maria lifted her hands and blessed God.

When the service was over, everyone prepared to go to the Cemetery, and then they would return to Holy Tabernacle for a repast. As Rob and Maria left the sanctuary, he offered to drive her and the kids. Genny and Papi voiced their eagerness to go in front of other members of the church who were leaving at the same time, so Maria agreed to keep the peace. They walked outside to his car, which was blocking another vehicle in the church parking lot. He gave Maria the keys and asked her to move his car – he would be right back, he said, he had forgotten something inside.

Rob went back inside the church and into the sanctuary. The service had a profound effect on him. He couldn't deny the presence he felt, especially during the sermon and the worship in song. After the last few people exited the sanctuary, Rob knelt at the altar and prayed, asking God to help him and show him what to do next. If nothing else worked, he would try God. *"Who knows,"* Rob thought, *"God might work."*

Chapter Twenty Two

Genny

Genny earned A's and B's on her report card, which placed her on the school's High Honor Roll. Her mother was glad to see and know that her daughter was not forfeiting her schoolwork for extra-curricular activities.

The girls' team remained undefeated through January, but they suffered a few losses in February to private schools with rosters of starting juniors and seniors who had mastered three point shots just as well as the girls from APHS. The coaches of the private schools scouted APHS and designed their team's play around the girls' offense and defense. It was a strategic move that Coach Milton was prepared for, so he, in turn, played his girls against the other teams in a man-to-man defense to stabilize them. The girls did well, but they were outplayed in the games where they suffered defeat.

Genny was researching the best internet sites for instructions on how to dunk, and though she followed every tip and applied herself without reservation, there was no difference in how high she jumped or reached. So she, Joanne and Bria came up with an idea to have Joanne kneel on all fours, and then Genny could jump off of and soar from Joanne's back. One day, the girls tried it before their practice when the gym was empty, and Bria stood as lookout. Joanne insisted that Genny first try from a chair, so they brought one into the gym. Genny was admittedly nervous, but she tried the first couple of times without the ball to be sure she could reach the rim, and she was able to with no problem.

Joanne passed the ball to Genny, who would try now to actually dunk. Bria pulled out her cellphone to record the attempt, and when she did she left her post at the gymnasium door. Chris Walker walked in to see Genny dribbling towards the chair, stepping on it and losing control of the ball as she went up. He was followed by a few players from the boys' team, and with a confused look on his face he asked, "What are you doing?"

"Bria! You're supposed to be looking out!" Joanne yelled.

Bria lowered her phone from her eyes and saw the boys standing to her right. "Sorry."

"Yo, I think these girls are in here trying to dunk," Chris said to the other players. They all started laughing, and Chris told them he would show them how it was done. The girls insisted they didn't need any help, but he was persistent, and he easily leaped off the chair and dunked the ball with one hand to the cheers of his teammates.

"We should do this," Chris said, as he landed. "What ya'll up to?"

"Nothing," an embarrassed Genny replied. She didn't want anyone to see her, least of all the boys, until she had perfected the move.

"If you really want to do this, you have to run all the way through. I watched you come down the court, and you were strong when you started, but you eased up when you got to the basket. You can't ease up." Chris took the basketball from her and dribbled back to three point range. He shot and missed.

"You should straighten your wrist and follow through on your shot," Genny said. She spoke low enough so that only he could hear because she did not want him to resent her giving him advice in front of everyone else. He just looked at her. At the same time, Coach Milton walked into the gym, and he told the boys to get the chair off the court so that the girls could practice.

"Sorry Coach," Chris Walker replied.

"Thanks," Genny said.

Chris nodded and then put the chair back in the rack of chairs that were stationed besides the bleachers.

"Let's go! Give me 20 laps around the gym!" Coach Milton said.

There were still a few minutes before their scheduled practice start time of 3:00 p.m., but the girls knew better than to talk back, so they started their laps. The rest of the team trickled in, as they usually did, up until 3:00 p.m. on the button, and Coach Milton let them know that their practice would include a new defense. He wanted to try a two-two defense (two man at the top of the key and two man at the bottom) with one player, Morgan, as the man out. She was tall and a shot-blocker, so she would be responsible to guard the other teams' three point shooters, and he needed the girls to master the new defense before the State Sectionals in March.

The weeks flew by, and the girls from APHS didn't lose another game. They played against their rival, East Ridge High School, in a deciding match for the Conference Championship, and when the fourth quarter started, the APHS girls were leading decisively, 50 – 33. Coach Milton wasn't willing to take any chances, however, so he insisted that Genny and Joanne keep hitting three pointers. Genny sank two, and Joanne hit one to bring their 17 point lead to 26. With four minutes remaining, Coach Milton called a time out and congratulated the girls on their win.

"We still play aggressive on defense, but I want to take it back to a two-one-two. Keep the hands up, and if you get the ball on a fast break, **do not** slow the game up. Score, and get back down on defense." Beaming with pride, he high-fived each one of the girls and led them in a huddle with their "1-2-3 Defense!" team chant.

Chris Walker and the rest of the boys' basketball team were in the stands. The gymnasium was starting to fill because the boys were playing after the girls, which was the usual order.

"Joanne, let's try that move when we get the ball," Genny whispered as they walked back onto the court.

"We can't do that, Genny. We don't even have it down yet," Joanne said with reluctance. She wasn't confident that Genny could pull it off.

"Yes, we can. I've been practicing at home with my mom's furniture. C'mon, let's just try it."

Joanne really didn't want to, but she did agree with Genny that it would be fun to at least try, and what was the worst that would happen? Coach Milton would get mad, make them run suicides and give them some long, drawn-out speech.

"What will your dad say?" Joanne asked.

"He'll be happy. He loves basketball, and he's so proud of you and Bria, too. C'mon, let's just try it. Stay ahead of me when we go for the fast break. When I nod, get down so Bria can post your man up like we practiced."

"Okay," Joanne answered. They gave Bria the signal, and she was excited to try it.

East Ridge brought the ball up, and their point guard was weak with her left hand, so Joanne forced her to go left, and she stole the ball. Joanne passed the ball back to Genny, who brought it up on a fast break, and Joanne ran ahead with Bria. The slower East Ridge girls were behind them, and Genny gave the signal for Joanne to get down on all fours. As she did, Coach Milton stood up from the sidelines and saw, for the first time in their school history, a freshman girl leap from the back of another freshman and extend herself as high as she could to reach the basket. It seemed to be happening in slow motion before the crowd of spectators, who watched in awe as Genny, Joanne and Bria pulled it off – Genny dunked the ball. The crowd went wild! Chris Walker and the boys' basketball team were jumping up and down in the stands, and they ran onto the floor behind Coach Milton. The referees were looking at each other with their whistles in their mouths unsure of what, if anything, to call. The girls on the APHS team were cheering, screaming and jumping up and down as well, but Coach Milton stood still and showed no emotion. Some of the spectators ran onto the court and high-fived Joanne and Bria, and then they lifted Genny up in the air. The coaches from East Ridge had to remind the referee to stop the clock, and it would be reset some 15 seconds once order was restored, leaving about three minutes left in the game.

Coach Milton never had a problem speaking his mind, but this left him speechless. While all the people in the gym were cheering and applauding, and the girls who sat on the bench stood and jumped with excitement, he sat down expressionless, thinking of what he would say to the girls in the locker room after the game. He didn't want fanfare behind tricks and stunts in the game, and this wasn't even anything they had asked him about. As long as they played well, everything else would come. Meanwhile, Rob and Maria sat in the bleachers with Papi. Maria was excited for her daughter, but she knew there would be some kind of repercussion. Rob was excited for his daughter as well, but he also knew that if Coach Milton stayed true to himself, he would probably have Genny sit down for a game or two because of what could be called "showboating," and no coach approved of that.

When the game ended, both teams shook hands, and then the boys' basketball team and several spectators ran onto the floor and celebrated with the girls. A newspaper reporter approached Coach Milton for an interview.

"Congratulations, Coach, on your win," said the reporter, Kevin Rollins, High School Sports Reporter for their local newspaper. He was dressed in black sweatpants and a navy blue hoodie, and he carried a worn notebook under one arm.

"Thanks, Kevin. At least you have the right colors on," he replied, taking note that Kevin had dressed in support of his team.

"Oh, I know how to dress when I come here. I better have on the school colors," Kevin said. He and Coach Milton shook hands. They had known each other for a few years. Kevin covered all the high school sports for both boys and girls.

"So, that dunk at the end of the game - that's a first, right? And, the players who did that were Genny Henderson, Joanne Hicks and Brianna Mitchell? All freshmen?"

Protective at all times of his players, Coach Milton answered defensively, "That's right."

"How are you feeling about playing St. Benedict's Prep Academy this year? You'll probably face off in the States."

Confidently, Coach Milton answered, "I'm feeling good about it, Kevin. We're a young team, but the girls can handle pressure, and we've made some adjustments to our game. We're ready to go up against them."

"Your team has always done well in the Conference Titles. Do you think your young players can get over that losing streak at the state level and compete in the state finals this year?"

Coach Milton thought for a moment. "That's a good question, Kevin, but I wouldn't characterize the efforts of my girls as a losing streak. We lose when we don't play our best, and this team has always played at its best. I've never been disappointed with any of my players or any of the results, and this year is no different. We will play our best, and if that sees us lose the next game, so be it. If that takes us all the way to the state championship, so be it."

Not convinced, Kevin replied, "That's a nice, humble way of looking at things, but c'mon, Coach, you want to win just like every other Coach. That philosophy was for our kids when they were five and six years old. You play to win. That dunk at the end of the game said it loud and clear. That sent a message to every other team in the state. Well, off the record, I hope you do win. I've always been a fan, and please tell the girls that I'll be rooting for them, too. But don't try that on St. Benedict's – their wing player is quick on the court, too. One of their assistant coaches was here tonight. You, my friend, just sent a message to them. Good luck in the tournament. The article will be in the paper tomorrow."

Kevin shook Coach Milton's hand again and looked over his shoulder, noticing the East Ridge coach by the team's bench.

"I need to go talk to the Coach from East Ridge before he leaves," Kevin said.

"Alright, thanks Kevin. We'll see you at the finals."

Coach Milton met with all the girls in the locker room and congratulated them on their win. He wasn't sure what he wanted to do about the slam dunk, so he told Genny, Joanne and Bria that he would need to meet with them the next day before practice. All three girls were still giddy and excited. One of their friends was recording the game, and their dunk was already posted on social media with many views.

Rob shook his daughter's hand when she came out of the locker room, and he and Maria hugged her and told her they were proud of her.

"I hope the Coach isn't too hard on you," Rob said softly in Genny's ear.

"Why would he be?" Genny asked.

"You didn't even tell *me* about that, so I know he didn't know," Rob replied. Then he laughed with his daughter for having the nerve and confidence to go after what she wanted. Genny smiled and told him that she didn't think she could pull it off, but she had been practicing with a chair at home.

"I found a few videos online of high school girls who can dunk, and that inspired me," Genny said. "It gave me the confidence I needed."

"Did anybody help you?" he asked.

"Yes, Joanne and Bria. We've been working on this since December." Genny didn't want to tell her dad that Chris Walker had also helped her. Her dad might think that she was fraternizing with the son of his sworn enemy.

"Well, what you did was pretty clever. Just be ready to handle whatever Coach Milton throws at you."

By the next day the video of Genny's slam dunk atop Joanne's back had gone viral. The sports section of their local paper had a photo of Joanne on all fours with a focused and determined Genny leaping from her back and soaring towards the rim. She used both hands to slam the ball into the basket, and the East Ridge players were visible in the photo with their faces aghast. The front page headline read:

"Freshmen Get Fresh With East Ridge"

Maria and Rob appreciated the press coverage, and Genny was hoping it would generate more support for the girls' team. When she came to school, the Principal mentioned the win in the morning announcements, and everyone in Genny's home room class gave her a standing ovation. Upperclassmen, who notoriously appreciated their school athletes, acknowledged and cheered for Genny, Joanne and Bria in the hallways. Chris Walker looked for Genny between classes, and he finally found her at her locker in the early afternoon. He told her she did a great job pushing through.

"That's how you do it, girl! How did it feel to fly?"

"It felt like the air was carrying me," she laughed. "Thank you for your help. I did what you said."

"I know you did. You wouldn't have made it if you hadn't. You can't ease up when you get that close. Don't ever ease up on it." Smiling, he said, "I'm proud of you, little sis. See you around." He turned to go in the other direction of his next class.

"*Little sis? Okay,*" she thought. "Wait," she said before he could leave.

"What's up?" he asked, turning around to face Genny.

"Your three point shot. If you just......."

Interrupting her, he lifted his right arm and extended his elbow, keeping it perfectly straight, and flicked his wrist. He kept his arm up to show her that he had taken her advice. "I know. Thanks, and I'll see you later, I can't be late to my next class."

After school, the girls met with Coach Milton before the start of practice as he asked.

"First thing, ladies, I am proud of all of you for your grades. Genny and Bria, congratulations on making the Honor Roll. That is an outstanding accomplishment. Every student athlete has to remember the priority of being a student first, and you have. Your education always comes first. Joanne, you just missed the Honor Roll, but I know that you'll pick up that grade in your Science class to make it next time. Genny, you did great in Science, so maybe you can help her."

"Sure, Coach," Genny replied.

Coach Milton paused and was silent for a moment. He took a deep breath and then continued speaking as the girls wondered what he would say next. His smile was replaced by a stern look.

"The second thing is.......I am responsible for educating you just as much as your teachers, and there is a lesson that I have to teach each of you. I thought about it and have decided that........Genny and Joanne, you will sit the bench for the next two games. Bria, you will start as point guard and take Genny's place. I am not running a circus. We do not need stunts or tricks to win basketball games. We were already winning the game yesterday. None of you came to me with this. Why not? Because you knew I would be against it? I'm the Coach. You can practice with everybody else, but you will not be playing in the next two games. That's it. 20 laps around the gym."

The girls looked at one another and then got up to run their laps. When the other girls arrived and found out from Genny and Joanne that their Coach told them they would sit the bench for the next two games, the team complained to him that he was being too hard on them, but he didn't care. Rhonda was the most vocal of all the players, to Genny and Joanne's surprise, and she threatened to sit the bench herself if he didn't let them play. Coach Milton called her bluff and told them that whoever wanted to leave could leave. Rhonda picked up her coat and walked towards the exit, but Bria and Morgan persuaded her to stay.

"We've worked hard all season long to get here, Rhonda. Don't leave. If you leave, we'll definitely lose," Bria said.

Rhonda stayed near the exit door, but she was determined to leave if her two teammates were forced to sit down. She directed her speech to their Coach.

"We need Genny and Joanne," Rhonda spoke with passion and fire. "They do everything you ask them to do. We practice when you are not here. So what they dunked – was it a mistake to you? You're penalizing us for making mistakes, Coach? We're going to make mistakes, that's a part of the game. That's a part of life. I'm not playing if they don't play, and Bria and Morgan, you don't have to either. We wouldn't have made it this far without them. Genny had her dad training you too, Bria. You wouldn't be where you are without Genny, so don't forget who helped you get here. Ain't none of us playing without Genny. We're a team, and we stand together."

Rhonda held her ground and didn't budge. Morgan and Bria grabbed their books to leave, and they stood by the exit door with Rhonda. Genny was in shock.

Now it was up to Coach Milton, and Rhonda, the street-smart and sassy one of the girls, knew it. She had showdowns with her gang member brothers before, so this was nothing to her.

"I'm impressed, Rhonda," Coach Milton said without showing any emotion. "That's what a good Captain does. She goes down with her ship."

There was silence in the gym for a minute. Coach Milton went and sat in the stands, and the girls wondered if their stand had backfired.

Coach Milton knew how to negotiate as well, so he decided to see their offer and raise it.

"Okay. Everyone plays. Thank your fearless leader, ladies, because if it wasn't for Rhonda, none of you would be playing."

The girls resumed their practice, but Coach Milton ran them harder than he had before. 20 laps around the gym became 40, and 15 minutes of suicides became 30. Though the girls did not complain, he knew that they were aware that their defiance caused their additional workouts. And even though Coach Milton promised that everyone would play, he didn't promise for how long. He was still the Coach, and he would limit both Genny and Joanne's playing time during the next two games to teach them a lesson.

The girls from APHS lost their next two games, but they qualified for a bye in the State Championships. They were seeded below the Top Ten in the State, and they would play against the #6 team in the Quarter-Finals, St. Mary's from Jersey City.

The Quarter-Final matchup was played at St. Mary's, and St. Mary's fans came out in full force. APHS had supporters who traveled, about 50 in all, but the sold-out crowd at St. Mary's had nearly 300 fans cheering in the stands.

"Maybe they dunk," Coach Milton said sarcastically to Genny and Joanne. "We'll see."

St. Mary's dominated the first half of the game. The St. Mary's girls hardly missed a shot, and the APHS two-two defense, one man out, wasn't having any impact. Coach Milton called for the girls to play man-to-man instead, and then he sat Genny and Joanne down. At half time, APHS was down by 13 points. Coach Milton kept the same five players on the court when the third quarter started, and their deficit increased to 17 points.

"Genny and Joanne, let's go," he told the girls who were sitting at the end of the bench. There was three minutes left in the third quarter.

"It's about time," Rob said to Maria. They were seated in the stands, watching and waiting for Coach Milton to put Genny and Joanne back into the game.

Genny walked onto the court, and Rhonda high-fived her. Then, Genny stole a pass from her opponent. She passed the ball to Joanne, who was already at the other end of the court, and Joanne scored easily on a layup. APHS girls maintained a full court press on St. Mary's and forced two successive turnovers. Joanne scored two points on an easy shot under the basket, and Genny dribbled back to three-point range and sank a shot, with a foul. She made her foul shot, and that cut their deficit to just nine points. St. Mary's called a time out, and the girls went over to Coach Milton who kept a poker face on as he told the girls to continue pressing the ball and take the three point shots.

It was St. Mary's possession, and APHS continued to press. This time, St. Mary's committed a ten second violation for not getting the ball past the half-court line. Genny took the ball out and passed it to Bria, who passed it underneath the basket to Morgan. St. Mary's had two players defending Morgan, so she got the ball back out to Bria at the top of the key. Bria faked the shot and then passed it back to an open Genny who hit another three pointer. It was now a six point game.

APHS pressured St. Mary's again, and they began to reveal a chink in their armor. They were nervous and intimidated. Rhonda liked to talk smack against her man, and the visibly shook guard Rhonda defended was stripped of her confidence. The ball was turned over, and APHS recovered it, scoring easily on a layup and cutting the deficit to just four points at the end of the third quarter. The fans from St. Mary's were now quiet, and the 50 or so APHS fans were cheering loudly and chanting "Let's go Knights! Let's go Knights! Let's go Knights!"

"I hope he doesn't have Genny and Joanne sit down again," Maria said to Rob. "He sat them down for most of the last two games, he made his point."

"Doesn't matter. All he's doing is making them hungrier. I do the same thing. He's a good Coach. It will be okay," Rob assured her from the stands.

When the fourth quarter began, the starting five for APHS were still on the floor. The jump ball gave St. Mary's the possession, but Morgan wrestled with her man and forced another jump ball. This time, APHS gained possession. Two players were guarding Genny every time she got the ball, and that was okay, because Joanne could shoot three pointers, too. Genny passed the ball to Joanne who attempted the shot and missed, but Morgan grabbed the rebound, scored and drew the foul. She made her foul shot, and it was now a one point game.

The fans from St. Mary's got back into the game, stomping their feet in the bleachers and shouting "Let's go Red Hawks! Let's go Red Hawks! Let's go Red Hawks!"

"Oh, be original," Maria said.

The two teams traded baskets for the next few minutes, and both teams were in a full court press. APHS was a little more adept at handling the press, having practiced against taller, meaner and stronger boys, and the girls capitalized on every possession. Coach Milton had only one timeout left, and when he called it, he told the girls to keep going for the three point shots. Morgan was to stay under the basket and rebound like her life depended on it.

Back on the floor, all Genny could think of was what her father told her: *"This is your house. You own it."* When she got the ball on offense again, she shook her opponents and took the three point shot from atop the key and made it. APHS now had the lead. They continued their full court press, and it must have been the girls' aggression and hunger that intimidated St. Mary's because it looked like St. Mary's was handing the game over. In the last three minutes of the game, APHS scored ten points and held St. Mary's to two. APHS won by nine.

Both teams shook hands, with APHS fans and supporters cheering from the stands, and Coach Milton went into the locker room that was designated for the visiting team.

Standing before them, he proudly said, "Great game, ladies. I am so proud of you. *All* of you. You played like a team today. You listened, and you followed through. You played with class, and St. Mary's has no choice but to respect you. Well done."

The girls upset the higher-ranked team, and the support Genny was looking for now came pouring in. If they won their next game against the #3 ranked Fairfield Regional High School, they would play in the finals against the #1 seeded team, St. Benedict's Prep.

APHS defeated Fairfield Regional, 43-35, and Coach Milton played all the girls for the entire game. They would play against St. Benedict's Prep in the Finals at Rutgers University.

This was the first time in over 20 years that the girls would be competing in a State Finals game. There were three days to practice before the Saturday afternoon final, and Coach Milton ran the girls for each practice. After 20 laps, he had them go shoot foul shots on one end and three point shots on the other. Mr. Henderson secured use of the Boys' and Girls' Club, where the boys' team, who were not as successful in their Conference matchups, were happy to assist by playing against the girls. Mr. Walker, Chris' dad, strictly advised the boys not to let up on the girls for any reason. Chris scored a few three point shots, and his father watched from the stands.

293

"He's been practicing," Genny said to herself.

Mr. Walker and Mr. Henderson shook hands, calling a symbolic truce to their feud for the sake of the girls. Mr. Walker was now a fan. For the first time ever, both dads were cheering for the girls on the court. Mr. Walker stood and applauded when Genny scored her three point shots. He was also impressed by the girls mastery of faking their opponents and then going up to the basket strong, drawing the foul the majority of the time.

"That's it," Mr. Walker said as Morgan drew a foul from one of the boys. "Go up strong!" he yelled. "This is your house, girls!"

When Friday evening arrived, Mr. Henderson and Mr. Walker were convinced that the girls had learned everything they needed to learn in order to win the game. Now, they were to get a good night's sleep and be ready to play tomorrow because St. Benedict's, whose girls played just as hard as APHS, were favored to win. The state-wide papers predicted their win would be by a margin of at least fifteen points, but Kevin Rollins, citing the teams were evenly matched in just about every area, predicted that it was too close to call.

The three freshman from APHS had become the darlings of the local papers and social media. Everyone, it seemed, rooted for the underdog, and even the local TV news sports channel had sponsored an event on social media where fans could vote and comment. The TV station would air the comments on their high school sports show, and the APHS girls were scheduled to be interviewed on air following the conclusion of the game.

On Saturday morning, the girls met the bus in front of the school. A caravan of cars filled with family, friends and spectators were lined up behind it, and they cheered for the girls as they high-fived Coach Milton before boarding. He stood proudly with Mr. Henderson and Mr. Walker, who were talking with him about the strengths and weaknesses of St. Benedict's. Mr. Walker had scouted their team, and he remarked that they played tough, yes, and they were strong ball handlers, but he didn't think any of the teams St. Benedict's had played against were really worthy opponents.

"A lion can kill a hyena all day long. It's not a fight until another lion shows up," Mr. Walker told the two men.

After all the girls arrived and boarded the bus, Coach Milton welcomed Mr. Walker and Mr. Henderson on board so that they could share last minute words of encouragement.

After shaking the hand of their bus driver, Coach Milton spoke to his team. "Ladies, let me have your attention, please." He waited for everyone to be seated and quiet. "I am so proud of each and every one of you, and I want you all to know that. You should be proud of yourselves. All of your hard work, discipline, training and commitment has brought you here today, and I am grateful to all of you for staying focused. Thank you."

The girls clapped their hands, and Mr. Henderson and Mr. Walker joined in.

Continuing, Coach Milton said "Thank you, everyone. We have made it to the finals of a state championship game, but the hard work has to continue on the floor today. St. Benedict's is the #1 high school girls' basketball team in the state, and they have what it takes to win today. They are not going to hand over this game to three freshmen, one junior, one senior and all our players from the city of Addington Park, no matter how hungry you are. You are going to have to win this game, and you will do that by playing solid basketball for four quarters. Some of the papers are predicting that St. Benedict's will win easily, but I am predicting that you will because *you* have what it takes to win. You've earned it. Let's play our game and let St. Benedict's know that Addington Park is in the house!"

Genny raised her hand to ask a question, and Coach Milton nodded for her to ask it.

"Coach, what makes St. Benedict's #1?" she asked.

Without pausing at all, Coach Milton answered, "They're not #1 yet, Genny. They can't be because they've never played against you girls."

The bus erupted with excitement, applause and cheers, and as the cars behind them heard the noise, they honked their horns in support.

"Now, before we head up to Rutgers today, you all know Mr. Henderson, Genny's dad, who was one of the best basketball players Addington Park High School has ever known. I know he's been training some of you, and it has paid off. We owe him our heartfelt thanks. He's going to share a few words with us before we go, so let's show him our appreciation."

The girls applauded as Coach Milton and Mr. Henderson shook hands, and then Mr. Henderson spoke briefly. He encouraged the girls to take heed to their Coach's instructions and remember that every player has a weakness, even the players from St. Benedict's. "Once you find out what her weakness is, press her."

Then, Coach Milton welcomed Mr. Walker, Chris' dad, who had been instrumental in helping him scout other teams. Some of the girls snickered as Mr. Walker came forward, but Coach Milton shot them a glare that demanded them to be respectful and listen.

Mr. Walker was straightforward with the girls. He told them that St. Benedict's was a powerhouse team with a deep bench, and watching them play was like watching Addington Park. They were quick, hungry, and solid on defense, good ball handlers and good shooters.

"They can play basketball, and they play as a team," he said. "However, and I do mean however, the schools they play against in their Conference are weaker, less aggressive teams. St. Benedict's is the lion in the jungle, and lions don't roar when dogs bark. Well, every team they've played against has been the underdog, so they've never been put to the test and challenged. They've never played against another lion, and Addington Park is the strongest lion in the jungle, you hear me!"

The girls applauded and cheered, standing and rocking the bus with excitement. The caravan of cars honked in support again, and the bus driver honked his horn in agreement.

Mr. Walker quieted the girls down, and then finished his pep talk. "You girls can run the entire game. Your conditioning is on another level! Ain't no underdog coming in this game today, partner! We roar! The papers are just giving them the game, it's a head game, but don't even worry about what they are saying. If you pay too much attention to it, it could take you mentally out of the game, and if you lose mentally, you're already defeated. We know who we are and where we come from. Three freshman, one junior and one senior dominating the sport, and *our* bench is deep! Coach Milton can ask any one of you to get in the game at any time! You all contribute. Today, ladies, we roar! We'll see how good this lion is now that another King of the Jungle has showed up. Roar! Let them know we're in the damn house!"

The girls applauded and cheered again, and the cars behind them continued to honk their cars in unity. When they finally pulled off, the girls were energized and ready to play.

The drive to Rutgers New Brunswick Campus was only 45 minutes along the state's Route 18 North. When they arrived, they were escorted by university representatives to the gymnasium and adjacent locker room, which had been designated for their use. A banner, which read "Welcome A.P.H.S. Blue Knights," hung over the locker room door, and the locker room was stocked with bottled water and fresh towels. Genny couldn't help noticing the NCAA Championship banners that hung in the gym.

"This is where I'm going," she told herself.

The girls got ready in the locker room, changing from their sweat suits into their shorts and sleeveless tops in a still silence. Outside the locker room, the girls could hear fans cheering and shouting, and they were excited to know that their families and friends had come out in good number. When Coach Milton came to get them, they were already lined up and ready to go out on the floor and start their layups.

Rhonda led the girls as their Captain. Coach Milton hugged her, and he could be heard telling her that it was going to be alright.

"I just wish my brothers could be here to see this," she said.

"We're all here for you, Rhonda. Play hard today for your brothers."

That seemed to make her feel better, and once she was settled, the girls walked out of the locker room and ran onto the floor, lining up in two lanes opposite the top of the key for their layups. There were many people in attendance, but only a small number of them looked like they were from Addington Park. Genny tried not to notice, following her dad's advice, and committed to just focusing on their game. The clock had started, and it was running down with just under 15 minutes to go before start time.

St. Benedict's came out from the locker room at the opposite end of the court, and the applause was so loud, some of the younger people in the stands were putting their hands over their ears.

Bullhorns and other noise makers sounded from the stands, and fans waved signs that read "St. Benedict's Prep State Champs."

"This whole thing is a mental game," Mr. Walker said to Mr. Henderson. They were seated in the first row of seats just behind the bench for APHS. Support had come for the girls in a greater than usual number, but it was no match for the fans of St. Benedict's who drowned out their cheers. "They are trying to take the girls out of the game before it even begins."

"Don't we do that?" Mr. Henderson asked. "They have our playbook and are running with it."

"So we're just gonna let that happen?" asked an agitated Mr. Walker.

"It's cool. The girls know how to play this game. They'll be alright."

St. Benedict's lined up in red and white uniforms with high top brand name sneakers that looked like they had just been bleached white. A loud noise maker sounded from behind the St. Benedict's bench, and all their fans stood and made a wave with arms raised high in the air that went around about 70% of the gym and back.

A St. Benedict's player ran underneath the basket and got down on all fours, as another player, dribbling the ball at the top of the key, backed up to the half court line. The fans were standing and clapping, shouting "Let's go Lions! Let's go Lions! Let's go Lions!" Then, the 5'11" St. Benedict's player dribbled towards the basket at top speed, jumping off her teammate's back and leaping into the air to slam dunk the basketball with both hands. The crowd erupted in a thunderous praise, and the St. Benedict's team high-fived one another on the court.

Mr. Walker and Mr. Henderson sat watching, but neither of them said anything. Coach Milton saw the whole spectacle, but he told his girls to keep shooting their layups and then shoot jump shots. The fans and noise makers were so loud, the girls didn't hear what he said. They only saw his lips moving.

It was a bitter pill for the girls to swallow, and as much as it bothered Coach Milton that St. Benedict's was mocking his girls and trying to unravel them, he knew, as a Coach, that it was needed. Mr. Henderson agreed, and he sat back in the stands as he usually did and would allow the girls to fight their own battle. The more vociferous

Mr. Walker, however, stood and shouted from his seat that APHS was the lion, the king of the jungle, and "ain't nobody here no punk." He was the self-designated spokesman for the group of fans from Addington Park, and he took his role with the girls just as seriously as he did when his own son, Chris, was playing.

Rhonda was upset with the turn of events, and she complained to her teammates that "these bourgeois chicks are out here trying to punk us," and "if my brothers were here, they would never have this."

"We can't let them take us out our game," Genny said, stepping up. "They're trying to take our heads out of the game. Forget that. We came to win. They haven't even played yet, and already they are celebrating like they got this in the bag. Mr. Walker is right."

"That's what I'm sayin'," Rhonda agreed.

"This is what we should do. They're trying to run with our playbook? Well, we take it right back and play it better than them. And, we use their 'good book' on them. They're a religious school, right?"

"Yeah, so," the girls responded. They gathered around Genny and Rhonda.

"Well, instead of mocking us, they should be praying. So *we* pray. We pray in their faces. They don't want to depend on God, then we'll depend on Him. We pray in their faces when the game starts and at the start of every quarter while we are on the floor. We pray when we are on the foul line and when they are on the foul line. That's what *they* should be doing. We take their playbook and their *good book* from them, and we use both against them. We'll win this game."

Her teammates stared and looked at her, and no one said a word. Joanne and Bria were the first two to agree, then Morgan and finally Rhonda who agreed that they could use all the help they could get.

"Should we ask Coach this time?" Bria asked.

Rhonda said she would tell him, and she ran over to him as he stood at the official's table.

The game was then set to begin with the meeting of the team captains and the referees. They were called to meet at center court, and Coach Milton asked Rhonda to take Genny on the floor with her.

"No problem, Coach," Rhonda replied.

Genny looked uncertainly at Coach Milton, but he smiled and said, "You are a natural leader, Genny. You are already the Captain, and I'm going to be depending on you next year."

After the meeting, the starting five players for both teams were introduced. APHS fans cheered, whistled and applauded from the stands. The St. Benedict's supporters stood and stomped their feet, mimicking a drum roll, and it sounded like lions were, indeed, roaring in the jungle. It was enough of a head game to intimidate players with little heart and focus, but to the inner city girls of APHS, and especially Coach Milton and honorary coaches Mr. Henderson and Mr. Walker, it was just the ding of a bell starting a prize fight, and the girls had come prepared.

"Bring it on, bitch," Mr. Walker shouted from the stands, but he was barely audible above the noise in the gym. "Hurry up and start this damn game. I can't stand these mother f------! They up in here like they *know* they got this. See, that's how they won against those other teams. Take their heads out the game. Playing against some damn hyenas. Not today!" he yelled. Then, even louder, he screamed, "You still gotta be able to play!"

A young girl of about 20 years was welcomed to center court, and the noise subsided. She sang a beautiful version of The Star Spangled Banner, and the referees blew their whistles to start the game. Again, cheers and applause filled the gym.

When both teams finally walked onto the court, the five APHS players bowed on one knee and prayed a silent prayer. The bold act of faith diminished some of the raucous from St. Benedict's, and Mr. Henderson smiled. This time, the fans from APHS could be heard from the stands.

"That's it, girls," he thought to himself. He knew that Genny had faith and believed in God, and if she could solicit the help of the Lord Almighty, glory to His name.

"Hallelujah!" Maria shouted as she stood in agreement with the girls. Then she bowed her head and prayed, *"Lord, please help them."*

St. Benedict's put two players on Genny as soon as the game started, and she wasn't able to get a shot off. Joanne made a few attempts at three-point shots, but she wasn't connecting, so the girls encouraged her to relax. Their opponents scored on three point shots and secured an early lead of ten points in the first quarter. When it closed, the score was 16 – 6.

Coach Milton motivated his players with a passionate pep talk. "Girls, you have to relax. They are doubling up on Genny because Genny is our top scorer from three point range. Joanne, we need you to make your shots. We don't waste our possessions! I want three point shots every time we go down. If Joanne misses, then Morgan you have to grab that rebound and go up strong, and come out on the two-two defense! Their shooters are wide open. We don't give anything away. Let's go. 1-2-3 Defense!"

At the start of the second quarter, the APHS girls knelt in prayer again. Morgan had the advantage in the jump ball, tapping it to Genny who raced down the court for an easy layup. The St. Benedict's players were careful to play her defensively, but they were playing cautious enough to avoid fouling her. Their coach told his team that he didn't want any fouls. "Hands up on defense! Make them earn every shot!"

Coach Milton was just as vocal from the sidelines, and he could be heard telling his girls to "Get back on defense!" and "Hustle!" Both teams traded shots in the second quarter, and when Genny drew her players into her, she threw a quick chest pass to Joanne, who set for her three point shot and starting sinking the ball, all net. She had found her rhythm, and Coach Milton's secret weapon scored three successive shots to bring APHS within two points. The St. Benedict's coach called a timeout with just under two minutes remaining before halftime.

He was screaming but could hardly be heard over the noise from the stands. A clipboard was thrown on the bench, and one of his starting players sat down.

"Did you see that?" Mr. Walker asked.

"Yup," Mr. Henderson answered.

"See, he ain't never played against another lion. We can win this game. He's frustrated right now, and if he takes it out on his team, they are going to wear that frustration on the court. All the girls have to do is press the hell out of them because they are going to break, mark my words."

"I know that's right," Mr. Henderson replied.

When the girls came back on the court, they had been instructed to play St. Benedict's tight in a man-to-man defense.

"They're shook," Coach Milton told his players.

St. Benedict's didn't go down easy. They were seasoned ball handlers, and they got the ball up the court in spite of the press. APHS was not giving up three pointers, and they pressed their players and stayed in their faces with hands high in the air every time a player picked up her dribble. When Rhonda's man attempted a two point shot, she blocked it with force and then roared in her face.

"Get that shit outta here!" Mr. Walker yelled, jumping to his feet.

"C'mon, man, stop cussing so much in here. These are kids," Mr. Henderson said to him.

"I don't give a damn whose kids they are," Mr. Walker replied. "Get that shit outta here!" he yelled again.

He could hardly be heard, fans were screaming and cheering all around the gym. APHS supporters had to be outnumbered about 4 to 1.

"They are trying to take our girls out, man. *We're* the lions in this damn jungle. Let's go!" he yelled at the top of his lungs.

Mr. Henderson just sat back in his seat. The two men were cut from the same cloth, and they were both fierce competitors. Their styles were different, but no one knew better than Mr. Henderson that Mr. Walker had their best interests at heart. So, Rob sat back in his seat and didn't say another word to him. Rob would enjoy the rest of the game, supporting the girls in *his* own way.

At halftime, the score was even, 27 – 27.

When they went in the locker room, Coach Milton high-fived the girls and continued to encourage them to press St. Benedict's. For the third quarter, he wanted the girls to stay in a two-two defense, but Rhonda should come out on the ball.

"If anything is bothering you, Rhonda, it's working for good today. Use that fire and energy against your players and keep blocking those shots. We are going to win this game. They are frustrated right now. They're used to winning against opponents who don't challenge them and stay in their faces. Stay in their faces! Hands up on defense. Fight! And let's win this game. 1-2-3 Defense!"

As the third quarter started, the APHS girls knelt and prayed again. Morgan won the jump ball and tapped it to Genny, who raced down the court for an easy layup and a foul. She sank her foul shot, and then the girls ran a full court press on St. Benedict's again. Rhonda intercepted a pass, threw the ball to Joanne, and she made a three point shot to give APHS the lead. Then, APHS set up for the full court press again.

"That's right! Don't give 'em nothing!" Mr. Walker yelled from the stands. "This is our house!"

St. Benedict's did get the ball in and up the court, and they slowed the ball down to set up their offense.

"Two-Two!" Coach Milton yelled from the sidelines, and Rhonda came out of the zone to stay on the ball.

A St. Benedict's player attempted to infiltrate the defense and go in for a layup, but APHS girls denied her, and she had to throw the ball outside the key. There were only 3 seconds left on their shot clock, so a player attempted a shot, which Rhonda threw off the court. A St. Benedict's player missed in her attempt to recover the ball, and she stepped out of bounds. The APHS fans and supporters went crazy! Then, Rhonda knelt and said another brief prayer.

APHS got the ball up, and this time the St. Benedict's coach changed his team's defense to man-to-man. That set Genny free, because Joanne would post Genny's man up so that Genny could take the shot. Their plan worked, and Genny scored two three pointers in a row, giving APHS a 12 point lead. The teams traded buckets for the rest of the third quarter, and Rhonda blocked another shot, after which St. Benedict's coach called a time out.

Coach Milton, Mr. Henderson and Mr. Walker were now standing. If the girls kept this up, they would win, and APHS would finally have a State Championship title to take home.

"Girls, your hard work, your dedication and your commitment are all making a difference today. We will win this game. Don't worry about the people in the stands. We are the State Champions."

"Coach, our prayers are helping, too," Rhonda said.

"Well then pray, and thank God in advance for this win. Can I get an Amen?"

"Amen!" the girls yelled.

"Can I get an Amen?" Coach Milton said again.

"Amen!"

The APHS fans cheered "Amen!" "Amen!" "Amen!" and the atmosphere was charged. The smaller crowd of APHS fans could be heard shouting "Amen!" over the more numerous supporters for St. Benedict's, and as the girls went back on the floor, they prayed again, and their fans shouted "Hallelujah!" and "Thank you, Jesus!"

"Hallelujah!" Rhonda shouted on the court, as she got back on defense. "Thank you, Jesus!" she yelled. "That's right! That's right! Aarrrgghhhh!" she roared.

When St. Benedict's attempted to get the ball in, Rhonda intercepted the pass again, roared, and threw it down court to Joanne and Genny who were waiting. Joanne scored an easy layup.

APHS pressed the ball, and St. Benedict's couldn't get it in within the ten seconds allotted, and then Morgan took the ball out for APHS. She passed it to Joanne, who dribbled up and passed it on a break to Genny. Genny scored easily on a layup and drew another foul. She sank her foul shot, and the third quarter ended with APHS up by 14 points.

"We run this mother! There's a new King of the Jungle up in here! That's right!" Mr. Walker shouted.

The St. Benedict's fans were quiet when the third quarter ended. Their #1 ranked team, top heavy with seniors who had been recruited by the best colleges and universities in the country, was suffering a beating at the hands of five much younger inner city girls who played and prayed. The fourth quarter started with the APHS girls, including the Coach and entire team, on bended knee. Morgan won the jump ball, tapping it to Joanne who ran on another fast break with Genny, scoring another easy layup.

APHS maintained their full court press, and the St. Benedict's coach could be heard screaming at his players to "come to the ball!"

Joanne noticed that her player telegraphed her passes just like the boy Mr. Henderson had her play against at the Boys' Club. She remembered Mr. Henderson's words that the player who does that *is a Godsend and is giving the game away,* and she was now fully charged to act. She stole the ball as her player tried to pass it inbounds, and then she dribbled back to three point range and sank a three point shot, also drawing the foul.

The St. Benedict's coach was livid. He slammed the clipboard on the floor besides the bench, and the referee called a technical foul. So, Joanne shot three foul shots, and she sank them all, bringing the lead for APHS to 21. APHS fans were cheering wildly, and Mr. Walker was standing and screaming something, but he couldn't be heard over Rob, Maria, Neicy and Tony. Joanne's mother, Ronny, was on her feet and in tears.

Brenda Miller came down to the floor and was standing at the end of the bench cheering for her twin sister and teammates. When Coach Milton saw her, he told her to come sit with her team. They embraced Brenda as she walked over and poured ice water on her head.

Bria's mother was in the stands crying with joy, and Morgan's mom and dad were in the stands beaming with pride.

"They did it," Mr. Walker said to Mr. Henderson.

"*We* did it," Mr. Henderson replied. "You played a big part. We couldn't have done it without you. Thanks, man," Rob said. He gave him a hug, and the two shook hands, ending the feud that was caused, ironically, by a basketball game between their children years ago. And now, Mr. Walker, who once called Genny "a mother f-----girl," was her biggest fan.

The minutes of the last quarter went quickly. Coach Milton insisted that they keep the pressure on in a man-to-man defense and full court press.

St. Benedict's had been stripped of their confidence, and they were not just mentally defeated, they were spiritually overcome. They missed their shots in the last quarter and committed sloppy fouls. APHS scored another five points from the foul line and increased their lead to nearly 30 points, which was unheard of against the top-seeded championship team.

With seconds ticking on the clock, Coach Milton told the girls to settle back in a two-one-two defense. The St. Benedict's coach cleared his bench and sent in five new girls, one of whom missed a three point shot at the buzzer, and the APHS fans cheered wildly and shouted from the stands.

"You see! They ain't never played against another lion before! How are you the number one team in the state when you've never *played* the number one team in the state? Explain that to me," Mr.

Walker said to Rob. He turned his black and blue cap around so that the visor was facing the back of his head, and then he adjusted his wire-rimmed glasses. It was a habit of his that he engaged in whenever he was making a point.

"Doesn't matter now. Now, *we* are #1."

"You are mother f----- right, we are #1," Mr. Walker replied.

The girls got several bottles of water and emptied them onto Coach Milton's head. He was a good sport and didn't ask for a towel when Kevin Morris came over to interview him. A representative of NJ's TV News 8 stood nearby to interview the girls for their show as well, but first his team needed to shake the hands of St. Benedict's and then have the ceremonial cutting of the net.

"Great game," Coach Milton said to Coach Peter F. Morrissey of St. Benedict's Preparatory Academy. The coaches shook hands as their players walked in two respective lines and shook hands.

"Great game to you. Your girls deserve it," he humbly said.

Brenda and Rhonda Miller came behind Coach Milton and poured an empty bucket of ice water on him. Kevin Morris caught it on camera. Coach Milton laughed, and he embraced the twins, and then they went under the basket to join the other players who were ready to cut the net.

Chris Walker ran onto the floor, and he hugged Genny, lifting her off her feet as he said congratulations. Then, just before their embrace would have been awkward, they both let go of one another and turned in opposite directions.

The girls of APHS were next interviewed for the NJ TV News 8 Station, and Coach Milton asked Rhonda, the only senior on the team, to speak on the team's behalf. Her interview, while the team could be seen cutting the net, was brief, and Rhonda was crying tears of joy. She shared that she would be going to a local University in the fall. Rhonda also thanked her family, coach and teammates for their support. The interviewer recognized her as Rhonda Miller, sister of Dante and Kasheem Miller, who had been victims of gang violence in Addington Park a few months ago, and he congratulated her for staying focused. "Good luck," was the last thing Rhonda heard before she ran back on the court to join her teammates.

The bus ride home was full of applause, cheers and songs. Parents had spray painted their cars before the girls came outside with

"APHS State Champs," "We Won," and "We're Number One." The police department had been on notice to have two patrol cars escort the team back into the city when they arrived, and the drivers honked their horns and waved as they drove behind their police escorts.

When Genny came home that evening, she knelt at her bed and said a prayer, thanking God for helping them.

"Thank you, Jesus. We couldn't have done it without you."

The next day, the local paper featured several photos from the game, including the St. Benedict's dunk routine with two of their senior players. Coach Milton was featured with the twin girls pouring water over his head, and there were several photos of the starting five in action. The headline was:

Addington Park's Starting Five Keep the Dream Alive: Blue Knights Pounce Lions of St. Benedict's

Coach Milton framed the article and highlighted Kevin's statement in his article that *"stunts don't make good basketball – good players do. Well done, Blue Knights."* He sent an email along with the article to all the players and parents, instructing his team to read the article and be prepared to discuss it with him briefly on Monday after school.

When the girls met Coach Milton as instructed, Genny promised not to resort to stunts or tricks anymore, and Joanne and Bria agreed. The lesson, ironically thanks in part to St. Benedict's, was learned.

"Now, if you can leap that high and pull that off on your own, more power to you," he laughed. "And I knew what you were trying to do when I saw the chair in the gym. This isn't an R&B stage, and none of you is a famous recording artist and dancer like……what's her name? Oh, never mind, just stick to shooting baskets."

They all laughed.

"We have a team dinner Friday at 6:00 p.m. I'll send an email to your parents. Everyone is welcome. I'll see you then."

"Is Mr. Walker coming?" Joanne asked.

"Sure, why?"

"He's funny, and he's like you, Coach. He has our back."

"Alright, then, I'll definitely tell him to come. I'll see you girls Friday."

With a heavy sigh, Genny added, "No more practices after school. This is gonna be so weird."

The rest of the girls agreed with her.

"Now wait a minute. All of you should come out and join the track team," Coach Milton suggested. "I'm going to be coaching the girls' team this year. Mr. Mathis just resigned."

"Ugggghhhhhh," Joanne and Bria replied.

Genny would consider running, but she would also look forward to the free time she would have to read the works of several recommended writers: August Wilson, Langston Hughes, Zora Neale Hurston, Sister Souljah and James Baldwin.

With a mischievous grin on his face, Coach Milton said, "20 laps around the track! Let's go!"

Chapter Twenty Three
Maria

Rob's phone calls became more infrequent as the weeks went by. Maria had laid everything on the altar before God, including Sophia's pregnancy, and she was satisfied that God was in control no matter what happened. There may have been some truth to Rob's allegations that he was not the biological father of Sophia's unborn baby for Maria had a few "visions" where she saw Sophia giving birth to a baby, in 3D image, which had two faces. When the baby's head turned in one direction, you could clearly see a distinct resemblance to Rob, but when it turned in the other direction, you could clearly see that the baby did not look at all like Rob. Maria believed that the Lord may have been revealing truth to her concerning the unborn baby, that it was not, in fact, Rob's, but there was no vision to reveal that he had never slept with Sophia. Even if the child did not belong to Rob, he was still sleeping with her.

"Lord, if this vision is from you, and you are telling me something, please reveal what you want me to do and grant me understanding," Maria prayed.

The newspapers and local TV news stations were giving more press coverage to the mayoral candidates, and Sophia's name and photo were now a regular item, along with the other nominees. When

Sophia made a formal announcement in March that she would not be running for office, she announced at the same time that she was three and one half months pregnant. She told the local reporters that she would focus her attention on her health and that of her unborn baby as her blood pressure had lately been higher than normal. Further questions prying into paternity and marriage were avoided as Sophia declined to comment and cited that she would be returning home to Pennsylvania. Lastly, she wished all of the other candidates well, and Mayor Bradley thanked her publicly for her principles of integrity, hard work and dedication that made his job easy.

"He is one lucky man," said Mayor Bradley before a televised audience at City Hall of dignitaries, city officials and residents.

Maria had watched the TV news broadcast at the insistence of Pam, who had re-surfaced once the news of Sophia's pregnancy was made public. Pam had advised Maria that Sophia had given notice to the Mayor, and they were planning an office party for her.

Pam called Maria to ask, "Can you believe 'this bitch'?' I'm so sorry, Maria."

"You don't need to be sorry for me," Maria replied. "I know it probably sounds corny to you, Pam, but I really don't care....."

"I know, you prayed about it, and God is going to handle it," Pam sarcastically interrupted Maria before she could go any further. "Girl, please. You are still a woman. You don't have to try and be so strong and act like nothing bothers you."

"Pam, you sound more irritated about it than I am. I don't care. God *is* going to handle it."

Maria became annoyed with the turn of the conversation as Pam tried to insist that Maria needed to be upset and "go check" Sophia. Maria told Pam she wasn't going to go and do anything, she would leave it in God's hands, and whatever would be would be. When that answer still didn't appease Pam, Maria asked her to come back to Holy Tabernacle, knowing that this would turn Pam off, and Pam replied that she would think about it and get back to Maria. Their phone call ended.

Neicy and Tony went on a cruise for two weeks, so Maria didn't bother her with trivial details. You would have never known that Neicy had just recently laid her mother to rest, she was just as jovial, thoughtful and caring as she had always been. Maria understood somewhat where Pam was coming from, but there truly was a peace with Jesus that surpassed all understanding, which blessed the soul to rejoice in sorrow. Pam wasn't yet able to appreciate how Neicy could sing with tears of joy at her mother's funeral. Neicy celebrated because she had faith to believe that the spirit of her mother was at home with the Lord, and Neicy knew that she, believing in Jesus Christ as Lord, would see her mother again.

"I don't know how people who don't believe in Jesus Christ get through," Neicy testified to Maria before she left for her cruise. "He comforts like no other. If I didn't know Jesus Christ, I would have lost my mind a long time ago. And, thank God that His peace is ruling in your heart, Maria."

"Yes, it is," Maria answered. "I am going to focus on Jesus, my kids, my studies and church."

That is exactly what Maria did. She was an active member of the PTA at both schools, and she attended all Board of Education meetings. She passed her classes at Hampton Bible Institute with high marks, and she served in the Women's Ministry at Holy Tabernacle alongside Mother Wright. The Women's Day Service in March went off without a hitch, and Maria was asked to open the service with prayer. Although nervous, she did well, and afterwards Maria was asked to be in the rotation of those who opened Sunday morning worship services.

Papi sang his first solo at Holy Tabernacle in June, and Rob did attend the packed Youth Service. His cousin, Walter, also attended, along with his barber, Mike Love.

"If you need anything, Maria, you know you can call me," Mike Love spoke to her as they shared a friendly embrace in the foyer of Holy Tabernacle.

"Thanks, Mike," Maria replied to their longtime friend, "I will."

"Giddy up," he jokingly said before they entered the sanctuary, recalling the All-Male Revue Night the ladies had spent together.

Laughing, Maria replied, "That was Pam. And how did you know about that?"

"How do you think? You know your girl can't keep her mouth closed." With a more serious look on his face, he continued, "Maria, it is good to see you laugh again. Live. Rob messed up, and he knows that he did. I don't know how he can ever make this up to you, I don't know if that is even possible or if it is even anything that you want. But you know that man loves you. He's sorry, Maria."

Maria appreciated the words of support and encouragement from Mike Love, but the truth was that he was a die-hard Robert J. Henderson supporter, and no matter what Rob did, Mike Love would cover for him. He hadn't come to support Maria, he was there to support Rob.

"Thank you, Mike," Maria graciously replied. "I appreciate your friendship, and I'm grateful that you came today."

Hoping that he now had a window of opportunity with Maria, he carefully maneuvered his conversation. "You know that I wouldn't miss this for anything. Lil' man singing in church, that's what's up. I'm going to tape him and play it over at the shop. Rob said he can really sing."

Maria just nodded.

"So, you know the Bible says that we are supposed to forgive each other so that *we* can be forgiven. Have you forgiven Rob, Maria? The baby may not even be his."

Maria didn't want to get into the conversation with Mike Love, so she offered that they should take their seats and refrain from talking before service began. He apologized, and then went to find Rob, who was still in the foyer talking with some people he knew.

Papi belted out a hymn entitled "Jesus, My Friend,"[116] like he had been singing gospel music for years. He was able to capture the spirit of the song, and the church rocked with him from start to finish. He wore a navy blue three piece suit that Rob had picked out with freshly polished black shoes. Papi removed the mike from the stand and held it close to his mouth, just like Minister Barrington had taught him, carefully enunciating every line of the mid-tempo hymn with a pure innocence and child-like faith that encouraged adult and child alike to look to Jesus:

> *All else I leave for Jesus*
> *My Lord who died for me*
> *All peace is mine, with Christ divine*
> *A constant friend is He*

All peace I have with Jesus
My Savior who set me free
Every burden and care, is Christ's to bear
A blessed friend is He

Jesus, my Friend!
Jesus, my Friend!
A trusted brother, like no other
Beginning and end!

Jesus, my Friend!
Jesus, my Friend!
He took my heavy load, what grace untold
Jesus, my Friend!

Papi repeated the chorus towards the end of the hymn, and Minister Barrington asked the Praise and Worship Team to join in. Minister Barrington and Papi traded lines of the song, going back and forth, and as Minister Barrington sang with runs and riffs showcasing his vocal prowess, Papi didn't miss a beat and mimicked him with perfect pitch. Reverend Wright stood and commended the young Papi, praying for him and for the mighty way in which the Lord would surely use him. Neicy beamed with pride, and the Mothers of the church stood with arms raised praising the Lord and blessing His name. Rob squared his shoulders when he stood, and Mike Love could be heard shouting, "Yeah, lil' man!" Rob appeared to "shush" Mike, but it didn't work. Mike shushed Rob back and shouted louder, "Go Papi!" At the end of the service, Rob shook the hand of Minister Barrington and thanked him. Then, he took his children along with Maria, Neicy, Tony, Walter and Mike Love out to eat at a local diner, where friends and family celebrated. Maria agreed because she believed it was the right thing to do. To her, it was about Papi, and Rob was still his and Genny's dad.

Over the summer, Genny participated in a travel basketball team with Joanne and Bria that was run out of the Boys' Club with Mr. Walker and Rob. Up and coming players from the Addington Park Middle School joined the travel team and showed tremendous promise. Both men were excited about the roster for the high school girls' team. To everyone's excitement, a repeat state championship title was highly probable.

Papi spent his summer with his dad at the Center for Young Men, and Mr. Henderson saw some of the same young men from the previous summer, including Marcus, Isaiah and Eric, as well as several new faces. Papi also went to karate lessons and passed his brown belt test.

At the end of the summer, everyone, including Maria, returned to school, and Maria would now focus in on Old Testament Studies, as well as courses in The Gospels, The Life of the Apostle Paul, The Epistles of the New Testament and Homiletics. From sunrise to sundown, she read the Bible, researched, prayed, sought the Lord for His help, prepared her papers, finished her coursework and assignments and studied the Word of the Lord. The work was easy for her, and her path and direction were clear. Now that she had submitted herself to the Lord and fully surrendered to His will, everything was falling into place.

Maria was scheduled to graduate from Hampton Bible Institute the following June. She and the other 12 students in her class were asked to prepare a 15 minute sermon on any topic they felt led to do in May. Maria chose forgiveness, since it was the area that she had grappled with, and she expounded on **Mathew 18:21-22**: *Then Peter came to Him and said, "Lord, how often shall my brother sin against me, and I forgive him? Up to seven times?" Jesus said to him, "I do not say to you, up to seven times, but up to seventy times seven...."* Her message was ***"Forgiveness You Can Count On."*** She spoke on the tender mercies and abundant grace of a God who gave His only begotten Son, Jesus Christ, that all who believe in Him should not perish but have abundant life.[117] Through Jesus Christ, we have forgiveness of our sins. Because of His abundant love, grace and mercy, we have been delivered from the chains of darkness and the perils of hell. How many times have we needed God to forgive us? If He kept a record of *our* sins, who could stand before Him?[118] Freely, He has pardoned our transgressions. We can do nothing to deserve God's grace. Jesus paid the price once and for all on the cross of Calvary, dying once to die no more. In spite of all the times we have sinned against Him, and still do, His blood was shed on Calvary's cross to atone for our sins and restore us into right relationship with our Heavenly Father. This is His love for us. We can count on His blood. We can count on His grace and mercy. We can count on His unconditional love because He is good, just, holy and righteous, and because He loves us so dearly. When the enemy tries to bring up our past, we can be certain that the blood of Jesus has cleared us of all charges, and freed by the Son, we are free indeed. Jesus was pierced for our transgressions and crushed for our iniquities that the penalty of our sins would fall on Him.[119] His blood was poured out for many for forgiveness of sins.[120] In spite of all the times we mess up in life, Jesus welcomes us into His loving arms and forgives us completely. Love doesn't keep a record of wrongs, and He forgave us to bring up our past no more. As far as the east is from the west, so far has He removed our transgressions from us.[121] Ought we not, therefore, to extend the same forgiveness to others so that we might be forgiven of our sins?

The following Sunday, Reverend Wright asked to see Maria after service, and he shared with her that he was exceptionally proud of her achievements at the Bible Institute. He wanted to give her the opportunity to cultivate her gift even further at Holy Tabernacle. Reverend Wright stated that he had prayed and sought the Lord for His will concerning Maria, and he wanted to know how he could help her.

"Please feel free to speak freely with me. What do you believe is God's will for you in ministry here?" he asked.

The distinguished older gentleman sat in a tall, high-backed chair in his office that looked more like a museum. There were religious artifacts situated on his desk and walls, and a tall, wooden bookcase full of Bibles was situated in the corner behind his chair. An old-fashioned rotary phone sat on a coffee table, and framed paintings of Jesus and a scene from The Last Supper hung on the four walls that seemed to close Reverend Wright in with so much of God's presence that he didn't have any choice *but* to be a pastor. Diplomas and degrees, certificates of achievements and plaques honoring him for his ministry were neatly displayed throughout his office, and a nearly full spring water cooler sat near a table with a coffeemaker.

Maria paused before she spoke, and then she shared with Reverend Wright that she felt a burning in her soul for teaching and preaching.

"Amen," he answered, his eyes focused on hers. "Gotta be called by God to preach and teach His word. A lot of folks preach and teach with no calling at all, and they know the Word of God, but the holy anointing is not there. Authentic Christians know the difference. We can't fool anybody, dear."

Maria didn't know what the good Pastor meant, and she, but for respect of him, was almost offended. She wasn't trying to fool anyone.

"I beg your pardon?" Maria politely asked.

"We have to be called by God to preach, Sister Maria. Man cannot call us, so if there is any man or woman here for that matter suggesting to you that you should preach, don't listen to them. Hear from God. He is the only one who calls His ministers."

Maria was shocked at his reply, but she knew what God was calling her to do, and she wasn't going to back down. "Pastor Wright, with all due respect, you preach the gospel, so that must mean God called you, right?"

Not backing away either, Pastor Wright said, "He most certainly did."

"Well, you had to know that God called you for yourself, and I have to know for myself, and I do. I know because I don't want to do this. I love Jesus, and I love His word, yes, but I didn't sign up to preach or teach. That's His will, not mine, and because I love Him, I will do whatever His will is for me."

"Everyone sounds passionate about Jesus in the beginning," Pastor Wright chuckled. "It's still early. When trouble comes, you may forget all about loving Jesus. You see, Sister, a lot of ministers come through these doors. Some are on fire for the Lord, and they maintain their course and go on to do mighty works in the name of Jesus. Some are on fire, but they don't last for whatever reason. I'm not here to judge you. As your Pastor, I want to help you reach your full potential in the Lord and in the things He has called you to do. I believe that there is a call of God on your life in ministry. He has kept you and your children on my heart since you first joined Holy Tabernacle. The Lord is with you. You are anointed. Are you ready?"

Maria smiled. "Ready? I can't tell you that I'll ever be ready to minister the awesome, sacred Word of a sovereign, holy God who seated in the heavens looked low enough at me in spite of me. I am unworthy and undeserving. Is any preacher ever ready to handle the sacred Scriptures but for the grace of Jesus Christ?"

Reverend Wright sat up in his chair.

Maria continued, "The more I come to know Jesus, the more I recognize I do not know. I read His word, yes, and I am ready, prepared and equipped to handle it, but at the same time I am still a sinner in need of His grace. Paul was a Hebrew of Hebrews, of the tribe of Benjamin, zealous and on fire for *persecuting* the church, educated and trained in the law, ready and prepared by the world's standards, but in order to be ready by God's standards, He had to lose everything that he considered of any value or merit for the sake of Christ. By the standards of men, Paul was ready, but by God's standards, Paul was not until He lost everything for the sake of knowing Christ.[122] If this is what determines whether or not I am ready, yes, Pastor Wright, I am."

Reverend Wright chuckled again. "I can see you have been paying attention in your classes and studying the Word on your own. Praise God."

Reverend Wright sat and didn't say a word for a few seconds. He appeared to either be praying or in deep thought, and Maria kept silent so as not to interrupt him.

"We are having ordination for new ministers in December, and I would like to welcome you to minister with us at Holy Tabernacle as an ordained Elder. Elder Daniels can give you information concerning the classes. Also, prepare a sermon on The Samaritan Woman at the Well to preach at my anniversary service in October. We're having service on that Friday, Saturday and Sunday, so there will be a few other speakers there, but I'll have you preach on Saturday at our brunch. The church Elders are in charge of the service, so I'll talk to Elder Daniels about that." Pastor Wright stood from his seat and extended his hand. "Welcome, daughter. He is calling you to preach. Now, it's still early, and there will be challenges along the way, but as long as you keep your focus on Jesus Christ, pray and stay in the Word, you and your family will be blessed, yes, beyond measure. I can't wait to hear the message He gives you. God bless you."

Maria could hardly hold back her tears, but this time they were tears of joy. She reached for a tissue from his desk and dabbed her eyes. Then she shook the Pastor's hand and thanked him.

"No, thank God. He is with you, and He will have his way. I have to do His will myself. If I didn't, I wouldn't be His servant. And, Maria, whatever we lose is profitable to the soul when we consider that we have come to know the Son of David.[123] For whoever desires to save his life will lose it, but whoever loses his life for Jesus' sake and the gospel's will save it.[124] The Lord will restore you, amen. We haven't lost or left anything worth having if we've lost it or left it for the sake of Christ, and He promises to restore us in His word. Read **Matthew 19:29**, daughter. God bless you."

Maria shook the Pastor's hand and then went to see Neicy at her home where she was tending to the petunias in her garden. The flowers were in an array of bright purple, pink and red. Hanging baskets of various flowers decorated the patio, and Neicy's other favorite flowering plants, Hibiscus, stood 48" tall in four green wicker containers at each corner of the patio. Bright yellow and orange flowers in full bloom beautified the small trees like ornaments on a Christmas tree. As Maria admired the gorgeous array of plants, Neicy handed her an aluminum watering can so that she could help water them.

Once Maria shared the news that Reverend Wright requested Maria to preach at his Anniversary Service in October, Neicy shouted, "Hallelujah! Praise the Lord!"

"I'm so nervous," Maria said. "I mean, I'm ready, but I'm nervous as heck. Look."

Maria placed her shaking hands in front of Neicy so that she could see for herself. Neicy laughed and told Maria that she had nothing to worry about. "Just let God use you. He knows what He is doing, and Reverend Wright would not have said anything to you if He did not believe that you were ready."

"It's funny you say that because he asked me if I was."

"You are, Maria. It's okay to be nervous. God's Word is nothing to trifle with. You have a healthy reverence of God's Word, and that will keep you humble before God and men. You're ready. I can't wait to see how God uses you. Amen!"

Their afternoon was spent caring for the flowers in Neicy's backyard. Neicy seemed to take extra care of the petunias, but she reminded Maria that these were her annuals, which would not come back next year. "I'm going to go to the cemetery and place some flowers on the gravesite for my mom. Would you like to come with me?"

"Of course," Maria replied.

When they arrived at the cemetery, Neicy took a small rectangular box full of the petunias, which she had gathered in three bunches and wrapped with white ribbon at the small stems. She gave one bunch to Maria and invited her to place them on the gravesite where her mother rested 6' below in the earth. Maria stepped forward, said a silent prayer, and laid the flowers carefully on top of the packed earth. Then, she walked a distance away so that Neicy could have time to herself.

Neicy stood to the right of her mother's engraved headstone and prayed softly. Then, she carefully placed the two bunches of pink and purple flowers on top of her mother's grave, kissing them before they were lowered onto the ground. She turned to join Maria, and the two ladies walked back to Neicy's car parked along the granite trail a few yards away. The sun shone brightly, and there was little breeze to cool the 80 degree temperature. Beads of sweat were just forming on Maria's brow as she stood in direct sunlight, so she walked underneath a large tree that provided enough shade to block the rays.

"Are you okay, Neicy?" Maria asked.

"Yes, I'm fine. Why do you ask?"

Maria hesitated.

"It's okay, Tony used to ask me the same thing. Do you want to know why I kissed the flowers?" Neicy asked.

"Well, not really, I know that it must have some meaning for you."

"It does," Neicy replied with a heavy sigh. "Maria, I'll explain it to you like this. I cared for those petunias as best I could, and we came today to lay those flowers on my mothers' grave. I bring them to be grateful for the life that my mother has eternally in heaven with Jesus, and I kiss them because I know that they will die, and I won't see *them* again. Flowers die. My mother lives because of Jesus Christ. I don't have to kiss her goodbye, and I will see her again, glory to God. The petunias remind me that she is not dead, only sleeping in the earth."

Maria didn't question Neicy. If that helped Neicy to feel better about the loss of her mother, amen.

The two women opened the doors to get back in Neicy's car, and they both saw a single bright pink flower that had been left behind. Maria picked it up, kissed it, and let it slip from her grasp onto the ground. She went over to the other side of the car and hugged Neicy, and as if Maria knew that she needed a hug at that moment, Neicy broke down and cried for the first time since her mother was buried. Neicy had such a tight grip on Maria that Maria didn't dare move. This time, it was Maria's turn to be the comforter.

Neicy hadn't cried yet, not really. Here and there, yes, she had teared, but there was a built up anguish and heartache that had not yet been released. Her own prayers had offered some comfort, and the prayers of her Pastor and church family some support, yes, but Neicy needed to cry and let it out. She was always the strong one who lifted up and encouraged everyone else, and she didn't dare allow anyone to see that she, too, needed Jesus' help. Tony had held her in his arms the evening of the funeral, but it was all so surreal to Neicy that she hadn't yet embraced the reality that her mother had passed on.

"I know I'll see her again," Neicy cried, "and I'm sorry for crying like this. I don't know what came over me." She took a tissue from her glove compartment, wiped her eyes and blew her nose.

"It's okay. You needed to let it out."

"Amen," Neicy agreed. She thanked Maria for being there for her.

"I love you, Neicy," Maria answered.

"I love you, too. Thank you."

The two women got into the car and Neicy drove out of the cemetery and back onto the main road towards her home.

Reverend Wright's anniversary service was scheduled for the weekend of Friday, October 16th through Sunday, October 18th. Sister Maria Henderson was listed on the church flyer as a speaker for the Saturday brunch at 11:00 a.m., and she was slated, per Reverend Wright and Elder Daniels, to preach on the Samaritan Woman at the Well, John 4. The theme of the anniversary service was "Living to Worship," and Elder Daniels explained to Maria that she could preach as the Lord led her on that theme.

The Saturday brunch was sold-out. It was held in the conference room of a nearby five-star hotel. When Maria arrived with Neicy and Tony, they escorted her into an adjacent meeting room where Reverend Wright, Mother Wright and Elder Daniels were seated. They prayed with Maria and thanked God for using her to bring the Word that morning, and then they went into the conference room to be seated.

After the meal was over, the praise and worship team sang a few selections. Reverend Wright then went to the podium and introduced his "daughter in the Lord," Sister Maria Henderson, as the speaker of the hour, and he asked everyone to keep her in their prayers for she would be attending catechism classes to be ordained as an Elder at Holy Tabernacle.

Maria nervously went up to the podium to speak. She gave honor to God, Jesus Christ, Reverend Wright and his wife, and all of the clergy present, as she had been taught. Then, she asked those present to please stand for the reading of the Word, and she read from **John 4:7-14**:

A woman of Samaria came to draw water. Jesus said to her,
"Give Me a drink. For His disciples had gone away into the city
to buy food. Then the woman of Samaria said to Him,
"How is it that you, being a Jew, ask a drink from me,
a Samaritan woman?" For Jews have no dealings with Samaritans.
Jesus answered and said to her, "If you knew the gift of God, and
Who it is who says to you, 'Give Me a drink,' you would have asked
Him, and He would have given you living water."
The woman said to Him, "Sir, You have nothing to draw with,
and the well is deep. Where then do you get that living water?
Are you greater than our father Jacob, who gave us the well,

and drank from it himself, as well as his sons and his livestock?"
Jesus answered and said to her, "Whoever drinks of this water will
thirst again, but whoever drinks of the water that I shall give him will
never thirst. But the water that I shall give him will become in him
a fountain of water springing up into everlasting life."

Then, she read **verse 24:**

"God is Spirit, and those who worship Him must worship
in spirit and truth."

Her topic was **"Living to Worship."**

Maria offered a verse-by-verse commentary on the scriptures
with a history of what life was like for a Samaritan woman in the
patriarchal society of ancient Israel. She recounted the enmity and
hostilities between the Samaritans and the Israelites, a long-standing
bitterness and division between the northern and southern kingdoms of
Israel dating back centuries over worshipping the God of Israel, race,
ethnicity and intermarriages, amongst other reasons.[125] Then, she
offered an overview of the complete Chapter, noting that this woman
had answered Jesus that she had no husband. Jesus told her that she
had five husbands, and the man she was with now was not her
husband.

> "Although many historians thought she was the
> recipient of a harsh rebuke from JESUS at Jacob's well,
> upon closer examination, it becomes obvious that the
> loving Savior was firmly, but gently, revealing to her
> the truth that because she had been destined for
> significance and greatness that would impact all of
> humanity, she could no longer look for fulfillment from
> imperfect humanity, who were threatened by her gifts,
> purpose, and destiny. Why would JESUS rebuke her
> for being married five times when women in that
> society had no power to divorce their husbands? Thus,
> upon closer scrutiny, it becomes apparent that she had
> not divorced her husbands, but rather they had divorced
> her."[126]

Maria's sermon was not an attack on the morals, or lack thereof, of a woman who had been with many different men and "couldn't keep any of them." It may have been according to the Law of the day that when the husband died, his wife was then required to marry the brother of her deceased husband to produce offspring to carry on her deceased husband's name (if the deceased husband had been living with his brother).[127]

If she were committing adultery, the Law commanded that she be put to death.[128]

Although Maria did not dare look beyond what was written, she questioned why the Samaritan woman was still alive if she were just the loose, immoral woman whom many commentators and expositors of the Bible made her out to be. Maria preached that the meeting between this despised outcast and Jesus at the sixth hour of the day was no chance encounter. It was no coincidence. Jesus strategically positioned Himself at Jacob's well because He who is omniscient would meet a worshipper who would not only live her life to worship the one and only true God, Jesus Christ, but who would go back to the men of Samaria, now wed in the faith to her true husband, Jesus Christ, and witness. Why weren't any men witnessing in Samaria?

This Samaritan woman was the one with whom Jesus spoke about true worship – that it was not specific to one geographic location or another, as the Jewish and Samaritan people misunderstood. Rather, the Lord wanted men and women to worship Him with the whole heart – not merely external actions in obedience to laws, rules and traditions, but by truth rather than ceremony.[129]

Conversations, advice, opinions and debates on the sacred scriptures at that time were the privileged responsibility of learned Pharisees, Sadducees, Scribes and Elders, who were male. Jesus entrusted this honor to a shunned, loathed and unnamed woman in John's Gospel, which, theologically, "is a persuasive argument for the deity of Jesus."[130] The Samaritan woman has for so long been vilified by prejudice, culture biases and gender discrimination that we for too long could not even appreciate the grace and mercy of a sovereign Savior who came seeking the lost. Her past, genealogy, address and status overshadowed the love of a merciful God who has compassion on whomever He pleases.[131] We are more concerned with who she is sleeping with. Well, we are in bed with the enemy if we are not with Jesus. Who are we sleeping with?

The Greek word for worshipping, Maria taught, was *proskynountas*, which suggests the willingness to make all necessary physical gestures of obeisance; to kiss the ground when prostrating before a superior; to worship; ready "to fall down/prostrate oneself to adore on one's knees."[132] The word implied a worthiness of worship, and God was worthy of our reverence regardless of what was going on in our lives.

To this statement, many in the crowded conference room stood and applauded.

Maria continued, preaching that Jesus had resolved a centuries' long feud in Israel over worship with an unnamed, ostracized woman at a well for God chose the foolish things of the world to shame the wise; God chose the weak things of the world to shame the strong. He chose the lowly and despised things of the world, and the things that are not, to nullify the things that are, so that no one may boast in His presence.[133]

"God did not choose philosophers, nor orators, nor statesmen, nor men of wealth and power, and interest in the world, to publish the gospel of grace and peace,"[134] Maria quoted. "He chose and chooses ordinary people who recognize their need for a Savior and who are willing, as this woman of Samaria, to drop what they are doing and go tell the lost, unchurched and unsaved, 'Come, see a Man who told me all things that I ever did. Could this be the Christ?'" [135]

"Jesus satisfied this woman like no other had ever been able to – like no one has ever been able to satisfy any of us. Was the woman in the text so different?"

Maria testified that she had only one husband in her life, but that *one* husband may as well have been five because there were five or more times that Jesus had tried to come into her life, and Maria refused Jesus. She testified that she previously didn't have any need of a Savior, because her one husband *was* her Savior. She thought she had everything she needed – what could Jesus offer? She was loved, self-sufficient, happy, and she had a nice home, money, a career and businesses. They went on vacations, their children were doing well, and they were all in good health. So here comes Jesus with His offer of living water. Well, Maria preached, she was living apart from Jesus, too. She played the harlot, as Israel, with other lovers whom she put before God.[136] She had been married to her money, and therefore, was serving two masters[137], unable to make Jesus a priority. She had cheated on Jesus by going after what she wanted in her life, so whatever His plans for her were didn't matter. Maria admitted that she had become her own god, and she neglected Jesus in favor of the other god in her life – the one fleshly husband she did have. She was comfortable in the world because she didn't have to submit or surrender to a God who wanted her whole heart, soul and mind.[138] If she surrendered, she would have to give up some things that made her happy, and she would have to take up a cross and commit to living *for* Jesus instead of *against* Him.[139]

Jesus wasn't even a close second – He was outside the door of her heart knocking as He stood outside the door of the Laodicean church in Revelation[140], Maria preached.

Clergy in white collars were seated at a table near the podium, and they all stood and applauded.

"Living to worship? Jesus gives fountains of living water, His Holy Spirit, to flow out of a heart redeemed by God.[141] The Samaritan woman did not go to the well in search of the living water that Jesus gives. No, she had a natural thirst that could only be temporarily satisfied by the natural water that she would draw from the well. The problem with the well water was that it could never keep anyone permanently satisfied. You still get thirsty after you drink it, and you have to go back to draw more. But the living water that Jesus gives, His Holy Spirit, satisfies the thirsty and longing soul, and Jesus' well never runs dry."

Reverend Wright stood and yelled with excitement, "Preach, daughter!"

"Living to worship? Yes, today, we are men and women in Church, and we are sold out for Jesus Christ. But, there was a time in my own life when I, like the Samaritan woman, didn't live for Jesus. I, too, kept going back to wells looking for water in all the wrong places, trying to find some, Amen, temporary…can I say it again, temporary satisfaction. Some temporary relief. Something to soothe my thirst, my appetite, my hunger, my flesh. Something to satisfy my carnal desires. But Jesus. Can I get an Amen?"

The members and guests shouted "Amen!" in unison that sounded like a well-trained chorus.

"But Jesus," Maria continued. "Jesus came into my life just like He did the Samaritan woman. I wasn't looking for Jesus, He was looking for me. God has a purpose for your life, and it isn't going to be blocked or hindered because of anything you may have done in your past or your present. She could have been killed according to the Law of that day if she were an adulteress. The Lord preserved her life, because His purpose for her was that she *would* live to worship Him. Hallelujah, there are some things that *should* have taken us out, but there is a divine purpose for your life, which requires you to live and not die. C'mon, Saints, say it with me, I shall not die, but live, and declare the works of the Lord.[142] Hallelujah, the power of life and death is in the tongue! Say Amen somebody!"[143]

The members shouted "Amen!" and "Hallelujah!" Neicy and Tony were standing at their table with hands raised, giving glory to God and praising His name. Mother Wright stood near them with head bowed, reverencing the Lord. As soon as she stood, several other Mothers, all dressed in white, stood with her.

Maria looked at Reverend Wright, and he nodded for her to continue as the musicians played softly.

"Tell it like it is, daughter. Preach on!" he shouted. "Say it! Take your time!"

"Can I take my time, Pastor?" Elder Maria asked.

"Daughter, say what God has told you to say. Tell it like it is. Take your time," Pastor Wright replied before sitting back down.

"Well, amen. God has a purpose for every Samaritan in this room. This despised, hated and ostracized woman in the gospel of John was honored by Jesus, vindicated and exonerated."[144]

"One of the main issues Jesus resolved with her was over worship. Enmity and disunity plagued the tribes of Israel throughout their history. In 2 Samuel 10, the Lord told King David that the sword would never depart from his house because David had Uriah killed in order to take Uriah's wife, Bathsheba. In 2 Samuel 15, King David's son, Absalom, led many Israelites away from their allegiance to the King. King David united the tribes of Israel, and they shortly after divided into a northern and southern kingdom with a temple in each. In 1 Kings 11, the Lord declared His reason for the division of the

326

kingdom was because Israel had not walked in His ways but had forsaken Him. King Rehoboam, the first King of a divided northern Kingdom, declared that the Jews no longer had to go to Jerusalem to worship.[145] He instituted calf worship and built a temple in the north. The division of Jacob's sons would see brother fighting against brother, Israelite against Israelite, for years. The nation would persistently walk away from the Lord in their pursuit of their neighbors' gods. Who do we worship and where?"

"Prophets were sent to rebuke the spirit of harlotry in the nation. In Jeremiah 3, the Lord speaks to His prophet and says that on every high mountain and under every green tree, Israel played the harlot. Lift up your eyes to the desolate heights and see: Where have you not lain with men? By the road you have sat for them like an Arabian in the wilderness, and Israel polluted the land with her harlotries and wickedness.[146] The Lord would proclaim in Hosea 4:12 that His people ask counsel from their wooden idols, and their staff informs them. God's judgment would ultimately result, and the nation would suffer famine, war, captivity, exile, dispersion, death and the fall of the northern and southern kingdoms to foreign oppressors, Assyria and Babylon."

"How are the brothers brought together again? Amen, how good and how pleasant it is for brethren to dwell together in unity.[147] How do we restore broken family lines? How are families reunited? When the relationship between the brothers was severed, the entire nation suffered. There was corruption in the nation's leadership. Heads of state and heads of families led their people astray. We need men to be in their rightful places in our homes, churches and communities, and we need men to be on one accord in the faith. The man is the head, yes, and the head must follow Jesus in order to lead."

"Jesus came seeking the lost sheep of the house of Israel. Will the lost sheep shout Hosanna or Crucify Him? The 12 tribes of Israel today are scattered. We need men to repent and believe in the name of Jesus so that they are in their proper places of leadership. Why? When a lady meets Jesus, her heart will become under new management. When a woman truly falls in love with Jesus, she would rather be by herself than be with any man who is not in love with Jesus, too. He has to learn how to love her as Christ loved His church. Proverbs 18:22 says that he who finds a wife finds a good thing, and

Proverbs 19:14 says a prudent wife is from the Lord. Jesus is the standard, and a godly woman will no longer settle or compromise. Faith is elevated."

"Amen!" several guests shouted.

"I read somewhere that this conversation in John's gospel is the longest recorded conversation between Jesus and a private individual in all of the New Testament, so the dialogue is of the utmost importance," Maria continued. "It isn't that this is a loose, immoral woman, but that Jesus is also settling a theological issue that caused separation in the brothers for centuries – they could not agree. Can two walk together unless they are agreed?[148] Jacob's grandsons and great-grandsons and great-, great-, great-grandsons are still fighting over who God is and how we should worship Him. The church is still divided. The brothers are still divided. When Jesus walked in the flesh, He was looking for fruit, and He cursed the fig tree. He taught parables about the Kingdom of Heaven, and He told the leaders of the day that tax collectors and prostitutes would enter the Kingdom before they did. He looked for the fruit of sincere repentance and faith, and He found it, glory to God, not in the religious leaders but in this woman of Samaria. Jesus reveals himself to a woman, He talks to her, and He settles the issue with her. She will take His message back to the unsaved and unchurched men. She knows what it is like to be hated and rejected. Yes, Jesus has vetted her, and yes, He has her background report in His hand. Any other employer may have thrown it in the garbage, but this employer is the Holy One of Israel who is merciful and gracious to us all. How does the adulterous and harlot church dare look down her nose on a soul Jesus has chosen? He knows all about her past, and He has an assignment for her anyway. 'On that prophetic day, He would exonerate all women by dealing with the injustice that had been inflicted on one Samaritan Woman in particular.[149]'"

"Amen!" several people shouted.

"Perhaps you are someone or know someone who has a past. You may go on a job interview and get the job, but then the employer later calls you into the office to tell you that something came up on your background report – maybe some type of infraction with the law or something on your credit report. That employer can let you go at will, and your application can be thrown out. Well, Jesus has this woman's background report in His hand, and it is His will to hire her anyway, wiping her slate clean. Have you ever needed Jesus to wipe your slate clean? Have you ever needed Him to throw your sins into the depths of the sea?[150] Has Jesus ever asked you to reason with Him and said that though your sins were as scarlet, He would make them as white as snow?[151] This woman's importance has been so minimized over the years that we, today, have been prejudiced to view a woman's biblical account through the interpretive lens of the same cultural biases and gender discrimination that Jesus destroyed."

The musicians played with more intensity.

"A spiritual restoration of God's people would occur as Jesus resolved the Jews' and Samaritans' dispute by declaring neither mountain would be of importance any longer. The Father wants us to worship Him in spirit and in truth, and His purpose is that we live to worship Him in spirit and in truth and are restored to right relationship with Him through faith in Jesus.[152] The testimony of Jesus Christ is so powerful from this Samaritan woman that she is able to witness to the unsaved brothers in Samaria where there were other gods. She is a powerful witness! Souls are saved. Territory is regained for Christ. Let's not be the same devils who hurled insults at her and looked not at the grace of God but at the past of a mighty woman of God, as if we, ourselves, have nothing in our past for which Christ saved and delivered us."

Several women came forward and brought freewill offerings to the altar as Elder Maria continued to speak.

"We discard her and write this account off as nothing more than a loose woman who can't keep a man, but this empowered evangelist has a mega church in her belly. Are we intimidated by the honor Jesus has conferred on her? Is it easier to keep our exegetical feet on her neck? Jesus honors her."

"Amen!" many women shouted."

"The Samaritan Woman, like many women in today's twenty-first-century world, was a broken woman. Therefore, history has reserved a place of great honor for her, even similar to that of the apostles. In fact, in Greek sermons from the fourth to the fourteenth centuries, she is referred to as "apostle" and

"evangelist." In these sermons, the Samaritan Woman
is often likened to the male disciples and apostles and
not diminished in comparison to them."[153]

"This daughter of Abraham was hated because of who her
parents were, and she was born into a society that had been living
apart from Jesus, which makes her a first generation believer. The
Lord uses her in a mighty way to break generational curses, and when
you are chosen to do this, you better believe you are going to have
some opposition. She was chosen to break generational curses in her
family and in the church that were not her responsibility or doing. Her
forefathers strayed from the worship of the Lord. This daughter of
Abraham was at a well, Amos was minding his own business, Moses
thought he could not speak, and Gideon thought that he and his family
were the least in all Israel. Peter cried out at Jesus, 'Depart from me,
for I am a sinner.'[154] God interrupted his mouthpieces and intervened
in order to bring about His holy purpose. We must honor this daughter
and not continue to spew sarcasm, prejudice and hatred in ignorance."

"In spite of the fact that her family was not worshipping Jesus,
she would. That takes courage and faith. She was not raised in the
Christian church or brought up in the faith. She goes against the grain,
the status quo and against the worship that her family and community
instilled upon her. She didn't have a choice up to now, she was born
into this. My God, to be hated by others because of the church you
come from. To be so despised that others walk around your town so
that they don't have to have any contact with you. How much can she
take? In spite of it all, this daughter will boldly go on to declare that
Jesus is the long-awaited Christ at a time when the intellectual, upper
echelon of the ecclesia, men of rank, nobility and pedigree, go on to
declare that Jesus is possessed by demons. Who do you say Jesus is?
Jesus would ask His disciples this question, and Peter alone would
confess Him as the Christ."

"Amen!"

"She recognizes Jesus as the Christ, just as Peter to whom the
Lord says flesh and blood has not revealed this to you, but my Father
in Heaven.[155] This woman has revelation, which means she can see.
The blind and hypocritical religious leaders of the day dishonored
Jesus Christ and sought to kill him. Jesus ministers for three and one-

half years, and they don't recognize Him as the Christ. How is it that one conversation is all it takes for this unnamed woman to recognize Jesus as the Christ? The foolish things of the world are used by God to shame the wise! She will share the gospel with others, namely, the bible says, with men. Well, amen. The church today is made up of mainly women. If there is a sister empowered from on high with that level of anointing to witness to unsaved, lost, idol-worshipping men and bring some brothers into the church, God bless her. Praise the Lord. Glory to God!"

The guests stood and applauded, and Pastor Wright could be heard saying, "Preach, daughter! Go ahead!"

"The separation would end, and the kingdom Jesus ushered in would welcome Jew and Gentile. 'Whoever calls on the name of the Lord shall be saved.'"[156]

"Jesus wants an intimate relationship with each one of us. His will is that we look to Him with our whole heart, soul and mind and put no other God before Him, no other man, no career, no plans of our own, and no pursuit of money. It is not God's will for you to remain separated from him and die without knowing Jesus Christ as your Lord and Savior. He doesn't desire that any should perish. He spoke through His prophet Ezekiel to declare to us that He has no pleasure in the death of the wicked. Rather, He is pleased when we turn from our ways and live.[157] We are all sinners, each one of us, and we all fall short of His glory. But the good news is that our Father loves us so much that He gave His only Son, Jesus Christ, so that we who believe in Him should not perish but have eternal life.[158] Amen, so that we may live to worship Jesus. It doesn't matter what you have done. Repent, and be saved. Jesus forgives, and He is love."

"In conclusion, the Lord says live. Live the abundant life that He came to give.[159] Live and not die. Live to worship the Lord, Jesus Christ."

Maria closed her Bible, which was open and on the waist-high podium before the conference room of clergy, members and guests. Reverend Wright walked from his seat to join Maria at the podium. There, he stood with one arm placed tightly around her, and he thanked her for bringing such a powerful Word. The guests applauded with respect.

"She is my daughter in the gospel," Reverend Wright spoke proudly. "My mother kept telling me, 'Sister Maria Henderson, Sister Maria Henderson.' Amen, I knew that the Lord was going to use her, but I am just so godly proud that He used her here today for this anniversary service of mine. 42 years in ministry......"

He was interrupted by a roaring standing ovation that didn't stop even when Reverend Wright asked them to.

"Hallelujah!" the guests shouted. "Hallelujah!" "Amen!" "Praise God!"

Reverend Wright thanked everyone, and after about a minute, the applause was stopped so that he could continue speaking.

"Amen, bless the Lord. 42 years, glory to God, and I am so thankful that the Lord raises up His own ministers. He chooses, and it is my responsibility as His servant to simply obey. God bless you, daughter," Reverend Wright said, turning to Maria. "The Lord used you today. You see, Saints, my anniversary service isn't about me. This is still God's church. He will use whomever He pleases. It is about Jesus Christ. If I were running His church doing whatever I wanted to do, I wouldn't be His servant. As the Pastor of this Church, I am bound to God first. I could not be His true servant if I were trying to please men.[160] So, we will allow God to use whomever He chooses to minister in His Church. Amen?"

The members and guests replied, "Amen."

Reverend Wright glanced at Mother Wright, and Mother nodded affirmatively. There had been some backlash in the church because Reverend Wright had asked Sister Maria to preach. Maria didn't have as much experience as those who were already ordained into ministry, so Reverend Wright made it a point to settle the controversy by allowing God to have His way. Sister Maria would preach, and the Holy Ghost would settle the controversy and speak for itself.

Continuing, Reverend Wright said, "And because the Lord had His way, I know that there is a soul in this room today who wants to give her life to Jesus. Hallelujah, He knew you would be here today. He used Sister Maria to bring this message today because there is an anointing on this word, and somebody needed to hear about living to worship. A Samaritan woman needed to hear that she was so important to Jesus that He was not going to leave her where she was –

apart from Him. A mighty woman of God with purpose and destiny in her belly needed to hear this message. A soul who was living for money or his career, who refused Jesus before, but wants to make it right today needed to hear this message about living to worship. A family member who needs to reunite with a loved one, separated from someone else over which church to go to. C'mon, daughter of Abraham, son of Abraham, I know you're in here. He's calling you today to live. Live, daughter! Live, son! Hallelujah!"

The musicians played softly, and clergy were asked by Reverend Wright to walk about the room and assist anyone who wanted to come down to the altar and be saved. Mother Wright walked past a few tables with her hands lifted up, and Ronny stood on her feet. Ronny was crying, and she walked willingly into the arms of Mother Wright who embraced her as if Ronny were her own child. Ronny looked beautiful in a long purple dress and white Cashmere sweater. Her natural hair was in tight coils that dangled just past her shoulders, and she wore pearl earrings and a single strand of pearls around her neck. She looked like royalty, and the transformation from scantily clad dancer was effortless. The musicians played with more intensity in a welcoming appeal for all who desired to accept Jesus Christ as Lord and Savior. Sis Maria's spirit-filled sermon lifting up Jesus and Reverend Wright's remarks blessing Christ were paired to prick even the most stubborn of hearts, and the high praise of the music only lent further spirit-filled support. One of the ushers handed Ronny a tissue, and Ronny wiped her eyes. Mother Wright held her hand, and the two walked towards the podium.

Ronny fell on her knees and bowed her head low. She wept before the Lord, and her tears flowed freely from her eyes, softly dropping onto the deep blue carpet.

"Hallelujah! Thank you Jesus!" Neicy lifted up her voice. She sang a few lines of the gospel hymn "I need thee every hour," by Annie Sherwood Hawks and Robert Lowry[161]:

I need Thee, oh, I need Thee
Every hour I need Thee;
Oh, bless me now, my Savior
I come to Thee

Then Reverend Wright led, and the guests and members lifted their hands to bless the Lord.

Out of the corner of her eye, Maria spotted Joanne approaching with Genny. Joanne released Genny's hand and knelt with her mother at the altar, and when Ronny saw her daughter beside her, the two hugged and prayed together. Neicy came over and draped a shawl over the two ladies, and then she squeezed Maria's hand.

"I didn't even know Ronny was here," Maria whispered in Neicy's ear.

"She came in late. I told her and Pam that you were preaching today. Pam couldn't make it, but Ronny said she would be here come hell or high water. Glory to God, you see why God put it in her heart to come."

"Hallelujah!" Maria shouted. "Glory to God!"

Neicy and Maria lifted up their voices and blessed God for the marvelous things that He had done.

Ronny and Joanne stood, and all of the women at the altar embraced one another and gave God all the glory.

Chapter Twenty Four
Rob

Two days after Papi's solo at Holy Tabernacle in June, Rob attended the APHS high school graduation ceremony, where James was receiving his diploma along with about 100 other students. He approached James after the ceremony's conclusion to shake his hand, and though James was somewhat distant, he did share a cordial hand shake, hug and conversation.

"Congratulations, young man. I'm proud of you," Rob said. He held a rolled up program underneath his left arm in the outdoor 72 degree temperature. The ceremony had been held in the football stadium in the rear of the school, where city officials, dignitaries, sorority and fraternity chapters, and administrators joined to celebrate and honor the graduating class of Addington Park High School. Rob was but one of a few local businessmen and community minded citizens who were happy to attend and pledge their support in the way of mentoring, counseling services, tuition assistance and scholarships, as well as job referrals and job placement.

"Thanks, Mr. Henderson. I appreciate everything you did for me," James said. He was smiling in his long black gown and cap, and the cap's tassel dangled in his face, brushing against his dark sunglasses.

"Let me see your diploma," Mr. Henderson said with eagerness.

James handed his handsome diploma in its padded and engraved cover to Mr. Henderson, who admired it with pride. James had beaten and defied many odds and stereotypes of a young, black man from the hood in a single-parent home. *"Statistically, James' life was disproportionately threatened with drugs, poverty, disease, imprisonment or death, but here he is,"* thought Mr. Henderson. James had a good head on his shoulders, and Mr. Henderson figured it would only be a matter of time before the young man sought him for his assistance with the business endeavors James had showed interest in.

As Rob read the text that honored James for his achievement, a young girl of about 17 or 18 years came over to them, and James reached for her hand. She handed him a garment bag, which he draped over his arm. Mr. Henderson noticed a small bump in the belly of the young girl, which may not have been visible but for the snug fitting orange and white dress she wore. A plaid orange, yellow and white belt was tied above her belly, and it looked like it must have been something the fashion forward James designed or picked out. James kissed the young girl softly on her lips, and she wiped sweat from his forehead. He removed his long, black gown and cap, and underneath he was wearing a white and yellow striped shirt, with plaid shorts in orange, blue and yellow. Only James could pull this look off, and his white leather belt, thankfully holding up his pants, was fastened with two shiny brass buttons in blue. His cashmere ankle socks were a navy blue and white, and his freshly polished calfskin leather penny loafers completed his classic urban, preppy look. The two apparently had dressed to coordinate with one another. Either that, or James was branching out into fashions for women as well.

James knew that his girlfriend's belly was protruding from her dress. Her naval could be seen through the white and orange dress she had chosen for the day, but he was unashamed of her pregnancy.

"Grace, this is Mr. Henderson. He owns the Robert J. Henderson Center for Young Men downtown and has been mentoring me." He then turned to Mr. Henderson and said, "Mr. Henderson, this is my girl, Grace."

Mr. Henderson stood still for a moment and looked at the young couple. He didn't want his shock to be apparent, and he certainly didn't want the young lady to feel embarrassed, so he stepped forward and hugged her, and she was receptive to him.

"It's nice to meet you, Mr. Henderson," she said. "James speaks very highly of you."

"Well, you have a fine young man by your side, Grace. James was one of my best students last summer."

Grace looked over her shoulder, and she saw some people waiting for her. "Excuse me, please, I need to go and talk with my family. It was nice to meet you, Mr. Henderson. James, I'll wait by the entrance, okay?"

"Sure, baby, I'll be right out," James said, kissing the young lady again before she walked off to talk with her family.

Mr. Henderson was a bit uneasy, but he knew that James was a mature and responsible young man. When he inhaled through his mouth and exhaled through his nose, however, James knew Mr. Henderson wanted to say something.

"Mr. Henderson," James began, "I'm a man. You can say whatever it is you want to say, sir."

Mr. Henderson was quiet. He didn't really know what to say to the young man, and he knew that James wouldn't really receive anything he had to say to him anyway. He decided he would change the subject.

"I haven't seen you around much, James. Are you still planning to go to the community college?" Mr. Henderson asked.

"No."

"Why not? You have a baby on the way, but that doesn't affect your education."

"Mr. Henderson, I have a baby on the way with my fiancé. Grace and I are getting married. No, it doesn't affect my education, but I'm not going to the community college. I'm going to Fashion Institute of Technology in New York. I applied for a few scholarships, and they came through," said James. He was holding his black gown in his hands, but he placed it inside the garment bag that Grace had brought over to him and zipped it shut.

"FIT? That's great, James. I'm proud of you," Mr. Henderson replied. He extended his hand, and the two shook hands again.

"Yeah, thanks, sir. Grace and I are moving to an apartment in New York on August 1st. Grace is the one, Mr. Henderson. And, you know what I have to do, right? I'm going to put a ring on her finger and take care of my baby. We're taking some counseling sessions at church, where Isaiah's mother goes. She set it up for us. That's what a man does, right Mr. Henderson?" James asked.

Mr. Henderson, feeling overwhelmingly and prophetically convicted by James for a second time, said, "Yes, James." However, Mr. Henderson needed to retaliate in self-defense against his paranoia that James was speaking indirectly to him, so he asked with sly sarcasm, "The child is yours, right?"

"What?" James answered in shock and disbelief. "Of course. Why, do you know something about her that I don't?"

"No, James, you know, I'm just saying. That's the question young men ask today, I guess. Girls are a lot different today than they were years ago," Mr. Henderson replied, fumbling over his words. "I'm just saying. But if you're sure, by all means, do the right thing. Congratulations," he said with insincerity.

James could see through Mr. Henderson's bumbling, so he reminded Mr. Henderson of his own words. "Well, you've always taught us that we should not make women 'baby mommas.' We should make them wives. So, I love Grace. I trust her. I know she hasn't been with anybody else, and I want to man up and do the right thing by her and my baby."

James lifted the garment bag over his left shoulder and waved to some passersby who congratulated him on his success.

"You know, Mr. Henderson, I'm glad we had that talk last summer. When Grace told me she was pregnant, at first I wanted to bail, for real. I'm just being honest with you. I had plans for college, and I wasn't really ready to settle down. Grace is cool, but she's just finishing high school herself. But then I remembered the research you asked us to do on single parent families in Addington Park, and I felt convicted. I want better for my family. So, I guess I can't only think about how her pregnancy affects me, I have to think as a man about how her pregnancy affects us all. So, I have you to thank. And, I'll tell you something else, when I talked to my man, Isaiah, about it, he suggested that I speak with his mom at their church. I went there and met with the pastor, and he prayed with me. Once I trusted God with the situation, He put everything together. I got accepted to FIT, they called me about available housing, and I have scholarships that total more than the cost of tuition. God is good, man! Call on Him. He will work it out."

Just then, Isaiah, Marcus, K'Shon, Jamarr and Eric came over to James, and they all shook hands. James told them that he had told Mr. Henderson about Grace, and the young men breathed a sigh of relief. Their conversation wishing James well and promising to support him and stay in touch lasted for several minutes before he told them he had to go.

"Let us know when the wedding is, man," Marcus said.

Laughing, Isaiah added "That ball and chain already got you."

"Whatever," James replied. "Grace's family will send out invitations, so keep a look out." He embraced his friends and mentor one last time and then hurried to join his fiancé and family.

"Alright, Mr. Henderson, we'll see you later. There are a couple of parties we are going to," Marcus said. "Well, that is all of us except Jamarr. We'll catch you later, man."

"Yup," Jamarr answered. He walked off to another group of young men who were dressed in gang colors, and the group exited the stadium together.

"I thought Jamarr wasn't running with that gang anymore," Mr. Henderson said.

The remaining four young men looked at one another, and then Marcus, their spokesman, replied, "We've been talking to him, Mr. Henderson, but that's what he wants to do. He has to make his own decision."

Mr. Henderson replied, "Yes, that's right. Okay, I'll see you all later. Come in next Tuesday at 9am, and we'll get started."

The young men left, and Mr. Henderson greeted several city leaders, school officials, parents and dignitaries before he walked to his car, which was parked a few blocks away. As he approached his vehicle and unlocked the driver side door, a black Jeep, driving at a moderate speed, passed him on his left. The rear tinted window was lowered slightly, and the barrel of an automatic weapon was pointed in his direction. Mr. Henderson ran behind his car and ducked low. The Jeep stopped short in the middle of the street, and laughter of young men could be heard. Then, the Jeep sped off in the residential neighborhood. Mr. Henderson did get a partial NJ license plate number, which he wrote down and threw into his glove compartment, but he knew he wouldn't do anything with it. Although it did shake him up a bit, he wasn't one to take to a random threat from a bunch of punks. After a few days, the incident was forgotten and written off as some misguided kids.

Rob hadn't spoken to Sophia much since she moved back to her parent's home in Pennsylvania. She was on a medical leave of absence from the City, and the last time Rob checked with her, she told him she needed to relax because her blood pressure was still high. He attended two doctor visits with Sophia, including one where she had an ultrasound to determine the sex of the baby, and the doctor advised them that she was having a boy. Rob felt no personal connection, however, to Sophia, and his gut instinct that it was not his child still remained. He finally met Sophia's parents, but they were not receptive to him. Her father was a short, stern looking gentleman who reminded Rob of the television personality, George Jefferson,[162] and her mother was a slightly taller woman who didn't talk too much and who was completely unengaged in any discussion they had. She responded to every conversation with one or two word responses – "fine," "yes," "no," "really" or "that's nice." Rob could usually win anyone over with his charm, but Sophia's mother was not interested in Rob, only in his plans for her daughter.

"We're going to talk about marriage after the baby is born," Sophia had offered, covering for Rob or avoiding an unpleasant conversation.

On August 13th, Sophia called Rob to tell him that she was in labor and at the hospital with her family. Rob drove with Walter and Mike Love to Pennsylvania, and he insisted that they come to tell him whether or not the baby looked anything at all like him. Sophia's labor lasted only five hours, and a perfectly healthy baby boy, Austin Robert Simmons, 8 lbs. 12 oz., 26" long, was born at 7:23 p.m. Sophia and Rob could not agree on using Rob's last name, so she used her own for her son.

As the three men viewed the infant from behind the glass looking into the hospital's pediatric unit and nursery, both Walter and Mike Love concluded that the beautiful and healthy newborn baby looked nothing like Rob.

"He is cute, and God bless him, but man, that baby looks white," Mike Love said.

"Yeah, bruh," said Walter, "and you are dark-skinned. Genny and Papi are rich brown. I don't know, man, I would question it, too. Even, what's her name, Sophia? She's not that light either."

Rob had his suspicions confirmed by his two closest friends. "I know. Ain't no way."

"So what are you going to do?" Mike Love asked.

"Get a DNA test. When it comes back, if it's mine, I will step up. If not, I'm out," Rob answered.

"And then what are you going to do? I hope you're not trying to keep Maria on a string," Mike Love said. "Stop messing her over, man."

"Mike, let me handle this, okay. It's my life," Rob answered. He was upset about the whole situation, and although he appreciated his friends being there, he didn't need another lecture.

"Well, handle it then. C'mon, Walter, I'm ready to go. Let's bounce," Mike Love said. He and Walter walked towards the elevator, and Rob told them he would meet them in the lobby. He wanted to say goodbye to Sophia.

She was sitting up in her hospital bed when Rob walked into the room, and her parents left when they saw him come in. Rob didn't need to be politically correct with them any longer, he figured, because it was clear that the baby wasn't his. He wanted her to tell him the truth, and he would not leave until she admitted that she had slept with someone else.

"How are you feeling?" Rob asked. He would take his time and get her talking before he demanded anything.

"Pretty good," Sophia answered. She was groggy and medicated. Her hair was in a disheveled ponytail, and she brushed it back with her right hand.

"Funny," he thought, *"how a woman can be concerned about how her hair looks after she has just given birth."*

When she reached for her cup of ice water on the tray beside her bed, Rob leaned over to hand it to her.

"Thank you," she said.

"You're welcome. I'm about to leave, the guys are waiting downstairs. Do you need anything? I'll try to come back tomorrow."

Sophia drank the entire cup of water, and then she held the cup in her hands, which were folded across her belly.

"Rob," Sophia began. She said nothing for a minute or two, so Rob asked her if there was something she wanted to say to him.

"I slept with someone else. The baby may not be yours. I'm sorry. I need to tell you the truth. We're grown, not teenagers, and I don't want to lie about this anymore."

Sophia had disclosed the truth to Rob in a cold statement that lacked emotion or feeling. She adjusted the back of the bed so that she was now in a reclining position, and it was as if she felt she told him the news and believed she could now relax.

There was a still silence in the room, and Rob could only hear the low sound of the television news that was on coupled with the nurses' station nearby where a telephone rang and a patient's room buzzer sounded. Rob looked in the hallway as he heard the footsteps of a nurse walking by. Thankfully, she was headed to another room.

"I know," Rob said. "I told you all along I knew I wasn't the father. Thanksgiving night, the washcloth on the counter – someone else was there, right? Was it Isaiah? He's mixed. The baby is light. Is Isaiah the father?" Rob asked. He spoke as softly as he could, considering the fact that she had just delivered a child, was medicated, had high blood pressure and was in a hospital room under medical care.

Sophia didn't say anything, but her lack of a response told Rob everything he needed to know.

"You should have just told me the truth all along. Does Isaiah know?" Mr. Henderson asked.

Sophia still sat there with no response. She pressed the call button by her bed and then asked Rob to please leave.

"I'm sorry, Rob. I'm not feeling well, but I did want to tell you the truth before this goes any further. Yes, I slept with Isaiah. Yes, I think the baby may be his. I'm sorry."

"Isaiah?! My student?!" Rob asked, raising his voice. "He's a kid, Sophia. Were you that hard up? And all this time, the two of you have been talking with me like nothing even happened."

"It was just sex, Rob, and it meant nothing. I had been drinking."

Rob stood at the foot of Sophia's bed and shook his head. "I can't believe you, but okay, I guess I should have seen this coming.

Well, you call him for whatever you need. Diapers, milk, clothes, food. Call *him*."

Sophia's parents walked into the hospital room. They heard part of Rob's conversation with their daughter, and they both asked Rob to leave and let Sophia get some rest. Rob shook Mr. Simmons' hand and acknowledged Mrs. Simmons as he left the hospital room, knowing that he would never see her parents again.

When Rob met his two friends in the lobby, his demeanor had changed, but he didn't say anything to either Walter or Mike Love. He couldn't admit to them that the other man was a 17 year old kid whom he had been mentoring.

"You okay, man?" Walter asked. "You look like you saw a ghost. Did everything go okay up there?"

"Yeah," Rob lied, "we just argued again."

"She still won't fess up, huh?" Walter asked.

"No, she won't, but it's alright. I'll handle it," Rob answered.

"Hey, since we're in Pennsylvania, where's a good place to get a good Philly cheesesteak? I'm starving," Mike Love asked.

The three found a good restaurant not far from the hospital, and they enjoyed Philly strip loin cheese steaks with caramelized onions, sautéed mushrooms and peppers, potatoes and provolone cheese sauce on soft wheat hoagie rolls. Rob hardly ate any of his sandwich, and when the server prepared it for him to go, Rob answered his friends that he didn't have much of an appetite anymore.

They returned home, and Rob thought about calling Isaiah, but he decided not to. He would wait until Isaiah came to him with the truth.

When the summer program ended at The Center for Young Men, Isaiah told Mr. Henderson that he needed to speak with him. Their discussion about Sophia in Mr. Henderson's office lasted for all of five minutes. Isaiah apologized to Mr. Henderson, and he stated that he never would have slept with her if she told him the truth.

"She told me that you were married, and she was single, and she was free to do whatever she wanted. I asked her if she was seeing you, and she told me that you were just friends."

"It's cool, Isaiah," Mr. Henderson said. He was embarrassed of how the whole situation had played out, and he would downplay his part by denying that he had any feelings for her anyway. "Yes, she can do whatever she wants, and I can't really blame you for wanting to hit that. So, the two of you can be together now that you have a son. What are you going to do?"

"I'm going to be there for my son, but it's no more than that, so if you still want her, you can have her."

Incredulous to Mr. Henderson, he just looked at Isaiah and allowed him to finish speaking.

"She was lying to me the whole time, using me to get at you. I asked her if there was a chance that the baby could be mine, and she told me no. *I* should have been at the hospital for my son. He can have *my* last name. She didn't come to me with this like she should have, for real."

Isaiah was upset. He would have been there for his son, and when he told his mother, she insisted that he be in his son's life and arrange for mutually agreeable visitation and custody. Mrs. Parker was livid that the much older future Mayor had seduced her son and taken advantage of him.

"A woman that old knows what she is doing, Isaiah. If she were 16 or 17, I might be a little sympathetic. He's your son, then you have the right to share custody and see your son. I'm not going to let some woman run all over you."

Mr. Henderson and Isaiah shook hands after their conversation was over.

A DNA test shortly after the baby's birth proved that Isaiah was, in fact, the father, and there was no further need for Rob to call Sophia any more. He would have to work his business deals without her, and he had done it before, so he would trust in his own instincts again to get things done.

However, Rob's luck soon after changed. His instincts and investment in his friend's karate school didn't pay off – the school closed, and the building was leased to a new tenant who would be opening up a convenience store.

The annual grant, which Rob usually received for his summer program at The Center, was not received. Maria usually did all the paperwork for him, and he had forgotten about it with everything else going on. She was busy with her Bible studies, and she was attending catechism classes for her December ordination. Her work with the church was hurting his business, and a surge of resentment was building up in the pit of Rob's soul.

"If Maria wasn't spending so much time with that church, she would have time for me," Rob complained to Walter. Walter was the only friend Rob had who would listen to his grievances, and he often encouraged Rob when he pointed the finger at Maria. Walter, too, was a divorced man, of some ten years, and he swore that he would never marry again. He had four children with his ex-wife, but they all lived in California where his ex-wife had relocated after their divorce. Walter was bitter, and he projected his sullen attitude about women onto Rob who absorbed it, in his already acrimonious state, like a sponge.

A new Mayor was elected in November, and new policies and procedures were implemented for city contracts. Maria had always done all of the paperwork for Rob, and Rob couldn't make any sense of it on his own when he picked up the applications at City Hall. When he called Maria to share with her that the baby was not his, in the hope that she might work with him again, she replied that she already knew.

"Mrs. Parker was very honest about everything. She and most of the people in this town know that Sophia was sleeping with you and her 17 year old son."

Rob decided after that conversation to just do the work on his own. He and Walter had been planning to invest in a few other projects within the city, and although they did get some of the paperwork in on time, none of their applications were approved. He was on a stream of bad luck that even salt thrown over his left shoulder, as his superstitious cousin Walter suggested, didn't change.

Rob was alone and running out of money. He continued to see his children on the weekends, but he was experiencing a depression that affected his moods with everyone else. He spent time with Walter, and the two would drink and get high, something Rob hadn't done since he was a teenager. It did help Rob forget about his troubles temporarily, but when he came home one day to an Eviction Notice on the door of his townhome, he was ready to give up. He had only $2,000 left in his bank account, and his credit was in poor shape due to several defaulted loans. Thankfully, he and Maria had worked out an amicable child support agreement between the two of them, and he knew that she would be patient with him. Walter agreed to let Rob move in with him in his two bedroom apartment, and Rob moved his personal belongings in with his cousin.

When Maria's ordination was held in December at Holy Tabernacle, Rob didn't go. He didn't offer any excuses or explanations to her, but he did watch a tape of it on social media that Neicy and Tony had posted. He told his children that he was not feeling well, and they didn't question him. Maria never asked him about it.

Genny's APHS girls' basketball team advanced to the Finals of the State Championship the next year, and they repeated their State Title over a northern New Jersey team by one point. It was a thrilling finish to the girls' 20-1 season, and Rob was even more thrilled when his daughter and two of her teammates were awarded Certificates by the School Administration for their academic achievement. Papi was excelling in his classes as well, and the school music teacher recommended him for solos in the school's chorus.

Maria continued to do well, and Rob understood from his acquaintances that she was preaching in a few local churches.

"Yo, man, Maria can preach!" Mike Love told Rob one Saturday afternoon in his barber shop. "She preached at my man's church, Deliverance House of Worship, over in Lakewood. They said she brought that Word."

"Whatever, man," Mr. Henderson answered. He didn't want to hear about it.

"Why are you hating? Aren't you happy for the mother of your children?" Mike Love answered.

Rob didn't respond. He was envious of Maria, and he wasn't able to camouflage it any longer. He had heard enough about his wife from others in the community, and their praise and kind remarks only heightened his resentment. Rob became increasingly indignant when the local paper did a feature story on "Clergy in the Community," and Elder Maria Henderson was quoted in the article. Rob was offended that neither his ex-wife nor the paper called him regarding the community event – *he* was the main community leader in the city. From that point on, Rob's spiteful and ill-natured disposition spiraled even further downhill and out of control. He resorted to attempts to

346

sabotage her ministry and defame her name to those whom he knew would regard and defer to his opinions.

When Maria was scheduled to speak at a community event in Addington Park on a Saturday in May, Rob called the organizer, who was a friend of his.

"She's a fraud, John. She doesn't want to do community events. She has never been interested in community events for as long as I have known her. She only does these things because I ask her to, and she's only doing this because she's afraid to tell you no. She doesn't want to do it."

His friend believed him, and John called Maria to tell her that they had overbooked the event, but he would have her again soon. It was a lie, but John believed what he was told and sided with Rob.

Maria was scheduled to speak at another community event in June, and when Rob found out, he called the organizer and told him the same thing.

Her graduation from Hampton Bible Institute was scheduled in June at an outdoor banquet facility in a neighboring town. Rob showed up late and complained about everything from his seat in the back row to the warm weather to the shrimp cocktail that weren't the right temperature to his liking, and he argued with one of the servers, causing some disruption in the service. It was immediately handled by the staff of the facility, however, and Robert J. Henderson was politely escorted out.

When Maria was asked to speak at a women's event in September for a new, young Pastor in nearby Red Bank, NJ, a friend of Rob's, Rob called the Pastor and suggested to him that he wanted to go to another church with his wife that day, and he asked him to excuse Maria. The Pastor agreed, and Maria was notified by the church that they had decided to go with another speaker.

On two Sunday mornings, Maria came outside to her car, which had a flat tire. The first time could have been her own fault, but the second.......Maria suspected Rob had something to do with it.

Maria's landlord, a friend of Rob's, sent her a certified letter advising that the rent on her home would be doubled if she wanted to renew her lease. Maria was at first a bit unnerved, but when she saw the landlord's wife in the supermarket shortly after she received the letter, she assured Maria that it had to be a mistake, and she asked

Maria to please forgive them for the error. The next day, the wife telephoned Maria to assure her that the rental price would not be doubling, and her husband "must have had a brain freeze when he sent the letter out."

"After all," she explained to Maria, "he didn't even talk to me about this, so I don't know where he got that from. We apologize for the error and for unnecessarily upsetting you."

Although Rob was secretly trying to damage Maria's ministry and frame of mind, Maria received even more invitations to speak at churches around the state and beyond the reach of his influence. When she completed and published a book, it propelled her into the spotlight, and Rob's envy was only inflated. He was upset that people were helping her, and although he didn't know who her connections were, he would have called them, too, if he did. It didn't take long for the book to become a success, and from what he was told by his children, "Mom is a bestselling author."

The most devastating blow came to Rob's ego when he went to his Center one afternoon and saw an eviction notice prominently displayed on the front door. He had been late with his payments before, and the commercial building owner had always been patient with him. His telephone calls to the building owner went unanswered. Rob left several messages asking for their patience, but he did not receive any return calls. He was three months behind in his payments, and the court date was scheduled in just four weeks.

Rob sat in his office and sulked, blaming Maria's heavy involvement with the church on his problems. She had always stayed on top of grants, finances and paperwork. He believed that she had stopped helping him purposely out of spite. He made mistakes, yes, but he admitted to most of them, and he apologized. What more did she want? He told her the baby wasn't his, and it wasn't. And she was supposed to be a Minister of God. *"Some minister,"* he thought. *"For that matter, some God. The hell with both of you. What kind of God sits back and lets a wife abandon her husband and go run off and hurt her husband's businesses, putting him in jeopardy and harm's way? I'm a man,"* Rob reasoned, *"she doesn't call the shots."*

It had been a long day, and he was tired and ready to go home. He would try and reach the owner the following day and work something out.

Rob left the Center at about 3:45 p.m., and as he walked to his car parked directly in front, he saw Jamarr, his protégé, approaching with another young man. They were walking quickly, and Jamarr's hands were in the front pocket of his sweatshirt. The other young man whispered something in Jamarr's ear, and then he turned and walked in the other direction.

"What's up, young man?" Mr. Henderson asked as Jamarr approached.

"Mr. Henderson, call the police right now," a nervous Jamarr said. He had fear in his eyes, a smell which Rob could easily detect.

"What's the matter, Jamarr? Are you in some kind of trouble?" Rob asked with concern.

"No, you are. These guys are all around the block, and they want me to shoot you. I can't talk to you anymore. I have a gun. Call the police."

Mr. Henderson looked at Jamarr with a blank stare. "Okay, Jamarr. It's going to be alright, son," he said.

Interrupting him, and raising his voice, Jamarr answered, "No, you don't understand! They want you dead! If I don't kill you, they will kill me and you. I'm sorry…."

"Jamarr, you don't have to do this……"

Jamarr lifted his hand from the front pocket of his sweatshirt. He held a small handgun, which he pointed directly at Mr. Henderson. Jamarr was nervous, and his hand was shaking. Mr. Henderson had only a split second to react, and he grabbed Jamarr at his wrist, spinning the gun away from himself. In a trained move he had learned in martial arts, Rob was able to keep his arm on Jamarr's wrist and take the gun from him.

"Jamarr, I'm keeping this gun, and if you ever come around me again, I will use it on you and whoever sent you. Go home," he said, looking Jamarr squarely in his eyes.

Mr. Henderson walked over to the driver side of his car. As he opened the door, a black Jeep drove up quickly from behind and opened fire, striking Rob in the back several times before he collapsed onto the pavement. Jamarr stood and watched the surreal scene in shock, and the passengers in the Jeep yelled at Jamarr to "Remember how Dante felt when he was shot! If this mother f----- hadn't taken his gun, he would have been able to protect himself. It's this nigga's fault

Dante is dead, and this is payback! Get in the damn car or get left behind!"

Jamarr stood motionless, and then he fell to his knees.

"Leave him!" someone yelled from the car, and the Jeep sped off with tires screeching.

Mr. Henderson lay beside his silver Mercedes in a pool of blood. Several people ran from nearby office buildings to the scene of the shooting, which had occurred in broad daylight. An off duty firefighter was among the people who attended to Mr. Henderson, and he called 911, frantic for an ambulance.

"A man has been shot in the back several times. There's blood everywhere! He's still breathing! Hurry!"

Jamarr was shaking uncontrollably on the sidewalk and unable to comprehend the words of some who ran over to him.

"Is he okay?" someone asked.

"He's in shock, but he wasn't shot," Jamarr heard a male voice say. Jamarr was short of breath and faint, but he could hear the sound of an ambulance siren approaching. That was the last thing he remembered.

Maria was eating a meal with her mother and children at home when she received a call from the police department. She nearly fell to the ground when they told her what happened.

"Maria, what's wrong?" her mother asked. "Where are you going?

"I'll call you in a little while, mom." She raced out of the house and drove as fast as she legally could to the hospital nearby where Rob was in emergency surgery. All Maria could do was pray. She pleaded with the Lord for Rob's life and reminded the Lord that the decision was not the doctor's to make, but His.

"Rob's days and times are in your hand, Lord, and if it is not your will for Rob to come home now, help him. Save His life, Lord, for what good is it for him to go down to the grave without confessing your name? His soul would be lost if he hasn't confessed you as Lord, and you didn't shed your blood on the cross that any man should die."

When Maria reached the hospital, she ran inside and was directed by hospital staff to go up to the third floor. Rob was in surgery, and Maria was asked to wait in the family room, and a doctor would be out to speak with her as soon as possible.

Maria never prayed so much. She knelt on her knees in the family room and cried out to the Lord. She used her cell phone to look up and read scriptures on the power of God to save, heal and deliver.[163] When Neicy called Maria, she and Tony prayed with her and promised to come right over. Mike Love and Walter called, and Reverend Wright and Mother Wright called. They all came over, and there was a powerful Intercessory Prayer Meeting in the family room of the hospital. Although the time went by quickly, when the doctor finally came out to talk to Maria, several hours had passed.

"Mrs. Henderson?" the doctor in surgical scrubs asked.

"I'm Maria Henderson," Maria said.

"I'll need to speak with you privately, please. Come this way."

"Is he okay?" Maria asked. She followed the doctor into another small waiting room, where there was a small table and three chairs. The doctor sat down with Maria and introduced himself as Dr. Horowitz, the Head of the hospital's Acute Care Surgery and Trauma Surgery Unit.

"Mrs. Henderson, your husband was very fortunate. He was shot three times in the back, but none of the bullets hit his spine or any major organs. Miraculously, they were only flesh wounds. However, he lost a tremendous amount of blood, and because of the blood loss, he is in a coma. We are doing everything we can."

Maria felt her eyes swelling with tears, but she fought back, believing that God was with him and would see him through.

"Thank you so much Doctor. How long is a coma?" she asked.

The Doctor explained that it all depended, but most were about two to four weeks. "The best thing you and your family can do for him right now, Mrs. Henderson, is pray. If you believe in God, pray. We've seen miracles happen before, miracles that medicine cannot explain."

Their brief meeting was interrupted by Mike Love and Walter, who were impatient and did not want to wait to hear about their friend. Maria asked the Doctor to please excuse the two, but he explained that it wasn't necessary. When they came out of the small waiting room, the Doctor shook Maria's hand and went behind the huge double doors accessible only to medical personnel.

"What's going on? Is Rob okay?" Mike Love asked.

"Yes," Maria answered. "He's going to be fine. He was shot a couple times in the back, but none of the bullets hit his spine or any major organs. The doctor says it was a miracle, and he asks us to pray."

Mike Love and Walter were in shock and disbelief. "Who would shoot Rob?" they asked. "What happened?"

"Well, that's not all," Maria said. She was bravely fighting back tears, and as everyone gathered around her, she explained that Rob was in a coma and might be for two to four weeks. "We need to pray, everyone."

Neicy and Tony hugged Maria, and Walter and Mike Love pledged their support to Maria to do whatever she needed.

For the next three weeks, Maria spent the night at the hospital in ICU and prayed at Rob's bedside. Genny and Papi had been told that their dad was in the hospital, and Maria's mom stayed at her house to help.

Rob looked completely helpless in his hospital room, with tubes hooked up to him and machines monitoring every detail of his body. This was hardly the strong, protective martial arts expert Maria had remembered, and Rob's condition reminded Maria of how frail we all are. Whether Rob lived or died was in the hands of a sovereign God who was still God, and who was still in control. All Maria could do was bow before Him and ask Him for His help.

Maria fasted and prayed, and the church was praying with her. Reverend Wright came to the hospital and prayed with Maria along with the other leaders and every Mother. Elder Daniels stopped in and encouraged Maria that everything would work out fine, and Maria was grateful for his fierce faith in Jesus. When Neicy and Tony weren't there with Maria, they were calling to check on her and Rob's condition.

The police advised that they were conducting an investigation into the shooting, and they did question a young man, Jamarr Moody from Addington Park, who was at the scene of the accident, but he was uncooperative. The police were unable to locate him or his whereabouts since the shooting, but his name and photo had been distributed to the media and television news stations.

"He won't get far," Sergeant Johnson, a friend of Rob's, said.

Three days later, young Jamarr Moody was found in a Virginia hotel room and brought back to New Jersey. He was further questioned by police, who charged him with accessory to murder after he admitted that the gun found at the scene was his. Witnesses who came forward told police that Jamarr had not been the shooter.

Rob came out of his coma three weeks and two days after the accident happened. Maria praised God and called everyone.

"Thank you, Jesus. Thank you, Lord," she prayed.

He remained in the hospital neurological unit for several days. His condition was improving, glory to God, but he had one disturbing discussion with Maria where he told her that he remembered calling the churches and community event organizers.

"Maria, if you had been there, none of this would have happened," said Rob. He sat in his hospital bed indifferent to his own situation and angry with Maria for what he deemed to be her betrayal and disloyalty.

"After all this time praying for this man," she thought, *"fasting and petitioning God on his behalf. Maybe he is still experiencing some kind of trauma or neurological damage, but Rob made too much sense."*

"Rob, you should thank God that you are alive right now. He saved your life," Maria said.

"No he didn't. He destroyed it. You spend all your time on church, Maria. That's all you do," he said angrily. "This accident would never have happened if you weren't so busy with everything else. It could have been avoided. God didn't save anything."

"Rob, maybe you should get some rest. You may not even realize what you are saying right now," Maria said.

Rob continued to argue with her about her disloyalty to him and her betrayal, so Maria left the hospital room and went home.

Rob was discharged soon after. He had to attend therapy every week. He distanced himself from his closest friend, Mike Love, who confronted him about his issues and refused to side with him against Jesus. This only further irritated Rob, who avoided Maria's calls and did not return any of her messages. He was still blaming Maria for his problems, and he was angry at his predicament. His Center was gone. His connections were gone. His money was gone. His family was gone, and his life had been attacked. Even though he was still alive and breathing on his own, Rob was resentful and full of anger at Maria and whoever was helping her.

"You can have her, Jesus," Rob argued with God one night. "Fuck that bitch."

When Maria called the next morning, Rob spoke to her bluntly, "You have violated our marriage, Maria. This is all your fault. Well, your God hasn't put it on my heart to return your phone calls. I'm done. Have a nice life. Bye." He hung up the phone.

That afternoon, Walter drove Rob to his nearby therapy session in Rob's Mercedes. The two men complained about the wrongs and injustices that they believed they had suffered at the hands of their ex-wives, and as Walter took a hit of the marijuana he had brought with him, he took his eyes off the road and drove through a stop sign. A small red pickup truck with the right-of-way hit the Mercedes on the driver side with force, causing Rob's car to spin in the roadway and a third vehicle to hit Rob's car on its passenger side. Both Walter and Rob were found unconscious at the scene by ambulance personnel and police minutes later.

Walter suffered a concussion, serious neck injury and spinal trauma that required hospitalization.

Rob's right arm was broken in the accident, and he also suffered a dislocated shoulder, facial lacerations, three broken teeth and some cerebral bleeding and swelling inside of his brain. He returned to the hospital, which had just released him, and stayed under guarded medical care. The second life-threatening accident to Rob, however, was somewhat of a wake-up call to him. When doctors advised that the medication to relieve the pressure in his brain was not working and they would have to drain the fluid by drilling a hole in his skull, Rob's eyes began to open. He didn't want to undergo surgery. He was physically, mentally and emotionally tired.

When Maria visited him in the hospital, however, his guilt surfaced, and Rob continued to take his frustration out on her.

"I don't need you here, Maria. I don't need your damn prayers. If I want God's help, I'll ask Him myself. Go preach about Jesus to everybody else. You're so busy running around trying to pray for everybody else, well then go, pray for everybody else. Don't try to come in here now and act like you care. You should have been taking

354

care of our business. I don't want you here. Just go," he told her as she came in to be with him the day of his scheduled surgery.

Maria had been fasting and praying for seven days, and she believed that Jesus would help Rob. Rob's demand that she leave his hospital room didn't really upset her because she knew Rob, as toxic as he was, was not fighting her, but the God in her. She left Rob's hospital room as he requested, trusting that his soul and life were in God's hands.

The nurses shortly afterwards came into the hospital room and advised Rob that they would be taking him in for surgery in a few minutes.

Desperate for help, and believing that there must have been something God was trying to show him, Rob finally stopped contending. This was not a prize fight or martial arts competition that he could win. Rob hadn't learned enough moves to disarm Jesus, and he knew it. He humbled himself and prayed to the Lord, Jesus Christ, for his Help, forgiveness and mercy.

When Rob came out of surgery hours later, Maria was there. The doctors advised Maria that the surgery went well, and Rob was expected to recover, but he would need rest and further evaluation for rehabilitation therapy. Maria stayed by his bedside until he opened his eyes for a brief moment only to close them and go back to sleep.

She gathered her handbag and jacket, which were in the bottom drawer of the hospital dresser. Genny and Papi had called earlier to check on their dad, and Maria returned their call to say that he was out of surgery and resting.

Maria stood from the hospital chair at Rob's bedside and placed her hands in his.

"Father, thank you for saving him. May he be full of your Holy Spirit and live to worship you, for your glory. In Jesus' name."

Then, she took a small vial of oil from her handbag and placed a few drops on Rob's bandaged forehead, anointing him in the name of the Lord.[164] Maria kissed him softly on the cheek, and then said in his ear, "Goodbye, Rob. Live to worship Jesus."

He was groggy, but he felt the soft wind of a touch upon his skin. He struggled to get the words out, but he managed to say, "Wait.....I think the Lord......."

Maria hadn't heard. By the time Rob got the words out, she was already in the hallway, headed towards the elevator. As she passed the nurses' station where several young ladies were discussing care for their patients, Maria thanked them for their care and attention. Then she got on the elevator, and when the doors closed, she fell to her knees and thanked Jesus for *His* care and attention.

"Thank You, Lord, for saving Rob's soul and life. Be glorified I pray, in Jesus' name."

Epilogue

"Wow, Jesus is able," Christina said, reclining in her seat. "What an amazing testimony."

The 11:00 a.m. To Jesus Christ, To Living Water Conference had long since ended, and though Elder Maria had reserved the ballroom for several hours, it was getting late, and the guests had all left. A server came over to the two women and asked if they needed anything, and Maria said they were just about to leave but could use a fresh pitcher of ice water.

"You got it," the server replied. The young man turned and walked through the swinging doors to the hotel's kitchen.

"Yes, God is able, to God be the glory. He is awesome, and He can do anything. He is working on him, and I'm happy about that."

"Is he okay now?" Christina asked.

Maria cleared her throat. "Yes, and it is a miracle, glory to God. Even the doctors say so. God blessed Rob to come through all of his surgeries, and he's still going for therapy, but he is a living, breathing miracle, glory to God."

Christina was amazed. "Glory to God. Well, do you still see him? I mean, have you spoken to him lately to find out how he's doing?"

"I haven't spoken to him in months," Maria answered. "My mom moved in with me and is helping with the kids. He's still going for therapy and isn't able to see the kids on the weekends as much as he used to. I've reached out to him to be sure he is alright, but he hasn't returned any calls. I met him at a few of his therapy sessions, and he said he didn't want me there, so I left."

"Well, did they ever find out who shot him?" Christina asked.

"No, and Jamarr isn't offering any information. I don't know if they ever will," Maria replied.

"And you're not angry or upset about any of this? I mean, his calls to get others to keep you from ministering - that was pretty mean. The flat tires on your car – geesch! I studied psychology in college, and I don't know everything, but he sounds like he's suffering from narcissistic personality disorder. Either that, or he's a bi-polar, toxic, controlling manipulator under the delusion of his image of himself. How could you stand it for so long? It would have been healthy *and* biblical for you to leave. The unbelieving husband is sanctified by the wife,[165] but *he* divorced you. And, all along he was the one committing adulteries. Don't you want to get back at him?" Christina asked. She didn't know if she could be as forgiving with her ex-husband.

"No, Christina. He is a child of God, and God is love. Jesus loves him, and Jesus helped me to forgive him just as Jesus forgave me. We are all sinners, and frankly, we all have some type of disorder that we need the blood of Jesus to cover. I forgave him. My trust is in the Lord, and He sees everything. It's all in His hands. I've done His will, so I will leave it up to Him to handle everything. He is my God, and He helps me."

The young waiter returned with a pitcher and two glasses, into which he poured cold water. Maria thanked him and sipped from her glass before continuing, clearing her throat again.

"Women always ask me how I am not angry or upset about what happened, but it doesn't even bother me. How is that possible? Well, I know you said you didn't want me to just quote scriptures, but the Word of God is true. You see, our Father in Heaven sent His only Son, Jesus Christ, to die for us and redeem us from our sins. This is how awesome His love for us, all of us, is. He blesses us with grace to do His will, so it is not of myself that I am able to forgive and let go, but of Christ who lives in me, and the joy of the Lord is my strength. He gives joy, unspeakable joy. His grace is sufficient, and I have learned to delight in weaknesses, in insults, in hardships, in persecutions, and in difficulties, for when I am weak, then I am strong.[166] Rob meant it for evil, but God meant it for good.[167] And, I can honestly say, Christina, it was good for me that I was afflicted for I have truly come to know Christ in the fellowship of His suffering.[168] God is good at all times, and without this experience, I wouldn't be here testifying to you or anyone else right now, and God wouldn't be glorified."

Christina shook her head in agreement.

"Yes, my marriage was toxic, and I am not advising any woman to stay in a marriage where she is suffering any type of abuse. Stay in prayer, and do what the Lord tells *you* to do. God will give you a word for your situation that agrees with His word, so seek Him for yourself. My husband divorced me, and God's word says that if an unbeliever departs, let him depart; a brother or a sister is not under bondage in such cases. For God has called us to peace.[169] Christina, Rob pushed me away. He wanted out. He filed for divorce and served the papers on me, and he fought against me all the way manipulating and deceiving me into thinking that the divorce was all my fault when he had already set it up so that he could walk out. I'm not perfect, maybe I could have done some things differently, but Rob actually did me a favor. He released me so that I could be married to my true husband, Jesus, and there is nothing diabolical about Jesus. Jesus was with me all the time. Jesus has a voice that is tender and gentle, yet powerful, strong and mighty. He is sweet, loving, faithful, generous, kind, protective, providing, caring, able, and He keeps His promises. He is a healer and a stronghold, a defense and a shield. He is beautiful and lovely, gracious and merciful, and He never fails. Jesus is good at all times. I never would have made it without Him," Maria continued. "It is by His spirit, His power, His anointing and His grace that we are able to get through the storms of life, and Jesus can save anybody who wants to be saved. There is no testimony without a test, and it is God who turns our trials into triumphs and our victimizations into victories for His glory. He is good, and His love endures forever. Jesus Christ is Lord. He is in control, and He will have His way. Besides, we are all clay on the potter's wheel, and He can do as He pleases for His glory. He kept me in the palm of his hand[170], and no weapon formed against me prospered.[171] Jesus tells us in **Matthew 10:36** that a man's enemies will be the members of his own household, but when my enemies came against me, they stumbled and fell. **Psalm 23** and

27 are great scriptures for prayer and meditation! The Lord prepared a table before me in the presence of my enemies, He anointed my head with oil, and my cup runs over.[172] No man has any power over God, and He has shown Himself mighty on my behalf so that men may know themselves to be but men. Their wrath, sweetheart, has only served to give God praise," Maria chuckled. She returned to seriousness and asked, "What do you want me to say? God is love, and He is good at all times. Count it all joy, Christina."[173]

Christina was blessed by the testimony, and she thanked Maria.

"You are most welcome," Maria continued. "The good Lord never puts more on us than we can bear, and God is love.[174] Being a follower of Jesus Christ doesn't mean we won't ever suffer affliction, but the Lord promises in His word that He will deliver us from them all.[175] God is faithful to His word. Give your burdens to the Lord, and He will take care of you. He will never permit the righteous to be moved.[176] Look to Him for His help, and keep reading your Bible. His Word is His testimony, and His Word testifies of His goodness."

"Thank you so much. I will look to Jesus for His help and guidance. God bless you, and God bless your ex-husband and family as well."

The two women stood at the table and hugged, and at that moment, Pastor Key came back into the room. She gave God glory for the conference and promised to keep in touch with Elder Maria as she and Christina left.

Elder Maria took her cell phone from her purse, turned it on, and returned Rob's call.

"Maria, you're never going to believe what happened," an exasperated Rob said. He had been waiting by the phone to talk to his ex-wife for hours.

"What is it Rob?" Maria asked. She hadn't spoken to him in months. "I've called several times, and you haven't returned one call. The kids are concerned about you."

Rob took his time, but he spoke clearly and without any of his usual pauses. "I just needed some time. Thank you for checking on me. Well, the first thing is I want to say is I apologize to you for the calls I made. I was wrong."

There was silence on the phone for a few moments. Maria didn't respond, and when she didn't say anything, Rob continued.

"And, I need to admit to you that I was unfaithful to you several times.........a lot of times, Maria, with about ten or fifteen different women."

Maria didn't know why Rob was calling her to tell her this, but she didn't really care. "Rob, why are you calling me with this nonsense? I don't care. Do you think any of your attempts to destroy me or my ministry have worked? They haven't. No weapon formed against me has prospered. The pits you tried to dig for me, you fell in yourself. And do you think that your affairs with all those women have destroyed my heart, Rob? They haven't. I have nothing but love for you. Jesus loves you. You haven't been fighting against me, Rob, you've been fighting against the God in me and the God who is for me. Maybe that's why you've been losing so many battles lately."

Maria was direct with Rob, and she felt led to be. "Your karate moves won't work against Jesus, Rob. God is wise and mighty, and there is no one who has ever hardened himself against God and prospered. You are just a man, created by the creator, and Jesus is Lord. You used to know how to pick your battles. What happened?"

Surrendered in his spirit to the God working on him, Rob spoke with humility. "Maria, I needed some time.........the Lord spoke to me."

"Well good, Rob, take all the time you need and listen to Him. Do whatever He says," she answered with forthrightness.

"He spoke to me, Maria," Rob reiterated. He wasn't sure Maria would believe him, but he wanted Maria's attention in a spiritual way, and he would not back down until he got it.

"Okay, Rob, He spoke to you. What did He say?" Maria asked, looking at her watch and waving to Neicy, who was waiting by the ballroom main doors.

Rob answered without hesitation. "He told me, '**Do not fear. I am with you.**'"

Marcia L. Boynton

INDEX OF SERMONS

Speaker	*Bible Verse(s)*	*Topic*	*Chapter*
Elder Maria	John 4	"To Jesus Christ, To Living Water"	Prologue
Pastor Wright	Luke 1:39-45	"He Told You"	12
Pastor Wright	Isaiah 41:8-10	"Chosen One, You're Not Alone"	15
Pastor Wright	Joshua 24:15 Matthew 7:13	"The Choice To Cross Over"	21
Pastor Wright	John 16:16-22	"Joy, Unspeakable Joy"	21
Elder Maria	Matthew 18:21-22	"Forgiveness You Can Count On"	23
Elder Maria	John 4:7-14	"Living To Worship"	23

INDEX OF ORIGINAL PRAISE & WORSHIP SONGS

Song Title	Singer	Chapter
"That I Thirst Not"	Ronny	Prologue
"Thank You For The Blood"	Holy Tabernacle Church Praise & Worship Team	Twelve
"Journey To Canaan"	Neicy	Twelve
"Closer to You, Jesus"	Minister Barrington and Holy Tabernacle Church Praise & Worship Team	Twenty One
"Home with My Lord"	Keyara Oliver	Twenty One
"Jesus, My Friend"	Papi	Twenty Three

Note: I Need Thee, Every Hour (public domain) appears in Chapter Twenty Three.

End Notes

Prologue

[1] Boynton, Marcia, © Marcia L. Boynton, "Journey To Canaan"
[2] A spontaneous gift or voluntary offering (See Exodus 35:29 and 2 Corinthians 8:2-4).
[3] Boynton, Marcia, © 2016 Marcia L. Boynton, "That I Thirst Not"
[4] See Acts 4:12
[5] See Philippians 2:9-11
[6] See Matthew 18:19-20
[7] See John 10:10
[8] See 3 John 1:2
[9] See Jeremiah 1:5
[10] See Jeremiah 29:11
[11] See Jeremiah 3:15
[12] See Romans 9:15
[13] See John 6:37
[14] "Benediction." Merriam-Webster.com. Merriam-Webster, 2015 Web. June 30, 2016. According to the Merriam-Webster.com page, "the benediction is the invocation of a blessing, especially the short blessing with which public worship is concluded."
[15] See Matthew 16:24
[16] See Matthew 10:37

Chapter One

[17] See Psalm 42:1
[18] See John 4
[19] See Luke 7 and Matthew 26
[20] See Hebrews 9:7
[21] What is the Day of Atonement (Yom Kippur)?, (©2002-2016). Gotquestions.org, Got Questions Ministries. Retrieved June 20, 2016, from

http://www.gotquestions.org/Day-Atonement-Yom-Kippur.html   Also see Hebrews 7 and 10
[22] See Hebrews 9 and Hebrews 10:19-20
[23] See John 5:1-15
[24] See Mark 5:25-34

Chapter Two

Chapter Three

[25] Fantastic Four in Film, (last updated September 10, 2016). In *Wikipedia*. Retrieved September 10, 2016 from
https://en.wikipedia.org/wiki/Fantastic_Four_in_film
According to the Wikipedia page, The fictional superhero team Fantastic Four featured in Marvel Comics publication has appeared in four live-action films since its inception. The plots deal with four main characters..."

Chapter Four

[26] See Matthew 18:20
[27] See Exodus 5:22-23
[28] See Hebrews 11:6
[29] See Mark 11:24
[30] See Luke 17:6
[31] See Psalm 34:19
[32] See Hebrews 13:5
[33] See John 16:33
[34] See Romans 5:3-5
[35] See Philippians 3:10
[36] See Galatians 6:9
[37] See Romans 10:17
[38] See Genesis 15-21
[39] See Exodus 14:21-22
[40] See John 11
[41] See Psalm 31:15
[42] See Jeremiah 29:11
[43] See 1 Corinthians 12:1-11
[44] See 2 Samuel 6:14

Chapter Five

[45] Austen, Jane. *Of Pride and Prejudice.* First published 1813. (n.p.)

[46] Frank, Anne. *Anne Frank The Diary of a Young Girl.* Everyman's Library, Oct. 19, 2010.

[47] Smith, Betty. *A Tree Grows In Brooklyn.* First published in 1943. (n.p.)

[48] Chopin, Kate. *The Awakening.* First published in Chicago: Herbert S. Stone & Co., 1899.

[49] Walker, Alice. *The Color Purple.* 1982. (n.p.)

[50] Jacobs, Harriott Ann. *Incidents in the Life of a Slave Girl (1861).* First published in 1861 by L. Maria Child. (n.p.)

[51] Angelou, Maya. *I Know Why The Caged Bird Sings.* Little, Brown Book Group, 2010.

[52] Peterson, Eugene H. *The Message: The Bible in Contemporary Language.* (n.p.)

[53] See Romans 12:19

Chapter Six

Chapter Seven

Chapter Eight

Chapter Nine

[54] Lee, Harper. *To Kill A Mockingbird, Enhanced Edition.* (n.p.)

[55] Bronte, Emily. *Wuthering Heights.* First published in 1847. (n.p.)

[56] Marquez, Gabriel Garcia. *One Hundred Years of Solitude.* English translation copyright 1970 by Harper and Row Publishers, Inc.

[57] Gardner, John. *Grendel*, Vintage Books Edition, 1989. New York: Random House Inc., 1989. Originally published by Alfred A. Knopf, Inc., in 1971.

[58] Morrison, Toni. *Beloved*, First Vintage International Edition, 2004. New York: Random House, Inc., 2004. Originally published in slightly different form in hardcover in the United States by Alfred A. Knopf, Inc., a division of Random House, Inc., New York, in 1987.

[59] Williams, Tennessee. *The Glass Menagerie.* First published in 1945. (n.p.)

Chapter Ten

Marcia L. Boynton

Chapter Eleven

[60] See John 12:32

Chapter Twelve

[61] Boynton, Marcia L. © 2016 Marcia L. Boynton. "Thank you for the blood."
[62] Boynton, Marcia L. © 2016 Marcia L. Boynton. "Journey to Canaan."
[63] See Psalm 30:5
[64] See Luke 15:7
[65] See Hebrews 4:15-16
[66] See 1 Samuel 3
[67] See Matthew 6:36

Chapter Thirteen

Chapter Fourteen

[68] See 1 Timothy 5:8

Chapter Fifteen

[69] See 1 Peter 5:7 and Psalm 55:22
[70] See Matthew 6:33
[71] See Romans 8:31
[72] See Proverbs 22:6
[73] See Matt. 18:21-22
[74] See Matthew 5:44
[75] See Romans 12:19
[76] See Luke 6:37
[77] See John 16:33
[78] See 1 John 4:4
[79] See Psalm 34:18
[80] See 1 Peter 5:7

Chapter Sixteen

Chapter Seventeen

Chapter Eighteen

368

Chapter Nineteen

[81] See Matthew 18:19-20
[82] See Matthew 4:1-11; Mark 1:12, 13; Luke 4:1-13
[83] See 1 Thessalonians 5:17
[84] See Psalm 76:10
[85] See Deuteronomy 31:6 and Hebrews 13:5
[86] See Matthew 19:9
[87] See 2 Peter 3:8
[88] See Romans 3:23
[89] See Ephesians 4:32, Colossians 3:13
[90] See Acts 9:1-9
[91] See Isaiah 64:8
[92] See Proverbs 21:1
[93] See Psalm 37:23
[94] See 2 Samuel 11 and 12

Chapter Twenty

Chapter Twenty One

[95] *NKJV Study Bible*. (2011). Thomas Nelson Publishers. (n.p.). Retrieved August 9, 2016 from http://www.christianbook.com/nkjv-study-bible-large-print-hardcover/9781418549961/pd/549961?dv=c&en=bing-pla&event=SHOP&kw=bibles-40-60%7C549961&p=1179517
[96] Matthew Henry's Commentary, (© 2004 – 2016). Biblehub.com. Retrieved June 30, 2016 from http://biblehub.com/commentaries/joshua/24-15.htm
[97] See Psalm 14:2
[98] See Acts 17:27-28
[99] Psalm 25:4
[100] Psalm 48:14
[101] Proverbs 3:5-6
[102] James 1:5
[103] See Hebrews 11:6
[104] See Proverbs 1:28-29
[105] Boynton, Marcia L., © 2016 Marcia L. Boynton, *Closer to You, Jesus*.
[106] Slain in the Spirit, (last updated June 3, 2016). In *Wikipedia*. Retrieved June 30, 2016 from https://en.wikipedia.org/wiki/Slain_in_the_Spirit
According to the Wikipedia page, "Slain in the Spirit or slaying in the Spirit are terms used by Pentecostal and charismatic Christians to describe a form of prostration in which an individual falls to the floor while experiencing religious ecstasy. Believers

attribute this behavior to the power of the Holy Spirit." Also, see Ezekiel 3:23, 43:2-3 and 44:4; and 2 Chronicles 5:14.

[107] See 2 Chronicles 20:17

[108] See Proverbs 31:25

[109] See James 4:8

[110] Boynton, Marcia L. © 2016 Marcia L. Boynton. "Home with My Lord."

[111] See John 11

[112] See Luke 7:11-17

[113] See John 11:26

[114] See Acts 2:24

[115] See 2 Corinthians 5:1

Chapter Twenty Two

Chapter Twenty Three

[116] Boynton, Marcia, © 2016 Marcia L. Boynton, "Jesus, My Friend"

[117] John 3:16

[118] See Psalm 130:3

[119] See Isaiah 53:5-6

[120] See Matthew 26:28

[121] See Psalm 103:12

[122] See Philippians 3:3-11

[123] See Philippians 3:8

[124] Mark 8:35

[125] Hatred Between Jews and Samaritans, (© 2016). Bible.org. Retrieved June 30, 2016 from https://bible.org/illustration/hatred-between-jews-and-samaritans Also, See 2 Kings 17:24, 2 Kings 17:29-41 and Ezra 9:1-10:44.

[126] Dowdell-Underwood, O. J., PH.D., p. viii. (2016). *Vindication of Broken Women Who Possess Deep Wells, The Samaritan Woman Principle*. Pittsburgh, PA. Dorrance Publishing Co.

[127] See Deuteronomy 25:5

[128] See Leviticus 20:10

[129] What does it mean to worship the Lord in spirit and truth? (© 2002-2016 Got Questions Ministries). GotQuestions.org. Retrieved June 30, 2016 from http://www.gotquestions.org/worship-spirit-truth.html

[130] Radmacher, E. D., Th.D., Allen, R. B., Th.D., House, H. W., Th.D., J.D., p. 1653. (1982). *NKJV Study Bible*. Nashville, TN. Thomas Nelson Publishers.

[131] See Romans 9:18

[132] "Proskuneo." Biblehub.com © 2004-2016, Retrieved June 30, 2016 from http://biblehub.com/greek/4352.htm

[133] See 1 Cor. 1:27-29

[134] Matthew Henry Commentary 1 Cor. 1:27, (© 2004-2015 Biblehub.com). Biblehub.com. Retrieved June 30, 2016 from http://biblehub.com/1_corinthians/1-27.htm

[135] See John 4:28-29

[136] 30 Bible Verses about Spiritual Harlotry, (Copyright 1960...1995 knowing-jesus.com). Knowing-jesus.com. Retrieved July 3, 2016 from http://bible.knowing-jesus.com/topics/Spiritual-Harlotry which includes Hosea 5:4, Hosea 4:12, Jeremiah 13:27, Psalm 106:39, Ezekiel 23:3-19, Numbers 15:39, 2 Chronicles 21:11 and Isaiah 1:21.

[137] See Matthew 6:24

[138] See Matthew 22:36-37

[139] See Matthew 16:24-26

[140] See Revelation 3:14-22

[141] What did Jesus mean when He spoke of living water? (© 2002-2016 Got Questions Ministries). GotQuestions.org. Retrieved June 30, 2016 from http://www.gotquestions.org/living-water.html

[142] See Psalm 118:17

[143] See Proverbs 18:21

[144] Dowdell-Underwood, O. J., PH.D., See p. 9. (2016). *Vindication of Broken Women Who Possess Deep Wells, The Samaritan Woman Principle*. Pittsburgh, PA. Dorrance Publishing Co.

[145] See 1 Kings 12

[146] See Jeremiah 3

[147] See Psalm 133:1

[148] Amos 3:3

[149] Dowdell-Underwood, O. J., PH.D., p. 9. (2016). *Vindication of Broken Women Who Possess Deep Wells, The Samaritan Woman Principle*. Pittsburgh, PA. Dorrance Publishing Co.

[150] See Micah 7:19

[151] See Isaiah 1:18

[152] See 2 Corinthians 5:18, John 3:16, John 14:6

[153] Dowdell-Underwood, O. J., PH.D., p. VIII-IX. (2016). *Vindication of Broken Women Who Possess Deep Wells, The Samaritan Woman Principle*. Pittsburgh, PA. Dorrance Publishing Co.

[154] See Luke 5:8

[155] See Matthew 16:17

[156] See Romans 10:13

[157] See Ezekiel 18:23

[158] See John 3:16

[159] See John 10:10

[160] See Galatians 1:10

[161] I Need Thee Every Hour, (last updated 8/7/2007). Retrieved June 30, 2016 from http://www.cyberhymnal.org/htm/i/n/ineedteh.htm According to the web page, the public domain lyrics were written by Annie Sherwood Hawks, 1872, and the music by Robert Lowry.

Chapter Twenty Four

[162] George Jefferson (last updated June 25, 2016). In *Wikipedia*. Retrieved August 2, 2016 from https://en.wikipedia.org/wiki/George_Jefferson. According to Wikipedia, George Jefferson is a fictional character played by Sherman Hemsley on the American television sitcoms All in the Family (from 1973 until 1975) and its spin-off The Jeffersons (1975 – 1985), in which he serves as the program's protagonist.

[163] Healing Bible Verses, (© 2014 Biblestudytools). Biblestudytools.com. Retrieved June 30, 2016 from http://www.biblestudytools.com/topical-verses/healing-bible-verses/

[164] See James 5:14

Epilogue

[165] See 1 Cor. 7:14
[166] See 2 Corinthians 12:10
[167] See Genesis 50:20
[168] See Philippians 3:8-10
[169] See 1 Corinthians 7:15
[170] See Isaiah 49:16
[171] See Isaiah 54:17
[172] See Psalm 23:5
[173] See James 1:1-4
[174] See 1 John 4:8
[175] Psalm 34:19
[176] Psalm 55:22

About the Author

Jesus Christ is Lord. He is the Messiah who was, who is and who is to come.

A servant of the Lord Jesus Christ, Marcia L. Boynton was divinely ordained to minister the gospel in 2001. Affirmed an Elder in 2014, Marcia's testimony today is as the Apostle Paul's: "I have come to know Christ in the fellowship of His suffering," and as Joseph's, "What others meant for evil, God meant for good." Years of homelessness and poverty only served to strengthen, by God's grace, her faith.

It is through the foolishness of the cross, Christ crucified, and the message of repentance, forgiveness and love that this servant labors to win souls into the Kingdom that she may be emptied and Christ glorified.

Marcia released a CD of original psalms entitled "Psalms from the Gap, Glory to God," in 2015 on independent label, Trower Music Group. This followed up a number one gospel house single on DJ Tony Humphries' international charts. She is currently working on additional gospel music projects.

Marcia L. Boynton

She supports the online Christian ministry and network of women, BWE, Inc., as a prayer intercessor and Teaching Elder of Saturday morning's "Women of the Bible Teaching Series and Bi-Monthly Book Club." Marcia was recently named the Director of BWE NJ/NY, a local chapter of the global online ministry.

A single mother of three daughters in college, Marcia gives all glory to God for saving her life and healing her brokenness. She lives in New Jersey and enjoys spending her time reading, writing, teaching and ministering, as well as sharing precious moments with her three daughters and two grandchildren.

Visit www.marcialboyntonpublishing.com for updates and new releases.